Pattaya
Confess

By Jack Corbett

Nirvana Publishing

Published by Nirvana Publishing Company

1st Edition
by Jack Corbett

For information address
Nirvana Publishing Company
505/Moo 5 Naklua Soi 16
Banglamung
Chonburi 20150
Thailand
http://www.alphapro.com
jack.corbett@gmail.com

Edited by Tom Crowsen
Printed by KDP
back and front cover design by Jack Corbett

ISBN-978-0-9848934-4-7

Other books by Jack Corbett

Death on the Wild Side
Welcome to the Fun House
Dick Fitswell the Man in Quest of the Perfect Fit
Extreme Guns and Babes For an Adult World

Table of Contents

The New Chairman of the Fun House

For the last time Herman the German was presiding over the Fun House's annual co-owners meeting. Addressing the thirty owners in front of his podium, Herman announced:

"For ten years I have been your chairman. But I have become very tired. I want to spend the rest of my life racing go-carts. Besides, under Thai law every committee member here must resign. If no one offers to replace a committee member that committee member can serve for another two years. But this time, I assure all of you that I will not offer to continue my services. To me, racing go-carts has become my life. And now that Pattaya has built the new auto racing track, I am now going to race real cars which are a lot more expensive and time consuming."

"So now I ask all of you, who wants to be on this committee?"

"I do," a lilting woman's voice resonated throughout the room.

To describe the woman as attractive was a complete understatement. Or even beautiful. She was stunning.   Her presence commanding. Blonde haired, she had a body that was as close to perfection as God had ever created. Her green eyes moved confidently from one face to the other as she stood up to address the condo owners.

"Can you tell everyone who you are, and why you want to be on this committee?" Herman asked.

"My name is Tatyana. I own a condo here. And I am Russian. And I don't want to be just on the committee. I want to be your new Chairman to replace Herman. If you elect me as your new chairman, I will bring the Fun House to new heights of glory. We face as a community new challenges that will make things more and more expensive for all of us. We face a lot of corruption in Pattaya. We will have to pay larger and larger bribes to the government agencies here. And because I am Russian, I know all about corruption."

"Do you have any special qualities that you wish to share with our fellow co-owners?" Herman asked.

"Yes. I do. I own many businesses here. And I have many

powerful Russian friends in Pattaya. And you all know that it's Russian money pouring into Pattaya that's transforming this whole city. We Russians can make things really happen. And I do mean the improvement of this entire community. I buy and sell condos, and luxury homes. I also own a few bars and other businesses. For you owners who want to sell your condos, I can get you prices that you never dreamed of before. And for you owners who want to rent your condos, I can find you renters who will pay you higher rental fees than you've ever gotten. Until now, most of my customers are Russian of course. But let's face the facts. Russians are trying to get their money out of Russia into more secure investments."

"You will all profit," Tatyana continued. "Immeasurably. If you elect me as your new leader, together we will make the Bahthaus the number one condo in the entire Wongamat area[1].

---

[1] Wongamat, a community in Naklua near the Wongamat Beach

The Background to the Short Era of Tatyana the Great

The real name of the condominium community where Fast Eddy and Herman the German lived was not the Fun House. The condominium was registered with the Land Office as the Bahthaus. Herman, Fast Eddy and a few other condo owners only called it the Fun House because of its being in Pattaya, Thailand. Which is probably the most fun city on earth and so much fun that Pattaya advertises itself as a "Disneyland for Adults." While its detractors call it "Sin City." Above all it's got the most beautiful women on earth. And nearly all of them are available. It's a place where even 70 and 80 year olds get to empower their manhood by taking ridiculously young sexy Thai women for girlfriends...for a single night, week, month or a lifetime.

"Herman the German was the founding father and developer of the Fun House. But when it came time for him to turn the Fun House over to the new owners, he had to have an annual Owners Meeting. This was a pivotal event. The first General Owners Meeting amounted to turning the financing and governmental reigns of the Fun House from Herman's corporation "Teutonic Visions, Inc." to the condo owners. So Herman assembled 30 out of the 62 condo owners in the Fun House Lobby where he had the owners vote for a committee to run the show.

At this first General Condo Co-owners meeting, Herman nominated himself to be on the committee, which all 30 of the condo owners attending the meeting approved. Then he nominated Frank to be on it also. He finally recommended a female lawyer friend of his, Shayla Sleight of Hand, to be the third member of the committee. Once again all the owners approved.

And of course, Herman the German made himself chairman of the committee, and became known ever since as the boss of bosses. And for the past eight years he ruled the Fun House with an Iron Fist. But there were still a lot of hilarious times during the reign of King Herman. And there were some serious moments too. Such as when the Thai kick boxers murdered Ted Buffalo by throwing him off the balcony which the police ruled as a suicide. Which Herman and several accomplices avenged by murdering the kick boxers.

Oh, those were great bloody days back then. But Pattaya had changed over the years, and so had the Fun House. Whereas in the beginning most of the Fun House owners actually lived in their units, the majority of the residents were now renters while most owners were living back in their home countries collecting their rent money. The comradery that had once existed among the owners had all but disappeared.

And things had long since gone downhill for Herman the German. Although he was a very talented and forceful leader, he had a bad habit of keeping his front door open. He did this to facilitate the airflow throughout his condo. He had a sea view unit facing the ocean. If he kept his door open, the sea breeze could course through his whole unit...So he wouldn't have to use the air conditioner very much. And of course there is nothing quite like having a sea breeze. The downside to Herman's keeping his door open was that it gave complaining owners easy access to the King.

Herman had long ago become very tired of all the complaining owners. Nearly every night someone had come up to his unit to complain about one thing or another. Every year it had gotten worse until Herman started calling most condo owners "That bunch of assholes" to his most intimate friends.

Herman figured that out of the 62 condo owners, all of them were completely selfish people with the exception of perhaps five owners. Although he enjoyed being the King of the Fun House, he decided to turn over all the condos' problems to somebody else.

So, at the eighth annual meeting of the Fun House Condo owners Herman suddenly announced that he no longer wanted to be on the committee. He was building a new house which would be close to the new race track Pattaya was building on the other side of town. And if there was anything Herman truly enjoyed the most out of life, it was racing cars.

He could already savor the sounds of loud engines and the addictive smell of gasoline and engine oil. He figured it would take another six months to finish his new house and only another two months before the new race track would be completed.

The owners voted to keep Frank on the new committee since he lived at the Fun House full time, and then they elected several sheep to be his followers.

But it was Tatyana who stole the show by becoming Queen of the Fun House. Most of the owners voted Tatyana to be the new

Chairman. Thankfully there weren't many American condo owners who would have voted against her because she was Russian. But the German owners could care less. And so could the British, Irish, Australians and Scots while the French owners saw Tatyana as the best thing since French bread.

Big Dicks

Big Dick's had not changed much through the years. Still, on Soi 6, it had become one of the most venerable short time bars on the soi. But Dick Fitswell had installed a new sign in front of his place. The sign read, "Ball realignment here" by the Angry Pussy.

Angry Pussy had not changed much over the past eight years. No longer in her twenties, Angry Pussy had become a tight little assed thirty-two year old. Her waist was just as slim as it was when she was twenty-four. And although her face betrayed her as no longer being in her early twenties, she could still pass for a twenty-eight-year-old. One thing that had changed, however, were her breasts which were courtesy of a silicon job that Dick Fitswell had payed for.

But unlike most women, Angry Pussy exercised heavily in the gym. An hour on the treadmill six times a week made her ass even tighter than it had been when Fitwell first met her. This gave Angry Pussy the right look for the part she was playing as the sexiest, toughest mamasan on Soi 6.

Fast Eddy first came into Big Dicks on a Friday night. Catching his eye immediately were all the big dicks that lined the wall behind the bar. They weren't real of course. A fact that Dick Fitswell announced to Fast Eddy as soon as he entered the bar.

"Those are plaster casts of the dicks of my best customers," Dick Fitswell said to Fast Eddy in a loud proud voice. Then he stretched out his hand.

"I'm Dick Fitswell. Welcome to my bar. There's no other place like it here on Soi 6."

"I can see that," Fast Eddy replied. "Why do you have all those dicks on display?"

"Well, you see, I haven't called my place Big Dicks for nothing. I tend to get a certain type of customer here. The kind of man who thinks he's gods' gift to women. Guys who are a lot like me."

"I've heard a lot about you, Dick. Such as your having an 18-inch penis."

"But that's in the past," Dick Fitswell replied. "I used to have an

18-inch dick but now that I'm sixty, my libido is just a shadow of what it used to be. While my dick's shrunk to fourteen inches. I'm not much good anymore unless I meet someone who really turns me on."

"Someone? What do you mean by someone?"

"It can be a woman. Usually it's a woman. But sometimes it's a lady boy who gets my dick to expand to its full 14 inches. And of course you know what a lady boy is."

"You bet I do," Fast Eddy replied. "It's a woman who's trapped in a man's body. In Thailand they call her the third sex."

"I have mostly ladies working here in my bar, but Angry Pussy's brother is a lady boy. She[2] gets over here pretty often when she needs money."

"So what's this about Angry Pussy giving ball realignments?"

"Rather than explain I'll just let Angry Pussy show you," Dick Fitswell replied.

Up until now, Angry Pussy had been busy behind the bar, getting Fast Eddy his beer while making a gin and tonic for another customer–a German sitting at the other end of the bar. After bringing them their drinks, Angry Pussy joined Fast Eddy, and sat on the bar stool next to him.

"Let me feel your dick," she asked as she gently rubbed Fast Eddy's balls with her left hand.

At first Fast Eddy didn't feel much of anything since he had long ago gotten accustomed to bar girls grabbing his schlong which still didn't rise to the occasion until Angry Pussy unzipped his shorts and started fondling his bare penis. But when she pulled his dick out of his shorts and started rubbing it with both hands,

---

[2]Lady boys are almost always referred to as she

Fast Eddy's penis swelled massively to its full eight inches.

"I've seen a lot bigger than yours, but it's not bad," said Angry Pussy. "Your dick shows some promise, but you sure aren't going to set any records with it."

"What do you mean?"

"But there's still hope for you. With the right kind of physical therapy, I think we can get a full nine inches out of it."

"What do I have to do to get to nine inches?"

"First, you must become a member here. Membership costs 30000 baht a year.[3] But for that 30000 you get a lot of free fucks and blow jobs."

"But I can get all the cheap blow jobs and fucks just about anywhere here on Soi 6," Fast Eddy replied.

"And it is costing you only one thousand baht that you must pay the girl plus 300 baht for the room," said Angry Pussy. "But your dick will still only be eight inches long."

"So what makes the difference?"

"You get a scientific schedule of treatments for a whole month from our special group of experts who work here," Angry Pussy replied. "These girls have the right knowledge and the proper techniques that I have personally taught them. And they have the right tools to get the job done."

"What do you mean by proper tools?" Fast Eddy asked.

"Such as vibrators and dildos, and custom-made dick extenders.

---

[3]There are approximately 31 to 35 baht in one dollar

And sometimes we will have two gals doing you at the same time. This works wonders for certain men."

Suddenly a loud voice rose from the other end of the bar.

"Get the membership," the German interrupted. "This really works. They tried it on me and now I've got the cast of my penis up behind the bar. My dick is a full 10 inches long now. And it works so much better because it shows women who's really the boss."

"I'm Fast Eddy. What's your name?"

"Ludwig. Be sure, if you don't get the Angry Pussy therapy, you are going to regret it for the rest of your life."

Turning to face Angry Pussy, Fast Eddy asked the shapely mamasan, "If I go through this therapy do I get to fuck you also?"

"Oh yes. Three or four times. But I have good idea for you."

"What's that?"

"You pay one-thousand baht now and three-hundred baht for room. I boom boom you upstairs, and then you decide for yourself if you want thirty-thousand baht membership."

Which was an offer Fast Eddy couldn't refuse. He had heard so much about Angry Pussy that he just had to try her.

Ten minutes later they were in an upstairs room. The room had a small plastic shower stall a few feet from the bed. But the toilet was down the hall. In the shower Angry Pussy immediately showed off her best feature to Fast Eddy. Which was her ass.

With her ass just inches from Fast Eddy's groin, Angry Pussy reached behind her back and grabbed his dick firmly in her hand until she felt him rise to a full erection. For a moment she took her hand away while pulling herself against him. With her ass touching his penis she pulled his turgid member up between her legs and started rubbing it against the crack of her ass.

Angry Pussy has a thing about asses...especially her own. It didn't take much longer than a few seconds of dick to her ass contact to make her start to cum. Which she now demonstrated by oozing her bodily fluid all over Fast Eddy's dick and the inside

17

of her thighs. Grasping his dick in her hand she started to rub his penis across her slippery upper thighs.

When she finally took him over to the bed, she had him bang her in the ass.

Like most of the other Fun House Residents, Fast Eddy had a Thai tilak who had been his live in girlfriend for ten years...who unfortunately still was. But if there was anything good to be said about their relationship, his live in kept him pretty well grounded in more ways than one.

The best thing about their relationship was having someone around his place nearly all the time. So loneliness was something he didn't suffer from. This home situation kept him out of the bars where he would surely be slowly drinking himself to death. So he didn't get out with his friends more than two nights a week.

These were his "sacred nights." And as far as his tilak was concerned, his right to get out on the town twice a week was something she should never question.

The First Meeting of the New Committee

The ex chairman ran the first half hour of the new committee meeting before he gratuitously left the room to let Tatyana take over the meeting.

When one of the new committee members asked Herman the German how many times he felt they should be having committee meetings, Herman the German replied, "I think two or three times a year should be sufficient."

But after Herman left, Tatyana said to her fellow committee members, "Forget everything this man just told us. We are going to start doing things differently around here. For now I'd like us to meet every month or 12 times a year. This tells our staff members that we are on the job and doing all the business necessary. If we only meet two or three times a year we will be telling our staff that we don't care, and that we are seeking the easy way out."

When the other four members of the committee agreed, Tatyana proposed that no salary or compensation should be awarded to committee members.

"There are five of us on this committee. If we meet every month and if each one of us is getting one-thousand baht for each committee meeting he attends, we could be costing our fellow condo owners as much as 60000 baht a year."

Once again all of her fellow committee members announced their approval.

Tatyana then turned to Koko, the condo secretary bookkeeper. And said to her, as she passed a balance sheet and profit and loss statement to the other committee members. "Koko, I want for you to show us that the cash balance in the bank book is exactly the same as what this balance sheet shows."

Tatyana had already rehearsed this with Koko. Years earlier while Frank served on the committee with Herman the German, he had trained her how to use the Quickbooks accounting system he had introduced to the Fun House condo office. So Koko was ready for this comparison between the two book balances. Bringing out the actual bank book that she had just updated at the bank, she showed the committee members that the balance sheet copies Tatyana printed showed exactly the same balances as the bank book.

Then Tatyana addressed the other three committee members. "I want all of you to know that Frank here is responsible for this accounting system."

Turning to Frank, Tatyana continued, "I want you to serve as vice chairman. I have heard that you are really good with accounting so I will want to learn as much as possible from you."

Death in the Bahthaus Swimming Pool

A crowd had gathered just outside the swimming pool. From his balcony overlooking the pool, Frank could see Herman the German, the condo secretary- bookkeeper, the security guard and several condo owners talking with two police officers. Frank knew it was necessary to do some repairs to the swimming pool grouting, and that the Bahthaus would have the repair work done soon. Which probably explained the rope that had been stretched across the pool entrance supporting a "Do Not Enter" sign.

Five minutes later, Frank was standing at the pool entrance next to Herman the German watching an attractive Russian woman performing CPR on a woman lying on the concrete at the far side of the pool.

"Who is it?" Frank asked Herman. "I hope it's not someone I know."

"Unfortunately it's Tatyana," Herman replied. "And I don't think Khristina will be able to revive her."

"What time did this happen?" Frank asked.

"One of the cleaning ladies saw her floating in the pool at 9:30 a.m.," Herman replied.

"What happened then?"

"The cleaner got Khun Toe to go to the pool. And you know Khun Toe. He didn't hesitate. He jumped right into the water and brought Tatyana to the side of the pool. By this time the cleaning lady got Khristina to go to the pool where Khristina and Khun Toe lifted Tatyana out of the pool."

"You know of course that the two Russian women are roommates?" Herman continued.

"I thought they were, but I wasn't sure. I do know they share an office, in front of our Bahthaus condo. And Tatyana is my neighbor in the condo directly beneath mine," Frank replied.

"Not are roommates," said Herman. "But were."

"What do you mean, Herman?"

"Because Tatyana is already dead."

"How do you know? Khristina is still performing CPR on her."

"Because as soon as I got here, Tatyana's body had already started to swell up."

"Then why is Khristina still performing CPR?"

"Because they are roommates. And because Khristina is a good lady. I'm sure she wants to give her roommate every chance even if she feels Tatyana is beyond help."

"Herman, we must get to the bottom of this to find out how and why Tatyana died."

When Khristina finally gave up performing CPR on Tatyana, Frank watched, horrified, as one of the police officers kneeled next to Tatyana's body as the other officer took pictures. "What are they doing that for?" Frank asked himself. "Taking pictures of Tatyana might be necessary, but what is this first officer getting into the pictures for? It's like these police officers are on an African Safari and one of them has just shot a trophy animal. And his partner is taking his pictures with the animal as he's holding up his arm in triumph. But these officers haven't done Jack Shit. And if someone's murdered Tatyana there is no way that they will be able to find out who did it due to their mucking up the crime scene."

Herman the German Talks about Tatyana's Death

Wilhelm hated Herman the German, which is why he swore Fast Eddy to secrecy about Tatyana's death.

"Whatever you do, don't tell anyone you heard this from me. I am warning you, Fast Eddy–especially that dictator Herman. I am almost ashamed to call myself German because I know him"

"Don't worry. I won't say anything to anyone. Now what is it you want to tell me about Tatyana?"

"As you know, Fast Eddy, whenever a Westerner dies here in Pattaya, they must do an autopsy. They must take the body to a certain hospital in Bangkok, which investigates the cause of death. After the autopsy is complete, the body can go back here or to the family. Wherever. But Tatyana is a special case. Someone put her body on a plane straight to Russia. No autopsy was ever performed."

"Now where did you learn this, Wilhelm?"

"I have a friend in the Land office. That's how I found out about it. I heard about it from one of the Thai higher ups."

"Come on Wilhelm. How in the hell is anyone at the land office able to find out what happened to this Russian woman? Why should anyone there even care? And even if someone did know why would he tell you about it?"

"Okay. Then don't believe me then. But I'm telling you."

"Okay Wilhelm. If what you say is true, then this smells of a Russian mafia killing."

But when Fast Eddy met Herman in the condo office to learn more about Tatyana's death, Fast Eddy was shocked to hear a different point of view. One that totally contradicted everything Wilhelm had told him with the exception of the Russian Mafia part.

"Herman, do you have any idea of why Tatyana died in our pool?" Fast Eddy asked.

"I am not sure," Herman the German replied. "But she had some kind of head injury. Either the day she died or the day before."

"How do you know this, Herman?"

"Because that's what the autopsy report said."

"So you read the autopsy?"

"Yes, of course. As chairman of the Bahthaus, that was my responsibility. I asked for the autopsy report which the hospital sent me. Next time someone dies this will be Frank's responsibility. As our new chairman it will his job to find out the cause of death of anyone who dies here."

"This reeks of foul play, Herman. A head injury? I do know Tatyana was a very good swimmer. And our pool is not even five feet deep. The newspaper and everything on the internet that has anything to say about Tatyana's death reports she drowned in our pool."

"That's not likely. I don't think that Tatyana drowned."

"Herman, is there anything else you know about this that hardly anyone else knows?"

"Recently there's been a red Ferrari that someone's been parking next to our condo. And I've heard that the owner sometimes comes into our building. Now you know, Fast Eddy, that any car that's made entirely outside this country has a huge tax on it. So if a BMW costs $100000 in the U.S. or Germany, it's going to be at least $200000 here. Which means the owner of the Red Ferrari must have paid at least one million American dollars for it. Practically the only people around here who have that kind of money are Russian mafia."

"Or rich Thais," Fast Eddy added.

"I must advise you, Fast Eddy, to not worry about this. Forget the whole thing. The Russians here have a lot of power. Tatyana's death concerns neither of us. The important thing to realize is, we aren't going to have any problems with our insurance. No one can sue us. Our insurance company told me that the Bahthaus is totally clear of blame for Tatyana's death."

"And one more thing, Fast Eddy. Frank needs good advice on how to run this condo. Even though you are not on the new committee, you and I have been through a lot together. Frank's a good man and he's tough. But sometimes he's not realistic enough. He's American like you. But he's too liberal. He's a democrat. You and I play hard-ball. I'm afraid that Frank is going to be too soft with the condo owners here. Almost all of them are self-centered assholes. We know how to deal with these people. So whenever the time comes, I hope you will get Frank on the right track. And that you will teach him to treat all the assholes with a big stick. He will be asking you for your good advice, especially when he realizes how weak this new committee is."

Thai Girl with blue eyes

"I'm telling you, Dick. The first time I saw Kit, I wanted her."

"Now how in the hell would you know that?" Dick Fitswell asked.

"Well, here I am coming down Soi 6, and I spot several girls in front of this bar. One of the girls is tall, and she's slender. Very pretty too. But another girl suddenly asks me to go into the bar with her. I quickly look away from the second girl, and look the tall girl straight in the eye. And ask her, "Can I buy you a drink?"

"Straight off she follows me into the bar. I take a seat on a bar stool as she goes behind the bar to get us our drinks. I ask for my usual–a bottle of San Miguel Light while she gets herself a Jager Bomb. But as soon as she takes the bar stool next to me, she starts grabbing my dick."

"That sounds about normal for Soi 6," Dick Fitswell replied.

"But she is much quicker than most of the other girls. It is almost as if she is a robot. Like you sit in a sports car, start the engine and immediately grab the stick shift on the floor. She has my dick in her hand that fast."

"She looks very young. Very cute, and right off, I notice that she has blue eyes," Fast Eddy added.

"What the hell!"

So I asked her if she had a Western parent. Then she told me, "No. I am wearing blue contacts."

"While she's still holding onto your dick?"

"Yes. She was non-stop except when she went behind the bar to get us our drinks."

"So you took her upstairs?"

"Yep. I didn't waste any time. But when we took that shower together I wished I hadn't."

"Come on Fast Eddy. It's always good having sex with these ladies. Even the ones who are not very pretty."

26

"Yeah, but you should have seen her in the shower. She was so thin. She looked like she came straight out of a concentration camp. I nearly told her to put her clothes back on and that I didn't want her. I mean, Dick, it was like, give me a refund. I'm sending this one back for a recall."

"So did you?"

"No. I thought I'd humor her. So I took her back into the room to see if I could get it up or not."

"So did you?"

"Yes. I did. I think she must have smoked me for a solid 15 minutes. She was relentless. Nonstop, like a windup toy. I came right in her mouth. And she didn't flinch. She didn't even wipe my cum off until after we went back into the shower again."

"So what happened next?"

"We go back downstairs and start drinking heavily in the bar. And she keeps feeling my dick. I mean this girl seemed totally devoted to my dick. Never seen the likes. Then, after an hour, I cave in and take her upstairs again.   Only this time I fuck her. And she's great. She straddles me. And with her being so narrow in the hips, my penis fits right up into her crotch. I cannot begin to describe it. But her being so slender gives me incredible penetration. She puts her pencil thin legs between my upper thighs and just sort of kneels there like that while she fucks me. It was like you keep crowing about, Dick. She's the perfect fit."

"Yes. The perfect fit. It's almost impossible to find, but when you do find it, you should never ever let go."

"That was only the first time I had sex with her, Dick. I banged her a lot after that."

27

The second Meeting of the New Committee

The four new committee members did not have to wait for Herman the German who was already waiting for them. Right on time.

"Let us begin right away. I won't stay long so after I leave the rest of you can talk all you want.

"Okay," replied Frank. "We will not try to interrupt you."

"All of you know that Tatyana died in our condo swimming pool. So, according to the rules of the Condominium Act we must replace her as soon as we have our first new committee meeting which is now. There are only four of you because of Tatyana's death. So you four must replace her as soon as possible. In the meantime you must elect a new chairman because tonight is the last time I serve as your chairman. Any of you want to volunteer?"

The room went silent.

"So there are no volunteers then. In this case, I recommend that you elect Frank as chairman since he lives here all the time. This means he's always available so when an emergency happens, he will be around to take care of the problem. This is not to mention his being on the committee several years ago so he already has experience. If anyone disagrees now is the time to speak out."

Once again the condo office went silent.

"Ok," said Herman the German. "So you all agree to having Frank replace Tatyana as the Bahthaus new committee chairman. I now recommend that you have a committee meeting only two or three times a year. That should be enough. I will now leave and let the rest of you continue on with the meeting."

Ghosts at the Bahthaus House Swimming Pool

All his life, Frank had maintained a rigorous physical fitness regimen, which he continued to keep throughout his new life in Thailand. Sometimes he would run 7 miles a day along the beach. Then he would start swimming. He had found that his running would go well for several weeks until he'd get injured from a multitude of causes. A knee injury or a hamstring. Sometimes it would be his feet giving out. This made him seek out alternative physical fitness regimens until his injuries had healed. He had always been a strong swimmer being able to swim long distances of a mile or more by using a variety of strokes such as a breast or side stroke. But from the time he was a child he never was able to do the Australian crawl very well finding that women, old men and even children could swim faster than he could on his best day. This is one of the many reasons he much preferred running having been the best cross country runner in his High School and having lettered on his college varsity Cross Country team.

Frank swam relentlessly. He was able so swim three laps underwater without coming up for air, especially if Tatyana was at the pool watching him. But Tatyana would never watch him swim again. His tilak was with him, lying on a plastic beach chair, helping him keep track of how many laps he had swum. Still thinking of Tatyana, he felt a hand touch him under the water.

It should have scared him, but it didn't. It felt like a hand. But it could have been something entirely different such as a discarded shoe. But even a discarded shoe would have sunk to the bottom of the pool or floated on top of the water. Whatever it was, it shouldn't have been there.

Frank shouted out to his tilak. "Something touched me under the water."

"Maybe it is Tatyana," his tilak replied. "She lonely. She want you to be with her. You scare me, Frank. Come out of the pool now."

But he kept swimming, while trying to keep track of his laps. He would do two laps doing the sidestroke. Then two laps using the breast stroke, followed by two laps free style After which he would do three more laps sidestroke. He did the tenth lap underwater, swimming forty feet as he held his breath which added up to 10 laps. And then he would repeat the sequence until he swam 130 laps.

Suddenly an old woman stood at the swimming pool entrance. And then the woman was gone. As if she had evaporated in the air. Once again, he called out to his girlfriend. "Did you see that old lady outside our pool?"

"No. No old lady come."

"I saw an old lady just outside our pool entrance."

"Are you trying to make me scare again?"

He kept swimming while losing track of his laps as he continued to think about Tatyana. And then, once again he saw the old woman standing just outside the pool entrance. Then the apparition disappeared. Grasping the edge of the pool in both hands, Frank pulled himself out of the water. Within seconds he was running through the pool entrance.

He followed the woman to Tatyana's car...a white Honda Civic. Then he noticed a younger woman following him who had just come out of Khristina's ground floor condo. The older woman heard his footsteps and turned around to face him.

Frank pointed at the woman while asking her. "Tatyana. You momma Tatyana?"

He watched the tears starting to course down the woman's face. Then she nodded as the younger woman approached Tatyana's car.

"She Tatyana's mother," the younger woman replied. "Me. Sister Tatyana."

"My name Frank. I am so sorry your sister die. I was friend of Tatyana's."

He couldn't speak a single word of Russian. So he beckoned for the two women to follow him back to the swimming pool.

When they walked back to the pool, he told the two Russian women. "I know Tatyana long time. I am her friend."

Tatyana's sister pulled a small notebook and pen from her purse and replied. "Phone number please."

After Frank wrote down his phone number, Tatyana's sister assured him that they wanted to visit him in his condo and that they would call him to set up an appointment.

Tatyana has been murdered

Frank expected the phone call from Tatyana's sister within a couple of days. But the phone call came one week later when another Russian woman called him to set up an appointment for the next day.

The next afternoon he greeted three Russian women in the condo lobby and escorted them upstairs to his condo.

The other Russian woman identified herself as the woman who had called him to set up the appointment, and that she would serve as an interpreter due to Tatyana's sister speaking only rudimentary English.

But it was Tatyana's mother who did most of the talking. In Russian, but the woman serving as interpreter was able to translate effectively.

"We think someone poison, Tatyana," the interpreter translated back to him in English.

"Do you know who?" Frank asked the three Russian women.

"No, we don't. We not sure."

"Let me ask you this then. Did anyone benefit from Tatyana's death?"

"Yes. There is a rich Russian man. He was Tatyana's partner selling and renting condos with Tatyana. If Tatyana should die, he would get Tatyana's share of the business."

"Which is Multi Land, House and Condo development," Frank added. "It's the same name that appears on that large sticker on Tatyana's car."

"Yes. Tatyana's car is owned by this company along with her lease on the condo she's renting to use as her office and home. And everything else. We are not sure exactly what Tatyana's company owns. But this man gets everything that belongs to the business."

"Do you know anything more about this man?" Frank asked the interpreter. .

"He drives a very expensive car. It's a red sports car that costs a lot of money."

Frank once again remembered the red Ferrari whose owner had recently parked in front of the Bahthaus a few times.

"Was it a red Ferrari?" Frank asked the interpreter.

The interpreter replied, after translating for Tatyana's mother. "Perhaps. But it was a very expensive and very fast car."

Danny the Fifth Member of the Committee

The committee held an emergency meeting to choose a new committee member to fill the position that had opened up because of Tatyana's death. The new committee member was an American from Los Angeles who had bought the condo next to Frank's. Since Danny was living at the Bahthaus most of the time and only visited the United States for three months of the year, he was the logical choice to serve on the committee.

Herman the German in his infinite wisdom had adopted a policy that would limit the possibilities for Thai office employees to embezzle money from his fellow condo co-owners. Although the day to day running of the Bahthaus was entrusted to the Thai manager, Herman had devised a method that would hopefully stop embezzlement by requiring all checks used to pay condo bills to be signed by two committee members.

No Thai could sign a check. Salaries to all Thai employees had to be paid by check each month. By Herman the German's edict, all bills to companies that provided goods and services for the Bahthaus were also to be paid by check–and never by cash. But unlike many other condo communities the Bahthaus office paid in advance for all water and electricity each condo owner used for his own condo private use. So each month, the Bahthaus office paid the electric bills and water bills for all 62 units, and billed each condo owner later for his share according to the amount recorded on the water or electric meter.

It was a great service most other condo communities didn't provide to their owners who had to pay their own bills direct to the water and electric company or through a Seven-Eleven, which earned a small commission from the utility company for performing this service. This amounted to each resident having to deal with only one bill which itemized what he owed for his water, electric, telephone, and his share of the television and internet service offered to all residents..

Because all checks had to be signed by two committee members, it was vital that committee members live at the Bahthaus most of the time. As it did very little good to have committee members living most of the time in England or Sweden or any other country outside Thailand because they wouldn't be in Pattaya when it came time each month for them to sign the checks.

Which is how Danny was able to get on the committee.

But Danny had many more important things to think about than condo business such as spending hours every week finding pretty massage girls to service his sexual needs. But although for the most part Danny nearly always chose 18 or 19-year-old girls, his sexual activities were really not that abnormal.

This was not the case with Harry, Danny's neighbor from Los Angeles, who had found Pattaya to be his tropical paradise many years ago and who had actually rented hotel rooms on Soi 6 for months on end. It had been Harry who had convinced Danny to visit Pattaya for his first visits to Fun Land. But Danny had come to his senses early and purchased a one thousand-three-hundred square foot two bedroom condo at the Bahthaus.

But Harry who had been renting hotel rooms on Soi 6, had become well acquainted with Dick Fitswell and Big Dicks, which Harry considered the most outstanding bar in Pattaya with the exception of Naklua's lady boy bar. And it was Harry who brought his pal, Danny, into the circle of enlightenment that oozed from Dick Fitswell's bar. Some would come to call this enlightenment the secrets to the next best thing to eternal youth whereas others would call it the effluents from a sewer.

Who is to Become Fitswell's Saint Peter?

"We have six of you here with us. Harry, Danny, Frank, Wolfgang, Scott and Fast Eddy. More will come later until we have 12 apostles to spread the word of the perfect fit as the Holy Grail all true men should aspire to. But it is going to be one of you six who will be our Saint Peter who will keep driving home the true message should any of you falter," Dick Fitswell explained to his followers.

"Harry, you show a lot of promise. But I've heard that you prefer lady boys to Thai women. This might present a problem because I really can't see any lady boy being the perfect fit. Speaking for myself, I've always preferred women to this other sex--what is often called the third sex here in Thailand. Would you please explain to the other men gathered here why your preference for lady boys might still qualify you as my number one disciple?"

"Dick. When I first started coming to Thailand, the Thai women were very different from what they are now. Thai women have become very greedy, lazy, and most of them have gotten fat. And I find that very few of them want to have sex with an old fart like me. But lady boys aren't really men. As you just said yourself, lady boys are called the third sex in this country. They are neither men nor women. They are women trapped in a man's body. Many of them have silicone breasts now while some of them have had their dicks cut off and had their privates changed into pussies. So let me ask you, Dick. If a manmade pussy is the perfect fit, and it is a lady boy who has this manmade pussy, doesn't the lady boy qualify as the perfect fit?" Harry asked.

"You do have a point there," Dick Fitswell replied.

"Now let me take this one step further," Harry continued. "Suppose then that a lady boy still has a dick. But she's got a great ass. And that ass fits me to a T. While the sex keeps getting better and better. Should we really disqualify this lady boy then?"

"Okay then. You have made your case. I'll just have to watch you over the next few months." Then Fitswell turned to Fast Eddy.

"Fast Eddy, you have this beautiful young lady. I believe her name is Kit. For some reason she is your favorite woman of them all. Yet you've had some great looking ladies with terrific bodies. But you keep sticking with Kit. So it would seem that you have already found the perfect fit. On the other hand, it seems to me that you are losing control. From what I've observed and from what you have told me, Kit has your number. I want you to know that in every relationship it's either the man or the woman who has the upper hand. Put another way, the partner who loves the other partner the most, has already lost."

"And you, Wolfgang, you show great promise. But most of your sexual partners are lady boys. You had a live-in girlfriend for four years. But you got tired of her. Then you started to go with the lady boys, and when one of your girlfriend's friends saw you on your motorbike with a lady boy riding behind you, your relationship with your girlfriend suddenly ended. And now you have a different sex partner with you practically every night. But you don't keep any of your sex partner's for long, which is great. You remind me of the younger Dick Fitswell I used to be, who was always on the prowl for the perfect fit. But you are like Harry. From what I gather. From what you have told me and what others tell me about you, most of your sex partners are lady boys so if I disqualify Harry as my number one disciple, I would need to disqualify you for the same reasons."

"But I'm completely bisexual," Wolfgang replied. "My stable of sex partners runs about 50-50 with 50 percent of them being women."

"Your point is duly noted, which brings us to Scott."

"Oh so it's my turn?" Scott replied. "I'm probably completely disqualified then because I never fuck any women anymore. The lady boys offer much better sex than any woman ever could."

"Once again," Dick Fitswell replied, "It all comes down to whether or not a lady boy can realistically be called the perfect fit. But, Scott, you do have this going for you, and probably more so than the other guys here. You are a total control freak. The truth is most people would find you to be a complete psycho. But I find your conduct to be admiral. I was the same way except I preferred women. Now I've heard that you brand your favorite lady boys. Can you explain this to the rest of us?"

"My full name is Scott Pruit. So my initials are SP. I created a wonderful tattoo that is based on my initials, SP, turned upside down. And I've used a special script so it's difficult to make out the SP unless you know what to look for. I had this favorite lady boy who I was completely in love with, but then I went back to the United States, and when I got back to Pattaya I found out she was cheating on me. And not only cheating on me–she actually had this new boyfriend of hers pay for a breast job. So I decided to punish her. She liked the tattoo I had created and then I offered her five-thousand baht if she would let a tattoo artist put my tattoo on her belly. When a lot of the other lady boys liked her tattoo I started offering five-thousand baht to each lady boy who would allow me to 'put my brand' on them. It's not a brand. It's a tattoo, but it's my initials so I've marked each one of them as my property."

"Now that's really sick, Scott. I love it," Dick Fitswell replied. "Which brings us to the essence of Saint Peter. Saint Peter has to be totally in control. And you are so much in control–well what can I say. You belong in a cage, Scott. You are a real predator."

"What about me?" Danny asked, in a voice craving attention..

"To be quite honest, in many ways you are a complete wimp, Danny, but you are like Scott in many ways. You like to control your women, even if most of the time it doesn't work. And one cannot argue with your success. You spend hours each day looking for the prettiest massage girls. And you get them at a very low price point. You are almost a pedophile since you prefer girls who are 16 or 17. But you are usually smart enough to make sure they are 18 or 19. Now most normal people find this to be reprehensible. But I find it admirable. Eighteen and 19-year-old girls are at their peak, physically. And in a place like Thailand where money can buy you any woman you want, why not settle for the best? However, I personally find most 18 and 19 year olds to be about as sexually attractive as a cow. And not because they are fat, but because they are pretty brain dead. There's nothing inside their heads. It's only when they go through the maturing process that they start to develop character."

"Well gentlemen: You all know where you stand. Fast Eddy, there's no question that you have found the prettiest girl around. I've met Kit several times and you have shown me dozens of pictures you have taken of her. She's cute beyond belief even if she's got the body of a scarecrow. But I must warn you. You must gain the upper hand with her. And Danny, you show a lot of promise. You like to get the upper hand with your women. And

you don't like lady boys, which is all to the good. And for you,
Harry, Wolfgang and Scott, a lot depends on whether in the long
run we consider lady boys to be women or men."

Embezzlement at the Bahthaus

Frank noticed something very odd with the accounts he was pouring over in the accounting system, as he considered the possible reasons why there was so little in the condo operating account at the end of each month.

There's an account in the accounting system called undeposited funds. At the Bahthaus, if a resident paid an invoice of for example one-thousand baht, this one-thousand baht would show up as undeposited funds on the Bahthaus balance sheet. But the one-thousand baht would not show up yet on the balance sheet as cash deposited in the condo's main operating account. And the reason was simple. The condo bookkeeper had not yet deposited the one-thousand baht the condo resident had handed her.

He spent more than two hours clicking on the main operating account figures appearing on the Bahthaus balance sheet to find out when the bookkeeper was actually making the deposits of money she had collected from the condo owners. For example, he would click on the amount shown on the balance sheet for June 15, 2014 for undeposited funds, and it would show 450000 baht in the account. Then he'd change the date on the balance sheet to June 28, 2014, and it would show 800000 baht. Finally he would click on the amount in undeposited funds for July 4, 2014 and it would show 200000 baht.

Smelling a rat, Frank pulled out the Bahthaus bank book for the condo operating bank account to check when the bank actually recorded deposits from the condo owners. And found the same pattern.

Checking the bank book more thoroughly, Frank ascertained that whatever Koko's personal problem was that had driven her to start embezzling money from the condo owners, it had worsened, and that she was finding it more and more difficult to pay them back. Which is why the July balance for 2012 for the operating account was 500000 to 600000 baht (he was checking various dates within the month which would show different cash balances) while it had dipped to 150000-200000 baht for July of 2014.

Which got Frank thinking: "What on earth is Koko borrowing all that money for?"

One scenario was that she was lending money out at exorbitant rates to Thai people who didn't have good credit ratings and who therefore could not get loans at a bank. He had heard stories of Thai mafia thugs lending money out at interest rates of 100% per month. Or possibly she might have invested in real estate, either a house or condo being built in which the total payments had to be made over the first six months. And that she had hoped to pay the Bahthaus back from the rent she hoped to receive once the property was finished.

Now that he had caught Koko embezzling, he now had to decide what to do about it. The solution would have been to call a committee meeting and have the committee make the final decision. But a phone call soon caused his whole decision process to be a no-brainer.

In the lawyer's office

Frank brought one committee member with him to the lawyer's office. Danny. Already waiting for them was Herman the German and Shayla Sleight of Hand , who had been Herman the German's personal lawyer for years, who had also become the lawyer handling all of the Bahthaus affairs.

"What's up?" Frank asked Herman the German and Shayla Sleight of Hand . "Why are we suddenly being called up to attend this meeting?"

"It's Koko," Herman the German replied. "She's been embezzling money from the Bahthaus for years and suddenly she's disappeared."

"How do you know that, Herman?"

"She hasn't shown up for work for the past three days," Herman replied. "I know you are the new chairman but you have only been at it for a couple of weeks now, and Koko's stealing has been going on while I was the chairman. And since I was the one who hired the present manager, the manager called me instead of you to report Koko's absence."

"So why does the manager think Koko's suddenly done a runner on us?"

"For one thing, the manager has seen you take a very unusual amount of time studying the accounting records. While you have asked both the manager and Koko many questions about why the undeposited funds were so high while our actual cash balance was so low. So I'm thinking that Koko must be thinking that you really know a lot about accounting, and with your complete knowledge of our accounting system that you are going to catch up with her."

"Any idea of where she is now?" Frank asked.

"We believe she's in Bangkok staying with her sister," Shayla Sleight of Hand suggested. "While Koko is not answering either the manager's phone calls to her or mine, I know her sister's phone number, and I am almost certain that I can get Koko to turn herself in."

"How's that?" Danny asked.

"I am going to tell Koko's sister that Koko's been stealing money from the condo owners, and that I am going to have Koko put in jail unless she shows up at my office on Monday morning," Shayla Sleight of Hand replied.

"And then what?" Frank asked. "You going to put her in jail?"

"Let me ask you, Frank. Would you rather put Koko in jail or would you rather have her pay the condo owners back what she's stolen from them?"

Before Frank could answer, Herman the German gently touched his shoulder as he tried to persuade Frank into following whatever Shayla Sleight of Hand advised him to do.

"If you ask me, Frank, how I feel about all of this is, I never want to see this bitch ever again. I hired her to look after our condo's money. She was working for me for two years before the condo building was ever completed. I trusted her completely. And I even lent her money from time to time. But now she's stabbed me in the back. So all of this is your decision now that you are the new chairman. But even though I never want to lay eyes on Koko again, I think it is much better for the condo owners that you don't press criminal charges against her. Which means that she won't be spending any time in jail."

"I suggest that you keep having Koko working for you, Frank. This is her only chance to pay back all that money she's stolen from the Bahthaus owners. You keep a close eye on her in the condo office for two months or three months, and when you have decided that she's paid back the money she owes, you can fire her." Shayla Sleight of Hand added.

"But how do we know, how much money she actually owes us?" Frank asked.

"That will be up to you," Shayla Sleight of Hand replied.

The Condo Owners Come out of the Woodwork to Get their Money

Frank didn't know and he didn't care how Koko was paying the money back, but somehow she was doing it. But as he studied the accounts receivable and checked which owners had paid their invoices and which ones did not, he noticed that Pieter owed 50000 baht for unpaid maintenance fees and utilities. Yet, Frank had gotten to know Pieter pretty well through the years. Pieter was loaded with money as he owned a few slot machine casinos in Holland. And in the past he had very good about paying off his Bahthaus invoices on time. For Pieter to become in debt to the Bahthaus office for 50000 baht just didn't make sense.

So he asked Koko, "I see here that Pieter owes us 50000 baht. And that he hasn't paid this for over two months now. Are you sure this is correct?"

"Not sure," Koko replied. "I talk with you later about it."

Two hours later, Frank came into the office again to ask Koko what she had found out about the 50000 Pieter owed. "See, I've taken care of it," Koko told Frank as she showed him Pieter's accounts receivable balance which now amounted to zero.

***

Two weeks later, Pieter returned to the Bahthaus from Holland. Frank didn't get hold of him until 6:00 p.m. after which he met him in Pieter's condo.

"Pieter, Koko our office bookkeeper had you down for owing the Bahthaus 50000 baht. Why do you think that happened?"

"What do you mean? I always pay back what I owe," said Pieter.

"Koko found out she had made a mistake and then corrected it to show you don't owe us anything. But I am wondering how this could have happened. Do you mind showing me some of your Bahthaus receipts for invoices you have paid?"

"I have to get into my safe. Just wait one minute, Frank, and I will be back," Pieter replied as he went to the bedroom to retrieve his receipts.

Five minutes later, Frank was studying the receipts Pieter had given him. Right off he noticed that they looked like the official Quickbooks[4] receipts but in reality they weren't.

Pieter then showed Frank some handwritten statements Koko had given him. One of these statements had Pieter paying 55000 baht cash to cover his upcoming maintenance and utility bills. Pieter made these large cash advances because he had a wife back in Amsterdam who had health problems. So he never knew when he would be able to come back to Thailand. So by paying 55000 baht and getting a credit for his money, he would be able to pay off two six month installment maintenance bills from the amount he had been credited.

Pieter, it so turned out was one of three owners to whom the condo routinely owed money due to their maintaining large credits with the Bahthaus front office. The trouble was that Koko had never credited Pieter for his paying his bills ahead of time in Quickbooks. And that's how Pieter ended up as a dead beat condo owner who couldn't pay his bills on time for over two months.

---

[4]Frank devised the official Bahthaus accounting system from Quickbooks, perhaps the most popular accounting software on the U.S. market.

Thai Military Raids Soi 6

Fast Eddy had been hearing rumors that the Thai military would soon be cracking down on the Soi 6 Bars and that a raid was imminent. So far, the Soi 6 bars had been under police protection so long as they paid their protection fees to the Thai police.

But he never gave any of this a thought, when Kit mounted him in an upstairs room. She was way too skinny, but by now he had gotten used to her painfully thin body. She was the prettiest girl he had ever found in Pattaya by far while her playful personality, attentiveness and inner beauty created a sexuality he had never found before–in any woman, anywhere in the world. Somehow she was able to squeeze her slender buttocks between his thighs, giving him awesome penetration he never had before. Experiencing it, was a dream, of having sex with thirteen year old virgins. Dreams he never had before or would ever have again because the very thought of banging thirteen or even fifteen year old girls disgusted him.

They had just finished, when he heard a great commotion coming upstairs. Suddenly three women burst into the room.

"Go downstairs now," one of the girls told him as one of the other women hastily gathered up his clothes, which littered the floor. Nearly out of breath from rushing up the stairs the woman handed him his shirt and shorts.

"The police are coming," one of the women shouted as Fast Eddy's eyes focused on the bed and floor looking for a place he could hide. If anyone could do it, he could. Because he was far more slender and muscular than 90 percent of the Soi 6 customers frequenting the bars. But there was nowhere to hide. It took him all of ten seconds to put on his shorts and shirt before one of the women started to push him out the door.

"Sorry, sorry. Leo Leo (which means hurry). The police are coming."

He managed to fasten two buttons of his shirt by the time he got to the bar downstairs where he found Kit, completely unconcerned, sitting on a bar stool.

But he had not had time to put on his underwear briefs which one of the women had scooped off the floor.

46

Fast Eddie ordered a Heineken for himself and a Jager bomb for Kit.

Then he went outside to watch the police conduct their raid.

This time the raid was to be for real because the military would be escorting the police while they made their rounds from bar to bar. There would be no favoritism toward the bars who had paid the police off because the soldiers would be there to stiffen the spines of any corrupt policemen who failed to do their duty. But the police and the military never came. I finally left thinking, "the putrescence here is absolute, on every level from the very top to the bottom of this cesspool."

Fast Eddy Meets Tatyana's Roommate

Most people believe from reading the newspapers and internet forums that Tatyana had drowned in the swimming pool. But Frank already knew a few things hardly anyone else was interested in. To most of the Bahthaus residents Tatyana was just a very attractive uppity Russian bitch. For over a year, Frank had been marveling at her wondrous figure as he watched her going into her condo at the Bahthaus. Yet he had never spoken a word to her.

Until one day when he was swimming with his girlfriend in the Bahthaus swimming pool. He watched Tatyana approaching them in a tight fitting bathing suit. Within minutes he was talking with her as they stood next to each other with the water coming up to their necks. They talked for over half an hour before he finally challenged her to a contest.

"I will bet you I can swim farther under the water holding my breath than you can."

"We will see about that," Tatyana replied. "But you go first."

Holding his breath, he was able to swim the entire 40-foot length of the pool underwater, turn around at the far end, and continue swimming underwater for another 40 feet. By the time he got back to the other side where Tatyana and his girlfriend waited for him, his tortured lungs were screaming for air. "Which is not bad," he thought. "Eighty feet under the water! That ought to impress her that I'm not like all these other old geezers who live here."

"Ha Ha. I am not about to try that. I was just teasing when I said I would do it after you finished." Tatyana told him with an impish smile on her face..

From then on, he would greet her with a friendly hello every time he saw her. Several times they sat in her car together, talking about cars and other subjects. But much more often he would join her on her patio near the pool where they'd smoke cigarettes together.

Once he asked her. "I have noticed that most of you Russians don't smile very often."

"Why should we if there isn't something to smile about," she replied.

One day while he was taking a shower in his small restroom overlooking the pool,, he noticed someone swimming in the pool during a heavy rain storm. "That has to be Tatyana," he started thinking, "because Tatyana's the only person living here who's crazy enough to do that, except for myself." And sure enough, it was Tatyana.

He had watched her swim many times, watching how she changed strokes from freestyle to a backstroke and then to a breast stroke and how she changed her strokes seamlessly.

There was no way she could have drowned in our pool, he had decided. For one thing it was less than five feet deep. And Tatyana was a wonderful swimmer.

One day he asked the German owner living down the hall about it. A man he often called Doctor German because the German was after all a real doctor. And how Doctor German had agreed with him that there was no way Tatyana had drowned.

Doctor German had asked Khun Toe about Tatyana's death. The day it had happened, Khun Toe had told Doctor German at 10 a.m. one of the cleaning women had found Tatyana floating on her back in the pool. So the cleaning lady came over and brought him to the pool where he swam over to Tatyana, and brought her to the side of the pool."

The conversation ended with Toe telling Doctor German that Tatyana did not drown in the pool.

A few hours later Frank decided to test Khun Toe's credibility by asking him the same questions Dr. German had asked him.

"So you pulled Tatyana out of the pool?" Frank asked Khun Toe.

"Chi."[5]

"And then you and the cleaning woman managed to get her to lie on her stomach once you got her out of the pool?"

"Chi."

"What happened then?"

"Tatyana roommate, Khristina. She try make Tatyana come alive again."

"You mean Khristina performed CPR on Tatyana?"

"Chi."

"Did any water come out of Tatyana's mouth or nose?"

"No." No water come out."

"Does this mean Tatyana not drown? Because if she have water in her lungs it must come out when Khristina try to make her come alive again." Knowing that Khun Toe probably didn't fully understand him, Frank pretended to be Tatyana heaving water out of her mouth. Then he pretended he was Khristina performing CPR on Tatyana by holding in his stomach and chest as he loudly exhaled. And said in Thai. "My Shy Nam." Which meant no water."

"Tatyana no drown," Khun Toe replied.

The next day Frank saw Khristina approaching her car in the condo parking lot.

Rushing up to her, Frank said, "Khristina. I am so sorry about Tatyana, your roommate."

"I am sorry also."

"I heard from Khun Toe that you tried CPR on Tatyana."

"Yes. It was me. But I already knew it was too late."

_____

"Why?"

"Because her body was no longer warm, and she had already started to get stiff. But I tried to do what I could even though I knew it was hopeless."

Malee

Fast Eddy was rapidly becoming a big fan of Soi 6. Like many long time residents of Pattaya having a live-in girlfriend, he found that Soi 6 offered him almost complete anonymity. Since most of the bars on Soi 6 were air conditioned inside and closed their doors to the street, no one could see what was going on inside the bars unless he entered the bar. Upstairs in almost all the Soi 6 bars were 300 baht short time rooms, which offered terrific opportunities to men who had Thai wives or live in girlfriends without getting their dicks caught in the cookie jar. The worse thing that could happen would be if someone who knew his Thai girlfriend saw him walking into a Soi 6 Bar. In such cases he could always tell his tilak[6] that he had gone inside the bar to have a beer with his friends.

As one of his neighbors at the Bahthaus had told him, not once, but many times, "What goes on at Soi 6 stays on Soi 6."

Fast Eddy had already had sex with a Soi 6 girl before he moved onto Dolls Go-Go which was the only go-go bar on the street. Dolls was every inch a go-go bar as the go-go bars on Walking Street. There was a main stage toward the back, and a second stage that was almost as large as the first a few feet away. He was having his second Heineken while slumping into a long couch behind the main stage when a slender girl asked him if she could sit next to him.

He bought the girl a tequila as she snuggled up next to him. Other than the girl not having the worn out jaded appearance of the typical Soi 6 girl, there was nothing special about her. But he found her attractive enough to ask her to do a short time with him.

"I want fifteen hundred baht," the girl told him. "A thousand baht for me and 500 baht for room."

---

[6] Girlfriend

"What do you mean by 500 baht for the room?" Fast Eddy asked. "All the Soi 6 bars are only charging 300 baht for their rooms. So I will give you one thousand-three hundred baht. Five hundred baht for the room and eight hundred baht for you."

"Okay," the girl agreed. "That is fair."

Upstairs the room was just another typical dowdy Soi 6 small room. He didn't find the girl to be all that spectacular either. And he didn't even cum, although he might have if he hadn't just had sex with another girl.

Fast Eddy didn't get very far after leaving Dolls when he ran into his third girl of the night. And when he took her upstairs, she did things to him the other two girls didn't until he climaxed.

One week later

He had been planning to go to the Walking Street go-go bars after going to Soi 6. But being already in the mood to get out for the night he decided to go to Soi 6 first. A couple of weeks earlier he had gone to Crazy House, on Walking Street, which had immediately lived up to its name. After having too many tequilas, he was urinating in the toilet when he felt one of the girls putting her arms around him.

He was still relieving himself when the girl started to fondle his balls. So it took him a long time to empty his bladder while a couple other girls watched. By the time he left he had even more tequilas as he sat with the girl near the stage. Yet drunk as he was, he was very horny. So horny that he nearly took her back into the toilet to have sex with her in the stall. Which she would have done since she was just as three sheets to the wind as he was. He thought about going to the ATM to get more money which would have paid for the 400 baht short time hotel across the street and still leave enough of a tip for the girl. But it was getting just too late for that since he had an agreement with his live in girlfriend to always come back to the condo before two a.m.

A few days later, he came to Crazy House much earlier, where he had a few drinks with the girl he had met in the toilet.

The go-go bar charged a one thousand-five hundred baht bar fine just to take a girl out of the bar. While charging just 800 baht for some of the girls including his new toilet girlfriend. The reason was, Crazy House was one of half a dozen of the Walking Street go-go bars that were owned by the same company. Upon finding out just how unreliable most go-go girls were, the company went to another company, which was to all intents and purposes an employment agency. It would contract with the second company for 20 or even 40 girls while guaranteeing this second company 200000 to 400000 baht a month.

The company that owned the six go-go bars would tell the newly hired dancers that they could earn over 20000 baht a month salary plus any tips their customers might give them for sex. But there was a catch that many of the girls never quite caught on to. The catch was that each girl had to get at least fifty lady drinks off her customers for every ten-day shift she worked.

Supposing a lady's drink, (which might be watered down orange juice, a small glass of coca cola or a cheap watered down Thai whisky) cost the customer 170 baht, this lady's drink cost the bar close to nothing. The go-go dancer would get the full 170 baht which would be credited to her account with the go-go bar. Then she'd work 10 days after which she would get a day or two off. After that she'd work another 10-day shift. One hundred-seventy baht times five drinks a night would come out to 850 baht a night or eight thousand-five hundred baht per shift. But, supposing she only averaged getting three lady drinks per night, the bar would then dock her salary 340 baht each night, which amounted to reducing her salary three-thousand-four hundred baht each 10-day shift she worked.

The term used for those dancers, who were under contract with the company, was Coyote. But the company employing all those coyote dancers had to make money off them due to their getting the full amount of money their customers paid for all those lady drinks. To recoup all that lost bar lady drink money the go-go bar owners started charging customers fifteen hundred baht bar fines whenever they took a girl out of the bar. However, to entice a girl to have sex with a customer, the company would kick back a couple hundred baht out of each bar fine to the girl.

Ever since this coyote bar girl plague started to hit the Walking Street go-go bars the main modus operandi of most go-go girls was to extort as many drinks as they could out of their customers in the shortest time possible. So the typical night out in a Walking Street go-go became–"Buy drink for me. Buy drink for mamasan. Buy drink for my sister (who was in most cases not

54

the girl's sister at all)."

His latest heart throb 'who he would call the "toilet girl", was not a coyote dancer, however. She worked for the Crazy House go-go, alone, as a house dancer. This meant that she did not have to go from bar to bar owned by the parent company, depending upon which go-go bar was short of dancers on a given night. Which amounted to the Crazy House only charging 800 for her bar fine. So, Fast Eddy wound up paying her eight-hundred baht bar fine the next time he saw her.

But, Sweethearts, the short time hotel across the street charged him 400 baht for a one hour fee. Later he would find out that most other short time hotels were charging between 200 and 300 baht for their rooms. But when he took the toilet girl to the cashier, the cashier had given the girl a voucher that he later found out was a kickback to either the girl or the Crazy House go-go bar. He ascertained this a few days later when he went back at one in the afternoon, when he asked for the price for a one hour stay in a room. And the cashier had told him the price was 300 baht--and not the 400 baht he had been paying.

He had found the girl to have just as good a body as he expected it to be. But unlike the Soi 6 girls most of whom he found to be pretty satisfying, she didn't try very hard in bed.

He never saw her again after that. But within a week he saw another girl at Crazy House, dancing on the stage. She seemed attractive enough, but nowhere near as sexy as the toilet girl. But he motioned to her to come off the stage to have a drink with him anyway.

She was shorter than she initially appeared on the stage in her high heels. But once she sat on his lap, she started to get down to work on him immediately. He soon found her massaging his balls as she stuck her hand up into his shorts. Then she put his hand deep into her privates. But she had already gotten several tequilas off him before he bar fined her.

Which normally would have been 800 baht. The same amount he had to pay the bar for him to take the toilet girl out to the short time hotel. But this week was the week of Christmas. So the Crazy House started offering its customers a Christmas special by raising its short term bar fine from 800 baht to one-thousand baht.

He decided to start taking advantage of the greediness of the Walking Street go-go bar owners by repaying their greediness in kind. Recalling the good old days when the go-go bar owners were only charging 600 baht bar fines, when they left it between the girl and her customers how much her tip would be and how long she could stay with him, Fast Eddy resolved on a long term plan of action that would ultimately cut the go-go bar owners out of their bar fines.

While Anne sat on his lap Fast Eddy offered her what he hoped would be a long term proposal that would benefit both of them.

"Anne, they have raised their bar fine to one thousand baht because it's Christmas. This is just too much. I will pay you one-thousand baht for short time from now on because the bar owners are charging too much for the bar fine."

Anne readily agreed. So whereas he had been paying her a one-thousand-five hundred baht tip for short time while the bar fine was 800 baht he would be reducing his cost from Two thousand-three hundred baht down to two-thousand baht. While hoping later on to offer Anne a two-thousand baht tip for staying all night with him. Anne would be doubling her money from him, while the bar would get just what it deserved which was nothing. He would also be getting her much cheaper drinks from his condo or by taking her to the Naklua bars where she would be viewed as a customer just as they viewed him.

Anne was much better in the sack than the toilet bar girl had been. And he had found her nether reasons to be simply exquisite. But he had soon gotten horny again after bringing her back to the bar. They sat together with her sitting on his lap as they French kissed each other. But by the time he left he had bought her another three tequilas plus the three tequilas he had bought for himself.

He was looking forward to seeing Anne at the Crazy House again. However, nearly all the Walking Street go-go bars didn't start admitting customers until 8:30 p.m. which is why he was starting out early at Dolls Go-Go on Soi 6.

He didn't want any part of the girls at Dolls that night because he was looking forward to short timing Anne for one-thousand baht. Fast Eddy headed straight to the bar hoping the girls would all leave him alone. "I mean what the hell," he told himself. "I'm going to have a bowl of free pop corn here so I won't have to eat right away."

His bottle of beer cost him 120 baht which was 30 baht more than nearly all the other Soi 6 bars were charging him. But a tall slender girl immediately sought him out as he sat alone on a bar stool. She stood close to him, and asked, "Do you remember me?" She was pretty. One of the prettiest girls in the place. At first he couldn't remember her and then it all came back to him. She was the same girl he had short timed for just 800 baht.

"Sure I remember. We went upstairs together. Can I buy you a drink?"

Surprisingly, she didn't ask for a lady's drink, being content to have a Leo beer in the bottle with him as he nursed his Heineken. But she snuggled up to him as they talked to each other over their beers.

He found her to be so cuddly, and so completely different from all the hardened bar girls dancing on the stages. She was so nice, so sweet looking... Fast Eddy felt as if they had known each other for years. And she was so much better looking than he remembered her being that time he took her upstairs.

"I am going to the go-go bars on Walking Street tonight," he told her. "And I'm taking notes which I will study later to put on my web site the most memorable girl of the night."

"I want to go with you tonight," she replied.

"I can't tonight because I am supposed to meet some of my friends on Walking Street, but I can see you some other night."

By the time he found Anne over at the Crazy House, he was already looking forward to seeing the girl from Dolls on Soi 6. Once again Anne charged him just one-thousand baht after he took her to the short time room across from Crazy House. But it set him back a 800-baht bar fine, 400 baht rent for the short time room and two-thousand baht for tequilas at the Crazy House. Once again, Anne completely turned him on while he was having oral sex with her in the room, but he got the feeling that she was just performing a chore and doing something she really didn't enjoy doing. Yet she had sworn him to secrecy about the one-thousand baht she was getting from him because she did not want to lose face with the other girls who were asking two-thousand baht for their short time tips. Which proved they were dumber than owl shit because Fast Eddy knew that most of them were lucky to be bar fined only once or twice a week tops.

But Fast Eddy still hoped to kick off the second phase of his plans for her which amounted to their becoming friends on his phone line application.   Later he hoped to get her to meet him outside the bar where he wouldn't end up having a bar bill of one thousand to two thousand baht and having to pay a one-thousand baht short time bar fine. Anne never replied to his messages. Although she would read them and usually make sure she was working in the go-go bar whenever he told her he was coming.

For a year he would never see her outside the go-go bars she was working in. But he would wind up seeing a lot of other girls. Especially Malee, who he would wind up listing as the "most memorable girl of the night" on his web site. But he would never find her ever working on Soi 6 again.

The Girl next door

"Fast Eddy, Have drink with me," Fast Eddy heard a woman's voice calling out to him as he was walking down Walking Street with Big John.

"Who is she?" Fast Eddy asked himself as the woman approached him. The woman was tall with a pretty face. But he just couldn't recollect where he knew her from thinking that she might have been a waitress at one of the Naklua restaurants or working at another legitimate job.

"I work at bar over there," she told him. "It's the Glass House. Come have drink with me."

"I can't. Big John and I are going to Super Girls Go-Go. But afterwards I come see you," Fast Eddy told the girl as he tried to recollect who the pretty woman was and where he had met her.

Over at Super Girls the DJ was playing that god awful noise Fast Eddy and his friends called Da-Da music. Da-Da is that frenetic electro music consisting of just two beats. The bar girls liked to dance to it, in spite of its sounding like a piece of steel scraping across a glass window.

The two men pulled themselves up on bar stools where they could get a good view of the dancers while still being close enough to interact with them. Big John liked one of the girls, who he had bought a few drinks in the past. By far the sexiest woman on the stage, as far as Fast Eddy was concerned, she had so eclipsed all the others, as to cause him no interest at all in any of the rest of the women.

He kept thinking of the girl who had approached him on Walking Street. Then he remembered. She was the girl from Dolls Go-Go Bar on Soi 6. He decided to abandon Super Girls with its mediocre girls and atrocious mind numbing Da-Da music to have that drink with her over at the Glass House.

Two hours passed by very quickly at the Glass House. Malee had no clue what her bar fine was since the bar had just opened, and she had just started working there. But when one of the other girls told Malee that her bar fine was one-thousand-five hundred baht, Fast Eddy decided to catch up with her later due to the bar fine being so outrageous. Deciding the bar was too greedy to justify his paying any bar fine, he decided to get her phone number to arrange a meeting when she was not working.

"My birthday is Wednesday," said Malee. "Will you come see me?"

"Yes. I will be here," Fast Eddy replied.

On Wednesday he bought her a small gift. Because after all, she was the girl next door and so unlike any other bar girl he had ever met. But she never showed up. Which left Fast Eddy having a few drinks with two of the other girls. But the bar fines were too high. Fast Eddy resolved to never step into the place again while chalking up Malee's unreliability as just one more "birds in the attic; no one at home" bar girl experience.

Catching the Embezzler

"Frank. Can you come to the condo office right now?" the new manager asked him on the telephone.

When he got to the office five minutes later, he found the manager already there with the condo technician and a locksmith drilling out the lock on the condo safe.

"We need to find out how much cash is in the safe," the manager told him. "This will tell us for sure whether or not Koko has been stealing."

After drilling out the lock, the locksmith found a metal box inside the safe. "Open it," the manager told the locksmith in Thai.

There was just two-thousand baht in the metal box. But there should have been 600000 baht there in cash deposits the Bahthaus owners paid to Koko to pay off their invoices that showed up on the balance sheet as undeposited funds.

"Now you can see," said the manager. "I had nothing to do with this. We continue looking for Koko who has still not been answering my calls."

"Our lawyer has found her already," Frank replied. "She's staying with her sister in Bangkok. She is to come back to this office and work for us until she's paid back everything she's embezzled."

On Monday Koko returned to the Bahthaus office. Meanwhile Frank had given strict orders to the manager to never allow Koko to have the key to the office again.

"She's a thief," Frank told the manager. "So she's going to pay us back what she owes us or she's going to jail. So you make sure that whenever she comes to work in the morning that she must ask you for the key. I don't want her in that office unless you get there first."

"You are wrong, Frank. The police are never going to put her in jail. All they are going to do is to help set up a schedule of payments which they will ask her to pay us back in installments."

"Just make sure she doesn't get a key then," Frank replied.

The next morning Frank found Koko inside the office working on the condo's books. But the manager still had not arrived for work.

But when the manager did come, thirty minutes later, Frank lashed out at her, "Oaf, didn't I tell you not to give Koko a key to the office?"

"Yes. You did, but Herman the German told me on the phone to give her a key and I did."

"Let me remind you, Oaf, that Herman the German is no longer the chairman here. I am. So when I tell you to do something, you must do it."

Stepping outside the office, Frank tried to call Herman the German who didn't answer. But two hours later while Frank was having lunch at the Heidelberg, Herman called him back.

"Herman, I told our manager not to give Koko a key to the office. But the manager gave her a key, and when I told her she had not obeyed me, she said that you gave her permission to hand over the key. I don't like it when someone goes over my head to contradict my orders."

"Frank. I never told the manager to give Koko the key. You are the new chairman now that I am finished. I would never do this to you, and I think you know that. The manager lied to you."

"I believe you, Herman. This is Thailand. LOL. Land of Lies."

The Manager Quits during the Second Meeting of the New Committee

The new committee met in the Bahthaus office at five p.m. in an emergency session. Frank wanted to update the entire committee on Koko's embezzlement of condo funds and what he and the lawyer had decided to do about it. As well as what to do about the manager's costing the Bahthaus 54000 baht for a pool tiling project that had no committee approval.

Although Frank was disgusted with the embezzlement of his fellow co-owners money, the manager's unapproved expenditure of 54000 baht on a swimming pool project outraged him.

The committee members had to wait ten minutes for the manager to arrive.

After updating the other committee members what steps he was taking to try to recover the missing funds, Frank turned to the manager.

"We have just spent 54000 baht to repair the swimming pool. You had workers you chose on your own to do that project. You approved this expenditure without even running it by me. Our condo rules specify that the manager can only spend up to five-thousand baht on her own. You should have known that you, as manager, must get the approval of at least one committee member for any expenditure up to 50000 baht. This can never happen again. Furthermore we as a committee must agree on what bidding procedures the Bahthaus must follow for all projects that cost more than five-thousand baht."

"I think we must require three bids for any big project," Kenny proposed.

"I agree," another committee member replied. "And all bids must be submitted in English. And that each bid must specify the estimated time it will take to complete the work, cost of materials, and the estimated labor costs."

After the committee approved the new bidding process, Frank returned to the embezzlement issue.

"Koko has already started working again in the Bahthaus office. Our lawyer was able to get in touch with her family. Then she convinced Koko that it was in her best interests to help us recover the money she's stolen from us. Obviously she cannot be trusted so I instructed our manager to never give her a key to the condo office. We had changed the lock to the office door and had a new set of keys made. I told our manager here to never give Koko a key, but she did. So I am bringing this up so it can be put in our committee meeting minutes and to see to it that this never happens again."

"I quit," the manager shot back in a loud voice. "Right now, I finish my work here."

Stunned, the entire committee watched the manager jump onto her feet as she picked up her purse and a folder of notes she had brought to the meeting.

"Why are you quitting?" asked Anton, a German who had served on the previous committee under Herman the German.

"Because I can no longer work under these conditions," the manager replied.

The committee members watched the manager storm out the office door.

"All I got to say," said Ian, another committee member who had served on the previous committee under Herman the German, "is good riddance to bad rubbish."

"What are we doing to do now?" asked Kenny. "We have a bookkeeper who has stolen from us already, and we no longer have a manager. We are up shit creek."

"This is a real emergency," Anton replied. "I know a fair amount about Accounting. And Frank has already had our lawyer's approval to work in the condo office as an emergency supervisor of sorts. I volunteer to work with him in the office until we can get things straightened out. But Thai law requires us to find a new manager within one month. And then we must still have an emergency meeting of the condo owners to approve a new manager."

"Speaking for myself," said Ian. "I am truly sorry that I didn't pay any attention to what was going on here while Koko embezzled all that money. I know that Herman the German is broken hearted over all this. We were all so clueless. No one on the old committee knew a thing about our accounting system and none of us wanted to learn about it. We just trusted Koko. She had done an excellent job for the few years she was learning how to do the accounting. And we all just went to sleep on the job."

"The situation is urgent," said Frank. "Anton and I will do the best we can try to run the condo office. But we must find a new manager within two, perhaps three weeks."

How Could Anyone Murder Tatyana Here?

Frank didn't doubt for one minute that Tatyana had been murdered. Her family was sure of it. And why did he feel a mysterious hand touching him while he was swimming in the pool? Which couldn't be a real hand because everyone knew that ghosts do not exist. Yet, he had felt something touch him under water. Which felt like a hand. Somehow Tatyana must have been trying to communicate with him from the dead.

Frank looked around the pool hoping to find clues. There were condos in the Bahthaus that overlooked the pool. And there were even more units in the hotel next to the Bahthaus rising over the pool. Tatyana had died in the pool around 10 in the morning. So if she had been murdered someone must have done it in broad daylight at a time when there was an excellent possibility that the murder could have been witnessed.

Deciding that the murderer would have taken a huge risk killing Tatyana in the swimming pool, Frank thought about the possibility that she had been murdered during the night before the sun had come up. Or that she had been murdered elsewhere and her body had been dumped in the pool.

But the problem with that is, Khun Toe had swum out into the pool and brought Tatyana over to the pool edge. Khun Toe would have told him and the German doctor that Tatyana was already dead because rigor mortis would have long set in long ago.

And then there was Khristina, Tatyana's roommate, who had performed CPR on Tatyana. If rigor mortis had set in, Khristina would never have attempted CPR.

But it is likely the murderer was Russian. And knowing that Russians have a long history of murdering people by undetectable poisons or even more exotic ways, Frank came up with an interesting answer to his dilemma.

"Poison. That's the likely weapon, he decided. "But if someone tried to poison Tatyana in her own condo, everyone who had been there the morning Tatyana died would be a likely suspect. So I must rule out the possibility that someone poisoned Tatyana in her condo. Also, when Khristina performed CPR on Tatyana, no water had come out of her lungs. If Tatyana had been poisoned, it would have taken her awhile to die. But, if a poison was used that acted instantaneously, she could have been dead before any water entered her lungs."

Looking around the swimming pool, Frank imagined Tatyana swimming laps in the pool. After all, the cleaning women had seen Tatyana walk to the swimming pool and had seen nothing unusual about her. Furthermore, unlike most of the other condo residents, Tatyana did not paddle around in the pool like an overweight falang. Tatyana would have been exercising hard in the water, doing her strokes meticulously as he had observed her so many times before. He reasoned that Tatyana went out to the pool, ready to exercise, and then just a few minutes later, she had died.

Poison! How does one poison Tatyana while she's swimming fast and hard? The killer can't just run up to her as she reaches either end of the pool and inject her because he is likely to be seen from one of the hotel units or Bahthaus condos looming over the swimming pool. So the poison must be delivered from a distance. That would obviously mean from either one of the Bahthaus units looking down on the pool or one of the hotel rooms next door.

"I got *it*!" Frank exclaimed to himself. "*A* blowgun could be used. The killer might have easily booked a hotel room that overlooks the swimming pool.   The only problem being that a blowgun would not have the necessary range to hit someone swimming in the pool. On the other hand someone might have been able to build a special type of blowgun that is powered by Co2 gas Or even an air rifle.   But neither will work because Tatyana's body is going to have a dart sticking out of it.*"*

Then he came up with still another solution. "How about an airgun or blowgun in which a thin monofilament line has been attached to the dart? The dart can be driven into Tatyana's body which then delivers the fatal poison. And then the murderer pulls on the monofilament line in order to retrieve the dart. So that no evidence is left behind. Or, the dart can be made up out of a biodegradable material which decomposes in water."

Kit Disappears from the Quicky Bar

Until recently Fast Eddy had never gotten a smart phone. He hated the entire idea of them. For one thing they were much larger than the cell phones he had been using. So they would be too heavy and bulky in his pocket. But he finally was forced to buy one after the Thai powers that be required their use in order to use the new telephone system that obsoleted all old cell phones.

He had already been text messaging Kit prior to her suddenly disappearing from the Quicky Bar.

So he decided to get her to meet him outside the Pattaya bars. Anywhere because it really didn't matter to him so long as they got together.

Then he found his girl next door again.

He had decided to join several of his friends who were going to the Walking Street go-go bars. One of their favorite go-go's was Oasis. But Fast Eddy didn't like the Oasis go-go girls nearly as much as he liked their happy hour specials, preferring to keeping his interaction with the girls to the barest minimum. But one night Malee came up to him out of nowhere as he drank a Heineken in front of one of the stages.

After they had several tequilas together, he asked her to do a short time with him, thinking they would go down the street to Sweethearts, the short time hotel in front of Crazy House.

"We have one room upstairs," Malee informed him. "But I not know if we can. I ask mamasan."

A few minutes later, Malee returned to tell him. "We can have room, but we must wait five minutes."

They drank two tequilas together, and then she took him upstairs. But there was no short time room upstairs. Instead they had to go through a small woman's dressing room into a room that was not much more than a closet. Several girls scrutinized them as they went into the room together. So apparently the room wasn't used very often for short times.

"Don't tell anyone here that you are boom booming me for only a thousand baht," Malee said to him as she undressed.

"Don't worry, Malee. No one will ever hear that from me."

Two weeks later, Fast Eddy and several of his friends went into a go-go bar they had never visited before. Or if they had, they had forgotten all about the place due to Walking Street having over forty go-go bars with most of them being pretty much alike.

Danny, the manager of the Doll House, looked about half asleep. Which was normal for him as Fast Eddy would realize over the many weeks and months he would keep going to the Doll House. What set the Doll House apart from all the others were the many drinks Danny soon bought for him and his pals.

Because of Danny, and the Doll House's outstanding happy hour specials, Fast Eddy started focusing his Walking Street prowl between the Oasis and its sister go-go bar, the Doll House. But the Oasis soon shut down its makeshift short time room. This forced Malee and him to do 400 baht short times at Sweethearts where Fast Eddy continued to pay Malee the same one-thousand baht tip.

He soon found another girl at the Doll House who was just as much fun as Malee. In her early twenties, Nid weighed less than 90 pounds, which made her just a little heavier than Kit although Kit was nearly three inches taller.

Fast Eddy soon found Nid to be very ticklish. He would start out sitting with Nid well behind the stage in one of the rows where most of the customers sat. In what Fast Eddy kept calling the peanut gallery. Many customers would sit in the Peanut Gallery because they were too shy to sit in front of one of the stages. While other customers would sit in the back with a Doll House dancer where they could do a lot of touchy-feely without being seen by practically everyone else in the club. Which amounted to a girl fondling a customers's testicles while the customer stuck his fingers into her privates, or giving him hand jobs and the occasional oral sex while the Doll House employees looked the other way.

Fast Eddy hardly ever indulged in such hands on activity anymore, having given it up ever since he had sat at a small stage over at the Misty's go-go bar with two girls. After buying the two girls too many tequilas, Fast Eddy rang up a five-thousand baht bar bill–while getting blow jobs from both girls as the girls alternated from one to the other as one girl sucked his dick while the other girl watched. It all went pretty well until one of the girls started to complain about having bubble gum in her mouth. Which was due to the other girl chewing gum while she smoked his penis. The bubble gum got stuck all over his pubic hair with some of it winding up in the woman's mouth.

By this time a couple of his friends and the mamasan were watching what was going on beneath the small stage. After being overcome by the smell of easy money, the mamasan kept coming up to the small stage to ask Fast Eddy to buy the two girls more tequilas.

Unwilling to give up an upcoming orgasm, a totally wasted Fast Eddy reached into his pocket for his Swiss Army pocket knife and started cutting off the bubble gum until he had removed all the sticky gum infested pubic hair with the knife's razor sharp edge.

It took awhile, but after too many tequilas, and while the mamasan watched, he was able to cum into the prettier girl's mouth.

Ever since that night, Fast Eddy tried his best to stop indulging in such mindless activity. So with Nid, he kept his sexual activity to a bare minimum such as kissing her ear lobes until her arms broke out into goose bumps. Then he'd kiss her neck, armpits, and sometimes her naval. But Nid would never break away. Because although her ticklishness was almost too much to bare, the jolt from being nearly tickled to death brought on just too much of a rush.

He also found Nid to be one of the few girls who seemed to enjoy French kissing him. Nid also enjoyed drinking a lot of tequila, and not just because she got a fifty baht kickback for every drink she could get off her customers.

But one night he found both Malee and Nid working at the Doll House. This was because too many girls were working at the Oasis while Doll House was short of girls due to some of them already having been bar fined while others simply didn't show up for work.

That night Malee wanted one-thousand baht. But Fast Eddy wanted to go to Soi 6 later on in the evening.

"Bar fine me and Nid together," Malee asked him.

"Are you joking, Malee?"

"Me not joke. You can boom boom me and Nid same time," Malee replied..

"I can't. Not tonight. But maybe tomorrow night. Or the night after tomorrow."

Fast Eddy had not been with Kit for two weeks. Meanwhile he had gone to his urologist who had given him a P.A. test for possible early signs of Prostate cancer. The P.A. test had suddenly gone abnormally high since the last one he had taken. Unfortunately Fast Eddy's MRI scan showed an abnormally large dark area in the upper portion of his prostate. Which convinced his doctor to perform a biopsy which kept him overnight at the hospital.

But the results of the biopsy would not be in for another two weeks. And here he was going to the United States for a three-week visit before the biopsy results would be in. However, his urologist had told him when they viewed the scans of the MRI together that the large dark area in his prostate had to be prostate cancer. Fast Eddy had told the doctor that he'd rather die of prostate cancer than to have his prostate removed which would have amounted to almost the same thing as having his dick amputated. But the doctor cut him off abruptly, informing him that although it normally took patients years to die of prostate cancer, it was usually something else that killed them. But in Fast Eddy's case the cancer appeared to be so far along that he'd likely die far earlier. Fast Eddy believed the doctor, because that large dark area on the MRI scan of his prostate showed even to his untrained eyes that the cancer would soon spread to his bladder.

All of this amounted to Fast Eddy having to go back to the U.S. in two weeks facing two choices. 1. Being terminal and not having much time left or 2. Never being able to have sex again.

On the brighter side, now he could have both Nid and Malee at the same time. But he had already had a three some with two women back in the U.S.. But that had been long ago, and he had never been able to cum because one of the two sisters sat on his face while the much prettier sister fucked him. The less attractive sister sitting on his face was just too fat, and since he was always turned off by overweight women, he kept thinking of the fat sister instead of the much more shapely younger sister.

71

But Kit. She was by far the cutest girl he had ever met in Pattaya. He wanted her far more than having two girls at the same time because of some unfathomable connection he had never yet found in any other Thai woman.

But there was one single compelling reason for doing a threesome with the two Doll House go-go dancers.

That was because although he was still having one-thousand baht short times with Malee, she had sworn him to secrecy because she did not want to lose face with the other girls. But if he was boom booming both Nid and Malee at the same time, one of them would be sure to tell some of the other girls. And then he would be sure to be labeled at the Doll House as a one-thousand baht man. Which meant he could later bang as many as a half dozen of the go-go girls for only one-thousand baht short time instead of the two-thousand baht most of them were asking.

By 11 p.m. he had returned to his condo from the Doll House where he immediately started messaging Kit to ask her to meet him at the Doll House go-go bar the next evening. Kit immediately accepted his proposal.

The next day, he parked his motorbike at a nearby hotel from which he could take a motorbike taxi to Walking Street. Where he called Kit on his phone.

His phone call with Kit was very odd. Kit seemed very evasive by failing to promise him that she would join him that night. So he went to the Doll House still hoping to get her to meet him while expecting her to stand him up instead.
He found Malee alone at the Doll House where they had a few tequilas. Yet he kept messaging Kit, who kept telling him she didn't know the location of the Doll House. Then she sent him, using Line, a picture of herself lying down in bed with her face in turmoil.

"My boyfriend and I finish," she messaged him. "I am very sick now and cannot go anywhere. I think I never see him again."

The next day she messaged him again, telling him, "I wish I had joined you at the Doll House."

But he had gotten drunk with Malee, who assured him that she and Nid would both meet him the next evening at the Penthouse Hotel.

72

Doing a Threesome at the Penthouse Hotel

Nid and Malee joined him at the Penthouse Hotel on time, at seven p.m. just as he arrived on his motorbike.

It cost him three-thousand baht for the room, which was one of many he could choose from. He had taken Ploy there once before for a five-thousand baht room which was around $175.00 for the night. But that other room was one of the largest at the Penthouse and it had its own Jacuzzi inside the room. The one he now chose was the Pool Side Premiere.

The room had sliding doors to the outside deck facing Soi 14 which looked a lot like the French Quarter in New Orleans. The deck also overlooked Boys Town, an area that attracted homosexuals looking for Thai homosexual men. On the deck there were cushioned chairs and a table on which management had thoughtfully placed a cigarette lighter and a clean ashtray. To the left of this balcony there was a narrow swimming pool about thirty feet in length. At its far end was a statue with water pouring out of its mouth into the pool. Fast Eddy had been in this pool over a year ago with Ploy, the prettiest girl he had ever met on Soi 6 until he met Kit.

Inside the room there was a large very ornate toilet with two shower heads. In the middle of the room there was a king size bed with a large mirror looking down on it and its occupants from the ceiling. Facing the bed was a television set on which the Penthouse played porn movies of two lady boys having sex together. Toward the end of the room was a low hanging trapeze which permitted one of two sex partners to sit while offering her partner easy access to her genitalia. A single step rose to a raised area at the far end of the room where there were a table and four chairs with a large bottle of champaign in the middle of the table along with four wine glasses.

The room also had a safe and a refrigerator that contained bottles of beer, wine coolers, and soft drinks. The room was also equipped with chocolate bars, bags of potato chips and other snacks, condoms, a hair dryer and a whole host of other things that its guests might want.

Down the hallway there was a winding staircase leading to a cavernous swimming pool with a trapeze similar to the one in the

73

room.   In addition to the trapeze there was a sliding board on which guests could slide naked into the pool.   Fast Eddy expected to find other guests using this pool, but he never found anyone else there.   Nor did he find any other guests using the narrow pool on the balcony that overlooked Soi 14/4. And although he would later wind up renting rooms at the Penthouse many times, he would never find anyone else using either pool.

After escorting Malee and Nid into the room, he asked them what they wanted to drink.

"I'll have Leo beer," Nid replied. "Ten big ones."

"I want Leo also," said Malee.

Which would cost him just 650 baht down the street at the Seven-Eleven.

Although he had often smoked cigarettes with Nid outside the Doll House entrance, he had never smoked in front of Malee. For that matter he had never smoked in front of Kit either, thinking both girls didn't want their sexual partners to have the aroma of smoke all over them. So he relished leaving both women in the room for a few minutes while he went to the Seven Eleven to get beer while smoking a cigarette on the way.

After returning to the room he asked the two girls if they wanted to swim naked with him in the swimming pool on the Penthouse deck. When they declined, he took them down to the cavernous swimming pool on the floor below them.

Fast Eddy was the first to take off his clothes while the two girls watched. Although he was able to get them to go nude, he could only get Malee to join him in the water.   There was a small table in the pool on which he was able to place his bottle of Leo out of which he and Malee drank to their upcoming carnal activities.

Back in the room, the threesome took off their clothes and got naked together on the large bed. Where Fast Eddy hovered over Malee, then Nid, as he orally savored each girl in turn before boom booming one, then the other, then back to the first girl he had started with, and finally to the second. But which one would he orgasm into? He finally stuck with Malee as Nid watched the happy ending.

Three weeks after returning from the U.S., Fast Eddy finally got his biopsy results back from his urologist at Pattaya Bangkok Hospital.

Here he learned what the doctor had originally diagnosed as prostate cancer, was likely to be an infection.

Those Wondrous Nights at La La Land

Fast Eddy soon found Kit working at another Soi 6 Bar after she told him on his phone where he could find her. He found her waiting for him just outside the entrance of La La Land, a small Soi 6 bar close to Beach Road. Radiant, with a smile he would never see again from any other girl, she took him into the bar and asked him what he wanted to drink as he seated himself in a small couch.

"Let's play game. I win. You buy me drink. You win, you buy me drink. Okay?" she asked him with an impish smile on her face.

Then she brought out that universal game all bars had to keep their customers focused on their bar girls that diffused the language barrier. This was Connect Four, which had been derived from Tic Tac Toe. Connect Four consists of a plastic frame containing six rows and seven columns. The object of Connect Four is to place 4 counters alongside each other.[7]

Kit beat him four times in a row. This was no big feat since most bar girls usually beat him due to their playing Connect Four for hours on end as they sat with their customers perfecting their technique. But he found that Kit was able to beat him so easily while showing so much delight each time she trounced him, that she unwittingly betrayed an innate intelligence that most bar girls never possessed.

Upstairs in the bedroom he found her to be absolutely exquisite. Starting out as playfully as a kitten, she would entwine her little body around him. But when they finally finished she would gleefully open her mouth to show him that she wanted to retain the essence of Fast Eddy in her mouth as if she were savoring a

---

[7] Surprisingly the game originated in the Soviet Union

fine wine.

They went downstairs afterwards where they had several more drinks as she snuggled next to him with her hand between his legs. Then they went upstairs a second time.

When he came back downstairs, he didn't go anywhere else, staying with her until the bar closed at one a.m.

Three Nights Later

Fast Eddy had just left the gym on his motorbike when his cell phone started to ring.

He heard her soft voice entreating him to come to her bar right away...that voice, soft and almost musical that he would find increasingly more difficult to resist. After promising Kit that he would join her at La La Land at seven p.m., he arrived right at seven only to find that she was not there. But another girl, who had seen him come in, rushed up to him immediately.

"Kit, eat now. She say. "You wait ten minutes for her to come. And I to get you beer."

So he ordered his usual Heineken, and waited.

Which he later found out to be a good thing. Normally he wouldn't wait for any girl no matter how pretty she was. But he put up with what would soon become her pattern. For one thing, she never was more than ten minutes late after they agreed on what time they would meet. While there were other times when he would arrive at La La Land on time only to be informed that she was in the toilet upstairs, and then she would come down a few minutes later.

At first he thought that she was doing short times outside the bar with customers which kept her reporting to work a few minutes late. Or that she was doing a short time with a customer upstairs while he waited downstairs drinking his first beer like a dim-witted fool.

But when he started to find that she was not downstairs waiting for him, he'd simply tell one of the other girls that he had gone to another bar. But after he had ordered his first beer in one of the many Soi 6 other bars, she'd call him within minutes pleading with him to come back to her at La La Land.

But whether she was loitering in an upstairs toilet or had gone out for a quick snack, he had never found her with another customer prior to his arrival at the bar. And as to her doing a short time upstairs, there was no back entrance to the bar. So any customer who might have been upstairs with her would have had to walk right by him as he waited for her.

Had she been socializing with another customer upon his arrival, he would have become so angry that he would have promptly left La La Land for another bar. Then he would have chosen another Soi 6 girl to take upstairs, if not in the first bar, certainly so in the 2nd or 3rd. Because this had never happened Kit soon became not only his favorite Soi 6 girl, but his only Soi 6 girl he would ever look forward to being with. While he was certain that he was her favorite of favorites out of all her customers.

Every night he came to Soi 6 he took his motorbike, speeding up to sixty kph as he overtook all the other traffic on Beach Road with the breeze in his face. Looking forward to being with his number one girl.

Then one night he took his camera. A Panasonic Lx10 which excelled in low light photography. He took pictures of her cavorting around and playfully posing on the bed. Prancing around the room she'd lift her t shirt over her eyes, laughing like a little child.

"But oh God, could that girl take pictures. Hardly any other camera could get the shots he got. Because the room was pretty dark, only cameras shooting with the fastest lenses at high ISO levels could begin to get what his camera could do unless they were using a flash."

So he had a thirty-inch by twenty-inch printout done for her, of one of her best poses, and brought it into the bar the next time he saw her.

Kit's portrait showed an inner beauty he'd never seen before in any Thai woman, or any Thai woman he would ever see.

Later on that night when he returned to his condo, Kit text messaged him on line, to show him the picture he had just given her, fastened to one of the walls in her room.

The Thai Mafia boyfriend

"How's it going now, Fast Eddy?" Dick Fitswell asked.

"Not great. I wasn't planning on coming to Soi 6 so early, Dick. But I just got back from visiting my tailor on Pattaya Klang and after ordering two new shirts from him, I decided to take a walk down Soi 6. As I started to walk past Quicky Bar, this older woman came out into the street to ask me to come into her bar. She told me she had something important to tell me. So I went in, got myself a soda because it was too early to start off drinking beer, bought the lady a drink, and that's when she unloaded on me."

"So what did she have to say?"

She said: "Fast Eddy. You very nice guy. I must tell you about Kit from my bar. I want you stay away from her."

So I asked her why and she replied.

"She have Thai boyfriend. He sell Yaba and other drugs. Not sure what kind but he drug dealer. He mafia. He go jail many times. Last time he go two-three months. Not sure how many. When Kit work here, he follow she into my bar. They argue too much. Very loud. He pick her up on motorbike when she finish here. I scare for you, Fast Eddy."

"You don't like Kit?" I asked the woman.

"She very quiet. I don't know where she is now. She leave bar me and I never see again. I worry her. She not tell me anything."

"So what else did you find out about your little miss Kit?" Dick Fitswell asked.

"Nothing except I thought this older woman was just one of the women working at the Quicky Bar. But it turns out she was the mamasan. And that for a while she was managing both the Quicky Bar and Foxy Bar next to it.

"So what are you going to do about it?" Dick asked.

"I'm not sure. But I'm not scared of any Thai boyfriend, mafia or no mafia. The mamasan was worried that this guy would get

79

some of his friends to beat me up or that they might shoot me. Right before I went to the U.S. when she sent me that picture on line, when Kit was so upset about losing her boyfriend, I thought she had lost a falang boyfriend. Who had been giving her a lot of money. But it looks like it's the Thai boyfriend she was so upset about. And apparently he was in jail and that's what made her so upset."

Hiring a New Manager

The new committee had two contestants to interview for the new manager's position at the Bahthaus. To keep the meeting a secret from the other condo co-owners the committee members decided to have the interviews take place in Anton's condo.

The first contestant was an attractive tall Thai woman who immediately sat next to Anton. Four committee members were present: Richard, Anton, Frank and Kenny.

"So your name is Amy?" Frank asked the slender tall woman. "And you are thirty-three years old. From your resume you have given us you were the manager of a large condo community of over 200 units. Where you were being paid 40000 baht a month. We are a much smaller community of just 62 units. Our past managers were getting around 25000 baht a month, but they only had to work four hours a day. Since there isn't nearly as much for a manager to do for a community of just 62 condo owners, we can't afford to pay any more than 25000 baht because only 62 units are paying maintenance fees here. What we have been looking for in the past is a manager who might have a second job or an older person who doesn't want to work full time. So why did you quit your 40000 baht job, and why would you be interested in working for us when we can't afford to pay anything like 40000 baht a month?"

"When I was working at the other place, there were just too many problems. The committee members were fighting between themselves, and we also had an assistant manager who was no good. I didn't get along with her and the committee. I also want to have more free time so that I can spend more time with my family," Amy replied.

"But still, there's a lot of difference between 25000 baht a month and 40000," Kenny interjected.

"Maybe we can work something out," Amy replied. "There's a lot of repairs that have to be made at any condo. Maybe I start for 25000 baht, and if I can save you money on all the repairs you have to pay, you can give me a commission on what I save you."

"That seems like a good idea," said Richard. "But we have another candidate we have to interview. We can let you know what we have decided in a week or two, Amy."

"I agree with you, Richard," Frank added. "Amy, you look pretty good according to your resume and your answers to our questions. We will get back to you soon."

Anton ushered the next candidate in after taking Amy down to the condo lobby.

"Your name is Ying, right?" Frank asked the second candidate.

"Yes," the woman replied, who was about the same age as Amy.

"And I see from your resume that you worked as number one cashier for a bank."

"That is right, Khun Frank."

"And you worked there for only two years. So why did you quit your job there, Ying?"

"I liked the job. But the bank also wanted me to sell insurance. My job was cashier for bank. Not sell insurance. And to tell the truth, their insurance was no good. So I was hurting people when I try to convince insurance good.."

At this point, Kenny stood up to get everyone's attention. And asked Ying, "You are the girlfriend of one of our condo owners here at the Bahthaus. And you live with him. I see a real problem here. If you and your boyfriend ever finish each other, how are you going to work in our condo office when you are seeing him take other ladies up to his condo?"

"I must separate my personal life from my job. I can do this. Believe me."

After Ying left, Frank asked his fellow committee members.

"What do all of you think of our two contestants?"

"Kenny has a point about Ying having a boyfriend and her living in his condo with him. This is called Nepotism," said Richard. "Which is not good. On the other hand Amy wants to get commissions from money she can save us for repairs and other expenses. But, a manager's job is to save us money. So, she should not expect to receive commissions from what she is required to do anyway."

"And I have talked to Ying's boyfriend about her. Not once but

82

many times," Frank added. "The boyfriend's contention is that most managers in most of the condo communities in Thailand don't really care if they make 20000 baht, 30000 baht or even 40000. They are after much bigger money than that. Here in Thailand the true repair costs are inflated hugely with people all along the food chain getting commissions and kickbacks. So let's just suppose that we have one repair cost of 200000 baht. It is likely that the manager is going to get 100000 baht out of that as a kickback. This one repair amounts to over an eight-thousand baht monthly increase in salary. So if Amy were getting 25000 baht a month, and we counted only this one repair we are really giving her 33000 baht a month. Not to mention the many other kickbacks she is bound to get."

"Let me give you an example of what I am talking about. A few years ago when I first started serving on the committee here before I ever became chairman we got a bid from another insurance company for our building insurance. We were already paying a one-hundred-thousand baht premium for insurance. I called up this new insurance company and I was the one asking for a bid. After two weeks I never got a reply. Finally the insurance agent insisted on seeing our manager. When I asked her why, she was stupid enough to tell me, "So I can work out his commission for him." Then she told me the manager was entitled to a fifteen-percent commission, which would have amounted to fifteen-thousand baht for the work I did. And most certainly not for "Cornhole[8] who was our manager back in those days. I was the one who got her the chance to do business with us. Cornhole didn't do jack shit. He just wanted to get his filthy hands on money he didn't deserve."

"I make a motion for us to call for a vote now," Richard announced to his fellow committee members. "I think Amy's a real phony. She's a part of what's wrong with most of these Thai

---

[8] Cornhole was the derogatory nickname for the manager in Welcome to the Fun House

managers who are out to get all the kickbacks they can. She's a real professional.   But we must think out of the box. Ying has an entirely different background. She's not part of all this corruption that permeates Thai condo communities. Let's try her out. Let's offer her a contract where she's on trial for three months starting at 18000 baht, and if we still like her after she's been here for three months we up her salary to twenty-five-thousand baht."[9]

"I second Richard's vote," Kenny replied.

Which both Jack and Anton agreed to.

---

[9] Roughly $700 to $800

The Bahthaus Hires a New Bookkeeper

For over a month Frank and Anton had been spending more than fifty hours a week in the condo office sorting out the accounting mess Koko had created to establish how much Koko still owed the condo owners. By the end of the month Koko was still performing her normal bookkeeping duties. While Ying took her place at the desk next to Koko to learn the Bahthaus accounting system from Anton and Frank.

Before the second month ended, the committee decided it was time for Koko to go since the balance sheet showed that she had somehow paid back the money she had embezzled.

This left Ying alone with a huge amount of work ahead of her.

It was Kenny who suggested an assistant to take Koko's place doing the bookkeeping and it was Kenny who told his fellow committee members, "I have the ideal person for doing this job."

The committee wisely decided to make Ying a vital part of the hiring process. Because, the two women would have to work closely together, there would be no room for jealousy or power plays between the two women.

A single woman applied for the job. Because Kamon had once worked for a company that had its office next to the Bahthaus office, Frank knew her very well. The company sold real estate and managed condo rentals for absentee owners for a fifteen-percent fee.   Frank had lunch with the woman many times at a small Thai restaurant just up the street. On several occasions she had taken him to nearby condos to show him units that his friends had asked him about. He had always been impressed with the woman's vitality and intelligence.

The committee members in the office asked very few questions. Leaving it to Ying and Kamon to do most of the talking. After Kamon left the building, Ying could hardly conceal her excitement, exclaiming to Kenny, Anton and Frank.

"I want her! I really want Kamon to work with me!"

"Done," Frank replied. "We will hire her. Do you two agree?" Frank asked Kenny and Anton.

"Yes. Absolutely," Anton replied. "We are lucky to have these two women."

*****

Wolfgang found Frank and Anton discussing the new Bahthaus management team at a neighborhood beer bar.
"Come join us, Wolfgang," said Frank. "We are talking about the new manager and bookkeeper we recently hired for our condo office."

"Do you think they are any good?"

"So far the manager is working very hard learning how our accounting system works from Anton and me. Anton and I have been working over 50 hours a week teaching her while we have been trying to recover all the money Koko has embezzled from us. And we just hired a new woman to take over Koko's job as bookkeeper."

"Is the new woman working for you now?" asked Wolfgang.

"Yes. She is learning the accounting from Anton, me and our new manager."

"So you have three women in the same office working together?"

"No. We just had our new manager fire Koko."

"How did you manage that? Did you have to give Koko severance pay? I am good friends with your new manager's boyfriend. He's German just like Anton, and me. I have met Ying a few times already."

"We are not paying that embezzler any severance pay," Frank replied.

"How are you getting out of paying severance pay? My understanding is once an employee works five years, the employee is vested. And for every year the employee has worked the employer must pay the vested employee one month's salary for every year she's worked."

"We got our lawyer to draw up a resignation letter for us. Which Ying handed to Koko. Koko signed it immediately."

86

"I wouldn't have done it if I were Koko. Even if I had embezzled all that money," Wolfgang replied.

"Well Wolfgang, you just don't know our lawyer, Shayla Sleight of Hand. Most of the other lawyers in Pattaya are terrified of her. She has connections you don't even want to know about."

"Well, it's very difficult to prove that someone's embezzled money here in Thailand. The courts tend to side with the embezzler. This is because embezzlers usually embezzle because they have real problems and the courts are sympathetic to such hard up people."

"We have bypassed the courts, Wolfgang," said Anton. "If we took Koko to court, the court would never have put her in jail. Instead the judge would have made the Bahthaus draw up a schedule which the embezzler would be expected to follow by slowly paying off what she has embezzled over a long period of time."

"How long?" asked Wolfgang.

"A hundred years," Frank replied.

"So what are you guys going to do now?"

"Ying and Kamon are very smart women. It shouldn't take us much longer to fully train them."

"Do you think they are honest?" asked Wolfgang.

"Anton and I think so."

"I beg to differ."

"Why?"

"From what I understand, the Bahthaus has all its residents paying off their invoices in cash which they hand to whomever is handling its books. In your case this is going to be Kamon. But keep in mind that the average salary here in Thailand is just 200 baht a day for unskilled labor. That's just $6.00 a day in U.S. money. But even talented college educated women are making just 12000 to 15000 baht[10] a month. Perhaps twenty-thousand if the woman is extraordinary. That's just $500 to $600 a month. Now, when you have residents bringing cash to your condo office, either your manager or bookkeeper can run off with two-hundred-thousand baht or even a lot more quite easily.   If your average resident is paying a twenty-thousand baht maintenance fee every six months, it's only going to take ten residents paying twenty-thousand baht in just one week for the bookkeeper to pile up two-hundred-thousand baht in cash."

"I don't think either Ying or Kamon would ever do that," Anton replied.

"Make it 300000 baht then. All it's going to take are fifteen owners paying their maintenance bills in a one or two week period. This is like putting 300000 baht on the table and asking the office girls, "please take this money. Why 300000 baht will buy a pretty nice house upcountry in Issan," Wolfgang added. So the gal simply disappears up in Issan and that's the last you will ever see of her."

"Well, I don't know," Frank replied.

"How much did Koko get away with at the most?" asked Wolfgang.

"I'd say she was holding back nearly one million baht from the owners which she was not depositing in the bank at times."

"There you go," said Wolfgang. "My case is closed. If someone's financial circumstances change for the worse, say an illness in the family, one's honesty is likely to change for the worse."

"I don't know what we can do about it other than to watch the women working in our office a lot more closely than the previous committee watched Koko," Frank replied.

---

[10]$375 to $470 a month at 32 Baht to the dollar

"I have a suggestion for you," said Wolfgang. "Why don't you make all residents pay their bills direct to the Bahthaus bank account?"

"You must be joking!" Frank exclaimed.

"They are doing that in Germany now. Not everywhere but where they are doing it, it is working quite well."

"I agree with you, Wolfgang. Being German myself I am well aware of such instances.," Anton added.

The Bahthaus Implements Direct Bank Payment

Ying and Kamon were very excited about making the residents pay their bills direct to the Bahthaus bank account. The first step was having Frank modify the invoices that the Bahthaus was sending out to all the residents. At the bottom of each invoice that the accounting system generated Frank put, "Please send payment to Bangkok Bank 866-3-08002-4, Bahthaus condo," And please notify our office of your deposit IMMEDIATELY or you won't be credited.

The two women then plastered signs on the office walls that read, "Our office does not accept cash." Which meant for anything and everything, and not just for payment of utilities and maintenance fees.

Residents could pay the condo bank account by three different methods. 1. They could go to the bank and give a teller a direct deposit to the condo bank account, 2. They could go to a nearby ATM machine and use their ATM card to pay their invoices (which took all of five minutes at most), or 3. They could pay by internet. Which they could easily do on their phones.

At first many residents resisted the new methods of payment. But after several months, everyone got used to it. Because neither Ying nor Kamon took any prisoners. Both women were disgusted by the embezzlement Koko had pulled off. And since both women were very honest (a rarity in most Pattaya condo offices) neither woman had one ounce of sympathy for anyone who did not follow the new rules.

Harry's meeting with Dick Fitswell

"Harry, what latest depredations have you been up to lately?"

"Just the usual shit, Dick. But last night I had a night that makes me proud."

"Oh really. Please tell me about it."

"It all started out at the Lady Boy Bar in Naklua. Although its real name is TJ Bar. It's a great place because every lady there is a lady boy. A lot of them have silicon tits now. One of the lady boys is from Laos. She only weighs 42 kilos although she's pretty tall. Nowadays most Thai bar ladies weigh more than that, and if there's anything I can't stand is a fat bimbo."

"So what happened?"

"I'm sitting on this bar stool where I start buying beers for, Kimi, the lady boy from Lao. Who starts feeling my dick. Then Kimi starts putting her hand up my shorts. Next thing I know is I'm putting my hands on her cock, and I start rubbing it. After it gets good and hard, she sits on my lap, pulls down her shorts and tries to stick my cock up her ass. But you know, Dick, it's damn hard to get your penis up someone's ass while you are sitting on a bar chair."

"So what did you do then?"

"I told Kimi that I had to go to the toilet which is the usual outdoor affair that's in its own building and isn't part of any bar. Suddenly she is walking with me to the toilet. We go inside together, and she follows me into one of the stalls, so we lock the door and remove all our clothes. Then she starts to smoke me while I'm sitting on the toilet."

"You fuck her in the ass, Harry?"

"You bet I did, and I shot my wad into her ass too. And you should have heard Kimi screaming with delight. But she started to scream so hard that one of the girls from the bar next door came over and started pounding on the door. Which made it harder to cum because I could no longer focus on what I was doing. But the bitch kept knocking and knocking and after awhile I started getting used to it. Finally I started cumming into the lady boy's orifice while the bar girl continued knocking on the door. It was great, Dick. And so deviant. I felt so wonderfully despicable afterwards."

"Why do you like lady boys so much Harry?"

"First off, I don't think many Thai ladies like to fuck an old geezer like me. Secondly, you know when a lady boy is cumming. With women it's awfully hard to tell. Thirdly, lady boys don't have any children, and I hate kids. And I am starting to dislike all women who have kids because we will never be number one with any woman who has children. Fourthly, lady boys are more extroverted than Thai ladies as a rule. So they are more fun to be with. Fifthly, a lot of lady boys are content to drink beer with me, so my bar bill ends up being a lot less. And last, almost all Thai bar ladies send most of the money we give them home to their family. To their worthless parents or their lazy brothers and sisters. Although a lot of lady boys do this also many of them don't, so I feel like I'm not throwing my money away. One more thing. The most beautiful Thai ladies are not ladies. They are lady boys, and as I mentioned earlier, most Thai women today are getting fat. But the lady boys exercise a lot more so they are in much better physical condition."

"You are making some very good points Harry. I am just blown away by what you just told me," Dick Fitswell replied.
"Dick, you ever eat chickens?"

"Of course I have."

"Hear me out now. Back in America over 60 years ago, farmers used to keep chickens around their farmsteads, and these chickens had to forage around the farm for their food. The farmer would throw his garbage and scraps all around the farm lot. So the chickens were all running around the farmstead competing against each other for their food. The farmers would butcher their own chickens. But they would also keep a few hens around the farm and these hens would lay eggs. So the farmers didn't have to go to a supermarket for either their meat or eggs. They also kept a few hogs which they would butcher so they could eat pork."

"But times have changed," Harry continued. "Nowadays farmers go to the supermarket to buy their eggs, chicken and pork. Most farmers today raise their crops which they sell. But a few farmers specialize in hogs, cattle, and chickens which they fatten up in

92

confinement enclosures. And the farmer who is able to fatten up a hog, chicken, or steer in the least amount of time at the lowest cost makes the most money. It's kind of like people who sit around all day watching television who get very little exercise. They get fat from all that inactivity. But getting back to the confinement pens. The farmers who specialize in hogs, cattle or chicken production keep their animals confined so closely together that they can hardly move. All this results in an animal that has put a lot of fat on in very short order, and when you end up eating its meat from the supermarket you are going get an oily taste in your mouth. The taste is horrible compared to what these animals tasted like when they had to exercise a lot from moving constantly about in a farmer's farm lot."

"Now stay with me, Dick. Here in Thailand you eat a lot of chicken which has not been raised in all those confinement pens. Just go up to these villages up in Issan, and you will find so many villagers having their chickens running all over their place. It's like America used to be. So chicken usually tastes a lot better in Thailand that it does in the United States. Even in Thailand's Kentucky Fried Chickens, chicken tastes so much less flabby than it does in an American Kentucky Fried Chicken restaurant."

"Now here's my point. As a rule fat people are getting a lot less exercise than thin people do. So when you are eating a slender Thai woman, you have probably noticed that she tastes a lot better than a fat woman. Unfortunately most Thai women are now getting fat because of all the junk food they are eating. So, if you are smart, you look for the skinny Thai ladies. But there's a lot more lady boys who keep in shape than there are Thai women, nowadays. This is a very important reason why I prefer lady boys to Thai women."

Issan Bar Girls Who Quack Like Ducks

"I'll tell you what, Dick. It's when she put that picture up in her room that put me over the edge with her. Now even you have to admit that this shows real appreciation. I can't think of a single girl in Pattaya who would do that. And then message me a picture of it on the wall. And she's soft spoken and so polite. How many of these women thank you for all the things you have done for them?"

"About zero," Dick Fitswell replied.

"And so many of these women start to quack like ducks with their Issan voices. While others talk like stupid cows. And Kit's far from stupid. Unless she's drunk, she's always alert. Doesn't miss a thing. She's also been very astute by keeping this online messaging going between us. For several months now. I don't care if she's sincere or not. She's clever. Want to hear more?"

"You've got my attention."

"We spend a lot of evenings at La La Land together, until the bar closes. Sometimes she would have one or two too many, and then she slips into the toilet where I can hear her puking inside. Then she comes out as if nothing had happened and slips into my arms on that couch. That little girl really has guts."

"I am finally able to get her out of the bar. One night it starts to storm so bad that all the lights go out on Soi 6. So the manager of La La Land decides to dismiss all the girls and closes down the bar for the night. Which leaves Kit totally bewildered. She wants to go back to her room, so I ask her to go with me to Walking Street. She watches me gesturing to her to follow me as I start to walk out of the bar. I really don't know what she's going to do, and I don't think she does either. Then I look back and see her standing just outside her bar wondering what I am up to. So I tell her: "Motorbike taxi. Walking Street. I give you two-thousand baht."

"Money." That magic word convinces her. At the end of Soi 6 I get two motorbike taxi drivers to take us to Walking Street. When Kit's driver shoots ahead of the motorbike taxi I'm on, I am not sure at all if anyone understands what I am up to. The other motorcycle taxi driver is going pretty fast, and Kit keeps looking back at me and my driver. It is like she has never been on a motorbike taxi before. Or has never seen the scenery flashing by her as her motorcycle taxi shoots up Beach Road. I watch her smiling and looking around, gleefully like a little girl riding a bicycle for the first time.

"Our two motorbike taxi drivers pull off right at the Beer Garden right before Walking Street. Where they have the Thai boxing arena and all those beer bars surrounding it. That's where we get off as I pay the two drivers nearly 200 baht."

"I walk fast down Walking Street–darting around all the tourists cluttering the street expecting Kit to lose sight of me. But there she is, walking quickly only a few feet ahead of me. When I turn to my left and go to walk down Soi Diamond, I'm hardly paying attention to her. Because I know my girlfriend has many friends, who would tell her that I have taken a girl with me."

"At the Doll House I find my manager friend, Danny, working on the first floor. Who joins Kit and me right after we are seated in the first row of the peanut gallery where most of the club's customers are sitting just a few feet in front of the club's main stage."

"You probably want your usual gin and tonics, Fast Eddy, which is your favorite happy hour special," Danny says to me. "But who is your lady you brought with you?"

"This is Kit." Then I turn to Kit to inform her that Danny is the manager of the go- go bar.

"What should I get her, Danny? Is there a happy hour priced drink you can recommend for her?"

"We have a concoction that is mango and vodka. All the ladies seem to like it. I guarantee you, Kit will like it."

"Five minutes later, a waitress is bringing us our drinks. They are two for one specials which cost just 75 baht apiece. Had I been buying for the go-go girls working there, I would be paying around 170 baht for each ladies drink. But Kit is a customer, same as me, because she is not working for the Doll House. This would continue from 8:30 to 10:30 during the Doll House Happy Hour."

"I am surprised to see that Danny can speak fluent Thai. I watch

Kit warm up to him straight off, as she speaks rapidly to him in that terrific voice of hers that betrays not one hint of that quacking Issan accent."

"By the time I down four gin and tonics and after Kit finishes off two of her Mango vodka happy hour specials I spot Kit and one of the Doll House girls exchanging glances. Then when the girl goes up to the stage and starts dancing, Kit asks me, "Can you buy girl drink?"

"When I reply, "Sure. No problem," Kit immediately calls for one of the waitresses who goes to the stage to inform the girl that Kit and I are buying her a drink".

"The girl soon joins us due to the policy followed by most go-go bars, that as soon as a man buys a drink for a girl dancing on stage, the girl has to immediately join the man who has bought her the drink."

"The two women speak to each other all of five minutes before Kit turns her attention totally on me. A few minutes later Danny rejoins us, and when I ask him why Kit wanted me to buy the other girl a drink, Danny replies: "They must know each other from another bar."

"Well, I don't know about Kit, but the girl working for you looks like a drug addict to me. Her movements are jerky and she has those eyes I've seen in so many drug addicts before." But as I share my suspicions with Danny, I am thinking about Kit while thinking of many drug addicts I had known before. I start speculating: "how I can bring a girl I know is on drugs into a crowd and the girl with me can immediately pick out another drug addict from among the crowd?"

"So maybe Danny is misjudging the two girls. Perhaps they had never met each other before, but Kit has picked her out from the Doll House group of dancers as a kindred spirit who shares the same addiction."

"But I can't tell for sure, one way or the other. Because whatever the connection is between the two women, by this time, Kit is getting drunk. We had started drinking tequilas as soon as the other girl sat with us. But Kit is totally into me. The other girl comes over to sit with us two more times, and each time I buy the two women tequilas, Kit barely pays attention to the other girl."

"The night ends with Kit getting totally trashed. By the time we leave the Doll House as we are walking down a back street to 2nd road, she is on wobbly legs. While her pace whether she is drunk or not betrays an oddity that I attribute to what might have been a childhood affliction. She's walking down the street and when she looks like she is going to fall down I grab her around her waist. But I must be nearly as wobbly as her. Both of us half carrying each other down to the junction of 2nd Road and Pattaya Tai where I put her on a motorbike taxi that is going to take her home."

Catatonic Kit

"Dick, I will never forget that night when Kit went comatose on me at La La Land. She's done that a few times since that night. I just don't know what to make of it."

"Let me begin with my telling you it was great therapy having Canada John back at the Bahthaus even if it was just for one week. Canada John and I met each other while we were exercising next to each other on the elliptical machines at the physical fitness center. I was trying to learn Thai from a USB that I always put in the elliptical machine. So here I am talking to myself while I am repeating the phrases I'm hearing from the USB. The guy sitting next to me thinks I'm crazy, and then he asks what I'm doing. One week later we are both trying to speak Thai while we are exercising side by side on the elliptical machines. Canada John and I quickly become good friends until the company John is working for moves him to China. But John never forgot Pattaya and all the great times he had there, so after several years working in China he buys a large condo at the Bahthaus."

"By this time I am seeing Kit several times a week. But most of the time I visit her at La La Land on Soi 6 even though I have been bar fining her to take her to the Doll House on Walking Street. But if there is any girl from Soi 6 who is as pretty as Kit, that woman has to be Ploy who had long ago moved onto bigger and better things. I had all but forgotten Ploy until I joined several of my friends who are visiting the new go-go bars on Soi Lemke".

"I am about to cross the street to join my friends in the Champagne Go-Go bar, when a motorbike pulls up next to me."

"Do you remember me," the pretty girl riding the motorbike asks as she pulls inside a gap between a long row of motorbikes.

"Sure I do, Ploy."

"I thought you forget all about me," the pretty girl replies.

"Like hell I forgot all about her, I tell myself. " I've only boom boomed her about a dozen times back when she was working on Soi 6." And I had also taken her to the Penthouse Hotel on my birthday. Where unlike Malee and Nid, Ploy had wanted to spend the entire night with me at the Penthouse, which I would have done except for the fact that I still had a live in girlfriend who would be waiting for me to return to her at two a.m.

"I also remembered one time when the condom I'm using blew apart on us and Ploy had told me, "No big deal. We are good friends anyway."

"Until I met Kit, Ploy had been by far the prettiest girl I had ever met on Soi 6. She is tall and long legged, and very beautiful in the face but back in those days she had been costing me only 800 baht for short time sex. But Ploy is a very talkative girl, who enjoyed drinking with me for an hour or two after we had sex."

"Turns out Champagne go-go is pretty dead so my friends and I go across the street to Lady Love go-go bar where I meet up with Ploy. But we don't stay long."

"So here I'm filling Canada John in about Ploy, and after I show him Ploy's line profile on my phone, Canada John starts giving me all kinds of good fatherly advice even though I am nearly 20 years Canada John 's senior."

"I think Ploy just might be a far better choice for you than Kit," Canada John tells me. "Kit's pretty flighty whereas Ploy seems to have her shit together."

"But look at this line profile of Ploy's, John. She's obviously had a tit job since I've seen her. And she's got over two-thousand friends on her Facebook page. While somebody's obviously bought her all that silicon. If you ask me, she's pretty high dollar now while Kit is a babe in the woods compared to her."

"Well, just give Ploy a shot. Just for me. I think she's a far better choice for you than Kit."

"I'm not wasting any time following my good friend's advice so I start text messaging Ploy online. When Ploy tells me she's working the next night at the Lady Love go-go bar, I promise to meet her at 9:30."

"It starts pouring rain the next night, but I had also promised Kit I would meet her at La La Land at 7:30. I arrive on time after getting soaking wet driving through heavy showers."

"Kit is waiting for me when I arrive. Sitting next to her, I start to explain my plans for the evening before I order our drinks."

"You have met my friend Canada John before," I start off telling her. "He's going back soon to Hong Kong so I agreed to meet him tonight at 10:00. So I can't stay here with you very long."

"Kit's face turns rigid".

"I gotta see Canada John . He doesn't come to Pattaya much whereas I'm seeing you very often. I might not see him again for six months."

"I watch Kit's body freeze up while waiting for a response from her."

"But no response comes from her mouth or body language. She just sits staring into space."

"I think you need a drink. Can I get you a Jager Bomb?"

Once again there is no response.

"Then how about a Tequila? One for you and one for me?"

But Kit continues to sit next to me like a statue, completely devoid of life.

"Do you want to go upstairs and boom boom me?" I ask her.

"No. I want to leave. I want to go back to my room," she replies in a little girl's voice.

"Look. It is still raining hard outside. And I don't care how much it rains. I promise you that I will come back to you before 11."

"I want to go my room."

"Kit, I have never lied to you. And you know that when I tell you something, I have always done what I have promised. And I don't care how hard it rains tonight. I will only leave you for two hours. Then I will come back here. To see you. Because you know I want you more than I want any other woman."

Suddenly Kit comes alive again. "Do you promise, Fast Eddy, you come back to me tonight?"

"Yes. I promise."

"Okay. I want tequila now. One for you also."

"I'm completely amazed at Kit's sudden metamorphosis as I watch her emerge from her statue like catatonic state. Once again she becomes her original self. A half hour later we are upstairs together as if nothing had ever happened".

"By 9:30 I've driven my motorbike to the Lady Love go-go bar on Soi Lemke. Where I go inside to wait for Ploy. I find myself sitting completely alone at a long padded bench in a line of customers waiting for their favorite go-go girls to appear from the dressing room. Finally Ploy shows up around 10 and comes over to sit next to me after taking her sweet time in the dressing room."

"Sawadee Ka, Fast Eddy. Where do you go tonight earlier?"

"I've been to Soi 6, Ploy."

"You are still going Soi 6 too much?" Ploy asks me while using the expression too much instead of often. Just like practically every bar girl I had ever met.

"You know I like it on Soi 6. You are a very pretty lady, Ploy. And Soi 6 is where I found you. So it's a good place."

"Fast Eddy, I have boyfriend now from England. I don't go with customers anymore. I only work here to dance and to make money selling customers drinks."

"I suddenly realize that I am making a mistake by admitting to Ploy that I had just come from Soi 6 and that I still liked going there. Because Ploy knows only too well that I am paying just one-thousand baht to have sex with the women there. So she is probably thinking that I am unlikely to pay the three-thousand baht she is likely to be asking for short time. Times had changed. And Ploy is no longer an 800-baht whore. She is obviously out for the big time money now and is used to getting it."

"When she tells me that she has to go back on stage to dance, I know that Ploy is not the girl for me. I can't wait to get out of the place. And when I leave after paying my bar bill, I drive as fast as I can to rejoin Kit down on Soi 6."

"I can hardly see out of my helmet through the torrents of rain splashing against my face. But I finally arrive back on Soi 6 which is practically deserted because of the evening showers. Where I find Kit still waiting for me at La La Land."

"I had been wearing my rain suit which helped me a little. But the two tequila shots I have with Kit helps even more. While the sex we have upstairs is awesome."

"But I will never forget how she had almost turned to stone when I told her I would leave her that evening. Even if it was for just two hours."

"Now what in the hell does all of this mean?" I keep asking myself that question over and over. "Does she feel some kind of strange connection with me? Or is there something wrong with her psychologically? Even so, how could my leaving her for only two hours trigger whatever psychological state I have somehow caused?"

"I gotta say one thing, Fast Eddy. I don't think you are ever going to be one of my 12 disciples. But I understand you. You have found the perfect fit." But you are not cut out to be one of my disciples. You care too much. Caring about any woman, especially a Thai woman, is the ruination of all good men."

Camera Magic

"With our date night set for Tuesdays and Friday's, Kit and I have it all planned for Tuesday night. But not everything. We'd meet at her bar on Soi 6. I'd bring my laptop so that I can show off her latest pictures at full resolution. A whopping 24 megapixels, which would probably do 45 by 30 inch printouts. I had never done printouts this large before. The Nikon can certainly do terrific 30 by 20 inch prints, but I knew it could do a lot better than that. And with the special lighting I would set up at the Penthouse Hotel I can expect phenomenal prints."

"I show her low resolution pictures on my Kindle Fire. But I want to show Kit how truly beautiful she is. And how I can zoom in on her pretty eyes. This is all part of my grand strategy for building up her self esteem. Which is working so far."

"I had done several photo shoots of her before. Once in the short time room at La La Land on Soi 6. And twice at the Penthouse Hotel using my Nikon with its magical 24-70 2.8 lense. Which had set me back nearly $2000 just for the lense. But it turned out that the picture I had chosen for her first printout was from the short time room. In far from ideal lighting conditions. And I had used the small Panasonic Lx-10 with its Leica lens shooting at 1/25th of a second without flash on a high iso setting."

"The print should never have turned out half as good as it did. Yet it did. But she isn't so sexy in this picture. She is simply a beautiful woman, with tender eyes. Betraying a soft heart. This is no Soi 6 girl. The picture is of a woman any mother can be proud of. I'm telling you, Dick. Any man would love to have that girl on his arm."

"Such as me. Especially me. I want her like I've never wanted any woman in memory. And she loves that 30 by 20 inch print just as much as I do."

"But she does something no other girl had ever done before. One week after I gave her the print, she takes a picture of it with her phone. Which she sends to me on line."

"I had taken pictures of Thai women before. And each time I had given the girl a 20 by 30 inch printout. But not one of them showed me she thought enough of me to put it on her wall. But Kit did, which proved to me that she was far above those other girls."

"She orders a San Miguel Light for me and her usual Jager Bomb for herself as we snuggle up next to each other in a booth. But I have no plans of shooting any pictures of her tonight. Instead of the Nikon I'm planning to take the laptop to the Penthouse Hotel so I can show her the latest photo shoot we had done at the Penthouse. That is the photo shoot using the Nikon with its primary flash controlling the second flash that we had placed around the hotel room to eliminate shadows."

"Anyway, that was the plan."

"But suddenly Kit comes up with an even better solution."

"Let's just leave your laptop in my locker here at the bar. Then we can go to Walking Street together."

"You are right, Kit. We can just go over these pictures in the short time room upstairs. Now why didn't I think of that?"

"She's a smart girl, Dick. I love her to death because she's so much more alert than all the other Thai women."

We have one tequila together. While sipping our other drinks. There's going to be no Penthouse Hotel tonight. So I decide to take her there again in a week or two to get even more pictures of her with the Nikon. Perhaps I'll teach her a thing or two about that wonderful camera and its even more wonderful lens.

During that last photo shoot, she had started playing with the Nikon in the room. Showing me, she loved what it can do. Which is pure magic.

Cheap Happy Hours at the Doll House Go-Go Bar

"Since Happy Hour at the Doll House runs from 8:30 to 10:30, we don't have any time to lose. Kit puts my laptop into her locker. Then I hand her one-thousand baht for her bar fine which she gives the cashier. Five minutes later we are out of the bar and on our way to hail a songthaew. She climbs into the bed of the small converted pickup truck. Without looking at her, I take the seat next to her."

"There is a reason for my not wanting anyone to even think that Kit and I are getting in the songthaew together. Because I have a live in Thai girlfriend at my condo, I know only too well how another Thai woman would love telling her about my infidelity."

"But I can't see all that well due to our sitting behind the driver which causes me to misjudge how close we are to Walking Street. Without much thought I push the electronic buzzer and the songthaew starts to slow down."

"One second later I hear a girlish voice crying out, "No.""

"We bail out and I rush up to the passenger sitting next to the driver, who is probably the man's wife, to hand her the 20 baht taxi fare. For Kit it must seem a long walk to Walking Street. She is wearing heels. I'm not. And I am in terrific shape. If she wasn't following behind me, I would probably run that last 3/8ths of a mile to Walking Street."

"Once again I notice that Kit's got a strange way of walking. One would probably not notice it in the small confines of the Soi 6 bar she works for. I start thinking that she might have contracted polio as a small child. Or been in a motorcycle accident that left her slightly impaired. But it doesn't matter to me. She seems so vulnerable. But she's game. I wait a few seconds for her to catch up. Then I cross Beach Road dodging between the cars and motorbikes that had piled up due to the traffic's being nearly at a standstill."

"When we get to the corner between Soi Diamond and Walking Street, we spot Harry walking toward us."

"Danny and Big John are still at Windmill," Harry tells us. "But the music is disgusting there tonight. I just can't stand all that loud music!"

"You mean Da Da music?"

"Yep. That electro crap they play with only two beats. Loud and louder."

"Okay, let's just all go to the Doll House. Big John and Danny can catch up with us later."

At the Doll House

"Kit is on the ball. Right off, she points out a row of empty seats. We are in front of the Jacuzzi where two naked girls are cavorting in sudsy water. Looking closely at the contraption, I decide that it really isn't much. The Jacuzzi is only a cheap plastic insert in a wooden frame. And the water is only about five inches deep. As for the go-go girls, they aren't that much either. Kit might be supernaturally thin, but she really has a nice build with narrow hips, an even narrower waist, flat stomach and a nicely flared torso."

"When Harry joins us, one would think that Kit would suggest "Let's go over there." But she's a woman of few words who would rather point to a vacant spot than to open her mouth."

"Several men who had been sitting in our normal spot close to the stage had just left. Which Kit, sharp as a tack, notices. So we take our bins[11] and our drinks to our new seats. Where we wait for Danny and Big John to show up from the Windmill."

"Kit orders four gin and tonics for me and two Vodka and Schwepps for herself. We had gotten to the Doll House early, around 8:30 which is the start of Happy Hour. Which offers two for one specials that come out to just 75 baht for each of our

---

[11]Restaurant or bar bill usually put in a small container

drinks which is a real steal. I figured I had almost saved enough on our drinks to pay for the one-thousand baht bar fine it had cost me to get Kit out of her bar."

"Let's see–I have four gin and tonics in front of me while Kit's got two Vodka and Schwepps. Six drinks times 75 baht comes out to 450 baht so figuring that most beer bars charge 150 baht for mixed drinks I've already paid nearly half Kit's bar fine already and we are just getting started."

"I can't really keep track of exactly what happens next. But I think Kit is on her second drink. Plus the two for one tequilas I had ordered. By now Big John and Danny have already joined us. When suddenly Kit receives a phone call."

"I must go to Soi 9 right now." To Central" (Pattaya Mall), but she pronounces it like most Thais do, as "Centrum." But oh well, so much for their respect for the English language."

"Handing me her purse, she promises to come right back".

"In fifteen minutes?"

"I come back quickly. Wait for me."

"Suddenly, she's gone, her drinks still on the counter while I'm holding her purse in my lap."

"Fast Eddy, Soi 9 is the police station, Big John tells me expecting me to read between the lines."

"So she's probably bailing somebody out of jail?"

"Probably."

"Good chance it's her Thai boyfriend, John. I was starting to think he is still in the penitentiary, or that she never had this guy in her life. But the mamasan over at Quicky Bar had told me Kit's probably on Yabba or ice and she has a little mafia snot for a boyfriend who's always in trouble with the police. And that he usually picked her up at the bar."

"I had concluded that the Quickly Bar Mamasan was figuring that Kit was no good to her anymore after leaving her bar and working at La La Land, and that the mamasan had lied to me about the boyfriend. But now I'm starting to wonder."

"I don't know what the hell is going on, John. We both know what her mamasan told me over at the Quicky Bar, but money is number one here and that applies to mamasans just as much as it does to bar girls."

"Ten minutes later I message Kit from my Phone asking her when she'll be back.

"I'm on my way now," she replies.

And good to her word, she's strolling into the Doll House five minutes later.

"I can't say exactly how many drinks we had. But I think we had one more Tequila together. This time Kit's drug addict friend joins us. And once again, Kit asks me to buy the girl a drink."

The Death of Madonna

"Madonna died last night", Big John told Fast Eddy one morning. "Her husband just called me."

"Did she die quickly? Was she in much pain?"

"Thankfully she died peacefully in her sleep."

"How old was she? I think she was 36?"

"You are right," Fast Eddy.

"We must go out tonight and drink tequila in her honor then," Fast Eddy replied remembering all the times Madonna had drunk tequila with him out of the bottle and how he had never seen Big John ever touch the stuff.

Big John was Fast Eddy's best friend. And probably the smartest out of all his friends. But in the United States, Madonna had been nearly as good a friend as Big John had been. Fast Eddy had met Madonna in a strip club in Washington Park, Illinois, a mostly black community adjoining East St. Louis where she was working as a prostitute. But he never had sex with any of the girls in the strip club where he had met Madonna which had become one of his favorite watering holes.

The Chameleon had a unique way of doing things. There was a backroom area behind the bar that had two rooms. One room had a Jacuzzi while the second room had a bed in it. Drinks were inexpensive at the Chameleon whose owner didn't even have a liquor license even though most of the customers drank beer from cans the bar owner bought at a gas station down the street. So if the police came in the owner would tell them that the canned beer had been brought in by his customers.

The Chameleon required a customer to make his own private arrangement with the girls. This arrangement was solely between the girl and her customer whether it was for as little as $40.00 or as much as $200. And then the customer would rent a towel from the bar for $25.00 which the owner could later claim was for using the bar's Jacuzzi.

The owner of the Chameleon had all his bases covered with the police. For one thing, his wife, Lulu, worked for the Washington

Park police department. But Jimmy had two other things going for him. He operated a towing service so whenever anyone speeded, illegally parked, or committed any other infractions, the Washington Park police would oftentimes have Jimmy tow the person's car to Jimmy's tow yard. In order to regain possession of his car, the car owner had to pay Jimmy in addition to paying court costs to the Washington Park municipality.

Fast Eddy oftentimes did beer runs for Jimmy to the local Clark gas station. He also did Jimmy's web site for him. For free in exchange for getting a lot of drinks free of charge, and having no problems taking out the girls after the bar closed.

But Fast Eddy didn't realize how connected Jimmy was until he got two tickets from an Illinois State police officer while driving home from one of the strip clubs he frequented. One ticket was for driving without a seat belt, the other one for driving without proof of insurance. After receiving the two tickets from the police officer, Fast Eddy resumed driving until he came up to the Chameleon.

He found Jimmy ensconced in his favorite chair near the bar's front entrance and handed his friend the two tickets.

"Who pulled you over?" Jimmy asked grinning from ear to ear. Illinois State or Washington Park Police?"

"It was a state trooper," Fast Eddy replied.

Jimmy started to make a phone call and walked outside the bar. Still, on the phone with whomever was on the other end. Five minutes later, he came back into the bar and handed the two tickets back to Fast Eddy along with the Illinois drivers' license the police officer had confiscated to insure that Fast Eddy would appear in court.

"That is most impressive, Jimmy. I know that you have the Washington Park police in your pocket, but the Illinois State Police? I never knew you had that much pull."

"Just forget that this ever happened," Jimmy replied.

So Fast Eddy had a special relationship with the Chameleon, which largely depended on his not fucking the whores there. The whores respected him a lot for it and so did the bar's owner. Although he oftentimes sat with the girls buying them drinks.

Because he was doing the web site for Chameleon along with a couple of other strip clubs in the area, he would shoot a lot of pictures at the Chameleon for the web site. But he often shot pictures of girls from other clubs he brought with him into the Chameleon.

Jimmy was a true Dr. Jekyll and Mr. Hyde. One night Jimmy took Fast Eddy on a tour of Washington Park, showing him one building after another and several vacant lots.

"There's a lot of vacant lots here now," Jimmy told Fast Eddy as he drove up to a lot that had just been bulldozed. "This one had a supermarket that did a lot of business just a few years ago. Back then there were very few blacks here. Now that's all you are going to see living here. Black people. I grew up here. There weren't any titty bars neither. Now there are six of them. It was a great place to live in those days."

On another night, Jimmy pulled out a sawed off baseball bat. "This is what I use to enforce the law here, Jimmy said as he patted his palm with his baseball bat. "I also have a 357 magnum here in this drawer where I can easily get at it. You should have been here three nights ago, Fast Eddy. One of my girls had this leeching boyfriend living off her. Because he didn't want her to work here that night, he came right into my place and started slapping her around, thinking I wouldn't notice. I was in the back room area checking the Jacuzzi out when I came out and saw him slapping the bitch. So I came over here and got this baseball bat to persuade him to never come into my club again. I hit him once with this which made him half ass fall down. And then I shoved him up against the door. Come over to the door with me and look."

"Look at this door. It still works," said Jimmy as he showed Fast Eddy some bent bits of metal trim that had nothing to do with the function of the door. "So I threw him out of the bar, and on the way out, he damaged this. Now I got him right here just outside my club, and I kept beating the shit out of him with my bat. Then I called the police who came right out. They took him to the Washington Park jail, but before they put him in the squad car I told him that he owed me fifty dollars for damaging my door. So I took twenty-five dollars out of his pockets while the police watched."

"How did you get the remaining $25.00?" Fast Eddy asked.

"I took that twenty-five from his girlfriend. As you know, Fast Eddy, all the girls must pay $20.00 to work here. And if they don't show up, I charge them $20.00 for not showing up. So I put the twenty-five dollars on her bill so to speak. Which I made her pay me as soon as she got it from a customer who fucked her in the back room."

One of the two prettiest girls at the Chameleon was Madonna who was probably making more money whoring than any other girl there. So whenever he came into the bar and Madonna was there, she would invariably shout at him.

"Get your bony ass over here, Fast Eddy, and buy me a fucking tequila!" And then after he did, she'd usually buy him a drink and oftentimes for any of his friends who had accompanied him into the bar.

But Madonna never allowed him to ever take pictures of her in the bar, which he was dying to do because she was the prettiest girl in the place.

One night while he was sitting at home in his apartment Madonna called him on the phone.

"Can you bring your car over and pick me up?" she asked him.

"When?" Fast Eddy replied.

"In ten minutes."

"In ten minutes? Why Madonna, I don't even know where you live."

"I live close to you, in Granite City."

Then she gave him directions. Fifteen minutes later he was pulling up to her house.

They went out to a couple strip clubs. Then she went home with him to his apartment where she banged him for free.

After that they became fast friends. Madonna would oftentimes call him to ask him to have lunch with him. Half the time he'd pay. The other half of the time Madonna wound up paying.

Madonna worked as a prostitute because she was terminal. She could never work full time at any other job due to her having a serious lung problem that she had been born with, and her addiction to cigarettes didn't help. Her doctors had warned her she would never live to see 25.

She had a series of very bad boyfriends. For that matter, Fast Eddy had found that most strippers he knew had boyfriends who lived off the money they earned in the clubs, but Madonna had just kicked her latest bad news boyfriend out of her house. When David kept returning to her house and started pounding on her door, Fast Eddy gave her a can of pepper spray. Which she used to spray into David's face while he was trying to force her front door open.

One week later David drove a screwdriver into his best friends brain. Which put David away for murder.

By this time Fast Eddy had become good friends with Big John who had a high-level executive position in Los Angeles. Although Los Angeles was over 2000 miles away from the St Louis area, Big John and Fast Eddy often visited each other. So whenever Big John visited Fast Eddy, they would visit the Washington Park strip clubs together. By then, Madonna had taken an old boyfriend back who was the father of her two youngest children. Because her boyfriend didn't have a job, like most guys living off their stripper girlfriends, Big John started to call him 'The Turd Pile'.

Madonna and Fast Eddy agreed that Madonna had been running around with the wrong kind of people. So Madonna sent the Turd Pile packing. Which the Turd Pile would never have done if it had it not been for Madonna's mother, who bartended at Dollies Playhouse and had the right connections with a local motorcycle gang living up the street from her.

With the Turd Pile gone, and David in the penitentiary, Madonna started to spend a lot more time with Fast Eddy, becoming his best friend in the St. Louis Metro East on the Illinois side of the Mississippi River.

A year or two after she returned from L.A. to her house in Granite City Madonna met her future husband. Jerry was making deliveries from his UPS delivery truck, when he encountered Madonna working at the Chameleon. The Chameleon just happened to be on Jerry's delivery route so he had always come into the Chameleon just to deliver packages, and never to fuck any of the women there.

113

Madonna had always told Fast Eddy that she could never love a customer because servicing the customers was just a job like shoveling shit. But she loved Fast Eddy and Big John because neither of them had ever paid Madonna for sex. And neither did Jerry who was just a tall handsome guy who worked hard for United Parcel Service. Jerry and Madonna fell in love, got married, and then Jerry moved Madonna and her children out to a nice middle class suburb in West County St. Louis.

But Fast Eddy never forgot Madonna's words of warning to him only a week before he moved out of the United States. "Fast Eddy, those women in Thailand aren't the same as the American women you have for friends. Even us whores. In Thailand the women will only see you as easy money, but over here, even us whores like you for yourself."

It was a lesson both Fast Eddy and Big John should have heeded a long time ago. But Madonna had just died, and now that Big John had followed in Fast Eddy's footsteps by buying a condo in Pattaya, they decided to get totally wasted.

Fast Eddy and Big John started off at Dolls Go-Go bar on Soi 6. But found the go-go bar to be far too noisy for them to be toasting Madonna. So they strolled down Soi 6 together looking for a much quieter place where they could reminisce about all the good times they had with Madonna. They passed a few bars when Fast Eddy saw a pretty woman smiling at him from the doorway of her bar.

After passing a few other Soi 6 bars, Fast Eddy said, "Let's go back to that bar where we saw that good looking girl."

Smoke and Kisses was divided into two parts. Inside, the bar was air-conditioned while the front section was open to the street. This outside section resembled a small beer bar where the bar girls and customers could look out onto all the Soi 6 drama passing by. There were food carts. And there were Soi 6 bar girls walking up and down the street looking for customers, food from the food carts, or going up the street to the 7-11 to buy cigarettes and snacks. There were other carts pulling up to the Soi 6 bars to sell shoes, t shirts, and dresses to the girls. As well as hundreds of potential customers prowling up and down Soi 6 in cars or driving their motorbikes. At the very front of this second section there was a long table and bar stools where several of the girls sat calling out to potential customers. Upstairs were five or six short time rooms where the girls could do their tricks.

The good-looking girl followed Fast Eddy and Big John to a booth in the air-conditioned section where the girl immediately asked. "Do you want anything to drink?" Then she turned to Fast Eddy, laughed, and told him:

"I want to suck your ass."

Fast Eddy ordered three tequilas, one for the girl, one for Big John and one for himself. The next half hour was filled with conversation between Big John and Fast Eddy about Madonna as Fast Eddy kept ordering more tequilas.

After finishing his last tequila, Big John told Fast Eddy and the girl, "Well I think someone has a little ass sucking to do so I will leave both of you now. I am supposed to meet one of the girls down on Walking Street and I had better get going."

Upstairs Fast Eddy found the girl to be true to her word by actually sucking his ass. But not for very long.

"Lie on your back now," she told him. "I want you to totally relax while I give you massage."

Ning started rubbing his feet, moving up his legs, slowly, as her hands gradually climbed to his thighs and then to his crotch. It was like getting an oil massage from Pattaya's massage girls. Which would oftentimes wind up being a happy ending with the girl jacking the customer off until he came. But it was much better than that because Fast Eddy knew for sure that Ning would do a lot more than simply jacking him off. After five minutes Ning took his whole penis into her mouth. Her mouth felt soft and very moist which made him almost cum. Then he turned her over to perform oral sex on her. After becoming very wet, she cried out, "Fuck me now."

She slowly put the condom on his penis in one uninterrupted smooth motion and told him, "Go slowly. Very slowly." But after five minutes she giggled and said, "Fuck me hard now. I want you to fuck me very hard."

He continued to see Ning over the next several weeks but then he ran into someone else after getting a haircut at a Soi 6 beauty saloon.

The Soi 6 Girl who Fucked 1500 Koreans

Relaxing with a Heineken at Dick Fitswell's Big Dick's bar, Fast Eddy just had to tell his mentor about the latest girl he had started fucking. Or to be more precise, he had resumed fucking since he had a spree with the woman a couple of times a few months ago.

"Dick, I just happened to run into her again, just as I started walking down Soi 6 after getting a haircut at a beauty saloon. This was around one in the afternoon, which was too early for a lot of these go-go and Soi 6 girls to be waking up. I had met this woman at the Red Point months ago. And man, she was just about the best looking gal there, being tall and full breasted, and I don't mean silicon breasted. She had nice luscious tits that I had just loved sucking on. But she must have liked me because she used to blow me until I was bone dry. But after only a couple of weeks she told me she was planning to hook up with some old fart for three months. She told me he was giving her 100000 baht for the three months, but she didn't know whether she could trust him or not."

She saw me walking up Soi 6 and ran out into the middle of the street calling out my name. And asked me to come into her bar to buy her a drink. When I asked her where she had been, she told me she hadn't been back to Soi 6 in ten months. And that she had been working in a Korean whorehouse for seven months. But it was still early afternoon, so I agreed to meet her later that evening.

"So was the sex still good with her?" Dick Fitswell asked.

"Funny that you should ask me that question. I thought you might ask me what the hell she was doing working in a Korean brothel for seven months."

"Well, was it any good?"

"Okay Dick, I fucked her twice that night. Big fucking deal. But yes, she was very good. Her tits were just as good as they used to be, and we did a lot of kissing in her bed before we got down to business. And I was sucking her tongue into my mouth as I came. Then we went downstairs to the bar where I had two Heinekens before going upstairs with her again. I didn't even

116

have to pay the 300 baht room charge again. Because it was her room so I ended up paying her two-thousand baht and a one time room fee of just 300 baht."

"What about her fucking all those Koreans?"

"She told me all about it. While she ended up saving over 2 million baht[12], which she's now using to build herself a house somewhere up in Issan. You know these sex traffickers come into Pattaya all the time looking for new bodies. I don't know if you could call these people she got in with sex traffickers because she ended up leaving Korea when she wanted to. But they do have these recruiters coming to all these bars in Thailand, and many of these recruiters are Thai."

"So how does this whole thing work?" Dick Fitswell asked.

"First off, the recruiter gets the woman all set up with a passport if she doesn't already have one. And of course any visa that the Korean government requires. Then they pay the woman's round trip airfare to Korea and back. I can't remember exactly what the Koreans are paying for short time sex in the brothel but I think she told me it's five-thousand baht. Out of that she gets one-thousand-five-hundred baht, the brothel gets two-thousand baht and the recruiter gets one-thousand-five hundred baht from each trick the girl does."

"How many guys did the girl end up fucking every day?"

"It varies, she told me. "They have a window that opens up to the street and there are several or more women inside that window. So potential customers can get a good look at what they are buying. A customer entering the establishment tells the people there which girl he wants. He has just 45 minutes to get off with the girl and out of that 45 minutes he has to take a shower before

---

[12]$62500 at a 32 baht to the dollar exchange rate

having sex and afterwards. But after 45 minutes they ring a bell, sound an alarm or whatever and then he must stop whatever he's doing right then and there. He either has to leave the brothel or pay a lot more for a few more minutes if he hasn't already climaxed. The Soi 6 gal told me she was averaging eight fucks a day."

"Which comes out to 360000 baht per month or 2,200,000 baht for the whole seven months," Dick Fitswell replied.

"Yes. I am not sure she fucked an average of eight men a day. That's because she told me she fucked something like one-thousand-five-hundred Koreans in that seven months. But at the rate of eight guys a day this would be 240 men a month or 1680 Koreans in the entire seven months. But come to think of it, Dick, yeah, that all about works out. She gets a couple of days off each month which means she doesn't quite have 1680 Koreans in her bed for the whole seven months."

"That's an awful lot of fucking, no matter how it works out," Dick Fitswell added. "So what else did she tell you about the Korean brothel?"

"Just think about this, Dick. If she fucked 1500 Koreans and the recruiters got 1500 baht from each trick she did, the recruiters got 2,500,000 baht and that's just off of one girl. This is huge business for everyone concerned, and it's something you will never hear about because the South Koreans don't want to own up to it."

"That's a lot of monkey business," Dick replied. "But getting back to my original question, what really goes on in these Korean brothels?"

"It's like a prison. They never let any of the girls out until their contract expires. They can't even go downtown to do any shopping. They must sleep overnight in the brothel and they must eat all their meals in the brothel. The people in charge simply dump out a lot of rice, vegetables and chickens for the girls, and they then have to do their own cooking."

"What did she think of the Korean men?"

"She had no thoughts about them at all. Because she had little

118

contact with any of them except for those 45 minutes while she was screwing them."

*****

Fast Eddy always wanted to take a woman to Queen Victoria on Soi 6 without his live in Thai girlfriend finding out. He had been going to this old English style restaurant and pub for years and had found the food to always be good there. And although Queen Victoria was also a hotel, he had never thought of it as a place for him to stay. Nor had he ever felt the need to due to his owning a condo where he had a series of four live in Thai girlfriends.

But now for the first time he gave serious consideration to renting rooms at Queen Victoria by the night because here he could keep his own alcohol where he could watch television with his short time dates. He could use his room as a base to take girls out to nearby Soi 6 bars to break up the monotony he so often found between boom booms. The potential here would be terrific because he could have sex with a girl and take her to a Soi 6 bar until he felt the urge again when he could take the girl back to his room for a second cumming.

Goi, the girl who had fucked one-thousand-five-hundred Koreans, would be perfect for this. So he invited her to meet him at Queen Victoria for dinner. But he also invited Wolfgang just in case someone who knew his girlfriend saw him having dinner with Goi. He had done pretty much the same thing with Ploy the night he took her to the Penthouse Hotel when he had his good friend, Big John, meet him and Ploy at the Beer Garden near Walking Street. His plan was to have Big John and Ploy sit next to each other. And after dinner Big John would walk with Ploy to one or two go-go bars while Fast Eddy walked behind them. That way anyone who saw Fast Eddy on Walking Street would assume Ploy was with Big John and not Fast Eddy.

This didn't work out so well at the Queen Victoria because Goi failed to follow his instructions to sit next to Wolfgang instead of Fast Eddy. Goi arrived on time, but sat with Fast Eddy. Even worse, Goi also kissed him a few times, which made it clear to everyone that she was Fast Eddy's date.

Fast Eddy soon found another problem with Queen Victoria. By the time he took Goi up into the room he had rented, he had realized that doing short times at the Queen Victoria did not offer him the anonymity he required. This was because access to the

119

rooms upstairs was through a door that opened to the only staircase going upstairs and this door was in the main part of the restaurant. Which amounted to anyone dining in the restaurant could watch him take a short time date up to his hotel room.

For Fast Eddy this was a fatal flaw because he had been living too long in Pattaya and too many people knew him who might tell his live in girlfriend about his short times at the Queen Victoria.

But he had a great time with Goi in the room, having sex with her two times while they had several beers and wine coolers together. Over the next two weeks he found that having sex with Goi was an all balls out take no prisoners marathon with Goi enjoying the sex every bit as much as him. Which he found a bit odd considering that Goi had just about every kind of sex imaginable starting with her fucking eight Koreans a day.

Goi should have been jaded to the point of not caring a long time ago. But for some reason she had always enjoyed Fast Eddy's company and had shared with him her darkest secrets.

Such as telling him about the old fart who had paid her 100000 baht to spend three months with him. Which had resulted with her being almost as much a prisoner as she had been in the Korean brothel. The cantankerous old man had expected her to spend all her time with him at his hotel out of which he seldom ventured to the point of preferring to eat nearly all his meals at the hotel restaurant.

Goi had found the old man to be reprehensibly boring.

Although this would be the first and last time Fast Eddy would ever take her to the Queen Victoria he would often visit her at her bar where she would take him to her room as many as three times. Between their sexual bouts they would go downstairs to party together in her bar, and then when the mood hit him again, he'd take her upstairs again while paying just a single charge of 300 baht.

Oftentimes he would visit her at 10:00 in the morning which worked out well for both of them. The mamasan would have Goi open the bar in the morning while she slept off her hangovers until noon when nearly all the Soi 6 bars opened. Sometimes a customer or two who wanted to start drinking early would show up at the bar which his why the mamasan started opening early.

One morning Goi started to give Fast Eddy a massage in her room. But after French kissing him passionately and after he had practically sucked non existent milk out of her luscious breasts, she squatted down on his very erect penis without using a condom.

"We have been good friends for a long time now, Fast Eddy. From now on I want to really feel you come inside me."

Goi had one problem though. Above all things Fast Eddy did not want his live in girlfriend to find out about his other girlfriends. Goi's problem was, whenever she wanted Fast Eddy she would call him. And not just once but as many as seven times a day. And each time she called while Fast Eddy was in his condo with his girlfriend, his tilak would ask, "Who is that? Who is calling you so often? You have other lady?"

Fast Eddy found Goi to be unteachable. Well. Almost.

Danny's Proposition to Fast Eddy and Kit

By now Fast Eddy had gotten into the habit of taking Kit to the Penthouse Hotel where they would have sex a couple of times. Then he would take her to the Doll House.

Like a laser, Kit would locate a place where they could sit together while still leaving a place for a couple of other people to join them. Fast Eddy never had to motion over a waiter or waitress because Kit had already anticipated his wanting his usual Gin and Tonic 75 baht happy hour specials while ordering two vodka and Mango cocktails for herself.

This was not lost on Danny, who came over to the peanut gallery[13] to greet them. When Kit went to the toilet, Danny offered Fast Eddy a few words of advice.

"This girl really looks out after you, Fast Eddy. I think you should take her under your wing before someone else does."

"What do you mean, Danny?"

"She's the real deal, Fast Eddy, and if you don't get her out of that bar she's working in, someone else will."

"But Danny. I already have a Thai girlfriend living with me for seven years."

"Then get rid of her. This one's much better."

"But you don't know my girlfriend, Danny."

"Take my advice. Take Kit out of the bar before someone else

_____

[13]The peanut gallery refers to those rows of
seats well behind the bar's stages

122

does. Trust me, I'm never wrong. I've been in this business for over 20 years. Kit does not belong in a bar."

"What are you suggesting?"

"Are you willing to pay her every month so she doesn't have to work in a bar?"

"Yes. If she is what you say she is."

"When she comes out of the toilet, I can ask her for you."

"Okay."

Fast Eddy was amazed at how fluent Danny was speaking Thai. Which got Kit speaking quickly in a melodic voice. It was a voice a man could fall in love with. Fast Eddy found that most bar girls spoke Issan. Which one might expect since most bar girls came from Issan, a region that is mostly rural, and most often associated with Thailand's poorer classes. Fast Eddy found the Issan dialect to be harsh. But Kit was no Issan girl. Later he would find out that she was a northern Thai from the Chiang Rai region.

"This is what she wants, Fast Eddy. She would like twenty-thousand baht a month in addition to her room rental. She needs ten-thousand baht for herself, five-thousand baht for her mother who takes care of her son, and five-thousand baht for her little boy. If she didn't have a son, she would be only asking fifteen-thousand baht a month."

"That sounds reasonable, Danny. Tell her she can quit working the bar right away."

*****

What Fast Eddy had in mind is not at all the way things turned out. Soi 6 bar girls were costing him one-thousand baht each time he took one of them up to the room, which set him back another 300 baht. Which was what he was already doing with Kit. But he had also been paying Kit's bar fine of 800 baht whenever he took her to the Doll House when he'd give her another two-thousand baht tip which often included having sex with her again at the Penthouse Hotel or the Sweethearts short time hotel on Walking Street. Like Danny he had been thinking that overpaying her would keep her out of the clutches of a worthless scumbag falang who didn't deserve her.

In addition to his paying her 20000 baht a month he put eight-thousand-eight-hundred baht into her bank account through his phone. But what he envisioned was his using her room to do short times with her. Because after all, it was his room since he would be paying for it.

One of his friends had done this a few years ago by renting a room for his girlfriend where he stayed with her whenever he visited her in Pattaya from the U.S. This had saved him the cost of getting a hotel room. Within a year, he had married his girlfriend and then he took her and her eight-year old daughter to the United States where they all lived happily ever after.

But one evening while he was driving Kit to a shopping mall on his motorbike, Fast Eddy offered to take her home. Which she readily accepted. After taking her home, when he asked to see her room, Kit fiddled around with her purse looking for her room key. While making a phone call to her roommate, she told him that her roommate was too busy having supper to bring them the key right away.

Which totally pissed Fast Eddy off, who wanted to scream at Kit, "whoever your roommate is, I'm paying for her part of the room. Your roommate should run down here and kiss my ass for paying her lazy ass's portion of the room rental!" Barely managing to control the volcano erupting inside him, he told Kit that he would go to the Oasis Go-Go bar next door to have a beer while he waited. His mood didn't get any better after Kit informed him that it might take a long time for the roommate to return to the room.

Fast Eddy swore to himself, "Whomever this roommate is who's taking her sweet time getting a key to us, I'm certainly not paying any rent on their room after tonight."

Renting a Room at the Penthouse Hotel

Instead of helping her pay for her room each month, Fast Eddy decided to get his own room at the Penthouse Hotel where he could do short times.

After taking Kit a few times to the Penthouse Fast Eddy had started to get on with the Penthouse owner pretty well. The owner was an Englishman in his early seventies. After getting a room from the owner several times and having to pay full price for the entire night, Fast Eddy soon found that he could pay half price for what the Penthouse called a short time stay. But, unlike Sweethearts which limited its short times to an hour after which one could pay extra for additional time, the Penthouse allowed him to extend his short time stays to three or four hours.

One afternoon Fast Eddy drove his motorbike to the Penthouse to ask about a more permanent arrangement. But when he asked the owner how much it would cost him to rent a room by the month, the owner replied: "It will be pretty expensive for you. You would do far better looking elsewhere."

"But I like the Penthouse," Fast Eddy replied. "If I get a room here, my girlfriend will never find out. For one thing no one wants to short time a girl at your going rates. Not when he can get a short time room for just 200 baht at a number of locations close to you. Or even 400 baht at Sweethearts. This means I will probably never run into anyone here who I already know."

That is very true," the Englishman replied.

"So what do you think we can arrange," Fast Eddy asked.

"We really don't normally do monthly rentals, Fast Eddy. One reason is we have every reason not to trust our customers who might get us into trouble with the police by bringing in underage girls, or who try to skip out on what they owe us."

"Don't worry about that. The last thing I want is a 17-year old girl. Or even a twenty-year old. I find them to be so boring. And, you can find me very easily if you have any payment problems with me. I have a large condo which I have owned for 12 years at Wongamat Beach."

"Well let's see, Fast Eddy.   If you rent something from me by the month, you will be getting the spare room we keep in mothballs in case we are full up. But we have never come close to renting out all our rooms. Why don't you take a look at it, and if it suits you, I'll rent it to you for 20,000 a month with a 20,000 baht damage deposit?"

Fast Eddy found the room to be much smaller than the Pool Deck Supreme room he had been getting. And although it had a sliding glass door opening out to the balcony, the balcony did not have the same view that overlooked Soi 13/4 and Boys Town. It was also much farther away from the long swimming pool.

But it still had a passable television, and the monthly rental included internet access. There was also a small refrigerator and a microwave, but the most important thing of all is that it provided him the anonymity that he required.

When he finally settled into his home away from home, he got an account with Netflix. Then he set up two users, one for Kit and one for himself figuring that Kit would have altogether different interests than his which would enable her to put the television shows and movies she liked into her favorites.

Fast Eddy had two motives for setting up Netflix in his Penthouse room. The 1st was so that he could offer Kit a source for good entertainment that she could not get anywhere else. The second reason was to help her learn English due to Netflix offering subtitles in Thai to its television series and movies that were in English.

When she saw the new room Fast Eddy had rented, Kit insisted on cooking supper for him. So he took her to the Villa Market supermarket for groceries which was only a short walk away from Soi 13/4.

At the supermarket, Kit behaved like a little child who had never been in a supermarket before. Fast Eddy allowed her to push the shopping cart around the supermarket by herself due to his not wanting to have any of his live in girlfriend's acquaintances see him with another woman.

Although her 80-pound body was painfully thin, he watched her scamper behind the cart pushing it forward until it gained enough speed to allow her to ride the the cart completely unaware of how much her little ass was taunting him. He watched her ride the cart again and again in total admiration with a stiffening dick.

He never saw this done before and couldn't imagine any other woman doing it. "Am I a closet pedophile?" he asked himself. "Does one part of her brain think she's only 11 years old? Am I really sexually turned on by 11 year olds?"

The idea of having sex with underage girls had always repulsed him. Which led him to ask himself, perhaps "I have been programmed to detest those who want to have sex with children by the social morales of my time."

He had learned throughout History that 14-year-old girls had been considered marriageable material by many cultures. "So why not? What's wrong with it other than the fact that my peers find pedophiles to be completely reprehensible. Perhaps for the first time, I'm finding out for myself that what I really want is having sex with young girls for which I would be put in jail practically everywhere in the world." But whether such thoughts were despicable or not, he knew he could get away with it because he knew that Kit was 24 years old.

"Was she insane? Quite possibly," he told himself," and would continue asking himself for many months on end. But this hardly mattered because he was starting to love that little shapely ass of hers.

They found that they could carry up to seven bags of groceries on his Yamaha Nmax motorbike by putting two bags into the large storage compartment under his seat and draping three bags on the hook just ahead of his knees, with Kit carrying the last two bags while she rode behind him.

Then they took the groceries back to his room at the Penthouse. Once they were inside the room, Kit took a beer out of the fridge and handed it to him. Then she cooked a noodle dish in the microwave. By the time she gave him his plateful of food, he was already watching Netflix.

"Here, you try it," he told her as he handed her the t.v. remote. "See here, this is for you under your user name, Kit." Then he showed her how to use Netflix and save her favorite tv shows and movies under her user name.

It didn't take her long to get onto Netflix. Fast Eddy watched her choose a t.v. series, and then he kept watching her as she sat next to him on the couch, totally focused on what she was watching while being totally unaware of anything else in the room.

After they finished eating, she scooped up their dishes, and started washing them in the little kitchen area the Penthouse had provided them.

The Hapless Thai Police

"Kwang[14], did our night time security guard inform you last night about the Thai police coming here to deal with a disturbance?"

"Yes, Frank. I got his full report."

"Good. You and the security guard are both doing your jobs well then. But I want to tell you the full story as what I am going to tell you will reflect how much we can expect from Thai policemen here at the Bahthaus."

"Here we go, Kwang. Last night's problem started when I was doing some computer work in my condo while my girlfriend was watching television. Everything is quiet until my girlfriend starts shouting "Oh my god, come come, Frank.""

"So I go inside one of my two toilets to watch all the drama through the window. A woman is sitting in the middle of the parking lot screaming at the night time security guard who is trying to scoop her off the pavement."

"Jenny, I hope that's not Terry's new girlfriend."

"I think, it is lady Terry," my girlfriend replies.

"It takes the security guard ten minutes to get the woman off the pavement.   Then I watch the security guard follow the woman to a car that is blocking the front entrance to the Bahthaus parking area. Eventually things quiet down and the security guard is able to get the woman to drive her car out of the front entranceway."

"Fifteen minutes later as I'm sitting in front of my computer, I hear a loud knocking on my door."

"It is the night time security guard, who as you know speaks little

---

[14]Is the manager of the Bahthaus

English but has proven to be very adept at his job in spite of the language barrier."

"My friend you," the security guard tries to tell me as I open my front door.

"Terry?"

"Chi."[15]

"Shit!" "I should have known. Terry is always getting himself into some sort of jam or another."

"When Terry opens the door to let me inside his condo, I see terror in his eyes. After letting me inside his condo, Terry shuts and locks the door behind us."

Then Terry informs me, "I don't want that bitch to come back in here."

"What is going on Terry? I saw your new girlfriend out in the parking lot making an ass of herself. She even blocked our front entrance to our condo so no residents can drive their motorbikes or cars through the gate."

"I took her drinking tonight to one of the bars over on Soi 7. And you know me, Fast Eddy. I get carried away with buying all kinds of ladies drinks when I get out. So here I am at this bar and I have my new girlfriend with me while I am buying several of the bar girls ladies drinks. This makes my girlfriend jealous and she starts going into a fit. She's got her own car, but by this time she's drunk on her ass. So I drive us back to the Bahthaus. When we go inside my condo she starts telling me that she's missing the key to her room and she's blaming me for it. Then she starts hitting and kicking me, and somehow I manage to muscle her outside my condo. Then I lock the door so she can't get back in."

---

[15]Means yes

130

"What do you want to do now?" I asked Terry.

"Well, I don't want to let the bitch back into my condo. I'd be too scared to go to sleep. No telling what she's going to do."

Fifteen minutes later, Terry changes his mind, goes just outside his condo to the hallway that looks down into the condo lobby and yells out to the security guard, "you can let her back in."

"But as soon as Terry's temporary girlfriend reenters his condo, all hell breaks loose. Lashing out at Terry in non stop broken English, the girl starts accusing Terry of stealing her money, wanting to fuck other girls he's buying drinks for, and stealing the key to her room."

"Then the girl tells me, "You good man. You good heart. Friend you, he big asshole." Then she starts kicking Terry but winds up kicking me between my legs. But her foot merely grazes my balls. So I'm not hurting that much, but it is just enough to tell both me and Terry that the longer she stays the more damage she can cause to anything she can get her hands on in his condo."

"By this time there's four people in Terry's condo with Manoon's just coming back from an errand he's doing for Terry."

"Kwang, you don't know him, but Manoon is a Thai man in his middle forties who has been living with Terry for a few months in Terry's spare bedroom. Terry is paying Manoon ten thousand baht a month to be his taxi driver and all around GG (go getter), which means that Manoon is at Terry's beck and call nearly twenty-four hours a day. Plus free room and board."

"As you are aware, Kwang, Terry is an enormous man, weighing over 350, but he can't walk more than one block. Instead of walking, Terry has Manoon drive him everywhere. And while most of Terry's friends don't mind walking all the way up Walking Street to go to their favorite go-go bars, Manoon takes the side streets into Walking Street so that Terry doesn't have to walk more than one block to visit his favorite go-go bars."

"So Manoon keeps trying to calm Terry's girlfriend down. Well, she's more like Terry's slut of the week. Terry had met this totally drunken bar girl on Soi 6 only one week earlier. But you know Terry. He's already thinking of moving this woman into his condo. Manoon has a firm yet gentle way about him, but he's

131

unable to calm the girl down."

"Finally the girl goes out onto the narrow part of Terry's balcony and either falls asleep or pretends to as she lies down with her back resting on top of the balcony's tiled floor."

"What should I do with her?" Terry asks me.

"Well, if were you, I certainly wouldn't let her sleep here. I would get Manoon to take her to the nearest reasonably priced hotel, check her into the hotel and let her sleep it off in one of the rooms there. I recommend Lek Villa. Should cost you one-thousand-two-hundred or one-thousand-three-hundred baht which is around $45.00. Lek Villa is close. And forty-five dollars is a cheap price to pay when you consider what she can steal here while you are asleep or how much damage she can do to your furniture, your t.v. or whatever. Just give Manoon fifteen hundred baht and let him handle it."

"But as hard as Manoon tries he is unable to get this bitch to wake up. Even though I still think she is only pretending to fall asleep so that she can stay all night in Terry's condo."

"I finally go outside Terry's condo into the hallway where I see the security guard just below him in the condo lobby. The security guard looks up at me, and asks me, "Police?""

"Chi. Call police."

"Only five minutes later three policemen arrive. When the police finally raise her into a standing position, she keeps calling, Terry a no-good asshole."

"When The police finally get her to walk out into the hallway, the girl continues to scream abuse at Terry. Then I go back to my condo to inform my girlfriend of the latest events. When I return to the hallway just outside Terry's condo, I find the three policemen still there. But the girl is no longer with them."

"Somehow the girl, as drunk as she is, is able to get by the three Thai policemen, reenter Terry's condo and lock herself into the toilet. Completely stumped, the three policemen shrug their shoulders and tell the security guard,"Mai Ben Rai Rai Rai." (Which basically means "shit happens")

132

Short Times at the Penthouse

Fast Eddy rented his Penthouse room primarily as a second or primary home for Kit. But Kit's catatonic fit when he looked up Ploy at the Lady Love go-go bar remained a complete cipher. " Did Kit feel such a strong connection with him that compelled her to insist that he stay with her that night?"

Although he never forgot that night, and what it might mean as a possible future for both of them, he kept smelling the everlasting presence of the despicable Thai boyfriend, who would forever be the turd in the ointment.

The everlasting smell of that turd in the fish bowl convinced him to bring other bar girls to the Penthouse room even though he had rented it for Kit's exclusive use in the hopes it would lead to Kit replacing his live in girlfriend. And then he would move her into his Bahthaus condo. But he would have to see first if Kit passed his Penthouse trial period.

Down Second Road from Soi 13/4, just 400 meters from the Penthouse Fast Eddy had found a bar whose main attraction was a nice looking bartender. But the bartender had always seemed aloof.

He found the bartender to be just too formal for his tastes. She controlled the bar, even though the bar had a mamasan who was officially in charge of the place. While the bar's mamasan got drunk far too often, she was a lot of fun to be around. Fast Eddy figured the bartender had a boyfriend already, and that this was the reason she never fraternized with the bar's customers.

And then, his live in girlfriend went home to visit her family up in Surin. When Fast Eddy discovered that he would be spending an entire week alone, he decided to have Kit spend the entire night with him. But when he asked Kit, she told him that she had to go back to her room to feed her rabbit. Which was total bullshit as far as he was concerned.

Whether the rabbit actually existed or not, Fast Eddy had been buying rabbit food at the supermarket with Kit. Since there was no reason for Kit to want to leave him to feed a rabbit, a totally pissed off Fast Eddy set out to get totally drunk.

He was planning on having the bar's mamasan as his drinking

companion for the rest of the night. While deciding to inflict his favorite drink on the mamasan—what he called an East St. Louis cement mixer.

The East St. Louis cement mixer had started out being a shot of Baileys with a shot of lime juice. But while he was living near East St. Louis Fast Eddy decided to improve it. But after making it better and stronger his favorite strip club started serving it to many customers. Later, when he moved to Thailand he got his favorite dancer on Pattaya's Drinking Street to drink East St Louis cement mixers with him.

The East St. Louis cement mixer was more a ritual than it was a cocktail, the ritual starting with filling a shot glass with tequila while filling a second shot glass with lime juice. Two or more people would then indulge themselves in the ritual while facing each other and pouring the contents of both shot glasses into their mouths. The catch was, everyone had to keep the contents of both shot glasses in their mouths for at least thirty seconds. So Fast Eddy would instruct his drinking companion(s) to hold two shots of liquid in their mouths, and then swirl it by shaking their heads. This would mix the tequila with the lime juice. And then they would finally swallow which would result in a rush that was far more powerful than downing a single shot glass of tequila.

With a little coaching he was finally able to get the bartender to bring him two shot glasses, one full of lime, the other filled with tequila. Both of which he chugged in full view of both the bartender and the mamasan.

"Song tequila" he told the bartender, meaning he wanted two while pointing to the mamasan and himself knowing that the mamasan was up to trying anything. Then as a second thought he pointed at the bartender and said, Som, with song meaning two and som being the word for three in Thai. To his surprise the bartender nodded so he bought three East St. Louis cement mixers.

He was completely surprised when the bartender asked him to buy her a second East St. Louis cement mixer. By then a customer had come in, and the mamasan had gone over to the other side of the bar to join him. After she had her second East St. Louis cement mixer with him, Fast Eddy was completely stunned when the bartender came over to his side of the bar and sat on the bar stool next to him.

By the time they were drinking their fourth East St. Louis Cement mixers the strait-laced bartender had completely lost her inhibitions. Leaning close to him the bartender started feeling the muscles in his arms. When her hand reached his crotch, he got an instant hard on. By the time they were on their fifth East St. Louis cement mixer, she was kissing him on his lips.

"I can bar fine you?" he asked the bartender.

"Yes. But we wait until two a.m. I must close bar."

Which the bartender had to do because by this time the mamasan had gotten totally wasted and had already gone home.

By the time they had finally gotten to his Penthouse room, both of them were completely trashed. Ten minutes later they were lying naked in bed together. But only after the bartender pressed her naked body against him while kissing him on the lips did he find her body to be up to his wildest expectations.

"I know what you want. I know what you need," the bartender cried out to him.

They had sex that night without using a condom as she French kissed him until he came. The next morning they did it again.

135

Death at the Bar

"Dick, that first night was my best night with the bartender. After that night things start to slowly go downhill. Because like nearly all Thai women I meet in the bars, the bartender always seems to be hungry. So when I bring the bartender up to my room at the Penthouse, she tells me, "I want to eat now." I grab myself a beer from the fridge, and then I ask her if she wants a mixed drink, such as a screw driver and she refuses it. I also had a carton of red wine in the fridge. But she doesn't want any wine either. I pour myself a glass, and then she keeps bitching until I cook her some food. Then she plants her lazy ass on a chair and takes half an hour to finish eating while I'm sitting around doing absolutely nothing. Finally we get down to business."

"Let me stop you right there," Dick Fitswell replied. "Here you are fucking this bartender without a condom, but you have to do the cooking. That seems a small price to pay for getting all the sex you are getting from her."

"Well Dick, here's what's wrong with it. First, she oftentimes must stay at the bar until two a.m. and that's too late for me to get started. I like to wake up early in the morning. I'm not like most of these bar girls who have nothing to do but party all night, and then they sleep until five in the afternoon. Second, I still have to bar fine her and that runs me around 800 baht because she's not just a bar girl. She's the bartender. So if I bar fine her early she has to get the mamasan to come over to the bar and take over for her. Next, it so happens she lives right down the street with four bar girls who work with her in the bar. So she's desperate. She wants to move in with me to get out of these horrible living conditions she's living with all these bar girls. Lastly, she insists right off on not using a condom so I think she wants to get pregnant. And if all that isn't enough she is no Kit. Kit cooks for me. Then she cleans up afterwards. This bartender expects me to wait on her hand and foot. She does not clean the kitchen. She doesn't do any dishes. There is a huge difference between these two women."

"I can see this great romance between you and the bartender coming to an early demise," Dick Fitswell replied sarcastically. "Good thing you are not going to have a baby with her."

"Well Dick, it didn't end quite that fast. I was still enjoying my times at the bar, and the bartender is a great fuck. But one night

I am sitting with her right up next to me when I look over at the bar next to hers. There is a gal serving drinks there, but there's only one customer in the place. Besides the woman serving drinks there are only two bar girls there. So I am looking at this guy sitting alone on his bar stool and all of a sudden I see him go over on his barstool. The guy winds up on his back only several feet from the bar, and he's not getting up."

"I hope you didn't go over to help him," Dick Fitswell replied. "Why's that?"

"Because if you do, the guy can sue you afterwards for any injuries you might have caused him, even if he suffered no injuries at all. Fast Eddy, if you haven't realized it already, most people living in Pattaya are scam artists. And most of the worse scam artists of all are those falang you think are trustworthy just because they are Englishman, Americans, Germans or whoever. Money number one[16] doesn't just apply to Thai bar girls."

"You've gotta frame this picture in your mind, Dick. Both bars are side by side and the two bars aren't very wide. It is almost like there is only one bar, and I'm sitting in the same bar with this guy. He's down on the floor out for the count with his eyes still wide open. The three women in the bar are kneeling over him trying to help him, but they have obviously never been in this situation before. I have to do something so I go over to him, and I'm kneeling over him while one of the girls is sticking smelling salts down his nose. He's not responding. But his chest is heaving up and down very quickly as if he's trying to get air. At the same time I don't want to put myself in the position of being a doctor, because I'm not. So I go over to this couch and pick up a pillow, which I bring over to the girls. And motion to the girls to put the pillow under the guy's head."

"Meanwhile you are not touching the guy, or are you?"

---

[16]Money Number One by Neil Hutchison is
highly regarded as a classic expose on bar girl culture

"No. I let the girls do that. One of them lifts his head while one of the other girls slides the pillow under his head. So now he's got his head off the floor. He's resting comfortably, but he's not feeling a thing. I put my face next to his and start talking to him softly. But there's no response. By now ten minutes have passed and he's still not come to. One of the girls starts kissing his mouth trying to blow air into his lungs, but there's still no response."

"And you still haven't touched him?" Dick Fitwell asks.

"No. I did. I feel his pulse and it's very faint. But his chest is still heaving rapidly up and down so he's very much alive. I ask the girls where he keeps his money, and one of them points at one of his pockets. I now motion to all the women around us that I am taking out his wallet so that no one thinks I'm trying to steal his money. I pull his wallet out of his pocket, and as the women watch I start to go through it. There's some money in it and I find a credit card. I had been hoping there's a hospital card so we know what hospital he wants to go to if anything happens to him. But there is none. Only the credit card."

"So he probably can use the credit card to pay his hospital bill."

"Yes. I happen to know that Memorial Hospital is only five or ten minutes away and it's pretty good. So it's either that or one of the public hospitals which will be much slower taking care of him. By this time the bartender is standing over him wondering what to do. So I take out my phone and look up Memorial Hospital, and I show that to the bartender. Then she gets busy on her phone. I figure she's calling Memorial Hospital to send out an ambulance."

"So did you guys get the man to Memorial Hospital?"

"No. We didn't. The guy's chest stops heaving up and down. His eyes are still wide open but he's not there at all. Then he starts pissing his pants. Urine starts to flow around his crotch. Pretty soon he's got piss all over him. About five minutes after he pisses all over himself, the rescue team arrives. There are three or four men and they start working on him right away. They've got the right equipment. Or at least it looks to me that they do. They perform CPR on him with this equipment. But nothing happens. Then they lift the guy off the floor and carry him on a stretcher to the rescue van. So he's gone, and I'm hoping that he will wake up in a hospital. I'm pretty upset. So I tell the bartender I'm leaving but I will come back later."

"So where did you go after that?"

"I went to Walking Street. You never saw me walk so fast, Dick. I went straight over to Beach Road and got a motorcycle taxi driver to take me to Walking Street. Where I went straight to the Doll House. I found Nid there and have a few drinks with her upstairs. It was nice having Nid with me. I always liked Nid and always will. But after a couple of hours I had another motorbike taxi driver take me back to the bar. My bartender friend was pretty upset. When I asked her if she knew anything about the guy who had been taken to the hospital she shook her head and replied"

"Dead. He die. He die in bar. We look at him when he die, Fast Eddy."

"Oh great. He die when he pee pee on himself?"

"Chi. He pee pee. He die."

"What killed him, Fast Eddy? Did you ever find out?"

"Well Dick, the bartender told me the man was Australian. He had been playing golf that afternoon, and that he never drank a thing. When he got to the bar, he was on his first beer. And then he just toppled over backwards with the barstool going over with him. I got just a glimpse of him as he started to go over backwards. This was only for around two seconds or so, but it looked to me that the guy was just relaxing in his bar stool enjoying his first beer of the evening, and he just leaned back a little too far. It could happen to any of us. The man just happened to have some really bad luck."

"What happened then?"

"The bartender and I were both pretty upset. We had just seen a man die while pissing his pants. So we went back to my room at the Penthouse where we got totally drunk together. And then we had sex, passed out, and I woke up late in the morning with her lying next to me."

"Your Penthouse room, Fast Eddy, did you bring any other girls there besides Kit and the bartender?" Dick Fitswell asked.

139

"I took Nid after bar fining her at the Doll House, and she was a lot of fun. But she just doesn't get into sex the way some of the other girls do. I mean she does it, but it's like I've got a huge cock and this huge cock is causing her a lot of pain."

"Well, I've seen your dick, and no offense, Fast Eddy, but it really isn't all that much."

"I have to agree with you, Dick. My dick isn't my strongest point."

"You didn't take any more women to your room at the Penthouse?"

"I took a lady boy."

"What! I didn't think you took lady boys, Fast Eddy."

"I don't. Shit, I mean I didn't know that she was a lady boy. She didn't talk like one. She was pretty small for a lady boy, and she had a nice dress on. I never dreamed she was a lady boy until she went into that room with me and undressed."

"Did you have sex with her?"

"Sure I did. And she was much nicer than most of the women here. After we had sex, she kept massaging me. And then we drank a few beers together, man to man. No, I'm just joshing you, Dick. We really had a good chat and I found her to be very truthful about her background, and her customers and so on."

"Did you see her again?"

"No!"

"Why not?"

"Because I'm not into lady boys. I love women. Especially little Miss Kit."

"Why do you like her better than the other girls?"

"She cooks for me. The other girls expect me to cook for them. She cleans the place up afterwards. The other girls didn't. She's the prettiest girl I have met in Pattaya bar none, whether other guys agree with me or not. And she's really weird at times and I

140

just can't figure her out. Then, we've got some kind of mental telepathy with each other. Like that night I went off to see Ploy and she went catatonic on me. And lastly she gives me the best oral sex."

"That last point of yours is the most important," Dick Fitswell replied. "But I want you to think again. Are you sure you didn't have sex with any other women at the Penthouse other than the ones you have told me about?"

"I almost forgot, Dick. And this was the most important one. One night when Kit was supposed to meet me at Penthouse, she didn't show. And when I called her on the phone, I asked her, "Where are you?"

Then Kit replied: "Bangkok."

Then when I asked her, "What are you doing in Bangkok?" she replied, "I don't know."

That pissed me off enough to make me hightail it down to Soi 6 where I ran into an old fuck buddy of mine. I had known this woman for about three years. She was a skinny little thing back then. But she never stayed at her bar for very long. But every time I caught up with her, she performed splendidly in bed, and made me cum every time. Well lady luck was running with me, because as soon as I drove down Soi 6 on my motorbike I saw her standing outside her bar. So I bar fined her for the night. But when I put her behind me on my motorbike, I saw Ullie standing just outside La La Land. So right off, I told Ullie that Kit had just stood me up, and that she was in Bangkok. Ullie replied to me: "Kit's got many problems." Then I responded without thinking before the words came out of my mouth: "Like Yabba."[17]

"Kit never knew about the other girls I took to the Penthouse

---

[17]Yabba is a very popular drug that is similar to Crystal Meth

141

room. But this time she had to find out because Ullie would tell
her everything."

Fast Eddy Gives Kit the Key

"But you brought Kit back to your Penthouse short time room didn't you? Now what brought you to that change of heart, Fast Eddy?" Dick Fitswell asked.

"As I already told you, none of the other women cleaned up afterwards. And then I talked with Harry about it. Harry compared Kit's situation to my live in girlfriend's. Essentially Harry told me, "Look, you put Kit in a little room, and all the time she knows you have a live in girlfriend staying with you in a large beautiful condo. Which has to make her feel like second fiddle."

"So I came up with an idea. I would make Kit feel this is her place, and that there would never be any other women allowed there. I decided then to give her own key and register her with the Penthouse as a co-resident. Who as a co-resident would have the power to evict unwanted guests. Or if her boyfriend should show up, she could have security call the police. Which is what I ended up doing. I had Kit bring her ID to the Penthouse owner to fill out a little paperwork. Then I gave her an extra key so that she could come and go as she pleased whether I was there or not."

"How did that work out, Fast Eddy?"

"Very well at first. I would often go to the Penthouse room, and she would be waiting for me, watching Netflix. She started staying over much later too, sometimes as late as three a.m. while she got completely addicted to Netflix."

"But eventually it didn't really work out, did it Fast Eddy?"

"Nope. Kit wanted me to introduce a friend to Danny, the manager at the Doll House, so her friend could get a job there. But I told Kit that her friend could do that without her help. Then one night while I was having a couple of beers down on Soi 6 at Passion Dance Club, Kit started messaging me that she wanted to go to the Doll House. I asked her, "you come alone?" and she replied that she would meet me at the Penthouse alone and her friend would not be coming along. When I drove my motorbike to the Penthouse Kit was outside wandering around the parking lot. And that's when I saw the second girl, going upstairs to someone's room. I caught just a fleeting glimpse of her. I can't even tell you what she looked like."

143

"So what happened, Fast Eddy?"

"Kit went upstairs with me to the room. She was still on her period so we started watching Netflix together. When Kit told me her girlfriend ran into one of the Penthouse guests, and didn't wait even five minutes before propositioning him for short time sex, I really lost it. I wasn't going to get any sex, but Kit's girlfriend sure was. I was so pissed off, and not just because Kit's girlfriend was having sex and I wasn't, but also because as far as the Penthouse was concerned Kit was my girlfriend. And a nice girlfriend at that because Kit always acts like a little lady."

"And then she brings this stupid little whore in to do tricks! So I told Kit that her girlfriend was making us look like trashy people."

"But there is even more to it than that. I was planning on taking Kit to the Doll House at 8:30 when Happy Hour gets started. While her dim-witted girlfriend is going to make both of us wait on her. For an hour, maybe even two hours. Well I sure as hell wasn't going to wait on that whore. So I took Kit out of the room, and up the street away from the Penthouse. We started walking up the street together. Then we took a baht taxi over to Soi 6, because by then I decided there was no way I would be taking Kit to Walking Street after the two girls had pulled that on me. We started arguing, and I started to walk really fast with Kit walking behind me. Then I turned left at Soi 6/1 while Kit kept walking on until she got to Soi 6. Then out of the blue Harry calls me to tell me he's on Soi 6 watching Kit walking over to her old bar, La La Land and what a cute bubble butt she has. But I never followed Kit into La La Land. Because I am I so pissed off that I decide to go to the first Soi 6 bar that suits me."

"And?"

"A tall slender women comes up to me in front of Happy Days, a bar that has only lady boys. Right off the woman says to me. "I lady. No lady boy." Then she points out the other sex workers who are standing with her in front of the bar, and says "Lady boys. Me no lady boy. I lady." So I take her inside where one thing leads to another, and I wind upstairs fucking her without a condom."

"Did you and Kit split up then?"

"Yes. Because the next day I messaged her that I had sex on Soi 6. Whch she took that to mean that I already had a lady, which

144

turned out to be completely untrue. I had sex with that tall woman just once because she turned out to be a real nutcase. I didn't know what Kit meant by my having lady already. Whether I had chosen another Soi 6 lady who I liked better than her or whether she meant my live in girlfriend."

"You and Kit split up for how long?"

About three weeks. Only about three days after we split up, I asked Malee to come down to hit a few Soi 6 bars with me. Which she did. By this time Kit was working again at La La Land, and once she saw me walking by her bar with Malee. She messaged me later on to say, "I see you with Lady."

"So what happened with you and Malee?"

"She lasted only about ten days with me. But she came with me to the Penthouse room a couple of times. We did it once without a condom. And Malee told me she was using no protection. She really got me laughing when she told me that if she had my baby I would have to take care of her."

"But one night when I bar fined her over at the Doll House, two of my friends were visiting the club when this god awful downpour started. My two friends were such pussies. Can you believe it, Dick? They must have stayed at the Doll House for over two hours waiting for all that rain to stop. While Malee and I walked in the rain all the way down Walking Street toPattaya Tai. The water had flooded that whole section of Second Road. It came up to well over my knees. But Malee and I were having a blast wading around in all that water. Then we got into a baht taxi which took us to the Penthouse. There were several of these old falang ladies sitting next to us watching us in a condescending way, like "what is this old fart doing with such a young lady?" So Malee and I started French kissing each other just to piss them off even more."

"So what caused you and Malee to split up. Seems to me she was a lot of fun, and Harry's been telling me she has one of the nicest asses on Walking Street."

"She stood me up. She was supposed to meet me on Soi 6 in

Passion Dance Club where I was telling Lamai[18] how reliable she was. Malee told me she was looking for me on Soi 6 but had never gone inside the bar. Which might have been true because Malee is pretty stupid."

"Like most bar girls, "Dick Fitswell replied.

"So you stopped chatting with Kit, you stopped seeing Malee and you completely blocked the nutcase then," said Dick Fitswell.

"All at more or less the same time, and as usual I was spending a lot of time at Passion Dance Club which became sort of a second home for me. Anyways, Dick, that same night after I left Passion Dance Club and walked up Soi 6 a couple of times, I saw a slender woman who appeared quite a bit older than the other women I had been seeing. So I decided that younger women were the problem, and on account of their being so young they had no idea how to treat a man. Figuring I'd give this older gal a try, I went inside the bar with her, paid for our drinks, the 300 baht room rental and took her upstairs."

[18]Lamai was the waitress at Passion Dance Club

Nang Queen of Vampires

"Dick, she was much more than I ever expected her to be. As soon as we started to shower, I start rubbing myself up and down her backside which had gotten to be smooth and slippery on account of all the soap I put on her body. If I were to describe her body in one word, that word has to be slithery. So I just start sticking my dick in her doggie style while we shower together. From then on we always did it without a condom. But when I got her down on that bed in the short time room, my God, did she cum. I really feel sorry for the couple who had to use those sheets after we got done with them."

"I must give you an A plus for that," Dick Fitswell replied. "First for doing it without a condom. And second, for making that gal lose all control. Looks like you are making the utmost of that cattle prod of yours even if I do find it on the small side."

"I'll tell you, Dick. Nang turned into a real stalker. About the third time we had sex together she mentioned doing long time with me just outside her bar. I bar fined her, then we went to her car together which she had parked a hundred feet away from her bar. I got in, and she started driving into a short alleyway to Soi 6/1. What I call lady boy alley because although it's only 100 feet from Soi 6 running parallel to it, it is crawling with lady boys. Now you gotta get this picture. Nang should have headed straight down Soi 6 which is a one way to Beach Road. Instead she turns into Soi 6/1 which is a one way heading the opposite direction to Second Road. So she winds up going against the flow of traffic. Soi 6/1 is very narrow and it's got cars parked all up and down it. And we've got cars and motorbikes heading right at us. Nang's wearing this baseball hat and she's behaving like it's no big deal, but all these cars are honking at her for blocking their way. She even grazes one of the cars that's parked along 6/1 but she keeps on going. It takes her all of ten minutes to go just 300 yards down 6/1. Then she makes a left onto Beach Road and we are finally on our way to Walking Street."

"Where in the hell does she park near Walking Street?"

"There's a big Buddha Temple where people can park their cars for fifty baht or so. When Nang drives in there, it's a lot bigger than I expected it to be and there must have been 500 cars parked there. There's hardly a place left for her to park, but after driving around that lot a few times, she finally finds a place. Then we start walking toward Walking Street together and she's got her arm all around me. I'm starting to think, "this woman adores me. She's the perfect replacement for Kit."

"Where did you two go?"

"She takes me to Baby Dolls. I know the manager there who sits with us for a while. It just so happens that just a few months ago, Nang was working at Baby Dolls. Then I take her to the Doll House which is also on Soi Diamond just off Walking Street. I try to explain how Kit and I always get the Happy Hour specials for 75 baht each, but Nang insists on having Blue Hawaiis which sets me back 250 baht for each drink."

"Did you ever take her again to the Doll House?" Dick Fitswell asked.

"One more time. And she's ordering Blue Hawaiis again. But the next time we go to Walking Street together, she takes me to Lucifers Disco. It's like a big cave inside there. Lucifers has a happy hour. I don't remember till what time, but at first our drinks are reasonably priced and then bottled beer goes up to 200 baht. Anyway, there are all these low life scumbags in Lucifers. That's because the guys who pick up ladies there don't have to pay bar fines. There's a lot of Indians and Arabs and cheap ass falang in there. And most of these guys are likely to stay there until four a.m. or so. But it's all the same in all these Walking Street discos. A lot of go-go girls go to them after being short timed from their bar. Looking for trick number two or three for the night."

"But just about everyone in these discos are total vampires used to staying up all night. I find most of these night owls to be so much wasted space because they have no life, sleep all day and do nothing worthwhile. And Lucifers is playing all that Da Da electronic crap music. The whole scene is so shitty if you ask me. With high-priced drinks and all these vampires hanging out there."

"Nang has the best damn body, Dick. But she never uses a condom with me so here I am having sex with a woman whose body completely turns me on. She's got her own car. So more often than not, she picks me up on Beach Road right at Soi 6. Usually she's right on time."

"So what's wrong with her?"

148

"One thing she did. We were in the Penthouse together and she tells me she thinks she might be pregnant. And get this, Dick. The reason she thinks she's pregnant is she's always fucking without a condom. So I am thinking she's trying to get money out of me because I am giving her a child. But at the same time she's telling me she's fucking all these other guys without a condom. This tells me she's stupid and she's a liar. Another thing, she is turning out to be a real stalker. Messages me constantly and wants me to be with her every day. I tell her I can't, and she keeps asking me why I can't. Then I tell her I'm tired because I have just exercised really hard, but she keeps asking me to meet her on Walking Street. One time I was sitting in a bar on Soi 6. She's on Walking Street so she wants me to meet her there. When I don't, she tells me she's at the Penthouse waiting for me. By this time I am just on the edge of getting back together with Kit."

"But the straw that finally breaks the camel's back is when Nang quits her bar on Soi 6. If I am banging her in the Candy Bar, it costs me just one-thousand baht for her tip and 300 baht for the room. But if I meet her outside the bar she insists that I pay her two-thousand baht. And then I have to pay for a hotel room also. Nang just never got it. She simply thought that I would rather pay one-thousand baht more for a short time, than pay her or any other girl the standard one-thousand baht short time price down on Soi 6. But what really ended it was what her mamasan told me one day at the Candy Bar."

"So what did mamasan tell you?"

"Nang has a Thai boyfriend. Mamasan even showed me pictures of the creep. So here I am paying this Thai boyfriend "his salary" through Nang. Mamasan also told me that Nang had been lying to her, and that she is no good. Mamasan doesn't tell me, but I've figured this out by myself. Nang's beautiful body is created by drugs. Not by God."

"How did you end it with Nang?"

"I completely cut her off. I blocked her on line and I blocked her on my telephone."

"Fast Eddy, when did you give up your room in the Penthouse?" Dick Fitswell asked.

"Not long after Kit and I split up. I just couldn't see keeping it

149

anymore. It was costing me around 20000 baht, and I had to keep cleaning it and stocking it with food. When Kit and I split up there was no reason to keep it. I rented it to be Kit's home and with her out of my life, I stopped my arrangement with the Penthouse as soon as I could."

Squirters

"Hey Dick, you ever have a girl piss in your mouth?" Fast Eddy asked.

"Uhh, no. I've done a lot of shit in my day but I have never had that done to me."

"Me either," Danny replied. "Did a girl piss in your mouth, Fast Eddy?"

"I am almost too embarrassed to talk about it, but yes. It happened to me last night. There was this gal hanging around right in the middle of Soi 6 pulling on just about every guy walking by her. She had a nice fine ass, the kind that looks like it needs to be fucked. She just came up to me and pressed her body into mine so I went into the bar with her. I got each of us a beer so she sits down on my lap. She was in no hurry so we had another beer together. Then she asks me to take her to her room where I can have sex with her there. I suppose she figured I was into drugs because she tells me, "I have everything in my room. Make you very happy. Me boom boom you and I have things you like. Everything you want to make you happy."

"Her room? Was she living in a short time room upstairs in the bar?"

"Many girls do who either don't have enough money to pay rent or for whatever reason want to stay down on Soi 6, Dick. But not her. When I asked her where her room was she said it was near Pattaya Klang."

"Did you go to her room with her?" asked Dick Fitswell.

"No. I was too scared to. I suspected she wanted to do drugs with me. Because I hadn't even short timed her upstairs yet. So why in the hell would she want to take me to her room when she didn't even know me?"

"Did you short time her upstairs then?" Danny asked.

"Sure did. But even before I took her upstairs I had to take a piss in the toilet. Like most Soi 6 bars they have a toilet downstairs. There's a curtain hanging in the doorway, so here I'm pissing in that urinal when the girl comes through the curtain and stands right up next to me watching me take a piss."

"That's really sweet of her," Danny replied.

"What's even weirder is what she does upstairs. We go up there and get naked together. She smokes me until my dick gets good and hard. I tell her I want to eat her so she straddles me and I start licking her. For some reason I must have had quite an effect on her because she gets wet in only a few seconds. She starts gyrating her little body around my mouth while pressing my face deeper inside her, and she gets wetter and wetter. It happens so quickly. She keeps cumming and cumming in my mouth and then her taste starts changing. Now I've never tasted piss before. I can only imagine. But she's completely out of control and my mouth is getting completely filled up with piss. You guys have no idea. I'm starting to think that this is a huge high for her. Like she's a control freak who hates all men but feels she needs to dominate the guy. To show him who's the boss while showing her complete contempt for him."

For the first time, Fast Eddy found Dick Fitswell to be speechless and totally detached from everyone around him, deep in thought.

"What do you think, Dick? You are being awfully quiet."

"I think it's quite the opposite, Fast Eddy. She's not trying to dominate you. She's letting you dominate her."

"Come again, Dick. I mean shit, this gal's squeezing my mouth between her legs while she's filling my mouth with piss and I am choking on it. Her urine is cascading down my cheeks. I'm totally disgusted with myself and with her even more. But, I've never drank piss before. I feel dominated, but it feels really good."

"On the contrary," Dick Fitswell replied. You should be quite proud of yourself. You have completely turned this woman on. God knows why because you really don't seem like that much to me. Look it up on the internet. Squirters or squirting. About 8 percent of all women in the U.S. are squirters. Most of them are closet squirters. Women have these tubes. One has cum coming out of it when the woman has an orgasm. The other carries urine. What happens to some women is the tube that carries urine ejects a bit of urine into her cum. The result is a liquid that tastes like you think urine tastes but it really isn't urine. Or at least not most of it. When these women go out of control during orgasm they start squirting. It's embarrassing for a lot of them so they try to hold back on their orgasms so they aren't completely out of control. Some of these women pull back right before they orgasm and you might even think they are lesbians. While a few of them simply let go, and then their sex partner suddenly thinks he's drinking a mouthful of piss. The key is the taste and the amount of fluid the woman secretes."

"That all sounds good to me," Fast Eddy replied. "If I ever see this woman again, I'm calling her Squirt. But I'll tell you guys something I'm not going to tell anyone else. I almost came while she was filling my mouth with squirt juice. And when I got around to fucking her afterwards my dick must have been about 15 inches long. Came right into her without using a condom because by this point I didn't care. I didn't care if I got gonorrhea. Hell, I didn't even care if I got HIV from her. I was so fucking turned on."

"I've never heard a story like that before," said Danny.

"Yeah, well it got even worse after that. It was great but I'm talking about later when we were showering together."

"What happened next?"

"She starts singing in the shower. But her voice is constantly changing. This strange voice keeps coming out of her throat like she's Mickey Mouse or some other cartoon character. It's like Linda Blair in the movie the "Exorcist." Her voice is not coming out of her throat at all. It's coming out of a ventriloquist's dummy. This gal is completely nuts. A real psycho."

"Well, are you going to do her again?" Because if you don't, my name isn't Dick Fitswell."

"Hell yes, I am."

The Dream

"Are you still seeing Kit?" Dick Fitswell asked Fast Eddy.

"Yes, I am, Dick, and it looks like I will be seeing her forever."

"You gotta be shitting me. Get lost, Fast Eddy."

"You are my father confessor so you must hear me out."

"Ok. I am listening. But please do not bore me to death with all this love bullshit."

"Here I am, split up with Kit for a month and I go into Three Angels. It's just another Soi 6 bar, so it's nothing special, but I want to have my first beer and a couple of cigarettes without any bar girls hounding me. Which doesn't happen because as soon as I'm seated, a pretty attractive girl sits next to me. I buy her a drink, and she starts kissing me. And I mean really kissing me, passionately."

"I'm going to try to make this short, Dick, but in no time we are upstairs together. She smokes me, swallows my cum, then she holds me down on my back and keeps French kissing me. Fifteen minutes pass like that and suddenly I'm fucking her without a condom."

"So you came twice in less than one hour? That's pretty good for an old fart like you."

"The gal was 23 years old, and she told me she hated working down on Soi 6. She wanted a good man, to settle down with, she told me. And she was pretty damn good looking."

"Sounds like the right girl for you. She puts lead in your pencil, enough to make you cum twice and you didn't pursue her? Is this what you are telling me?" Fast Eddy.

"Yes. Didn't even get her phone number, but what happens next is I go into Sex in the City the next day and there's a good-looking gal in the bar. So I bang her. She has a pretty good body, but her legs are too short so her ass doesn't quite hang right. Her body's nowhere as good as Kit's, with those long skinny legs that accentuates her beautiful little bubble butt."

154

"Oh shit. Here we go again. With you, Fast Eddy, it's Kit, Kit, Kit. I should kick you out of my establishment."

"You won't, Dick. Not when you hear what comes next."

"Okay, Fast Eddy, go on. If you insist on continuing to bore me with your lovey dovey tales of true romance, have at it."

"The second time I take this young woman upstairs at Sex in the City, I'm banging her upstairs. And she's not that bad, but I just can't cum. So I start to think I'm with someone else to help me get my mind off this mindless cranking my dick into her pussy exercise. She's getting off, but I'm not. So I start thinking about Kit and Kit giving me a blow job. Which almost always makes me cum. I've got my mind totally on Kit now, but I still can't cum. By now about an hour goes by so I fake an orgasm just to make this whore feel good about herself. Then I take off the condom, which has nothing in it. But I don't want her to see that, so I take the condom into the toilet, wrap it in toilet paper and throw it into the waste basket."

"You are such a helluva nice guy, Fast Eddy. You make a Soi 6 whore cum, and then you hide the completely dry condom from her so she won't start feeling sorry for herself."

"You are not going to believe this. But as soon as I take the woman downstairs, my phone starts ringing. And it's Kit. Who has just tried to call me three times. So now I'm talking with her, and of course she wants to see me. But here's my point. She's been trying to call me already while I am thinking of her as I am trying to cum. This means there's some sort of mental telepathy going on between Kit and me."

"I don't think so," Dick Fitswell replied. "I think it's all purely coincidental."

"Not at all, Dick. Because when I go back to my condo that night and fall asleep I have this dream. In the dream I am taking Kit to her home up in the village to meet her family. I'm dreading it because I don't want to meet her family. I've been there and done that only too often. The family only cares about the falang's money. And while he's visiting the family, he's paying for everything. Their food, their beer and gas money when he's taking the whole family around on their errands"

"Anyway, I'm off to see Kit's family and suddenly I'm approaching their house. It's a lot bigger and much better kept up than I thought. And then I see several cars in front of it, all of them belonging to Kit's family. One of the cars is a very powerful race car. Which has to be very expensive, so I start thinking, "Just what the hell is going on here? Kit's family has a lot more money than I ever thought it had."

"Dick, the whole thing gets pretty whacked out after that. I'm now at the kitchen table and Kit's in the kitchen cooking dinner for her family and me. She's got three brothers sitting with me. But now, we are no longer in Thailand. And her brothers aren't Thai. They are Americans. Suddenly my mind has been transported from Thailand to rural Missouri in the U.S. and here I've got these country boys sitting around me who claim they are Kit's brothers. Then one of the brothers says something to me, and it's something I will never forget so long as I live."

"What did this brother say?" Dick Fitswell asked.

"He said to me, Fast Eddy, it is very important that you keep Kit with you, no matter what happens. You must never sever this link between our family and yourself. No matter what you think of her, never leave her."

"That is unbelievable, Fast Eddy. Did you really dream that up?"

"Yes, I did. And it was the same night I was thinking of Kit while I was trying to cum into that other woman. And Kit's trying to call me right as I was trying to climax. That might have been, as you say Dick, coincidence, but that very odd dream coming into my head right afterwards, this surely can't be two of "these things" or pure coincidence happening one after the other."

"What does this all mean to you?" Dick Fitswell asked. "What are you planning on doing with Kit?"

"What it means is no matter what Kit is. If she's a drug addict, mentally deranged, a child in a woman's body, or schizophrenic, there's an inseparable bond between us that cannot be broken by any other woman, or anything else for that matter. On one level or another, Kit is to be my woman for as long as I live."

Reconciliation with Kit

"So how did you two get back together? I find all this to be most incredible. First you actually believe you are on some type of mental telepathy with Kit. And believe me, Fast Eddy, there's ample evidence for you to believe in it. Then you have this dream warning you to never give up on the girl. No matter what she is, whether she's psycho, lesbian, retarded or what have you. Any one of us would have given up on her long ago. What do you think of all this, Harry? I might be Dick Fitswell, the man who claims to have all the answers. But this time, I have none."

"I don't get it either, Dick. Looks like our friend here has his tit stuck in a ringer." Staring intently at Fast Eddy trying to read his friends thoughts, Harry finally adds:

"You are together again. Just how did you and Little Miss Kitty happen to manage that?"

"She messages me on line.[19] "I am very sick, Fast Eddy. Help me please."

Then she meets me down on Soi 6 one, which I keep calling Lady Boy Alley because it's chock full of lady boys. But I've parked my motorbike on Soi 6 in front of a bar where I've been having a beer with another condo owner at the Bahthaus. When I bring Kit around the corner to Soi 6, I introduce her to my friend. Then I take her to Shabushi, one of the Japanese restaurants at Big C. Kit looks very tired. Her face is drawn the same way you see these women on television dying from typhus or cholera. And this

---

[19] The most popular text messaging application in Thailand

fellow Bahthaus co-owner,[20] who has no manners at all, tells me:

"You really know how to pick them, Fast Eddy. This girl looks like she's on death's door. Why did you get yourself involved with her?"

"That's a very good question," Harry replied. "None of these women care one rat's ass about us. Which is why I like lady boys. Your friend's name is Sam if I remember. He's a complete asshole to say that in front of Kit. But he's right."

"I had to help her, Harry. Kit and I have just been through too much together for too long."

"So what did you do for her?"

"Well, Harry. I took her to Shabushi which is a Japanese restaurant. The next day I took her to a doctor who's prescribing sleeping pills for me at Bangkok Pattaya Hospital. He's a shrink. He works in the department of mental health. Kit is too skinny at 35 kilos, but by now she weighs just 33 kilos."

"What are your conclusions for what's causing Kit to get so run down?" Dick Fitswell asked.

"I was thinking since she wasn't getting any money from me that she had money problems. I was also thinking that Kit might be on drugs. A lot of these gals do drugs to enable them to put up with so many slime ball customers. Especially Soi 6 girls who have to fuck guys with two heads and diseased minds. I also thought she might have a parasite or even HIV. So I asked the doctor to give her a complete drug test. But when I asked him for a complete blood test I was thinking they would be testing her for drugs and if she were on them, this would show up on the blood test."

---

[20] A fellow co-owner at the Bahthaus. Not Big Jim

"Did the hospital give her a CBC blood test?"

"Yes. And she passed it with flying colors. As you know Dick, a CBC stands for complete blood count. This test is for any irregularities in the red blood cells. Red blood cells carry oxygen. So among many other things, this test detects anemia, infection and leukemia. But it also tests the white blood cells which fight infection. Since HIV attacks the immune system it might very well be detected by a CBC test. If the CBC test is abnormal showing an abnormal blood platelet count, one would want to test further for something like HIV. So although this test is by no means conclusive, it would tend to show that Kit does not have HIV. It will also detect to some extent drug use, particularly amphetamines. But urine analysis is a much more reliable test."

"Let's hear from Harry about these tests," Dick Fitswell replied.

"I get tested all the time for HIV and other genital diseases because I'm having sex with a lot of lady boys," Harry replied. "Chances are, Kit does not have HIV due to her getting such good marks on the CBC test. But she should still get other tests to get more reliable results. As for drugs, urine tests are far better indicators than a CBC test. Fast Eddy, did you have her get tested specifically for drugs?"

"I didn't. But after she had her blood tested and it came time for me to pay her hospital bills we were still in the Mental Health waiting area. So I went back into the doctor's office and asked the doctor if he had tested Kit for drugs. He said, no, he didn't but if I wanted her to take a drug test, he wanted to ask her first. So I took Kit back into the doctor's office and the doctor asked her if she would submit to a drug test. To my surprise, Kit said that she was willing to do the urine sample tests for drugs."

"Did she?"

"No. Because the doctor told me that he didn't think Kit was on drugs. The doctor said: "Her eyes are clear, and her teeth show no evidence of her being a drug user. So I told the doctor, "if Kit says she's not on drugs and you say she isn't, then I have to believe she's not on drugs." So I asked the doctor not to have her do a drug test."

"Did the doctor give you and Kit any advice?" Dick Fitswell asked.

"He asked Kit what bothered her the most. Kit told us she was extremely worried about her four year-old son. I took this to mean that she was extremely worried about money. Or lack of it. This is very normal for many if not most people. From this I reasoned that Kit is not very worried about money so long as I'm giving it to her and operating as her safety net. I took this even one step farther. If I kept encouraging her to see her son fairly often and I gave her the means to do so, she would view me as her number one friend in her life. But the doctor also told Kit to do a lot of swimming. I'm sure he thought she was living with me and that she would have access to our condo swimming pool and also the pools at Centara once I paid a membership fee for her."

"But she's not living with you is she?" Dick Fitswell asked.

"No. She hasn't even spent one entire night with me. Obviously the doctor must have gotten her mixed up with my live in girlfriend."

"So how did you feel after you and Kit saw the shrink?"

"I felt I should strongly encourage her to keep seeing her son and offer her money to see him every couple of months or so. I also decided that I needed to start giving her money again so she would feel that she never has to work in the bar again."

Boom Boom Buddies

Big Dicks Bar on Soi 6 had become many things. First and foremost, it had become the leading hangout for Dick Fitswell's pals, one of whom would become Saint Peter to spread the message of what all real men should aspire to. While becoming a confessional where Dick's converts could confess their inner most thoughts to a select few, who would actually listen. Lastly, it was serving as a springboard to the many neighboring Soi 6 bars where Fitswell's converts could satisfy their sexual needs cheaply and efficiently so they could get onto more important matters. Such as getting totally wasted, which oftentimes leads many of us to a true understanding of Thai bar girl culture.

"You are here pretty late. So what have you been up to tonight?" Dick Fitswell asked a not yet drunk enough Fast Eddy.

"I have been shopping with Kit for a suitcase over at Central Pattaya Festival Mall. We picked out a nice Samsonite that she can treasure for years to come. Then we took it to Sandman where we had a few drinks together, did a short time upstairs, and then we walked up Soi 6 to Second Road where I put her on a motorbike taxi. Tomorrow Little Miss Kit gets on a bus to see her son way up in northwestern Thailand."

"What? You are giving her a few days time off from seeing you?" a totally intoxicated Harry asked. "I wouldn't be sending her off anywhere. I'd be having her smoke me every night to justify what I was paying her."

"You forget, Harry, that I'm taking my girlfriend to the U.S. day after tomorrow so I can't be seeing Kit anyway."

"I'm surprised that Kit walked all the way up Soi 6 with you," replied Dick Fitswell. "We all know that she doesn't want to be seen anywhere near Soi 6."

"I got her pretty drunk on tequilas at Sandman, Dick. So she didn't care who saw her tonight. All the bar girls at Sandman saw us with that suitcase. They knew I had just bought it for her. And we walked right by Smoke and Kisses and Ning was watching us. Ning's always asking me all kinds of questions about Kit. "

"We all know all about Ning," Wolfgang replied. "And how she keeps telling you the latest about her boyfriend and her customers. You two are the most classic case of two fuck buddies I ever saw."

"Speaking of Ning. What makes her so good in bed? I prefer the lady boys myself," Harry replied. "What does she do for you that makes you claim she's better than any lady boy?"

"I'm nice to the ladies who often reciprocate. And you aren't, Harry. So do you really think any of these ladies gives a rat's ass about you?"

"They are all users and whores," Harry replied. "Every last one of them."

"They might be that, Harry. But I guarantee you that while Kit is with her family that she's going to be one happy woman. And that she will be messaging me like crazy while I'm in hotel rooms in the U.S. wishing I was back in Pattaya."

"But you will be with your girlfriend."

"And we are as good as finished, Harry. This upcoming trip to the U.S. is going to fill me with a sadness that I've not experienced since my mother died. She's been a good lady, but as B.B. King used to sing, 'The thrill is Gone'."

The Real Turd in the Punch Bowl

"So you finally split up with your live in girlfriend? Fast Eddy."

"Yes, Dick. Over the past couple of years I did so many short times with so many girls, it was bound to finally happen. By this time I wanted my freedom, unless I would be living with Kit, which would have curtailed any more short times with all those other women. Several times Kit would sharply reprimand me for having a live in girlfriend. Which would have meant her becoming just as jealous as my live in. But as I keep telling you. There's no one like Kit. Whenever I have any other woman on my arm, it just doesn't feel right. But when Kit's with me, it's like there's no other woman in the room. The other girls might be there, and I might be talking or joking with them, but Kit's always the center of my attention. I would give up a lot of my freedom I have with other women so long as I have Kit living with me. So when my girlfriend finally left me and took all her things with her, I started to prepare my condo for Kit to move in with me."

"What do you mean by preparing your condo so Kit could move in, Fast Eddy?"

"I took all the things that belonged to my ex girlfriend out of the condo. Clothes she had left behind for example, and pictures, especially the large one of my ex that I had hung on the wall."

"Then I got rid of all my old dishes and other kitchen items my girlfriend used. I bought a new set of plates, soup bowls, and utensils. And I replaced all the kitchen knives my ex had used for food preparation with a knife set that I had Kit help pick out for me. I wanted my condo to have a slightly different appearance, one that Kit could help me with. For example, I had the kitchen floor replaced by a new one, and I had Kit help me pick out the tiles."

"But she's not jumping at the chance to move in with you, is she?"

"She most certainly isn't. She never even brought her own toothbrush over. That's what a lot of Thai women do when they want to move in with a man. They will usually start off by leaving a neckless, a ring, ear ring or even a purse behind. Then they start bringing in even more of their stuff until you finally realize that you have a new roommate. But the real capper is Kit's not spending any nights with me. Sure, she might stay with me until

163

one a.m. or even as late as three a.m. This would often infuriate me, because I know that any woman who does not sleep with her guy has another person in her life. Someone she loves far more than the guy who is preparing the new home for her."

"That would be her Thai boyfriend?"

"Either that or a tomboy lover. But either way, whether it's a lesbian girlfriend or a Thai boyfriend, whoever she keeps going back to her room for, is the real turd in the punch bowl."

"Did you ever find out for sure if she has a tomboy lover or Thai boyfriend?"

"You can bet your ass I did. Terry who lives on the floor under mine at the Bahthaus has a good friend who used to be a manager of a Soi 6 bar. Now this ex manager has something like two-thousand friends on his Facebook pages and most of them are women. One of his Facebook friends is Kit. Now, although Kit hardly ever posts on Facebook, she does every once in awhile. Eventually she posts a few pictures of herself with this Thai boyfriend of hers. And this was at the same time my girlfriend and I were splitting up. A couple of the pictures show her and the Thai boyfriend on this bed together. And although, none of the pictures show them naked, they are still quite revealing."

"How's that? What do you mean when you say revealing?

"They show her smiling while she's lying down with this asshole. Sometimes she's holding hands with him."

"So did you tell Kit that you were now 100 percent certain she had a Thai boyfriend?"

"You damn right I did. I started messaging her on line that I was 100 percent sure she had a Thai boyfriend because a friend of mine had shown me pictures. But I made it clear that I had never asked for them, and that I had never gone to her Facebook pages, nor had I ever paid a detective to find out whether or not she had a Thai boyfriend. And I most certainly did not tell her that the mamasan at the Quicky Bar warned me to stay away from her and her Thai boyfriend."

"How did she respond to your accusations?" Dick Fitswell asked.

"At first she said that the pictures were meaningless because people can put her in pictures even if she doesn't want to be in them. Then she said, "You bore me with your talk of a Thai boyfriend. I am going to cut off all internet contact with you within 24 hours." But I knew she wouldn't do that on count of all that money I was giving her."

"Did she cut you off?"

"No. She couldn't afford to as I was too much of an ATM for her. And then just one or two days after she threatened to sever all contact with me she asked me to help her with a big problem."

Kit's Big Problem

For a few moments there's dead silence in Fitswell's bar. A completely wasted Harry's almost asleep while Wolfgang is listening intently, taking it all in, while calmly smoking a cigarette.

"So what's Kit's problem this time?"

"I knew you would ask, Wolfgang. She tells me she has a very serious problem with her arm and hand. I knew she had two small blemishes, one in her hand, the other one on her forearm, but I have been looking at those blister like bulges in her skin on the internet, and I had concluded they weren't very serious.

"So how serious is her arm problem?" Dick Fitswell asked.

"Very serious. I took her to Bangkok Pattaya Hospital. And they did two MRI's which showed the entire internal composition of her arm and hand. This equipment costs over a million dollars, and Bangkok Pattaya Hospital is the only hospital in Pattaya that has one. The two MRIs cost me almost $1000. I got the results from Dr. Sonchai.

"Can you tell us what you found out about Kit's condition, Fast Eddy?"

"She's had two Haemangiomas on her hand and forearm for 20 years, but there's been rapid growth in them over the past five years. In her case, she now has a large tumor that extends from her elbow into her hand. This tumor is a gelatinous mass that is entwined by a large number of blood vessels in her arm and hand. The only recommended treatment is a series of injections that will hopefully control further growth of this tumor. This is a lifelong affliction so she will need to get injections for the rest of her life. He told us this injection procedure is very dangerous.

"I take it then that you would be having to pay large amounts of money to Bangkok Pattaya Hospital every few months for the rest of Kit's life," Dick Fitswell replied.

"No. Dr. Sonchai strongly advised me to have another hospital perform the injection treatment because Kit was not insured. Because if she wound up in intensive care, it would be far cheaper for me to pay the bill at a public hospital than a private hospital such as Bangkok Pattaya. He then set Kit and me up for an appointment with a colleague who worked out of Chulalongkorn Hospital in Bangkok."

"How did that appointment go?"

"A few days later we met again at Bangkok Pattaya Hospital with Dr. Sonchai and his colleague. The young doctor strongly advised Kit to go to King Chulalngkorn hospital because Kit did not have insurance and Bangkok Pattaya Hospital would be too expensive for Kit and me. So he gave us a date to show up in Bangkok when the specialist who does injections on Haemangiomas has office hours."

"So how was Kit's arm at this time, besides it hurting a lot?"

"One finger of her left hand is bent back nearly 90 degrees. It's unusable. Dr. Sonchai explained to us that the tumor was pushing up against a nerve that travels to that finger. So for the rest of her life she will no longer be able to use that finger because the nerve has atrophied too much. She also had lost the partial use of her left thumb and she's not getting it back for the rest of her life.

Fast Eddy Does Another Threesome

The next week things were very quiet at Big Dick's Bar. Angry Pussy had gone home to her village to visit her family and the other guys never came, which left Fast Eddy and Dick Fitswell to themselves drinking beer and tequila.

"So how did that appointment with the hospital in Bangkok go, Fast Eddy?"

"Real Shitty Dick. The whole sorry episode was very unfortunate. My girlfriend had just moved out. Packed all her stuff and left me by my lonesome. But she had kept warning me not to move any other woman in with me until I got to know the woman really well. She had already been hearing a lot about Little Miss Kit and figured I was going to move Kit in as soon as she left me. So Kit and I both decided that I shouldn't have her staying with me for a few weeks until the dust had cleared. By this time I had become friends with a Cambodian woman who was working at Sandman Hotel and sports bar on Soi 6. It had been a hotel. But recently the authorities have been clamping down on short time hotels in Pattaya. So officially Sandman was no longer renting its rooms out unless a customer was taking one of its own bar girls upstairs for short time. Kit was now just a customer, like me, but my Cambodian friend would allow me to take Kit upstairs for short times provided I paid the 400 baht short time room rental. Later on several of the other girls would rent me a room for short time. So Sandman became a meeting place for Kit and me."

"How old is this Cambodian gal?"

"About forty. She used to get Malee and me short time rooms on Soi 13/2 near Walking Street when I used to bar fine Malee from the Doll House. After Malee went home or back to her go-go bar, I'd often head back to the bar just to drink with Noi. So by the time Noi started working on Soi 6 we were already good friends. Sometimes Kit and I would drink tequilas at Sandman with Noi or a couple of the other girls there. Then we'd do a short time upstairs and after that we'd oftentimes go over to Big C to have dinner and to do some grocery shopping together."

After Kit and I agree to leave for Bangkok at three a.m. in order to get to the Chulalongkorn Hospital before five a.m. We meet at Sandman around six p.m. I tell Kit she should stay with me at my condo until three a.m., and then we will take a taxi to Bangkok.

Which made perfectly good sense to me. But after we have a couple of drinks at Sandman, Kit tells me she has to go back to her room before she can meet me back at my condo."

"I'll bet that pissed you off."

"You bet it did. Because there's absolutely no reason she can't go with me from Sandman to my condo after we have dinner at a Big C restaurant. I figured there was only one conceivable reason why Kit should insist on returning to her room from the Sandman."

"I get it," Dick Fitswell replied. "She has to say goodbye to her Thai boyfriend."

"Exactly. You cannot imagine how angry this made me.. I tell Kit I am going a couple of doors down to MK Kitty bar which is a new go-go bar on Soi 6. So I go into MK Kitty bar where I find Dowel and Lamai. I walk back to the Sandman to tell Kit to follow me to MK Kitties and then I go back to Kitties and wait ten minutes for Kit but when she doesn't show up, I go back to Sandman. By then Kit must have become very angry with me because she had left Sandman and had probably gone back to her room. So I head back to MK Kitties where I get totally drunk on tequila with Dowel and Lamai."

"Who in the hell are Dowel and Lamai?"

"Lamai had been the main service lady at Passion Dance Club while Dowel was the prettiest girl in the place. Passion used to be a very wild place. Twice I had seen friends of mine getting blow jobs while they were sitting right next to me. Including Harry. I never did, but I used to take Dowel upstairs for short times. I had known both girls for two years, and then they closed Passion down. The Night Wish group bought the premises and created two new Night Wish bars out of what had once been a lot like a go-go bar."

"Okay, so these two gals are good pals of yours and one of them is a fuck buddy."

"Yep. Anyway I get totally wasted on Tequila with Dowel and Lamai, and they manage to convince me to take them both home with me for short times. Cost me a bar fine of nearly two-thousand baht for the two of them and another one-thousand baht each for their tips. But I soon have them following me two up on a motorbike taxi. But they don't have my phone number. So here am driving down Naklua Road with the motorcycle taxi behind me, and I keep looking back to make sure I haven't lost them. Because I drive real fast even when I'm drunk. I keep looking back at the girls, but I'm not paying enough attention to what's right in front of me. I hit the curb and boom. My bike's down on the side of the street, and I'm down on the pavement right next to it."

"Sounds pretty crazy."

"I was. Still am. But I got right on up on my feet and start lifting my motorbike off the pavement. The girls and the taxi driver are helping me. My left arm and left leg are bleeding like a stuck pig, but I'm not feeling a thing. I tell the girls, I can drive my motorbike back to my condo when Dowel tells me to get on the back of the motorbike taxi with Lamai. She won't let me back on my bike. So she heads straight to my condo, driving my Nmax with Lamai and me following her on the motorcycle taxi. Which surprised the hell out of me because Dowel already knows where I lived. When we get to the Bahthaus, I take both girls upstairs."

"Where you had a threesome?"

"Yes. A threesome. I don't remember all we had to drink. The bar had only given us two hours, then the two girls had to be back at the bar. But we are all drinking beer and tequila. Then we all get naked together and head to the bedroom."

"And?"

"It was no really big deal. I had Lamai sitting on my face while Dowel had her face between my legs. Keep in mind, Dick, that Dowel was one of the best girls at sucking the cum right out of my dick. But I had never had Lamai naked with me before. All I could think of was Lamai's pussy which I was completely exploring with my mouth. As my excitement kept building, I kept focusing on Lamai. Until I exploded into Dowel's mouth."

"Did you finally meet up with Kit?"

The girls have to go back to the bar. By now it's about one a.m. and I'm alone. I'm having another beer out on my deck and I start messaging Kit. She tells me she will be at my condo at two a.m., but she doesn't actually arrive until a quarter till three. She's got this fat woman as her motorcycle taxi driver. I take her upstairs where she sees several empty beer bottles, an open bottle of tequila and several other liquor bottles on my kitchen shelf so she knows I've had plenty of company. A few minutes later we take my motorbike to the Lek Villa hotel where the taxi that's taking us to Bangkok arrives at three a.m.

Bad Times at King Chulalngkorn Hospital

"So Dick, here we are, Kit and me, in this taxi at three a.m. heading to Bangkok. When we arrive at King Chulaingkorn Hospital at 4:30 a.m. there's already over thirty people in line. But the hospital does not open until 8 a.m.

"There must be around five floors or more in this hospital, Dick, and we aren't even allowed on the floor Kit needs to go to until after eight. And there has to be over 200 people in this room where there's a big board facing most of the people who have gathered there and it's all in Thai with all these numbers on it.

"So how long did Kit have to wait before she saw the doctor?

"We didn't get out of the place until 3 p.m. Then we spent another two hours in a taxi that took us back to Pattaya. The doctor told us, "I not do injections today." So I thought the doctor would do the injections in one month. But when we got back to Pattaya, Kit showed me her appointment card. Her new appointment was for next year,

"Brother, what a clusterfuck", Dick Fitswell replied.

"Dick, I was so upset. Right then I decide that we should go back to Bangkok Pattaya Hospital to see about having the injections done there. I had talked with the underwriter of my health insurance company figuring she knew just about everything about the hospitals in our area. And she told me that if I told the doctors at Bangkok Pattaya Hospital that Kit didn't have any health insurance, we would get a big discount on her injection treatment. I mean, Dick, this tumor of hers is growing. She's already lost the use of a finger and much of her thumb. If we wait a year how much of her arm is she going to lose?"

Thailand's Xenophobic Caste System

"Fast Eddy, I wouldn't do what you are doing, for Kit," said Wolfgang. "None of these bitches are worth it. When it is finally said and done, Thais look after Thais, but they sure won't look out after you."

"You are right, Wolfgang. These women and their families will take everything you have if you give them the chance. We are only an ATM for them, and when the ATM has finished they have run off to find the next sucker," added Harry.

"I am on the same page as the rest of you," Fast Eddy replied. We all know money is number one here. Since birth most Thais are taught that their country is the number one country in the world. To them we are aliens and hardly human at all. I'll take this one step further. They have a caste system here in Thailand, with the rich Thais being the elite caste. I've seen pictures that resemble cartoons. The first image is of a very handsome Thai man. He's got his hair just so. He's wearing nice clothes and his skin color is very light. There's a caption underneath this image that reads in Thai, "handsome man". The second image is of a second Thai man, but this Thai man is not handsome at all. His skin color is almost as dark as a Negro's, and he's got kinky hair like an African black man. His caption reads "Ugly man" in Thai. Here's what's happening here. The ruling classes here are based in Bangkok. Most rich people in Bangkok are Chinese Thais so their skin color is very light. You will notice that most Chinese and Japanese have legs that aren't tanned at all. You will also notice that in all the supermarkets here, Seven Elevens, Family Marts and Mini Lotus they have all these whitening products.. Even deodorants are advertised as having whitening agents in them. So white skin is good, and dark skin is bad."

"I'd hate to be an American black man here having to deal with all these racists," Harry replied.

"The way this thing works is dark-skinned Thais are associated with that portion of Thailand known as Issan. Issan is mostly rural. It's where most farmers come from. People have to work hard if they are Thai farmers. They are in the hot sun all day and they have to do a lot of manual labor. In general they are very poorly educated. The white skinned Bangkok elites look down on these people. Whereas the darker skinned Issan Thais look up to their white skinned superiors. It's a pure caste system here. The

173

poor people do the manual labor while the rich Thais very seldom get their hands dirty."

"From what you are telling us, Fast Eddy, since we Westerners are light skinned, all Thais should look up to us," Dick Fitswell replied."

"Nope. To them we are an entirely different species. Our culture and values are very different. As a German friend of mine once told me, "For most Thais we are the untermenschen." Which means in German subhuman. He knew I understood too well what untermenschen means. It's what the Nazis called Jews and Russians who they deemed inferior races."

"This is what I mean," replied Wolfgang. "Except for our money most Thais don't even want us here. But when it comes to the Thai family, whose Thai bar girl daughters we are supporting, we aren't even human beings. They are all sisters and brothers whereas we are the infidels. So the game is to separate us from as much money as they can so they can give it to their families. If we cave in and go bankrupt, they could care less because we are not human at all."

Kit Faces a Terrifying Operation

"Dick, I found a new hospital in Si Racha which is about 30 miles from my condo. I took Kit back to see Dr. Sonchai at Bangkok Pattaya hospital who agreed with me that having to wait a year to see that government hospital in Bangkok was totally unacceptable. So he got Kit and me together with Dr. Yosuite who practices at the Queen Savang Hospital in Si Racha. I reminded Dr. Sonchai and Dr. Yosuite that Dr. Sonchai had told us the injection treatments were very dangerous because of the large number of blood vessels in Kit's arm surrounding the tumor. But Dr. Yosuite informed us that the procedure was not as dangerous as Dr. Sonchai had originally explained to us due to his hospital seeing a lot more similar cases than Bangkok Pattaya Hospital has to contend with. Dr Yosuite explained that the injections would be limited to one section of her arm and hand at a time which would require 3 to 5 operations to complete the entire treatment.

Most of Dick Fitswell's disciples congregating at Big Dick's were anxious to hear about Kit's moment of truth which is what's going to happen to her while she's getting the injections since it's a potentially deadly procedure. Kit had cried when the doctors from Bangkok Pattaya Hospital had laid it all out before her and Fast Eddy. And even though Wolfgang, Harry and Scott had hardly any empathy for any Thai woman, there was still a gnawing concern for Kit that had somehow seeped into the blackest hearts among them. But it was Dick Fitswell, who was the most concerned.

"Fast Eddy, what was it like for you and Kit on the eve of Kit's having all those injections."

"Dick, I hate to admit it, but I was having a lot of bad dreams about this procedure going terribly wrong. I really was starting to feel that they would be wheeling her into the operating room, and that I would never see her again because she had just died from a brain aneurysm or heart failure. There's so many arteries in and around that tumor, that whatever they are using in the syringe can go just about anywhere. I've looked her affliction up all over the internet, and I cannot find anything definitive at all on what she's got. So I decided to do all I can to get her mind off what she's about to go through."

"What kinds of things did you do with her?"

"Dick, first thing I did, is I lined up our taxi driver to take us to the Si Racha Khao Kheow zoo. Most tourists go to the Tiger Zoo in Si Racha. And don't get me wrong the Tiger Zoo is a great place. But not too many tourists are directed to Khao Kheow. It's world class. I think it's the best zoo in the world. The way I do it is once I get there I rent a golf cart. The zoo's just too large to get around by foot. It's about a mile by 2 miles long. There's a huge aviary at Khao Kheow that's about four levels high. It's the best I've ever seen multiplied by four. And as far as tigers, they've got Bengal tigers there, white tigers, Indochinese tigers, and they have lions, jaguars, leopards and all kinds of other large cats. And you get to see them up close and personal. Once I almost jumped into the cage with a jaguar. I can't explain it but that jaguar and I had this kind of telekinetic connection between us. I got this feeling he wouldn't try to hurt me and he wouldn't try to run away either. There was a way I could have gotten in behind the pen. But I didn't do it. I always thought about it afterwards though."

"I've never been there," Dick Fitswell replied. "Tell us more about it."

"There's monkeys running all over the place. Deer too although there is one area where the deer all walk up to you. If you have something they like to eat you can stroke and pet them. There's about thirty deer in that area alone. You can also feed elephants and giraffes. Right out of your hand. But I like feeding the rhinoceros. They have them behind this iron fence, which is less than five feet high. You can buy this grass they like to eat for twenty baht and have them eat right out of your hand as you stroke their heads. I'll bet you have never thought you could do that with a rhino before."

"No. Rhinos are considered to be one of the most dangerous African big game animals of them all," Dick Fitswell replied.

"They can hook you if they want to. But the caretakers there told me they have never had any problems with the rhinos. They explained that the rhinos are very territorial so if you jump the fence and get in with them, they will try to kill you, but so long as you keep on your side of the fence they will never try to hook you with their horns. But they can because that fence is just too short."

"How did Kit like the zoo?"

"She loved it. But I knew she would. Kit's got about the softest heart I've ever seen when it comes to animals. She told me many times she liked dogs but hated cats. And she used to show me these cartoon dog videos on the internet, laughing like a little six-year old. One night I took her to Nam's restaurant next to my condo and then I took her to Khristina's condo on the Bahthaus ground floor. Khristina was just so nice to her. She's just so charming, and not at all the way you expect Russian women to be like. She has two cats in her condo and shop. Kit just went right over to those cats and started petting them. So as soon as we got to the zoo, I got us a large bunch of bananas. And told her we would feed the bananas to the deer and other animals but she didn't believe me when I told her that deer would eat just about anything. When we got to the deer, she was like a little six-year old when all those deer kept nuzzling her back and rubbing themselves against her legs."

"That sounds like some zoo," said Harry.

"You bet your ass it is. Once I was having Thai food there in one of the little el cheapo restaurants at the zoo's front entrance. They had an Orangutan in that restaurant on a chain perched on a stool. I only had my shorts on, with my shirt off because of the heat. I got too close to that orangutan, and that orangutan grabbed one of my nipples in its hand and started to squeeze it really hard. God, that sure hurt."

"Glad to hear Kit liked the zoo," Dick Fitswell replied.

"She loved it. Anyway, after the zoo, Kit had this great idea. She knew of a place up in Chonburi where she told me she could get some special food she can't get anywhere else at a small market. But she surprised the hell out of me when she suggested we take both of my motorbikes, the Nmax and my Triumph. So she met me at my condo. She got on my Nmax and I took the Triumph. I looked the route up on Mapquest and Chonburi is over an hour away by car. We did it in about 45 minutes on my two motorbikes."

"You two must have been driving pretty fast," Harry replied.

"Funny thing is Kit does not have a drivers license. But she takes off like a bat out of hell on my Nmax. Once we get on Sukhumvit she knew exactly where we are going and she's driving as fast as 90 kilometers per hour, which is pretty quick for zipping in and around Thailand traffic. But when the traffic starts to pile up, we are squeezing in between cars and have to often drive on the shoulder of the road to get around slow moving cars. And let me tell you, Kit's damn good on a motorcycle."

"When she finally got the injections how did that go?"

"Dick, when she gets this kind of injection treatment the doctors tell us she cannot drive and she cannot ride on the back of a motorcycle. So I got Khun Toe to take us. We got to the hospital pretty early, around 6:30 a.m. but once again we had to wait in a long line just to get in the main building. And then we had to wait a few more hours until the hospital had a room available for her."

"What was the room like?"

"It was better than I thought, Dick. There were six or seven other women in that hospital ward, but the beds seemed just as comfortable as the ones I've been in at private hospitals such as Bangkok Pattaya. Anyway, we all knew Kit would not start her injection treatments until the next day. I think Toe, and I left the hospital around four p.m. and here we had all been there since 6:30 a.m."

"Did you go see Kit the next day?"

"Damn right I did, Dick. The thing is I had no idea what would be really going on during that injection treatment. I thought she would get these treatments several times during the four days she actually stayed at the hospital. It turns out there was to be only one treatment. When the hospital staff took her out of that ward I was scared to death that I might never see her again. So you can imagine how I felt when they brought her back and I saw that she was alive and never had to go into intensive care. But she had about fifty injections. I could see the needle marks all over her forearm and her hand."

"So what did you make of the Si Racha Hospital?"

"I think the doctors there are very competent, and being a government hospital it's very inexpensive. But we had to keep waiting for hours on end in long lines before we could see Dr. Yosuite or the surgeon. And we had to go to the hospital many times before Kit finally got to go in for her treatment. On the fourth day when Toe and I arrive to pick Kit up, the nurses tell us she can't leave because her condition has not completely stabilized. But later the doctor tells Kit she can leave. By now

178

Khun Toe and I had almost gotten back to the Bahthaus when Kit calls us to come back for her."

"Sounds like a bit of a clusterfuck," Harry replied.

"Absolutely. But it only cost me 13000[21] baht for the entire surgical procedure, nursing care, and three and half days in the hospital. Had this been Bangkok Pattaya Hospital there's no telling what it would have cost. But I tell you what really pissed me off, Harry."

"What's that?"

"When the nurses told Kit on the fourth day that she couldn't go home yet, Kit started to cry. I think even Khun Toe realized that she wasn't crying for me and all that I had done for her. She was crying because she missed her room. Not just for the room though but for the people in that room, starting with her Thai boyfriend. And I'll bet not one of those so called friends of hers even bothered to visit her in the hospital."

---

[21] At 32 baht to the U.S. dollar this is $406.25

Driving Like a Bat out of Hell to the Hospital

"Fast Eddy, what's the latest on Kit's hand and arm?"

"Glad you asked, Dick. I've been spending about four days or nights with Kit every week since she received those injections. We had to go back to the Si Racha Hospital about four times already. We had an appointment with Dr. Yosuite on one Friday, then on Wednesday we had an appointment with the surgeon. We spent four hours in the hospital only to learn that the surgeon had taken the day off to teach at the medical school. He's supposed to be there every Wednesday and we had a bona fide appointment with him, but we had to come back the following Wednesday."

"Are you still taking taxis?"

"No. We are taking two motorbikes. Only before or right after she gets injections is the hospital requiring Kit to go by car. So I had her driving my Nmax while I follow her on my Triumph."

"Is she still driving like a bat out of hell?"

"Damn right she is, Dick. And a lot of times she manages to hit the holes in the traffic just right. And when I get up to her the holes have suddenly closed which puts me behind four of five cars which are driving a lot slower than her. I might wind up a quarter of a mile behind her. But Dick, she looks so small and fragile on my Nmax. I see her weaving in and out of traffic and I start to think about how devastated I will feel if she has a serious accident and that I might lose her forever. But my Triumph has so much torque. I can jump on that throttle and just blast by all those cars while still managing to weave in and out of traffic nearly as well as she can on my Nmax. I just love my Triumph. It's awesome."

"So how's her arm and hand?"

"She's still showing all those injection needle marks. I understand now why Doctor Doom, that heroin addict friend of mine in the U.S. was shooting heroin through his knuckles. She says most of the pain is gone now but she still can't use that finger or most of her arm."

"How are things going between you two?"

"Even aside from these hospital visits we are seeing each other three times a week."

"Is it going good or badly between you two?"

"Both Dick. You just about name it and we are doing it together. Take restaurants for example. She especially likes Shabushi and Yayoi, both of them Japanese. Then there's Nam restaurant right next door to my condo. And Surf and Turf down on the beach which many people claim is the best beach restaurant in Pattaya. I've taken her to the lady boy bar twice and once to Cocktail bar on Naklua Soi 33. We go shopping together. We go to the Big C supermarket. And wouldn't you know it, she's still riding around in that grocery cart like a little child."

"So what's going wrong for you two?"

"For one thing, she never spends the entire night at my condo. She will leave at 12 or as late as 1:30 a.m. or so. I am pretty sure she goes out with her friends all night after that. She's like a vampire like so many of them are. These Thai karaoke bars are open all night I understand. And I think this is one of the reasons she gets so run down. Here's another thing. I am now having her meet me at my condo. Whereas before I had her meeting me at Sandman on Soi 6 and from there we'd go to a restaurant or shopping at Big C. Now she meets me in my condo lobby or she might even go upstairs to my condo to surprise me. You would think she would have the motorcycle taxi bring her right up to our condo front entrance. Instead she's usually walking down Soi 16 from God knows where. So it makes sense that she's being dropped off by somebody she doesn't want me or the security guard to see. And that someone's the Thai boyfriend."

"Why not a girlfriend?"

"Dick, it could be a girlfriend, but the mamasan from Quicky Bar on Soi 6 where I first met Kit told me the Thai boyfriend was always picking her up to take her home. She also told me they argued constantly until she had to kick the prick out of her bar. Patterns tend to repeat themselves. So I believe he's dropping her off so he can control her just as he had been doing on Soi 6."

"If this is true, I'd get rid of her right now?"

181

"I might have to. But I'm not completely sure yet. Plus, Kit has some great qualities. She never lets me down. She always comes and hasn't stood me up for over six months. She's just about always right on time. And she won't let anything stop her. When she's sick, she will still show up. If it rains, she will meet me regardless. If she's on her period she still shows up and in the room she will still smoke me even while she's on her period. In the supermarket she knows what I need and what I've run out of. She knows her way around my condo and she cleans up the kitchen for me. Shit, Dick, almost all my falang friends are unreliable. They don't show up on time, and those who do, won't show up if it's raining. Kit's got every one of my male friends beat by a mile. And she's been my internet buddy for years now. I'm talking to her every day. My phone would not be entertaining at all if it wasn't for her. And if that's not enough, she's the prettiest girl I've ever met here, and she will never ever get fat."

"But she's still got that Thai boyfriend," Harry replied.

"I think so. I keep waiting for her to wake up and see how worthless the son of a bitch is. The one thing going for her is she's no longer 20 or even 23. She's about to turn 26 and the way I have it figured most women start to really wake up when they get to be around 28, 29 or 30."

"What do you mean?"

"Dick, it's because by the time they are 29, they realize they are about to turn 30 and they start to think of themselves as getting old. About that age most of the women start to really think about what's best for them. And when it comes to Thai women what's best for them is to latch onto a nice falang who's got enough money to take care of them and their families for years to come."

Bar Girl Vampires

"Harry, for awhile I thought you were right about my ex live in girlfriend and Kit?"

"What do you mean? Fast Eddy," replied Harry who was already on his sixth beer at Big Dicks.

"Remember your telling me when I had that room at the Penthouse how I was making Kit feel like she was second fiddle to my girlfriend. Here I have this large very posh seaside condo at the Bahthaus with my girlfriend staying with me there while I was putting Kit in a small room at the Penthouse like she was my kept whore."

"Yes. I remember."

"After my girlfriend left, I took Kit down to Index to help me pick out a new set of plates, bowls and a set of nice carving knives after which I threw all the old plates, bowls, and kitchen knives out. Replacing the kitchen and dining room tiles came next so I took Kit down to Homepro where we picked out the new tiles together. I did all this to make Kit feel that she was a vital part of my condo. I even got each of us a pair of loafing shoes that nearly matched each other with Kit picking them out at Big C."

"All nice touches that would make Kit feel that your condo is his and hers," Dick Fitswell replied.

"First thing she does when she comes to my condo is she puts those slippers on, then she goes over to my couch and starts watching one of her Netflix television shows. Well by now she's meeting me at my condo but a lot of times she goes straight over to Nam's restaurant. Three or four times we get pretty inebriated there with Nam. Nam's got the strongest tequila. It's gold in color and she has it in these small bottles. But one thing really started to bother me."

"What's that?" Harry asked.

"I figure Kit to be a vampire, and that she has all these other vampires living with her. What I mean by vampire is all these young Thais, most of them bar girls and their Thai boyfriends staying out all night and sleeping all day long. These people have got nothing going on in their lives other than their going out and having fun all night with their deadbeat friends. I can't say for sure, but Kit seems to have a problem. I might be wrong but I think she is staying out late in Karaoke bars until six or seven in the morning. Because she often messages me early in the morning. After that she will crash until seven p.m. or so, go out to have dinner with her friends or Thai boyfriend, and return to her room and then she starts messaging me again at nine or ten. Then she'll run off to resume her night owl activities."

"If you are having fun with her, why should that bother you?"

"Because lately I've gotten to know a lot of Thais who are damn good at what they do and who have to work very hard for a living. Or Nam who runs the restaurant next door. She has to drive all the way back nearly to Sattahip after she closes the restaurant, and each afternoon she must drive all the way back here. And as Nam explained to me, all her food is fresh so each morning she has to buy all the ingredients for the food that she will cook for her customers that evening. Then there's that tech who works for Homepro. When he measured my kitchen area for the tiling, he used a laser for his measurements because a measuring tape was not good enough for him. And that tiler was a real perfectionist. Then there's that high powered technician who troubleshot my entire television and audio system. The man was as reliable as the sun comes up and he really knows his shit."

"So you found these people to be a lot different from bar people, Fast Eddy?"

"They are worlds apart. This Thai time crap is a load of shit made up by a bunch of racist foreigners. I've found that foreigners here are less reliable than this group of Thais I am describing to you. And Kit's been very reliable even though she's a bar girl."

"So maybe she's not a bar girl at heart," replied Harry.

"Maybe not. But, even if she's not a bar girl at heart she's hanging around with all these bar people who have no concept of being on time or any sort of work ethic."

"But let me continue. It really bothers me I am endorsing a bar girl lifestyle for Kit, and I'm probably giving a lot of her lazy friends a lot of that food I'm buying for her."

Thai Mafia Kills Fast Eddy's Favorite Bar Owner

For 14 years TJ bar continued to be a Naklua bar legend. Long term expats oftentimes call it the Lady Boy Bar because every bar girl there is a lady boy. Although Naklua had a couple great bars that put women on the menu, both were long gone. There was Girl Beer Bar that had been owned by a group of Germans that once offered a great selection of delectable bar girls. But the Germans sold it after one of the German owners went off the deep end and got rid of one of the best mamasans Fast Eddy had ever known.

Only several bars away from the Lady Boy Bar a savvy Thai woman had owned the Sabai Bar for years. Waan had hired three Thai musicians to work in her bar paying each man one-thousand baht a night which was way over the top for any beer bar, especially in Naklua. Waan's business acumen had soon paid rich dividends. Although she was no Harvard MBA with a sound university background in marketing analysis, Waan clearly understood her market.

Unlike Pattaya which attracts the majority of tourists and short timers staying for holiday in hotels and second rate condos, Naklua is primarily residential. Since it is relatively quiet compared to Pattaya, Naklua has long attracted men seeking permanent residence, and since most of these long term residents are German, Naklua is often called Little Germany.

Waan was smart. Seeing through the widespread view of the no nonsense humorless German stereotype, she had long ago seen the other side of so many Germans. Who were on the whole a very outgoing group of guys who had no use for a bar filled with naive tourists. Sabai Bar soon became the favorite watering hole for Naklua's long term expats community.

Whereas nearly all Pattaya bar mamasans kept asking their customers to buy them a drink, Waan would often buy a customer a drink. And then she would tell him, "Thank you so much for coming to my bar."

Waan was also sharp enough to realize that most of her prospective customers were older men who wanted to relive their youth. So she had her trio of Thai musicians play English and American oldies such as Paul Anka's "Diana" and Credence

Clearwater Revival's version of "Suzie Q".. So the expats continued to come to Waan's bar in droves, again and again, especially the Germans who contrary to the average American's impression of the typical German, were great fans of all the old English and American classics.

Unfortunately Waan had a fatal flaw. Although her bar continued to have great success, her gambling addiction got her into debt with the Thai mafia. Which caused her to sell the bar to a clueless new owner. Waan was shot to death driving her car home on Sukhumvit Road.

Which left the Lady Boy bar as the only really popular bar with Naklua's expats community. Where Fast Eddy and Wolfgang sat drinking together on their bar stools, discussing the current state of affairs.

"Fast Eddy, a lot of people here in Pattaya don't realize these are probably the best looking lady boys in the entire area with the exception of all the professionals performing for the tourists at Alcazar."

"Very true, Wolfgang, which is fine for you, Scott and Harry, who prefer lady boys, but I like real women.".

"What you are saying isn't accurate, Fast Eddy. You have been here often enough. How many times have you been drinking a few beers at TJ's when a lady boy comes up behind you and starts massaging your dick?"

"More times than I can remember."

"Did it feel good?"

"Well yeah."

"Did you think of the lady boy who's massaging your dick as a man or as a woman?"

"As a woman of course."

"And did your dick get hard?"

"Why sure it did."

"And during those times, did you ever feel like you wanted to come in your pants?"

"Of course. But I never took any of them home with me from this bar."

"So, you have had sex with a lady boy before?"

"I don't tell many people, but I have, but I was very drunk when I did it."

"We can talk more about this later. I don't have a lot of time and I sure want to fuck somebody pretty soon."

"And it doesn't matter if it's a woman or a lady boy?"

"It doesn't matter to me at all. It all depends on who's close to me at the time and whether I am attracted or not to her."

"I can understand that, Wolfgang. I still prefer the ladies by far to any lady boy."

"Changing the subject, what's the latest between you and Kit?"

"I sent her home. She hardly ever gets to see her son. One reason is she never saves enough money."

"Fast Eddy, I think Kit might even expect you to pay her so much each month while she stays up north with her son and never comes down to see you."

"That might very well be true, Wolfgang, but I won't ever let that happen. Anyway, Kit has a brother who lives in Bangkok and every so often Kit's mother goes to Bangkok to visit him. Thing is Kit's mother keeps Kit in the dark when she's going to Bangkok. She tells Kit she's bringing Kit's son to Kit's brother's house, but she never gives Kit a firm date. And then when she tells Kit she's bringing Kit's son with her, more than half the time she changes her mind. Which is unfair to Kit because her mother waits until the last minute to tell her that she's changed her plans. So I found a way that Kit can turn the tables on her mother."

"So how do you figure on doing that?"

"Kit comes from a medium sized community called Prae. I looked up Bangkok Airways and Air Asia to see what flights they have between Bangkok and Prae. Turns out there aren't any. Then I did a little research on Prae on the internet. And although I found many interesting things about Kit's city, there was no indication that there was an airport there. Then Kit told me that Prae has a small airport and that it is serviced by Nok airways. And only by Nok airways. So one night while Kit was with me in my condo we got on my desktop computer where I booked a two-way flight between Bangkok and Prae and put it on my credit card. Only cost me about $100.00."

"So what happened? Did Kit actually get on an airplane?"

"Yes. It was the first time she took an airplane. So I got Kit and me a taxi which took us from my condo to Don Mueang Airport. It took over two hours. We had breakfast together at the airport. I hand held her all the way. Took her all the way to the security line. Kit had no idea of what to do. She even asked security to allow me to take her through the line, but of course security wouldn't let us. She was like a little child and I was her father. I watched her go all the way through security until she disappeared out of sight. Then I went outside to find myself a taxi to take me back to Naklua."

"So how did all that turn out?"

"Kit stayed with her son for five days. She kept in constant touch with me using line and even had me video conferencing with her and her son. It had to be quite an adventure for her. But she completely screwed up her return flight. She was to fly out of Prae to Bangkok at 11 a.m. But she arrived at the airport ten minutes too late so they did not allow her to board. She would have been okay if she only had a carry on but she had packed all her things in that large suitcase I had gotten her. So she didn't have enough time to check her luggage. Turns out she blamed her father for driving her to the airport on a motorcycle and that he was driving very slowly."

"I can see that," Wolfgang replied. These village idiots have no clue about anything."

"Yep. And Kit is used to getting up real late. I can see her family telling her. "You have plenty of time, Kit", and there's no way she's going to disagree with her papa or mamma even if she knows better. So she's at the airport and she's messaging me that she's just missed her flight. She tells me she's taking a bus."

"So why didn't you let her take a bus and teach her a lesson?"

188

"Because I wanted to be sure that she learned the entire procedure of how to get around in these airports and how much time it all takes. So I booked another flight, a one way to Bangkok which was to fly out of Prae at four p.m. So Kit had to spend another five hours waiting around in the airport waiting for that new flight. But I also gave her clear instructions to tell the taxi driver to use the toll way, which would save her a lot of time getting through all that horrible Bangkok traffic."

"I take it she didn't follow your instructions."

"Exactly. I figured she would arrive at the Bangkok airport around five and from there it would take her around two and a half hours finding a taxi and getting back to my condo. So I went next door to Nam's restaurant around six thirty where I waited. By this time Kit's messaging me to tell me exactly what's happening. At first the taxi driver doesn't want to take her. Because he figures she doesn't have enough money to pay him. He's probably had a lot of Thais fuck him out of his money. Had it been me, being a falang, there would have been no problem. So Kit puts me on the phone with the driver and I tell him I will pay him. Then it takes forever for her to get to Nam's restaurant. After an hour I figure the taxi's gotten out of all that Bangkok traffic, but Nam and I figure Kit's hardly gotten out of central Bangkok. It takes her four hours in that taxi before she finally meets me at the restaurant. It's nearly ten p.m. when the taxi finally pulls up to the restaurant. Meanwhile Nam's rolling her eyes at me. Letting me know how badly she thinks Kit's screwed up this whole thing and how little regard Kit has for my money. Well, it turns out that the taxi driver never uses the toll way. I don't know. Maybe Kit told him to but clearly he doesn't trust her a bit so he takes the cheapest way to Pattaya figuring that Kit's not going to pay him the toll way expenses. Anyway, it's a total screw up and Nam's about to close the restaurant."

"So how are you and Kit doing now?"

"There's a bad sequel to this, Wolfgang. I am planning on having Kit visit her son every two or three months by having her take an airplane instead of her using a bus. Or having her rely on her mother to bring her son to Bangkok, but just one week later, Kit tells me her mother is bringing her son to Bangkok again. I tell kit, "it looks like you and I won't be seeing each other for a while," and she replies, "I will bring my son to your condo." Then right before her mother is to bring her son to Bangkok, her son suddenly gets sick again. Maybe I'm wrong but I am thinking there's something fishy going on here, so I am telling Kit on line that her son might not be as sick as she thinks. I'm thinking her mother is spoiling the child, and every time the kid gets the slightest cold or headache her mother is taking him to the hospital and giving Kit all the bills to pay."

"What makes you think that?"

"This happens to a lot of Thai boys, Dick. Nothing is expected of them and the whole family is making all over them. They don't do this for the girls who are expected to pitch in on family chores at an early age. Anyway, I'm not so foolish as to tell Kit her son is spoiled and that he cries over the smallest things, but I am telling her to make up her own mind how sick he really is."

"I'll bet that didn't go over very well with Kit."

"Kit's totally pissed off at me for insinuating that her little boy might not be so sick after all. So she tells me that she doesn't want my help anymore, and that she will use her own money by going back to work again."

"What did you do then?"

"She told me not to pay her any more so I stopped giving her money. That lasted for a week or two and then she started messaging me again on Line. I have no idea what she was doing to make money. I couldn't believe she would tell me she didn't want my help any more over such a small thing as my suggesting that her four-year old son might be acting more sick than he actually was.

The Drug Addict

Fast Eddy, "Who's the best fuck you ever had on Soi 6?" Dick Fitswell asked as he watched two men staring at the plaster casts of big penises lining the wall where liquor bottles would normally have been placed.

"Why do you want to know that?" Fast Eddy asked.

"You might just become the Saint Peter of Big Dicks who will spread the good word of the Perfect Fit," Dick Fitswell replied. "And as we gaze at all those big dicks before us, think of those who gave their penises to have those casts made for future posterity."

"I'd say it's Ning, although it could have been Goi. But Goi's gone now while Ning's still a great fuck buddy of mine. Maybe Kit because I keep thinking of her while I'm having sex with other girls. Although all things considered Ning's the best performer of them all"

"So how is Ning these days?"

Just last week Ning asked me, "Fast Eddy, how are you and Kit?"

After giving her a complete update on Kit, Ning suddenly becomes quite angry almost shouting at me. "She is very bad lady. I thought she good lady for you. Not now. I no have Thai boyfriends. Thai boyfriends have no money, and I like money too much." Then Ning points upstairs. "You want to fuck me?"

"Well of course I do," I reply, "Sure."

In the room Ning escorts me into the shower, turns the tap on, and hands me the bottle of Listerine she always keeps there. Five minutes later she has me lying down on my back as a prelude to one of the best fucks I've ever had on Soi 6.

"Now a lot of times she will put a towel over my face, but this time she tells me, "Close your eyes, Fast Eddy. Relax. Think of nothing but me," as she sticks her luscious breasts into my face."

They might have been silicon but they aren't. Ning's breasts are full. She has nipples that are large enough to make you think they are fake. But they aren't overly large. In my mouth, they expand to being much more than the proverbial mouthful.

But I see nothing while I am able to feel everything. Ning slides her body down my stomach and legs to my feet. With my eyes still closed I imagine myself getting a full oil massage from JJ, the Cambodian massage girl, who has never given me a happy ending. But with Ning I know what's coming as her hands slither from my feet to my thighs. By the time she inserts my cock into her moist mouth, I'm fully erect. And by the time she finishes smoking me, I imagine myself cumming in Kit's mouth. I'm sure I could come in Ning's throat but Ning is not going to have any of that."

 "Now your turn," she tells me softy as she turns over on her back and spreads her legs wide. "Go slowly now. I want you to go slow," she tells me as I probed the upper part of her vagina with my tongue until my mouth tastes a touch of urine. But I know it isn't urine, because I already know her fluids are not going to overflow out of my mouth the way they did with Squirt. Ning only starts to taste differently which tells me how turned on she's become. But I still want her to go so out of control that she squirts in my mouth."

"After her cum starts to flow down her ass, Ning has enough. She suddenly pulls away from me screaming, "Fuck me now. I cum already." So I turn her over onto her back. While she smiles at me, looking into my eyes while she puts the condom on my erect penis."

"It takes only five minutes for me to ejaculate as I squeeze her body tightly into mine while her smiling eyes keep urging me to cum."

"Then I leave her and run off to two more Soi 6 bars before returning to Smoke and Kisses. But Ning's already gone home. But I spot a second girl whom I had barely noticed during my most recent trips to Smoke and Kisses. She has a nice trim little body and a face that's pretty enough. But her eyes are incapable of showing any emotion whatsoever.

"But I buy her a drink anyway. And eventually take her upstairs for my second fuck of the evening."

"She has silicon breasts that are nearly as ample as Ning's. And while she smokes me well enough, I feel that I can never cum in her mouth as I had done so many times with Kit and had wanted

192

to do with Ning. I find her mouth to be too dry to make my penis erupt into uncontrollable squirting."

"But when I am fucking her, she switches to the rear entry position until I finally cum into her backside while she keeps pushing her firm buttocks against my groin."

"I bang Zara two more times at Smoke and Kisses. The fourth time, I pay a nine-hundred baht bar fine and take her back to my condo after we agree to do a short time that should last only two or three hours...because she tells me she wants to go to Walking Street to play pool with her friend. I'm okay with that, because I really don't want to have just anyone sleeping in my bed all night and my having to wake her up early the next morning to watch her lazy ass sleeping until noon."

"I take Zara on my motorbike back to my condo using the back way to avoid the police at the Dolphin Round About. Then I watch her stretch out on my couch as I turn the volume up on my surround sound system."

"Zara doesn't waste any time undressing. We are soon engaging in oral sex. I take her into my master bedroom to give her a twenty minute massage after she starts complaining about a massage girl screwing up her back the day before. While I start thinking, "these girls should all be paying me for what I am doing for them." Then I fuck her without a condom as she shifts through several positions while I'm keeping my penis inside her until I finally erupt into her vagina."

"Suddenly she exclaims as if it is all such a big surprise to her. "No condom!"

"She stay all night?" Dick Fitswell asked.

"Unfortunately yes. After I bang her, she falls fast asleep. I get up at seven and work all morning on my computer. I thought about having breakfast at one of my favorite German restaurants, but I don't want to leave her in my condo alone. I would have taken Kit to the restaurant in a heartbeat because Kit always looks presentable even when she's looking at her worst. Eventually I wake Zara up at noon and take her on my motorcycle to the market near her room, which turns out to be only five minutes from the Bahthaus. But just before we get to the market she points at a little soi on the left and tells me her room's on that street."

"Did you see her again?" Dick Fitswell asked.

"Twice. Actually three times although I only saw her for a few seconds the last time. I was with Canada John hitting a few bars on Soi 6. Canada John wanted to watch the tennis championships at the Nature Bar which was directly across from Smoke and Kisses. So when I saw that Zara was at Smoke and Kisses we went over there. Zara sat next to me as I stroked her legs, which are very firm, especially her thighs. She wanted me to take her upstairs right away, but I was onto her now."

"What do you mean?" Dick Fitswell asked.

"Ning had told me all about her. And since Ning had never lied to me before I half-believed her. I said half because Ning knew that Zara was competing with her for my money so it would be in her best interests to disparage Zara. Ning had told me that Zara doesn't like fucking older men and that she prefers young guys. She also told me that Zara does a lot of ice (crystal meth) and that she likes to go to Walking Street to meet up with her boyfriend."

The night Zara spent the whole night with me I got her line account on my phone so I could message her. But when I looked at her line profile I saw two pictures of her with this younger guy who appeared to be in his early forties or late thirties. It was very obvious to me that this was her boyfriend. Later when I showed Ning the guy's picture, Ning told me that the guy had been in jail. So I figured that Zara wanted to take me upstairs and fuck me to get a thousand baht off me so she could get down to Walking Street by 12 to do drugs with her boyfriend."

"You take her upstairs then?"

"Fuck no. I told her I would long time her. And that I wanted to take her back to my condo for an all-nighter. Then she asked me to come back at 11 when the bar fine would be cheaper. So I went down to MK Kitties to have a couple drinks with one of the girls and came back to Smoke and Kisses at 11. Where Zara becomes a complete bitch when I keep insisting on long timing her. So I just went across the street to the Nature Bar where I find Canada John still watching tennis on the tv. But by then Canada John is bored watching tennis so we sit at the front of Nature Bar. From this spot we have a perfect vantage point from which we can watch everyone walking up and down Soi 6 and the girls sitting across the street in the bars. I keep watching Zara

194

who is sitting in front of Smoke and Kisses looking gloomy and sorry for herself. She's looking real flighty also and that's when I know that Ning has been right all along about her. She's obviously coming down from drugs, and that's why from that point on, I decide to call her the drug addict.

"What happened the next time you saw her?"

"Thailand had two Buddha days in a row. So they were closing all the bars down at midnight until midnight two nights later. There were five of us going down to Soi 6 together. We meet at Smoke and Kisses. Ning's there so I introduced her to the guys and buy her a couple drinks. Zara is in her room, but I keep staying in touch with her on line. We end up closing MK Kitty go-go at midnight, but by then Zara and I have agreed to meet at her room and then I'd take her back to my condo."

"Trouble was, I didn't know where her room was. I thought I knew what Soi she lived on and that it was one or two streets before the market. Anyway, I have Canada John on my motorbike behind me and we go down two of the sois[22] right before the market but there is no Zara in sight. So I take Canada John back to Soi Poitasan where he hires a motorbike taxi while I continue to message Zara. Finally I take a picture of the 7-11 across the street from me and send it to Zara who walks over to the 7-11 five minutes later."

She is pretty angry with me for missing her street. But it is hard to see at night with the sois packed so closely together. "It is all my fault," which Zara makes painfully obvious to me. You know how all these bar girls are. It's always the falang's fault. But Zara can't get her lazy ass onto her street so I can see her. So I swallow my pride and take her back to my condo where I fuck her again without a condom.

I gotta say one thing about her though. She has got to have just about the perfect ass. And she's so firm all over. She's got this

---

[22] A soi is a short street, e.g. Soi 6, Soi 8, etc

trim little waist so when you bend her over doggie style she looks just about perfect. She wants to go back to her room, so she winds up staying only a couple of hours. But I pay her only one-thousand baht and tell her she had done a short time, and that's all I'm paying for short times.

Then a couple days later on Monday when all the bars reopened, I ask her if she is working on Soi 6. She reads my message but she never replies. So when I get down to Soi 6 that night I find her working at Smoke and Kisses. There are a lot of guys in the place. I speak to her, but she is complete bitch, so I leave after just five seconds and head down to a few other bars and wind up fucking somebody else who I had never been with.

"How did that go?" Dick Fitswell asked.

"This gal is always real friendly to me. I had a couple drinks with her in her bar two or three times. Where she's always feeling me up but I had always left after a half hour or so and had gone elsewhere. But even though I had not seen Kit in three weeks and had told her I never wanted to see her again, she had called me twice. To ask me to buy her some food and help her with her room situation. She was to meet me at five p.m. but she flat ass stands me up, which is the first time in over a year. I am horny as hell, and wind up taking the gal upstairs. She turns out to be a real wildcat in bed and I end up coming in her without a condom. Afterwards I find out she is living in one of the rooms upstairs in the bar. She asks to come back to my condo to spend the night with me, and that's when I tell her I want to just short time her upstairs. I think she would have spent the rest of the night with me for free because I had already paid her one-thousand baht short time. I just couldn't see having her spend the whole night, Dick, and then having to wake her up late in the morning. And because she has such a shitty room to live in, there's a very good chance that she would never want to leave my condo."

"You did all right, Fast Eddy. But I am warning you, you keep comparing other girls to Kit while you are fucking them. And she's been god-awful to you."

196

Best Motorbike for Thailand under $3000

Last night I saw a motorbike accident. I want to get back to my condo fast as it had just started raining. My only rain suit was under my seat, and I expected a big downpour any minute. Time was of the essence, and speed was my only way out, so there was no time for fooling around with a rain suit. I'm doing about thirty miles an hour up Naklua Road with the Bahthaus just five minutes away. I'm at full alert, fully expecting drivers of cars and motorbikes to do all kinds of stupid things, and my visibility is impaired on account of the rain. Then I see a motorbike just behind me and to my right slide right underneath its driver. "Boom", I can hear the bike hit the concrete. It happens so fast. One second the other driver is just driving straight up Naklua Road. as far as I know, just like me. The next second the bike is up in the air, and down with its driver sprawled out on the pavement.

But I continue to drive on completely confident that my Nmax is not going to let me down. I see the driver of the other bike lying prostate on the pavement. Don't know if he was falang or Thai. Or if he was wearing a helmet. But I'm not about to go back to help. Because the number one rule in Pattaya is "don't get involved", because you might end up having to buy the idiot a new motorbike, especially if he's Thai. That's the way the police work here. If they see a well off Westerner getting involved in an accident they are going to figure out the poor Thai person needs to have his bike replaced or repaired. And that the Westerner has the money to get it done, while the poor Thai cannot afford to pay.

But my Nmax is unflappable. It always is, regardless of the road conditions. It weighs just 280 pounds, about the same as a Honda PCX 150, which is an excellent bike no matter what its detractors contend.

Honda was selling a shit load of PCX's. Which is why Yamaha decided to aim its cross hairs right at the PCX and better it in just about every way. The PCX is very comfortable with a smooth ride for a scooter.[23] And it's got enough power to get its driver all over Thailand in a variety of road conditions short of high speed expressway driving.

I didn't buy one although I got one for my live in girlfriend because it is very good. But I didn't buy one for myself because I always wanted a sports car type vehicle, and with a sports car you give up the smooth ride for maximum performance. I also wanted a motor bike that offered the utmost safety to go along with sports car like handling on two wheels.

Such is the Nmax. It takes just eighty-thousand baht to buy one. But for this eighty-thousand baht Yamaha designed the Nmax from the ground up to be a world beater. Rule of thumb is you can't get good high speed stability out of little 13 inch wheels. Yet Yamaha designed the Nmax around 13 inch wheels with the kind of high speed stability you will never find in any other bike I know of that has such small diameter wheels. Yamaha must have thought long and hard how it could engineer nearly perfect balance into a motorbike with such small wheels. But those small wheels have fat tires on them that keep the Nmax glued to the road.

The Nmax has disk brakes and ABS on both wheels so the front wheel never locks up. Which is unheard of for a motorbike that costs just $2500. It will stop you faster and more safely than just about any bike I can think of. Even the Nmax's bigger brother, the 300 cc. Xmax won't stop you as fast as the Nmax will.

My Nmax has 155 cc.'s to the Honda PCX's 153. Yet its engine is

---

[23] A scooter has a floorboard. Technically an Nmax, Pcx and many other "scooter like machines are called under bones since they have a steel tube connecting the front of the bike to the rear which makes the bike far more stable. The under bone bikes have the front and rear connected at two points..at the floorboard and another point a few inches above the floorboard.

so much better. It's got variable valve timing, which acts a lot like a racing cam once you start pouring the power to it. While if you are just cruising along at moderate rpms, the engine's valves just sort of close down to give you superior fuel economy. But keep the throttle pinned all the way back, and this bike just doesn't want to run out of rpms. Which is why the Honda PCX 150 can only get up to 115 kph while the Nmax will keep charging all the way up to 120. The Nmax makes about 15 horsepower, which is about 1.5 horsepower more than you will ever see out of the PCX.

Now a lot of people will complain about the lack of smoothness of the Yamaha Nmax 155. But smoothness in a small motorcycle like this comes at a price. Yamaha just decided to pay the price to build a small motorbike that offers the best handling, best braking, and highest load capacity of anything in its class. The Nmax is much better for handling two up riding because its suspension and shocks are much stiffer than the PCX's. Ease around real slowly in a parking lot, and the Nmax is a bit jumpy whereas the PCX's throttle response is much smoother. But believe it or not take both bikes up to 115 kph and the Yamaha is more stable than the PCX in spite of its 13 inch wheels.

As I keep saying, Yamaha built this thing from the ground up to be a superior handling machine. And those 13 inch wheels with the Nmax's fat tires give it very quick precise handling that you are never going to get out of any Honda PCX.

Its 15 horsepower variable valve engine will get you around cars and other motorbikes very quickly. While its very quick turning and superior braking will allow you to slow down quickly into a slot between other bikes and cars in case you suddenly see another vehicle heading right at you while you are passing three or four cars. You can't do this with any other bike.

So getting back to that accident. The driver of the other bike probably hit his front brake hard enough to lock up his front wheel. I really can't say what he did wrong. Or maybe he had put crap tires on his bike. But I will say this. Short of a flood, rain hardly causes me to slow down when I'm driving my Nmax. The Honda PCX 150, as good as it is, drives like a boat compared to the Nmax. But oh well, a lot fat guys like driving boats because a boat is much easier on a fat ass.

Amy

"Alright guys. We all know the name of the game is finding the perfect fit. So right now, who's the perfect fit in your estimation?"

"Dick, you know I prefer lady boys," Harry replied. Over at TJ Bar on Soi 16, there's this lady boy who gets hammered at least three times a night by different guys. She's got great tits. She's full of herself and rightfully so. I had her two or three times, and she's got the tightest little ass with the firmest buttocks in Naklua. She don't like me anymore, but I still have to give her my highest rating."

"Speaking of Lady boys, how about you, Wolfgang?" Dick Fitswell asked in a voice that betrayed more than a little antipathy toward Lady boys.

"I'd have to go with that lady boy who stayed with me a few months. She Looks just like a woman. She was that sexy. I wouldn't have traded her ass for anything, but she turned out to be crazier than Dr. Lecter. Who's entirely fictional of course, but he ate people and you don't get any loonier than that. But that lady boy? She'd be a match for Dr. Lecter, but she sure gave the best blow jobs and she had the greatest ass."

Turning to Fast Eddy, Dick Fitswell pointed his finger into Fast Eddy's chest, demanding a reply knowing Fast Eddy would name a woman who would be likely to best any lady boy.

"When you get right down to it Dick. A lady boy is still a man. Sure, when you are drunk in a bar when the lady boys are heavily made up and looking their best you might think they are women, but when you think about how they are going to look the next morning, you will know without a second's thought that they are men. Me. I love women. So now that you bring up the subject of who's got the best ass, I have to say, that I love Little Kit's fine little butt. I love everything about it. But then I just happen to really be attracted to Kit. But if you consider a woman's ass alone and not consider her personality, mannerisms or anything else I have to go with Amy whom I just met a few weeks ago."

"So where did you meet her at?" asked Wolfgang.

"At the Nature Bar on Soi 6. From the first time I met her and practically every time after, Amy was always poising with her back toward me. She had the sexiest ass on Soi 6 and knew it. Sometimes she would put one of her legs up on a bar stool or table top to accentuate how sexy she looked from behind. And she would shake it back and forth pretending that she was having sex in the rear entry position."

"How was she like when you took her upstairs?" Dick Fitswell asked. "Perhaps I might want to try her out myself."

"She never asked for more than the usual one-thousand baht, so that was good. She has one of the most terrific bodies I ever saw, so sometimes after I got her upstairs I'd start off giving her a body massage. But she has this large bag that is almost as big as a small suitcase.   She keeps all these lotions inside that bag, condoms, Vaseline. All kinds of stuff. She is the opposite of Kit who never carries anything more than a very small purse. She gives a pretty good blow job at first but she won't stay at it for very long. Then I start to go down on her, but that never lasts very long because she will always spoil a perfect moment by crying out, "Boom boom." But before she lets me bang her, she starts to lube up after putting a condom on me. But I don't think I ever was able to last more than five minutes before cumming."

"What was she like downstairs in the bar?"

"She was pretty good at getting two or three drinks out of me. Sometimes more. Anyway it turns out she lives in Naklua about a mile from me although I never saw her room. But I brought her to my condo three or four times although she never stayed more than two hours. And that would cost me two-thousand baht plus her bar fine. So after that I'd just have sex with her in the bar because it is more cost efficient for me."

"Since you weren't seeing Kit while you were doing Amy, were there any other girls you were having sex with?" Dick Fitswell asked.

"Well sure. About every time Ning was working on Soi 6 which was about half the time, she would spot me driving my motorbike down Soi 6 as soon as I got there, so I was doing her a lot. Once in awhile I'd do that drug addict who works with her. And a few others I was meeting here and there."

"Tell me more about Amy. Why aren't you seeing more of her now?"

"For one thing she is working only about half the time at her bar. And obviously she has a lot of customers so when she keeps saying she is going home for a few days, who knows? She's 28 years old so her shelf life isn't going to last forever. Which is a good thing. But she's too damn popular and she knows it."

MK Kitty Go-Go Bar, the Worse and Best Bar on Soi 6

"Dick, before I tell you more about Amy, I think I should let you know about the worse god damn bar on Soi 6."

"Fast Eddy, now why in the hell would you want to be telling me about the worse bar on Soi 6?"

"Because it's still been one of my favorite bars, and not only for me, but also for several of my friends."

"Please enlighten me."

"I used to do short times upstairs there. It's also directly across from La La Land where I spent so much time with Little Miss Kit. Its owner is a Thai woman who lives close to me in Naklua, who I have known for years. This owner used to play all that god awful "Da Da" music. Still does although there are times the bar plays a lot of good stuff. The owner has totally remodeled the bar and turned it into a go-go bar."

"What's the name of the bar?"

"MK Kitty bar."

"Yes. I know the place. It's a total rip off."

"As are most go-go bars."

"Why do you go there then?"

"For one thing I've got several unique connections there whereas I have just about zero connection to any of the Walking Street go-go bars anymore. Danny used to be the manager at the Doll House. When he quit, an English pal of his became the manager, and then he quit. I knew the manager at Baby Dolls really well. That's Larry who used to manage Secrets. You will remember Larry. The Thai police set him up. Probably because the Pattaya Secrets forum members got too critical about the police and other powers that be in Pattaya. Anyway, a customer comes into his bar and asks Larry to hand some money over to one of the girls while she's dancing on stage. Larry hands the money to the girl without giving the matter a moment's thought. Then suddenly all these police come out of the wood work and take Larry down to the police station. Since the money had been for a bar fine, the police charge Larry with prostitution. Later Larry tells me that the whole thing wasn't a big deal–nothing that a million baht didn't take care of. As you remember, Dick, Larry quit his job at Secrets right after that. He had been set up by the police. Much later he became manager at Baby Dolls, and several months ago he retired."

"Yeah. I know Larry. He's one helluva nice guy, and the girls who worked for him really liked him."

"There's a couple gals I have a connection with at MK Kitty bar. There's Dowel who I short timed a lot when she was working at Passion Dance Club. Then there's Lamai who had been my waitress who always looked after me. At the price of my buying her a lot of drinks of course. They are the two women who did that short time with me back at my condo that night I took Kit to that government hospital in Bangkok. That was the same night I got pretty banged up in that motorbike accident when I had the two women following me on the motorbike taxi. Turns out when they went back to the bar later on to report to the owner, they told all the girls how I had bled all over the place and thought nothing of it. So let's just say, I got pretty well known at Kitty bar as one tough crazy motherfucker."

"Which is always a good reputation to have."

"Also as you know, Dick. I enjoy smoking cigarettes but I don't smoke around the girls I'm banging. Unless a gal likes to smoke also. Women who don't smoke don't like the smell of smoke on a man. But the girls I already knew at MK Kitty bar know I smoke and are used to me smoking. And Dowel smokes herself. So when I go into Kitty bar Lamai will run off and get me an ashtray and even light my cigarettes for me."

"Okay. I can understand where you are coming from, Fast Eddy."

"The drinks are higher priced than they are at the other Soi 6 bars with the exception of Dolls Go-Go which is right across Soi 6 from Kitty's. Both places are go-go bars with prices that are the same as the Walking Street go-go bars. And like most go-go bars, the girls keep pressuring the customers for drinks at Kitty's. So that's really shitty. But, they have a lot of pretty girls there who are just as good as you will find in the best Walking Street go-go bars. So although I've had both Dowel and Lamai up to my condo, I was figuring on getting a couple of the other girls to go with me also."

"I get it. Kitty's is damn expensive but you are setting your sights on perhaps some prettier girls."

"You got it Dick. I am banging Ning at Smoke and Kisses but I simply won't smoke a cigarette there. And I'm also banging that drug addict who works with Ning. Once in awhile I will go to Nature bar to have a drink or two with Amy or one of the other girls, and Amy will smoke with me. But when I have sex with Amy or one of the Smoke and Kisses girls I don't want to go to another Soi 6 bar where I'm constantly being pressured to take one of the girls upstairs. So Kitty bar has become kind of a refuge for me. To a lesser extent Dolls go-go across from Kitty's is another spot where I feel I won't be pressured so much by the girls to have sex with them."

"But it's a go-go also. And you and I both know that the name of the game at nearly all go-go bars is for the girls, mamasans and waitresses to constantly try to pressure the customers to spend too much money on drinks."

"Dick. The one thing I have going for me at Dolls is I know before I go into the place that there's no way I'm going to try to bar fine one of the girls. I know that ahead of time because even if a girl agrees with me to do a short time with me for one-thousand baht the mamasan is going to tell me I must pay her at least two-thousand baht. Then there's the one-thousand-five-hundred baht bar fine. So i'm not going to get really caught up with any of the Dolls go-go girls. So I just go there, have a beer or two even though they are more expensive, eat some pop corn and try to stay away from the girls."

"Have you been successful keeping away from the gals?"

"Not always. I can even sit in the corner alone and the girls will still come up to me. I had one join me and another girl who actually bought me a drink."

"So you don't hate the go-go's as much as you say you do?"

"Soi 6 is different. First, most of the go-go girls on Walking Street live in South Pattaya. Whereas some of the girls at Mk Kitties or Dolls live in Naklua, which means close to my condo. Also, I figure that the girls at these two go-go bars are not constantly fucking so many guys due to the bar fines and short time asking prices being so high. So they are not as jaded as most of the other Soi 6 girls. Which means there is actually a fleeting chance of actually finding a more normal type of woman at either of these places."

"Normal? Are you saying most Soi 6 girls are not normal?"

"Hardly. Look at Ning. She's really hard-core. Or the drug addict. Or even Amy or Kit."

"So how are you getting along with Lamai and Dowel?"

"Lamai always wants to be around me. She's constantly giving me massages. I can sit with her for two hours and she will keep massaging my legs and if she gets pretty drunk she will massage my dick for an hour or more, kiss my nipples or French kiss me. She's very alert. And older than most of the other girls. I've seen a couple of the younger girls falling down drunk and it's usually Lamai who rushes over to pick them up off the floor or take them to the toilet while they are puking their guts out. As for Dowel, I've pretty much had it with her. She keeps getting these watered down tequilas which she calls tequila lights. Dowel can easily drink eight of them in a row on my dime. She might have been my favorite girl when she was doing short times with me at Passion Dance Club but now there's no chance to do a short time with her upstairs at Kitty bar."

"Meet any other interesting girls at Kitty's?"

"Yes. And I'm going to tell you about them now."

"Mind if I intrude," asked Harry, who had just walked into Big Dicks.

"Not at all," Dick Fitswell replied. "We were just talking about MK Kitty bar."

"Kitty bar! That place is absolutely disgusting."

"Then why do you go there?" Fast Eddy asked, "if you hate the place so much, Harry?"

"Because you go there, Fast Eddy. And I have to go into that revolting place just to make sure you keep out of trouble."

"But you still go there," Fast Eddy replied.

206

"Unfortunately. There's that girl who used to give me blow jobs at Passion Dance Club. God, what a cock sucker she was. Whenever I find her at Kitty's I give her 100 baht just to stick my hand up her pussy."

"Then you remember Bo. Don't you?"

"Oh yes, Fast Eddy. What a hottie. I'd like to stick my dick right into those fake titties of hers and cum right in her face."

"That's the spirit," Dick Fitswell smirked.

"Hey. Bo really likes me, Harry. She's now my favorite Kitty girl."

"What a money pit. She wouldn't come near you, Fast Eddy, except for all those drinks you keep buying her."

"Okay Harry, we all know you hate just about all women. So I'm now going to ask you to please keep your comments to yourself while I have Fast Eddy tell me more about Bo," Dick Fitswell replied.

"The first time I met Bo, there was a whole group of us in MK Kitty Bar, Fast Eddy replied. Big Jim was there, Big John, Danny, me and a couple of other guys I can't place. A girl who had dyed her hair a dark blonde color greeted us at the door and took us over to two tables in front of the stage. Before the waitress even got to us, she was taking all of our drink orders. I thought that Anne, the owner, put this girl in charge of the whole bar as the mamasan. Not only was she the prettiest girl in the place. She was also the friendliest, most alert woman, hands down. I can't remember whose lap she sat on. But I think it was Danny's or Big Jim's."

"Who is Big Jim?" Dick Fitswell asked.

"He's the biggest dick around," Harry replied. "Why I'll bet his dick is twice the size of mine, and I've got a pretty big dick."

"Be as it may," Fast Eddy replied. "Big Jim's the horniest guy I've ever met. If he's getting laid only once a day, Jim's thinking he's getting over the hill."

"I want to know more about Bo. Perhaps I need to get her working for me, here at Big Dick's."

"I don't think she would, Dick. And I wouldn't want to see her ever work for the likes of you. She's too bubbly and she's too young for me to see her banging five guys a day for you," Fast Eddy replied. No offence Dick. Anyway, after that first night, I found myself sitting with Lamai most of the time. But there were a couple memorable times when Lamai wasn't working, and Bo would sit with me. Then there were a few other times, when I told Lamai, "Look, the last time I bought you drinks, I didn't buy Bo one drink, so tonight I'm buying drinks for Bo. And Lamai was okay with that."

"Whatever happened with Dowel?" Fitswell asked.

"She went home for something like a month. Or that's what she told everyone. Back to her Thai boyfriend I suspect after she had made enough money to stop working for a while. But with Dowel gone, the three girls I bought the most drinks for were Bo, Lamai and a tall slender girl who went by Pim. Bo had a lot of customers while Lamai, who was not nearly as pretty as Bo used to hang outside the club's front entrance. I think Anne had hired Lamai to lure potential customers into the bar. I'll tell you one thing. Whenever Lamai saw me walking by the bar, she'd rush up to me to ask me to buy her drinks."

"But let me tell you about Pim. Once in awhile I'd see her sitting with a customer who was usually Chinese, Korean or Japanese. But more times than not she would be dancing on that long stage. Two or three times when Bo was with a customer and Lamai was not working, she would join me. We'd wind up drinking a lot of tequilas together and before long we'd start making out. And if she didn't like French kissing, she sure acted like she did. She was very pretty but the most striking thing about her was her smooth soft skin. I loved touching her and kissing her face. She is also very ticklish so when we get drunk enough I'd stretch her across that long bench seat behind the tables and start kissing her armpits and belly."

"But before I tell you more about Bo I should tell you about this girl. One night they had a new waitress. I think the main waitress had taken a week off so this new girl was just kind of filling in. After I check binned and she brought my drink tickets over to me, I saw that she had charged me three-thousand baht, which was ridiculous because I had only been buying drinks for myself and Pim. Pim got really upset with the waitress. As I watched her going over each ticket, I could see her getting angrier and angrier. Then she called the waitress back, handed her my tickets, and said something to her in Thai. Two minutes later the waitress came back with a new bill for just one-thousand-eight-hundred baht. I'm telling you that Pim is sharp even if she can't speak English very well. And I always got the impression that out of all the girls in the entire bar she would be the best keeper if I were to get a new live in Thai girlfriend."

"You've told us enough about Pim and Lamai. I want to know more about Bo."

"For one thing, Dick, if Lamai and Bo were both sitting with me, Lamai would be feeling my dick a lot, but she was also into giving me massages. But she was very mechanical the way she kept massaging my penis. To tell you the truth it got boring after awhile. Especially after I've already fucked one of the other Soi 6 girls. But Bo. When she felt my dick, she always made me hornier than hell. And even Lamai would oftentimes say to me, "Bo really is in love with your penis, Fast Eddy." Sure Bo would also give me massages. She'd also kiss me on the lips, but she really seemed to get into giving me a hard-on and keeping me hard."

"I'm going to give you guys a better sense of what Bo's like. One night she was sitting next to one of the older gals. I was in a very good mood that night. Can't remember why but I even bought the other girl a couple of drinks even though I thought she was stupider than owl shit. I must have ended up spending five-thousand baht in drinks but Bo and I sure got drunk together. I started showing her how American strippers do lap dancers on their customers. I'd sit on Bo's lap and move my ass around on top of her, and I would even straddle one of her legs like a dog cocking its leg around a tree to take a piss. Bo thought the whole thing was funnier than hell. The other girl found it funny too so I lap danced her also. But Bo and I got really trashed and we finally got up on the stage together where I started to pole dance with Bo standing right next to me. Then we started dancing and I'd be grabbing Bo by her ass, bending her over, and start humping her in front of everybody. Looking back on it all I think I was really gross, but Bo didn't think so."

"Anyway Dick. I've been doing a lot of talking. What I liked about MK Kitty bar and Dolls go-go, I felt that although I was getting ripped off by their high-priced drinks, expensive short and long times and outrageous far fines, I was meeting a different type of bar girl than I was meeting in all the other Soi 6 bars. They were making a lot of money on drinks by getting 50 baht for each lady drink, so they didn't have to be fucking one guy after the other to make a living. Because both Dowel and Lamai had come to my condo, I figured that I could have others come for a lot less than the three-thousand to five-thousand baht their Chinese, Japanese and Korean customers were paying."

Big Jim joins the Apostles at Big Dicks

"Hey, what's going on here?" the newcomer asked Danny, Fast Eddy, and Wolfgang while making his grand entrance into Big Dick's.

The newcomer was gigantic. Watching him tower over the small gathering of Fitswell converts, Fast Eddy figured the man to be about six foot seven and over three-hundred pounds. Fast Eddy also noticed a resolute determined attitude straight off, reflecting a mind set he had only found once before. A mind set that the great mentor himself, Dick Fitswell alone possessed.

"Let me turn your question around," Fast Eddy replied. "What brings you here to Big Dicks when there's a lot of other Soi 6 bars to choose from?"

"I'm looking for Fitswell. Is he here?"

"He should be back in a few minutes," Wolfgang replied while looking up from his Thai whiskey and soda to size up the newcomer. "So what's your name, and can you state your business?"

"They call me Big Jim. I think you will all agree why I might have arrived with a name like that."

"Yes. You are bigger than fuck incarnate," said Danny. "Is your dick big also?"

"As a matter of fact it is. And that's why I came here to see Fitswell?"

"Here I am. What do you want with me?" asked Dick Fitswell who had just entered the bar."

"I have a problem," Big Jim replied. "I think about pussy all the time."

"Don't we all," said Wolfgang. "About everyone who comes in here thinks about pussy all the time."

"Tell me about yourself. So what makes you so special?" Dick Fitswell asked the newcomer.

"I am American. I go to strip clubs at least three times a week when I am in the U.S. And what can I say other than I can't help myself. I love looking at pussy. I dream about pussy every night. To me there is nothing more beautiful than a naked woman spreading her legs in front of my face."

"You are enormous, Big Jim. Does you dick measure up to the size of your body? My dick is a lot bigger than most people might think considering I'm only around five foot six," said Danny."

"You bet it is. And not only is it huge. It begs to be fed at least once a day. And all the better if it feeds at least twice before I go to bed at night."

"So how do you feed it?" Dick Fitswell asked.

"I get a shit pile of lap dances from all the strippers I encounter in the clubs. If the girl is any good, I nearly always cum during these lap dances, and when I don't have the time to go to a strip club, I watch porn and masturbate a lot."

"Okay. So you are a really horny motherfucker," Dick Fitswell replied. "Any other reasons you are looking for me?"

"I've heard a lot about you, and how you are trying to get a very special group of men to follow you. I want to become one of your strongest supporters."

"It's going to cost you to get started. Are you good with that?"

"Yes."

"Okay, I'm going to hand you over to Angry Pussy for an assessment of your, uhhh, qualifications."

Sitting behind the bar riveted to her phone Angry Pussy finally emerged next to Big Jim, smiled lasciviously at the newcomer, and invited him in an Issan accent: "You come upstairs with me now, Big Jim. I want to see what you've got."

An hour and a half later, Angry Pussy, came back down the stairs followed by a gleeful giant of a man.

"Big Jim. He very big here. I think someday he become big leader here at Big Dick's so I add him to special class right away."

"Why put me in special class, Angry Pussy?"

"Your dick same same trunk big elephant, but Dick Fitswell here. He bigger than you. I want to make you improve so all ladies want you." Angry Pussy replied.

Dick Fitswell Starts his Second Bar in Naklua

"Big Jim, Angry Pussy thinks the world of you," Dick Fitswell assured the newcomer.

"Really? Is my dick really that big?"

"Yes. It really is and that's why I am calling on you to lead a special mission."

"I know it has a really large circumference. A lot of women are scared of it."

"It's not just your large dick that's of supreme importance, Big Jim. It's your attitude."

"What about my attitude?"

"You have an unquenchable thirst for pussy. You tell us you dream of it constantly. And you keep mentioning your addiction to American strip clubs when you are in the U.S. I think it's fair to say that pussy is your Holy Grail, and that your quest for the perfect vision of it is constantly on your mind. I can only compare it to my eternal search for the perfect fit."

"Yes, Dick. Our visions are quite similar."

I don't want to get too Biblical about it, Big Jim, but if you recall, Jesus Christ came unto Saint Paul on the Road to Damascus. Where he struck Paul blind until he finally embraced Jesus Christ and the resurrection as the one and only true path to eternal life. I see you as my Saint Paul who was Saul of Tarsus before he came to embrace the Christ. Now Paul was a Gentile and not a true Jew so Jesus felt it was very important to send Paul to Damascus to spread his word to all the other gentiles. Thus assuring the ascendency of Christianity throughout the entire world and therefore not limited just to Israel. I want you to do the same thing for me that Paul did for Jesus."

"What do you want me to do, Dick?"

"I want you to go up to Naklua where all the Germans live and start a new chapel for me. I mean bar."

"What the hell, Dick. I don't want to go up there and have to live with all those Germans."

"Think about it, Big Jim. You will head a new bar and with it comes access to all the girls who will be working for you. And speaking of Germans, think of all the power you can hold over them."

"The idea is tempting. But how am I supposed to do all of this?"

"Well, you already have a lot of experience with American titty bars, don't you?"

"Yes. I've been going to them constantly ever since I was seventeen. I even had a fake ID made up for me so I could get into all those strip clubs."

"I want you to take Angry Pussy with you. She will help you set the new bar up. With her helping you run it, it will be a cinch for the two of you to be very successful up in Little Germany."

"When do you want me to start?"

"I'd say you should start looking for the right place immediately. And don't worry about the money. I can help you with that."

So what are you wanting to achieve there exactly?"

"I need to find more apostles to spread the true word of the perfect fit, Big Jim. Already all I have now is Harry, Frank, Scott, Wolfgang, Fast Eddy, Danny and now you. That only makes seven. I think we can find a few more up in Naklua where you and Angry Pussy can convert them."

The Cocktail Bar

Deep inside Little Germany, which is what the English and Americans call Naklua, there's a small bar on Soi 33 one block off Naklua Road. This bar is revered by many of the most knowledgeable Germans. Ferrari Willy is one of them. Less well heeled Germans call him Ferrari Willy because back in Germany he owns a Ferrari, a Lamborghini and a high-powered Mercedes. The Cocktail Bar is also Canada John's favorite watering hole which Canada John used to call "The German Bar". The reason Canada John called it the German Bar is due to his waking up one morning with such a huge hangover that he was unable to remember the bar's name.

The Cocktail Bar had been Canada John 's favorite bar while he was still living in Pattaya. But his visits became few and far between once he moved back to China to teach the Chinese how to build casinos in Macau and bridges like the one that now joins Macau to Hong Kong.

Thanks to Ferrari Willy and Canada John , Fast Eddy soon learned to appreciate the virtues of the Cocktail Bar where he could get totally wasted without having to spend a fortune down on Soi 6 or in the Walking Street go-go bars.

The Cocktail bar is a small bar that one can easily miss even if he's walking right by it on Soi 33. But once Fast Eddy had actually counted 27 customers. The main secret to the Cocktail Bar's success was Yah, who had successfully run the bar for seven years. Yah had two assets that most Thai bar owners do not possess. Number one, Yah's a genuinely kind person who wants to see everyone around her having a good time. Which goes for all people, whether it's the Thai women working for her or her customers whether they be German, English, French, white or black. Her second valuable asset is her unique ability to give her customers exactly what they want. And since most of her customers are Western white guys, Yah plays the bar's music according to their tastes. The key word here being "tastes" which implies none of that Da Da electronic crap. But sometimes most of her customers are Thai and when it's Thai people who are buying all the drinks, she will play a lot of Thai music.

There's a table when you first enter the bar which is open to the street like most beer bars. Canada John and Ferrari Willy call it the Soc table which is short for sociable table. It's got seating for up to eight people although several more customers can sit close to it perching on their bar stools.

One never knows who's going to be sitting at the Soc table. Sometimes high level policemen will be sitting there or close by talking quietly together at the bar. One night Fast Eddy saw a beautiful Thai woman wearing a nice dress talking with her friends. The woman wound up buying everyone in the bar several rounds of drinks. Which included Fast Eddy.

Most of the time Yah would invite him to join whatever group was sitting at the Soc table. Which was Yah's way of making everyone feel welcome.

But until now Fast Eddy had only bar fined one bar girl at the Cocktail Bar. It might be said that the bar girl was prettier than most of the other girls had it not been for the drab clothing she was always wearing. Fast Eddy never gave the woman much thought, regarding her as just part of the scenery except for her giving him damn good massages nearly every time he came into the bar. He had always given the Cocktail bar a pass when it came to buying the bar girls out of the bar. For the very reason of keeping it as his favorite drinking bar. Not to mention his not wanting to stir up any trouble due to a girl getting jealous should he stop bar fining her or showing too much interest in one of the other girls. But, one night he got just too drunk, and after getting too turned on by her massages he had caved in and brought the girl back to his condo for long time.

In his bedroom once she had taken off her nondescript clothing, he found that she had a great body and that she was much more slender and firm than he had originally thought. He wound up banging her twice without a condom and woke up the next morning with her arm still around his chest.

She had tattoos though, and he just couldn't see having her for a live in girlfriend no matter how good a performer she was. So he purposely avoided going into the bar for over a month hoping that she would move onto another bar.

When he finally went back into the bar, the other girls told him she had gone home due to her not making enough money to justify her continued existence in Pattaya where the price of food and housing was so much higher than it was back in the village.

He found a new girl there, but he never said a word to her until he had already gone back several times. The new girl was tall and slender, but she never asked him to buy her a drink or expressed the least interest in him.

Until one night a young European was having his birthday party there. Getting even more drunk than usual Fast Eddy started to show off his pole dancing abilities, as the young European watched.

"Try it," Fast Eddy said to the young man who was still celebrating his birthday.

Which he did. And unlike most other men who never managed to actually get their feet off the stage, he was actually able to pole dance.

"I can't believe how you can do pole dance so good," said the young man. "How old are you?"

"60."

"No way. No man who is sixty can do it the way you can."

Everyone was in a great mood that night. Before long most of the customers and bar girls were all dancing when one of the older bar girls approached him to bar fine one of the other girls.

"I know what you like, Fast Eddy. You like small lady. I see you before with girlfriend. She very small."

The woman was obviously referring to Kit who he had brought into the Cocktail bar several months before.

"Look look look. See lady. Her Meow. She small. She tall. She never work bar before. Meow very good lady. Good for you."

Suddenly the woman was right in his face holding Meow's hand. "Meow. Here is Fast Eddy. He very good man. He very good customer."

Within three seconds Meow was sitting on his lap. Fast Eddy found her to be just like the much older woman told him, having a firm body with great legs and a really fine ass. Before long they were kissing each other passionately until the older woman interrupted them.

218

"Bar fine her, Fast Eddy. Meow perfect for you. Take her back condo you."

"Yes. I come to condo you now. You bar fine me?" Meow asked.

"How could I refuse a body like this?" Fast Eddy asked himself. Fifteen minutes later he was leading her into his condo living room. Before he could even go to the kitchen to get her a drink, Meow sprawled out on his couch and pulled him on top of her. Kissing him passionately she unzipped his shorts, pulled out his appendage and started to go down on him.

Fully five foot six, her body looked sensational to him after he got her completely naked in the main bedroom. But when he stuck his head between her legs he saw something he had never seen before. Her vagina was a bright red. Could it be the alcohol or was it a figment of his imagination? But for the first time he realized the real meaning to the words, "She is red hot."

But he was drunk and Meow was only too anxious to please. He entered her without a condom. But there was something about the angle that just wasn't quite right. So they wound up having oral sex with her smoking him for what seemed to be an hour before he finally came.

Soi 6 Shenanigans

"Come buy me drink." Kit finally messaged him from her line app.

"Where are you?" Fast Eddy typed back.

"At bar, Soi 6," Kit replied.

"Which bar?"

"La La Land."

Which was no surprise to Fast Eddy who had long ago discovered Kit to be a creature of habit. She felt comfortable at La La Land. He just knew she'd be back at La La Land if she ever came to Soi 6 again.

"You come buy me drink?" she asked again.

"I can't, Kit. I busy now."

"Please come?"

"I cannot."

"Why should I come see her on Soi 6?" Fast Eddy asked himself. "She's the one who refused my help. She's the one who got angry because I even suggested that perhaps her little boy wasn't as sick as she thought."

But he went anyway, driving his motorbike down Soi 6/1 which could not be viewed by anyone on Soi 6. He used the rear entrance to MK Kitty bar instead of the front entrance which faced La La Land. Where he ordered a Heineken from the waitress.

Bo saw him come in. A few minutes later it was her turn to come off the stage. Joining Fast Eddy at a small table, Bo broke out into a huge smile as she told him in a bubbly voice. "Kit's working at La La Land tonight, Fast Eddy."

"I know, Bo. She finally messaged me and asked me to come buy her a drink."

"Are you?"

"No. I will buy you drinks instead of her. Hey Bo, you know everything. How she has that big problem with her arm. And my taking her to all those hospitals. Spending all that money. And she wants to work at La La Land again?"

"I understand. You very good man, Fast Eddy. I look at Kit. She no look good. She so small."

"I haven't seen her for a month, Bo. So I don't know what she looks like now."

"I go look at her now."

Like a fourteen-year-old girl too anxious to please Bo scampered out the front entrance door. A few moments later, she returned grinning from ear to ear.

"She standing outside bar now. She look very bad. Kit look like she sick."

"Yeah, I can just imagine," Fast Eddy replied.

"Buy me drink, Fast Eddy."

"Ok. I buy tequila. One for you and one for me."

After several more Heinekens and two more tequilas, Fast Eddy had just about had enough. He thought about bar fining Bo. Which would cost him one-thousand-five-hundred baht for the long time bar fine or one-thousand baht short time, which would be good only for an hour or two and not enough time if he took her back to his condo. He thought about walking out the front entrance with Bo on his arm so Kit would see them together. But Kit was smart enough to see that he was angry with her if he threw another girl in her face. Which would be just like someone like Robby would do. Fast Eddy thought about Robby for a moment, and how Robby had been shoving other women in his ex girlfriend's face. He compared his situation with Kit to Robby and Mint. "No, I'm not like Robby", Fast Eddy said to himself, almost loudly enough that Bo could overhear him. "I won't give Kit the satisfaction of seeing through my anger and perceiving me as a juvenile idiot. And I really don't want to hurt the girl anyway."

Bo must have gone outside the bar three or four more times to check up on Kit. The two bars were across Soi 6 from each other so if Kit were standing just outside La La Land and Bo stood at the

MK Kitty bar front entrance there would be only 30 feet separating the two women.

"I don't think Kit go with customers upstairs," Bo reported. "Maybe she get two, three drinks from customers. Then they leave."

"I don't think she make much money, Bo. Fifty baht for each drink she has. Maybe she gets 150 baht for all night. I think not many customers like her if she is as thin as you say she is."

But he couldn't be sure because he knew that La La Land had only four or five girls working there and all of them were fat and ugly.

He took the back way to Cocktail Bar. Half a kilometer from Cocktail bar he passed a big building that sold sex shows to hundreds of Chinese tourists at one-thousand-five-hundred baht a ticket. Here he could find hundreds of Chinese who had been delivered by over fifty tour buses which had parked up and down the street.

The sex shows were of no interest to Fast Eddy who considered all the Chinese waiting to get into the building as a mass of dimwits. Turning left in front of the sex show building, Fast Eddy drove several more blocks down a very dark street to Soi 33 which took him straight to the Cocktail bar.

He looked around the bar for Meow. Who wasn't there, but Yah was. When he asked Yah what Meow was up to, Yah told him she had gone to a nearby restaurant to eat with friends. Fast Eddy stayed two hours at Cocktail bar drinking with the bartender. But there was still no Meow.

"She's obviously doing a short time or long time with a customer," he told himself. "As far as Yah telling me she's having a long dinner with friends--well . . . we know what time it really is."

But before leaving he had one more little chit chat with Yah.

"I guess Meow's with a customer now. I don't care Yah. But what about that bartender who used to work for you? The one who was here for years who had a tomboy girlfriend."

"You mean Ohm?"

"Yes Ohm. I like her. I like the bartender you have now. But I always liked Ohm."

"You want her to come here now?"

"Not now, Yah. It's getting late. Another time maybe."

"I call her now for you."

Before Fast Eddy could stop her, Yah started video conferencing with Ohm. Fast Eddy already felt three sheets to the wind and didn't feel up to video conferencing with anyone. But it was too late. Suddenly Yah put her phone in his hand and here he was too intoxicated to have very much to say.

"You want me to come?" Ohm asked.

"Not now, Ohm. I really drunk."

"When do you want to see Ohm?" Yah asked. "I tell her now."

"One week from now." Fast Eddy might have been feeling pretty drunk but he still had his wits about him. One week from tonight would be July 21 which was Kit's birthday. He knew that he would be thinking about her that night. So he wanted to make sure that he'd have a drinking companion who would make him forget all about Kit. And the right woman would be Ohm.

Although he liked the current bartender well enough, he really liked Ohm. The present bartender was fat and not very attractive. But she sure knew her music, and she could judge the bar's crowd and play whatever was appropriate. Fast Eddy often bought her drinks and smoked cigarettes with her. Most of the time he would keep suggesting various musicians to her such as the Grateful Dead, Mick Jagger, the Searchers, and she would play whatever he asked her to play.

But Ohm was really something. She could make drinks for all the customers in the bar, keep track of what each person owed and still be able to spend a lot of quality time with him. She could match him shot for shot with tequila and still be up to doing all that multitasking. She loved dancing and when he got drunk enough she would really get him going. But every night he came in the bar she would ask him to pole dance for her. When she was working, he would never buy another girl a single drink.

Normally he got along well enough with her Tomboy lover. Who

223

was also pretty good at playing good music for the bar's customers. But Fast Eddy could always tell that the Tomboy was very jealous over how much fun Ohm was having with him.

Lamai Keeps an Eye on Kit

Fast Eddy went back to MK Kitty Bar two nights later. Once again he parked his Nmax along Soi 6/1 where Kit stood practically no chance of finding out that he was on Soi 6. He walked though the go-go bar's back entrance and sat at the same little table he had been drinking with Bo. But before he could even order his first beer, Lamai pounced on him.

If Lamai didn't have a customer, she could nearly always be found standing twenty feet in front of the club's front entrance where she could lure potential customers into the bar. Although he oftentimes sat with other girls, especially Bo or Pim, most of the girls considered Fast Eddy and Lamai to be an item. She had after all been his favorite waitress when she was working at Passion Dance Club. But the club had been closed for over six months now and had been resurrected by the Night Wish group into two separate Night Wish bars. She had gone to his condo four or five times. Twice with Dowel and two or three times by herself. One night she had gone back to his condo with him where they had sex in the bedroom. Then afterwards he had taken her to TJ's, which he and his friends always called the Lady Boy Bar. And after that he had taken her to the Cocktail Bar which she liked very much.

Once again he had three or four Heinekens and several tequilas but this time he was having them with Lamai, not Bo, who was already sitting with a Korean customer. But just like Bo had done before, Lamai kept going outside the club to spy on Kit. And not that Fast Eddy had asked her to. Lamai knew more about Kit than any other girl in the bar. No matter what kind of problems he kept having with her, Lamai knew that Kit was always and would forever be his favorite girl.

Like Bo, Lamai was alarmed by Kit's appearance. "She can't be making any money," Lamai kept telling him. "I don't see how any customers would like having sex with anyone that small."

The night ended up pretty much like it had with Bo with Fast Eddy making a beeline for Cocktail bar where he could keep his bar bill to a reasonable limit. Kitty's might be a lot of fun, and he certainly knew some attractive girls there, but he had found out the hard way that spending more than two hours there simply put too deep a dent in his wallet.

By the time he finished his second beer at the Cocktail bar, Fast Eddy had clearly formulated his plans for Kit's birthday. He would spend it at Cocktail bar where he would spend most of his time drinking with Ohm. But Fast Eddy knew that Kit would remember how she had spent his birthday with him just four months earlier when they had dinner with two friends at the Surf and Turf restaurant. And they're having a few drinks with Nam at Nam's restaurant next door to his condo where their two friends had joined them. And how they finished the evening at the Lady Boy Bar.

"Kit will never forgive me if I forget her birthday." He was sure of that. On the other hand she sure as hell didn't deserve much of a present. Due to her leaving him for the greener pastures of Soi 6 and all because of a few remarks he had made about her five-year-old son.

Since Bo was the prettiest and most charismatic girl out of all the MK Kitty go-go bar's women, he would once again go into the bar through the back entrance where he would hand her one thousand baht for Kit and a thousand baht tip for her trouble...while instructing her to go right into La La land to give Kit her one-thousand baht birthday gift. By this time Fast Eddy would be back at the Cocktail Bar having one helluva good time drinking with Ohm.

But things didn't quite work out the way Fast Eddy had planned it. The next morning his phone went off four times. When he answered it the fourth time before he even had a chance to make himself a pot of coffee, he heard Kit's voice on the other end.

"It's my birthday today, Fast Eddy. What are you going to give me?"

"Uhhh. I don't know. I not wake up yet. No coffee yet. But, you want to see me tonight?" he asked due to his not being able to think of anything else to say.

"Yes. I come see you tonight," said Kit.

"Okay. Come to my condo at 18:00."

226

Angry Pussy Bar

Had gotten to a great start. If there's one thing Angry Pussy had over Yah, her command of the English language was extraordinary for a Thai woman who had come out of the Thailand bar scene. And she had Big Jim with her to help guide her. Between the two of them, they had if anything an even better idea than Yah about what Naklua customers wanted.

Now Naklua is an entirely different kettle of worms than Pattaya even though the two municipalities adjoin each other. Naklua is mostly residential whereas Pattaya gears itself primarily toward tourists who are here today and gone tomorrow. Not that Naklua doesn't have a lot of tourists. Its hotels such as Centara and Pullman attract a lot of wealthy tourists but most of them are Asian because most Europeans, Australians and Americans feel that spending $150 to $300 for hotel rooms is a waste of money. But the Germans compose the largest segment of Naklua's long term residents. And Germans are by nature a very thrifty people, who despise all the price gouging that goes on in the Walking Street go-go bars.

It was Big Jim who steered Angry Pussy over to Soi 33. He already knew Yah who he thought the world of. There's also a large Italian restaurant directly across from Cocktail bar that is owned by Italians. Whose staff is also largely composed of real Italians, who speak like Italians who have that unique style that many Italians have. The Italian restaurant would allow its customers to have their food delivered to the Cocktail bar as well as Angry Pussy's.

Although one could have said that Yah and Angry Pussy were rivals, the two women got along quite well, with Angry Pussy oftentimes seeking Yah's advice. Angry Pussy's music was very similar to what they were playing at the Cocktail bar. And like Yah, Angry Pussy nearly always drank with her customers. Bar fines were low at both places. While neither bar ever cheated or took unfair advantage of their customers.

Although Angry Pussy had done very well running Big Dicks over on Soi 6, she knew only too well all she needed to know about Soi 6 women. They were fickle, most of them were practically brain dead, while 90 percent of them had Thai boyfriends. Angry Pussy knew that the Germans simply wouldn't put up with all those Thai boyfriends hanging around her bar. So she had made it her cardinal rule to never employ a Soi 6 or any other bar girl known to have a Thai Boyfriend.

*****

Fast Eddy wanted to make Kit's birthday party a night she would never forget starting out with a birthday present of five-thousand baht. He then went over to the five star Centara Hotel where he had his fitness membership to look for a birthday cake. Just inside the Centara's front entrance was a gorgeous bar that overlooked Centara's opulent gardens, swimming pools and the Gulf of Thailand. In the front of the bar there were two large displays of cakes, sandwiches and snacks where Fast Eddy was pleased to find a large strawberry cheese cake. He also bought a set of birthday candles and took the whole lot over to Angry Pussy's bar.

Two days later, Fast Eddy went to Big Dicks where he found Dick Fitswell alone and in an amiable mood.

"Dick, Kit's birthday was an interesting night with a sequel the next night that left a bitter taste in my mouth."

"Kit and I had dinner at the Italian restaurant just across Soi 33 from the Angry Pussy Bar. "I had my favorite fettuccine dish while Kit chose a pasta laden with shell fish."

"By the time we got over to Angry Pussy's bar, Big Jim and Big John were already there as well as Danny and a couple of other friends. One of them was there with his girlfriend, an attractive enough Thai woman in her early thirties who had a regular job and who had never worked in a bar. Big John's young girlfriend was there also."

"Angry Pussy was utterly amazing, doting on Kit as if she were Kit's mother. Big Jim was okay also, more or less taking Kit under his wing while making sure she had enough hard liquor to drink. While Yah, who normally would be attending to her customers next door came over to our table to make Kit feel welcome."

"Ohm, my bartender friend arrived at the Cocktail bar much later than she said she would. And when she arrived I felt torn between taking Kit out of Angry Pussy's bar so we could party with Ohm and staying longer with our birthday party group."

228

"By the time Angry Pussy brought out Kit's birthday cake, Yah had joined us from Cocktail bar. Where I went to ask Ohm to join us for some cheese cake. But not just Ohm—I had invited several of the other girls to join us for cake, but no one came except for Yah."

"It was a precious and as it turned out funny moment when Kit tried to blow the candles out. I don't know how it happened but somehow the candles turned out to be the joke candles that are impossible to blow out. I watched Kit blow as hard as she could, not just once, but several times as the candles sputtered as it they were going out, then burst into flame again. Perhaps the candles I had gotten from my condo were gag candles my ex girlfriend had bought. Or possibly it was Angry Pussy who might have substituted gag candles for the real ones I had gotten at Centara. But Kit was so precious trying to blow the candles out seeming so frail and shy in the pictures and video I got of her hovering over that strawberry cheese cake trying to put out those little candles."

"By this time Big Jim and Yah had achieved a fair amount of success getting Kit drunk. I watched her go to the toilet once, and when she didn't come out right away I figured that she was throwing up. Which would make the Angry Pussy bar to be the fifth place Eye had lost her supper. The first two being the Doll House and La La Land. Followed by my condo, then Cocktail bar. I still insisted that she go with me to the Cocktail bar where I could have a drink with Ohm.

"I wound up taking her to the motorbike taxi drivers at Lek Villa and sent her back to her room where I knew she'd wake up with one helluva hangover."

Caught out with the Sleeze Ball Thai Boyfriend

"I already know what Fast Eddy's going to tell you next, Dick. Because he's already told me all about it. I keep telling all you guys, all these Thai women are cunts!" Harry shouted at Dick Fitswell and Fast Eddy.

"You gotta get the picture, Dick," Fast Eddy continued. "At the time of her birthday I had been getting a lot of sex from a variety of different women. There was Amy, and Ning of course. Then there's that drug addict who worked with Ning at Smoke and Kisses and four or five others I've almost forgotten about. But the night after Kit's birthday, I went to Nature Bar where I bought Amy a drink. That's when Robert called me. I couldn't hear a thing on account of all the loud music so I had to go inside the toilet to hear what Robert was trying to tell me."

"Amy pretty much knew why I suddenly jumped up from our table and rushed off to the toilet on my phone. Robert's voice was urgent."

"I just saw Kit down at Big C with her Thai boyfriend," a hard to understand voice told me.

"Are you sure?" I asked as I raced to the toilet to escape all the bar Noise in order to hear what Robert was trying to tell me.

"Almost 100 percent. I know it was Kit because I just saw her last night at her birthday party. Anyway, she walked by me and as soon as she saw me she looked down at her feet. She was walking with this Thai guy holding hands."

"Shit. So after I gave her that five-thousand baht birthday money she goes out to spend it with that loser little boyfriend of hers."

"Sure looks like it, Fast Eddy."

"Wait till he tells you what happens next," Harry smirked.

"I was so pissed off that I hardly said a word to Amy when I went back to our table. However, I did buy us a tequila or two. So right off I text message Kit in line: "Robert see you with Thai boyfriend tonight.""

She immediately replied: "When?"

I text messaged Kit back: "Big C. Not long ago."

"What time?" she wrote back.

When I called Robert back he told me just half an hour ago, at around 6:30, so I messaged her back, "around 18:00."

To which she replied. "I was with Japanese customer. You forget, Fast Eddy, that I still work bar."

"Once again I got back on the phone with Robert who told me that the guy sure looked Thai to him, but he couldn't be totally sure."

"So what did you do then?"

"I was so completely pissed off that I vowed to get totally wasted. And I sure as hell wasn't going to get drunk with Amy, who liked all those high-priced drinks like Jager bombs. And I really didn't feel like fucking anyone that night so I went to MK Kitty bar. I found Bo there and also Dowel who had gone "home" for a month."

"So did you take Dowel back to your condo or Bo? Which one was it?" Dick Fitswell asked.

"Neither one. I bought both of them several drinks. Dowel kept telling me that she had seen Kit at a party on her birthday night. Dowel also made the point without my even asking that Kit was not with a Thai boyfriend and that she had been partying with a bunch of girls. I couldn't really see Dowel telling me that because she was always telling me, "Kit your number one. I number ten for you." So it would have been in Dowel's best interests to tell me that she had seen Kit with a bunch of Thai guys."

"So what do you really think?"

"I really don't know, Dick. At the time Kit was weighing only about 75 pounds and she had enough to drink at Angry Pussy's to be sick the entire night and to be royally hung over the next day. Maybe I am wrong but I just can't see her staying out so late to party with a bunch of Thais. On the other hand, it doesn't matter how much I have done for her or how much money I've given her over the past two years. Or that I got her all those injections which might have saved her left arm. Bottom line is she's Thai and with most of these girls we falang don't count for as much as a pet dog. So in her mind her real party, the one she was really looking forward to, was to be with all her Thai friends even though not one of them has done jack shit for her."

"In the mood you must have been in I'm really surprised you didn't bang one of the MK Kitty girls," Dick Fitwell replied.

"I tried to. I told Dowel I wanted to take her home with me straight off, but she told me if I waited until the bar closed, there wouldn't be any bar fine. But around one a.m., she told me she was not going to go back to my condo with me. So I decided right then that I would never ever buy Dowel a drink again."

Meow goes Ballistic in the Bar's Toilet

When it came down to Soi 6 girls, Fast Eddy felt Pawn actually liked him. Although most of the time whenever he went by Foxy's he would make excuses for not going inside to buy her a drink. But when Harry called him to tell him that he was in Foxy's with Big Mike, Fast Eddy decided to make Foxy's his first stop of the evening.

"I'm surprised you got down here so fast," Harry announced as soon as Fast Eddy entered the bar.

"And I am equally surprised you got Big Mike here to join you," Fast Eddy replied.

"Yeah, can you believe it, I actually was able to get Harry down to Soi 6 to get away from all those lady boys at TJ's he's been bonking," Big Mike responded with a smirk.

"Yeah, yeah, yeah. Aren't you the one to be discussing my lady boy business," said Harry. "As if you never go to TJ's, Big Mike."

"Let me buy both of you a beer," said Fast Eddy. "Because it's the only way I'm going to keep you guys from getting over to that lady boy bar too early tonight."

"You forget that I don't drink," Big Mike replied.

"Just tonight, Mike, have a few with Harry and me."

"I would, but I might get too carried away and get angry with a customer and beat the shit out of him."

Big Mike looked the part of a man who could beat up just about anyone. Six foot two and just over two hundred and fifty pounds one might easily make the mistake of thinking he was just another overweight Pattaya beer hound. But a much closer look showed off his thick muscular arms, wide chest and thick neck. Big Mike had often boasted of having too many bar fights in his past which was the reason he had given up on alcohol.

The bartender was already getting the three men their drinks, including a coca cola for Big Mike when Fast Eddy noticed that Pawn was still standing next to him.

233

"Come sit here," said Pawn, as she pulled one of the chairs out for Fast Eddy. The three men sat together talking for a few minutes while Pawn sat up close to Fast Eddy before he noticed that he hadn't bought her a drink yet.

"Pawn. Let's you and me have a tequila."

"You want two tequila. Me and you?" she asked.

"Yes. Kap kun kap."[24]

By the time the bartender brought them their tequilas Pawn was playing with his balls.

Which prompted Harry to tell her. "Pawn, you are my dream girl. I wish I had a woman as good to me as you are to Fast Eddy."

"Hey Fast Eddy, can you get Pawn to go outside and bring in a couple of girls for us?" Big Mike asked.

"Sure, Mike. Will do." Then he turned to Pawn and asked:

"Puying ti non (while pointing outside to the beer bar portion of Foxy's). Preun tini chop puying mak mak." Which means, or so Fast Eddy thought he meant, "Ladies over there. My friends here want ladies very much."

"Whether he had spoken in clear Thai or not, Pawn got the idea, which prompted her to immediately go outside to bring back two slender girls whom Fast Eddy considered to be pretty mouth watering.

By this time Harry had already had two bottles of Heineken which along with whatever else he drank earlier, brought him to that supreme moment of Harryness, which had made him infamous on too many occasions to recount. Meanwhile Fast Eddy had already

---

[24]Thank you

234

had two tequilas with Pawn who was so busy French kissing him that neither of them noticed Big Mike fiddling with his smart phone.

"That's it, Big Mike, get your camera ready. I want you to take a few pictures of me eating out this lush pussy who's sitting next to me!" Harry shouted out loudly enough for the whole bar to hear.

Then Harry turned to the girl to offer her a proposition she could hardly refuse.

Pointing at his crotch Harry entreated her to suck his dick so that Big Mike could shoot a few pictures.

"If I give you two hundred baht will you smoke me?" Harry asked the girl.

"Smoke you."

"Yes. For five minutes,' Harry replied. "Suck my dick now," he repeated while pointing at his groin.

"Ok. Pull dick you out. I smoke you now."

There was an empty booth close by. Quickly, almost in a blink of an eye, Harry lay on the booth's table and pulled down his shorts which exposed what must have seemed to the girl an enormous cock.

"Suck me off, now baby."

The girl obeyed by putting Harry's erect penis between her lips, which she mouthed gingery at first as Big Mike snapped several pictures with his phone. Until Harry shouted out to her, "Put it all in. I want to fill your mouth completely with my dick."

Which she certainly didn't understand until Big Mike towered over her while jamming her head into Harry's crotch.

"That's it baby. Now...Leo leo (which means quickly) put it deep inside your mouth now."

Which she did as Big Mike continued to shoot more pictures.

"Very good,' Harry told the girl. "Now, I want to eat you while Mike here shoots even more pictures. I give you 200 more baht," he added as he put two hundred baht into her hand.

"Here let me help you," Big Mike told the girl. Who he picked up and put down on the table as soon as Harry stood up.

The girl smiled at Big Mike, as she obviously savored the fact that she was making 400 baht without even having to go upstairs to do a short time. Then she pulled off her shorts, opened up her legs and allowed Harry to lick her out for another five minutes while Big Mike kept shooting pictures.

"I want boom boom you now," Pawn told Fast Eddy. "I want you make me cum."

Which he would have in a heart beat. But he had other ideas on how to spend the rest of the evening. Betting that he had a seventy-five percent chance of still finding Meow back at the Cocktail bar, Fast Eddy decided to give Pawn a pass.

"You going to fuck Pawn now?" Harry asked. "You really should. She loves you. And I'll bet her pussy is so delicious."

"I don't think so, Harry. Not if I can find Meow back at the Cocktail bar."

Luckily he found her still there. But immediately, before he could even buy her a drink, Meow asked him:

"I want go your condo. Customer, he ask me go with him. But I want you better."

"Okay, Meow," Fast Eddy replied. "We can go back to my condo right now."

Five minutes later he had her on the back of his motorbike. And five minutes after that he was already pulling into the Bahthaus entrance gate while Meow was massaging his balls.

She staggered into the condo still clasping his balls right in front of the security guard as Fast Eddy smiled forlornly at the guard as if to comment, "I can't help it. She's doing it. I'm not."

Before he could even get her into the large bedroom, Meow was already sitting on his lazy boy taking her clothes off.

Whereas it had taken her almost one hour to get him off on her first visit, this time, was totally different. Perhaps it was her complete wantonness, or perhaps it was because he wasn't nearly as drunk, but he came inside her mouth in just five minutes. Eagerly sucking in his cum, she held it in her mouth and motioned for him to kiss her on the lips. Which was something he had never done before. As soon as he pressed his lips firmly against her mouth, she stuck her tongue down his throat, and exhaled. He felt a salty liquid filling his mouth. Then Meow pulled away. Laughing at him.

She stayed all night with her arms wrapped around his waist. By the next morning his penis felt like it was eight inches long. Which put him firmly in the rear entry position so once again, he did her without a condom.

Meow's room was upstairs in the Cocktail bar. It took him just five minutes to get her home due to the traffic being so light that early in the day. But Meow couldn't get into her room since no one was awake inside the bar. While Fast Eddy waited, she called one of her roommates who came down to open the large front door of the bar up to let her inside. But before she said goodbye, she said to him, "Fast Eddy. I want you long time. Take me now before it is too late."

On his way back to the condo, Fast Eddy kept thinking, "She's probably the best looking bar girl by far in Naklua. But her staying with me long time? Now that oughta cost me plenty with her having three children. If Kit expects five thousand baht for her only child, Meow would probably want 10000 or even 15000 baht just for child care. Not to mention the 15000 baht or even more she will expect for herself."

By this time Fast Eddy and Kit were doing a lot of text messaging on line. But whereas sexually Meow was totally more than satisfactory there was something about her that was completely wrong. She had been nearly telling him she was in love with him. And then she had given him what he considered to be an ultimatum that amounted to "take care of me and my children or I will soon find someone else who certainly will." While several times he had gone to Cocktail bar only to find out that she had been obviously bar fined by someone else. Not that this mattered to him. But if she was really smart she would never allow any other man to bar fine her so long as she felt she had a chance with him.

He would have probably gone for it. She was really into him or at least had given him the outward appearance of being so. She had gone all over his condo and had even pulled the picture away from the wall that showed him at his High School Graduation when he was just 18 years old. But she clearly was not smart enough for him. She could have moved in with him within two or three weeks but she just couldn't hide the fact that she was doing all these other guys.

Meow knew all too well how often he was going to the Soi 6 bars. Because he had made no bones about how much he liked Soi 6 to the bartender or to Yah. So when Meow accused him of liking Soi 6 so much, he admitted: "Sure I do. I know a lot of people on Soi 6 and I just have so much fun there. And the girls only cost me one-thousand baht for a short time."

But Meow was not just a very sexy girl. She was charismatic, energetic, and totally off the wall. So when he went back to the Cocktail bar just two nights after Meow had made him swallow his own cum, he resolved to bang her again, whether she had three children or not.

They must have had at least four beers together. But whenever Meow had to go to the toilet or get up to bring their beers over to them, Fast Eddy was busy text messaging Kit. Oftentimes when Fast Eddy thought she was talking to one of the other bar girls, he would be text messaging Kit only to find that Meow was watching him over his shoulder. Once or twice she even grabbed his phone so that she could look at his messages.

When he finally had to go to the toilet to let out some of the beer he had drunk, Meow hurdled through the door while he was pissing in the urinal. Within seconds, she was kneeling at his feet smoking him. But knowing that the Cocktail bar discouraged people from having sex in the toilet he put his penis back into his shorts, and walked out of the bathroom only to find Yah standing in front of him with the bartender. But Yah smiled at him.

"Because she knows how innocent I am," Fast Eddy said to himself.

He ended up taking Meow to TJ Bar where there must have been fifteen lady boys, most of them without customers. It didn't take Meow five minutes before she started chatting with the lady boys. Although he couldn't speak Thai very well, Fast Eddy could often pretty well size up a conversation by cherry picking a few words. He heard Meow mention Soi hok (Soi 6) to a lady boy several times and heard the lady boy say "Chi" several times back to her meaning that she[25] agreed with whatever Meow was asking her.

Fast Eddy concluded "Obviously Meow is all bent out of shape about my liking Soi 6 so much so she's asking the lady boy what she knows about me and Soi 6. Which is a lot because I've made no secret about my great love for Soi Soi 6 to the lady boys"

So Fast Eddy decided to take Meow down to Soi 6. But he'd only take her to MK Kitty Bar, because it was a go-go bar where most of the customers and girls were relatively well behaved. And certainly not to any one of a number of Soi 6 bars where she might just go in and see a girl blow a guy right in front of everybody.

Shooting the shit at the Lady boy bar

" Fast Eddy, did you ever take Meow down to Soi 6?" Harry asked while fondling a lady boy who was sitting on his lap.

"Sure did Harry. And it didn't go well."

"What happened?"

"I took her into MK Kitty bar where I got me a Heineken and a Tequila. I started to order a drink for Meow when all of a sudden Bo shows up. Bo, of course, is curious as hell over this new girl I'm suddenly bringing into her bar so she asks me if she can join us at our table. I agree. Then I order Bo a Tequila. Bo is being her normal gleeful self, and she simply is the cutest girl in the bar.

I hear the name "Kit" come up in the conversation so I know Meow is asking a lot of questions about Kit. It's obvious that Meow doesn't like the place so I take her back to my condo after staying less than one hour at Kitties."

---

[25] Lady boys are always called "She"

The next night, I went back into MK Kitties, and once again I'm drinking with Bo who tells me how much she disliked Meow. Bo had me laughing my ass off due to her ability to size Meow up as one helluva jealous controlling bitch.

The Night Terry almost Died

"I am going just nowhere with all these bar girls, Dick. I've had Amy over to my condo several times, but as I have said before she thinks it's okay to come over for a couple of hours and my paying for a two-thousand baht long time. Lamai has been over a couple of times after twice coming over with Dowel. Meow almost makes the grade but I am already realizing her short comings. I am banging both Ning and the drug addict at Smoke and Kisses and had the drug addict over to my condo twice. Then there's a few others that I've all but forgotten about. So I just head down to Soi 6 to get the lay of the land. I grab a large 70 baht slice of pizza to go at Slice Pizza, and head to the Nature Bar for my first beer."

"Amy's there so we start off having a couple of drinks together when suddenly my phone starts ringing. It's Terry and he's already tried to call me several times."

"You must come to my condo immediately," he tells me. I have to go to the hospital right now and we can't get an ambulance to come."

"Luckily, I've driven my Yamaha Nmax to Soi 6 which I have parked in front of Nature Bar. I pull out my wallet and tell Amy I must leave immediately. She's back with my change within three minutes. Although she doesn't know me that well, Amy knows this is no drill, and that something awful has happened."

"I must have been doing over 40 miles an hour on Second Road. But I haven't even finished my first beer which I've left half empty on our table. It takes me just five minutes to get to my condo."

"The security guard tells me: "Terry very bad. We try take him to hospital. Ambulance no come.""

"Terry is sitting on the edge of his bed, in considerable pain."
"He can barely talk, but he manages to blurt out: "Fast Eddy. There's a chair next to my bed. You gotta help me get into that chair. Then take me to the hospital in my car.""

"Now, Dick. You have never met Terry but you gotta picture him. He weighs 350 pounds and if he walks one block he's walked one block too far. He had Manoon living with him at his beck and call, but now Manoon has got a job in Bangkok so Terry doesn't have anyone living with him except for his girlfriend, Mut. He's bought an Nmax which he lets Mut drive, but now that he no longer has a driver, he's somehow been able to drive the car by himself to shop for groceries and do other errands. But he hasn't been to a bar in over six months. He lives to cook, and when he cooks meat, he roasts it for four or five hours. And he makes the best chili in the world."

"Putting a 350-pound guy in a chair is nearly impossible for the average guy. But I must hand it to Terry. Although he's in a lot of pain, he does his utmost to help lift himself up to keep all that dead weight off me. Somehow we manage to get him into that chair. It's really hard on me, but I am able to scoot that chair out of his condo and down the hall into the elevator. And get the elevator to the ground floor and continue to scoot the chair over to our parking lot."

"Terry tries to get me to drive him to the Hospital in his car, but I'm thinking the police might stop me. Because even though I've had only half a beer with Amy I had a couple at the Cocktail bar before I went to Soi 6. Besides, I have a lot of trouble with my night vision when I'm driving a car here in Pattaya."

"But I'm in luck. There's several Thai guys in our parking lot. It turns out at least one of them works security for the Singha beer family which owns some land across the alley next to our building. Terry and Mut know the guys because Terry gets iced coffee nearly every day from a vendor who sets up next to the Singha family's property."[26]

The three Thai men are able to take Terry to Bangkok Pattaya Hospital and bring his car back to the condo. Since they strike me as a trustworthy and very caring group of guys, I don't go

---

[26]Singha is the largest beer company in Thailand. The Singha Family has a 200 meter long property that extends from the Bahthaus to the Gulf of Thailand.

with them to the hospital. Because I've done everything I can, and I cannot do anything at the hospital for Terry. He's lucky to have Mut with him and I figure Terry will be sedated upon his arrival in the emergency room.

"But I'm all torn up inside because Terry is one of my best friends and I don't think he will live through the night. I am one of the few people to know that Terry is already terminal with a heart condition the doctors have told him will kill him in one or two years. So knowing I will not be able to sleep without a lot of alcohol in me I head to the lady boy bar."

"For one thing it's closer to Bangkok Pattaya Hospital than our condo, so if Terry or Mot calls me I can be at the hospital in five minutes. I want one thing only, and that's beer and Tequila because I sure don't want any lady boys trying to seduce me. I've known Emmy, the bar owner for fourteen years. And find her sitting at the bar where I tell her that one of my best friends will likely die tonight so please tell the lady boys to leave me alone."

"I must confess that I enjoy drinking with the lady boys at TJ's, but tonight's not the night. Then I get a message from the drug addict on my phone. She wants to come to my condo so I figure she's about out of drugs."

"From the first moment I met the drug addict I thought she was one of the hottest girls on Soi 6. But she's got a pretty rotten personality. Like the first time I met her, Dick, and I asked her if she wanted to go upstairs to do a short time with me. And she replied, "Well, okay, (I might as well because what else do I have to do in a dive like this?). But about the third time I took her upstairs at Smoke and Kisses we had a lot of drinks together afterwards when she told me about her life."

"She was a straight A student in High School," she told me, then she went to some kind of junior college or even a university afterwards where she was doing well until she got knocked up by a Thai guy. "That completely destroyed my life," she confessed, "and one thing led to another and here I am on Soi 6 going nowhere."

"That's what she wanted you to believe," Dick Fitswell replied.

"Well be as it may. Turns out her English is quite good. She's also 39 years old. And one time when I went into Smoke and Kisses, I didn't even recognize her because she only looked twenty. Had her hair made up and everything. And you know I don't like all these really young girls. But as I keep telling you, she's got one of the nicest looking asses I've ever seen. She has silicon breasts too, which I don't really much care for, but wow, she's one of the best fucks I ever had."

"So did you short time her or long time her?"

It turned out to be long time. We got drunker than shit together. And since my neighbor Danny was back in the United States, I didn't have any neighbor around to complain about my stereo being too loud. I've got this USB with a lot of great music on it. Makes you want to dance, and I use that USB to put in the elliptical machine at Centara. So I was playing my music really loud. And we danced and we had sex and then we drank a lot more and played that USB even louder until about five a.m. when I heard a knock on my door.

"Who was it?"

"The night time security guard. So I turned down the music and the next night I asked him who had complained. Turns out it was Missy, the Thai woman who went with Kit and me with her boyfriend to my birthday party at Surf and Turf who later started beating her boyfriend up. Now Missy is an ex Soi 6 gal and she's got a really big mouth. So the security guard just laughed when I told him I didn't give one shit about Missy's complaining about me. And you can bet your ass that he empathized with me because he knew what I had done for Terry the night before."

"I'm getting a little ahead of myself though. I still didn't know if Terry made it or not through the night so I woke up the next morning at ten or so with the drug addict fully naked in bed lying next to me. I woke up with a big hard on and took one look at her beautiful naked ass and Oh God, did I ever want to put it to her again. But I kept thinking of Terry, and I felt that if he died later that morning, and I had missed seeing him because I was obeying my stiff dick that I was one turd of a friend."

"So you woke the drug addict up and took her home?"

"Yes. I gave her one thousand baht. But I was in so much of a hurry to see Terry. Dropped her off in front of her place and was at the hospital inside of two minutes. Later I realized that I owed her another thousand baht because that was what I was giving her for long time. Wound up messaging her the day after I looked in on Terry and had her meet me just outside her apartment building so I could give her the extra thousand baht."

"You are such a nice guy," Fast Eddy.

"Well, back to Terry. Turns out he had a life threatening blood clot in his leg and the doctors told him that if I hadn't gotten to him as fast as I did that he would have either died or lost his leg."

"Why couldn't he get an ambulance to take him to the hospital?"

The security guard told me that practically everyone tried but no one came. Terry told me that he had tried to get two of his friends to help him before I got to him that night. There was Demon, an American guy. who used to be a Night Wish manager on Soi 6 who was staying with him a lot. And there was Andy, an Englishman Terry had become friends with after Andy sold him some kind of gee whiz internet box that could get everything imaginable including a direct connection to both God and Jesus. But Demon was in the Walking Street go-go's where he probably couldn't hear his phone. And Andy tried to get an ambulance to pick Terry up but he really fucked that all up."

"What do you mean?"

"Andy called one hospital but the hospital asked Andy if Terry had insurance or not. That really pissed Andy off. Andy told me later that whether Terry had the money or insurance to pay for an ambulance or not it shouldn't make any difference to the hospital. So Andy told the hospital that Terry didn't have any insurance even though he knew that Terry has insurance. So the way I got it figured the hospital decided not to send an ambulance because it might not have been reimbursed for the ambulance's cost."

"Sounds like Andy really screwed up."

"Dick, had it been me, I would have told the hospital, "why sure Terry has insurance. He's got two thousand dollars in his policy to cover the cost of that ambulance. And not only that. The policy says that anyone who picks Terry up in that ambulance is guaranteed a long time with any girl he chooses out of the Walking Street go-go bars.'"

"How was Terry doing when you visited him the next day?"

"Terry nearly died so he looked really bad. He was coughing and in a lot of pain. They put him in intensive care and they kept him there for four days. Then they put him in a regular room for another five days."

A Jealous Meow Gets into Fast Eddy's Phone

Fast Eddy knew he had hurt his back the night Terry went to Bangkok Pattaya Hospital. Which didn't stop him from visiting him every day. But he ultimately came close to having a back operation.

With Terry still in intensive care, Fast Eddy decided to bar fine Meow. Which started out badly enough before he even got her out of the bar. He was still doing a lot of text messaging with Kit. And to a much lesser extent with Lamai and the drug addict. Time and time again he caught Meow looking over his shoulder while he was messaging the other girls. Who had the audacity to snatch up his phone while he was talking with the bartender so that she could get a closer look into who he was text messaging.

Back at the condo, Kit started to message him before he had finished his second beer when Meow suddenly took his phone away from him, ran into the main bedroom and locked the door on him.

But he had two keys to the large bedroom in the wooden key box he had hung next to the front door to the condo.

Meow didn't hear him come into the bedroom. Fast Eddy found her sitting on the floor on the far side of his king size bed, totally engrossed in reading his text messages to the other girls.

"Kit, Kit, Kit!" Meow screamed at him when she finally saw Fast Eddy hovering over her. "You love Kit too much."

"You know I like her," Fast Eddy replied. "Now get off my fucking phone right now!"

Fast Eddy had never had a girl do this to him before although he had put up with her looking over his messages in the bar. And when she had snatched his phone away from him in the bar, he had told her to never do it again. But locking him out of his own bedroom was simply too much. Before Meow could react, he took the phone away from her and went into the living room where he sat back into his couch to see what messages Meow had been looking at.

Meow just didn't get it. He should have expected much more out

247

of her considering she was 29 years old. Before he could react, she straddled him and once again grabbed the phone out of his hands.

He tried to pry his phone out of her hands. While Meow clung onto it with all her strength. For a few seconds they wrestled each other for the phone until the heavy couch suddenly overturned. Which sent Meow and him sprawling.

Luckily the telephone did not appear to be damaged.

She should have known that phones are nothing to trifle with. And that his private business is just that. His business and no one else's. "Who is this twenty-nine-year old woman who thinks she can get into my private business and take my telephone away from me? This bitch has gotta go," he told himself, not caring if she heard him or not.

"You gotta go back to bar now, and I mean Now Now Now. Doney kap," he repeated in Thai. "Va".[27]

A day or two later, his back started to go down. His groin had been hurting him already, but he had expected that. This was because he had two hernia operations within two years of each other, in almost exactly the same spot. His doctor had explained to him that the pain was caused by a lot of scar tissue from the two operations and the cutting of nerves.

He had manhandled all 350 pounds of Terry, which would have been enough to give him his third hernia. But he didn't start to experience much pain until after this latest Meow incident. More than manhandling Terry the complete suddenness of the couch going over on them might have caused a sudden twisting of his spine.

---

[27] Donee kap means "now", while va means "go".

248

But he found out after getting an ultra sound at Bangkok Pattaya Hospital that he didn't have a hernia at all. The surgeon recommended a few weeks of rest which would have been the normal treatment for a muscle pull, which was unfortunately in his groin. So he figured on looking forward to not having much sex for the next few weeks.

Should have, but didn't because the same night he had Bangkok Pattaya Hospital do the ultra sound, the Drug Addict text messaged him on line. Which led him to picking her up on his Nmax and bringing her back to his condo.

As they sat drinking beer together on his couch, Fast Eddy explained his predicament to the drug addict.

"Maybe we still can have sex?" she suggested.

"I don't know. It hurts me right here," he told her while pulling up his shorts and pointing out the scar that had been left by the hernia operations.

"I can smoke you. Not hurt too much I think."

"Yes. Smoke me then," Fast Eddy replied as he pulled off his shorts and lay back in the couch.

"I can fuck you too. I do very softly."

She started off by giving him an exquisite blow job, but when she started to lower her body onto his face, he wanted that and so much more. After he had eaten his fill, the drug addict gently lowered her beautiful little ass onto his erect penis and slid him inside her without a condom.

There's something about having sex without a condom a man will never get using protection. Both Danny and Harry always went bareback. For the primary reason that it's oftentimes difficult to maintain an erection by going from oral to suddenly having to insert an erect penis into a woman's privates. Condoms are not the easiest things to deal with. There's all that fumbling around that goes with unfolding the condom and sometimes the damn thing doesn't even fit. But with the constant dull aching in his groin, Fast Eddy found the drug addict to be the perfect antidote. She was gentle with him. And whereas in the past she had normally orgasmed with her tight little body convulsing at high rpm, tonight he found her to be a miracle of restraint. With no condom to restrict his release of precious bodily fluids while feeling her wet warmness, he felt the muscles in his groin relaxing.

Using Gravity Inversion Boots to Avoid a Back Operation

Fast Eddy was starting to feel that all was right with the world in spite of the constant pain he was feeling in his groin. "It will be all over soon," he kept reassuring himself. " It's only a muscle pull and I can deal with that." Until he felt his lower back starting to go out due to the nerve endings being crushed between the compacted vertebrae, which the x-rays had picked up many years ago.

"But I can deal with that also," he told himself once again. "I still have those gravity inversion boots and the gravity inversion bar that I fastened into the door frame of my large lavatory."

He still had the strength to pull himself up on the bar wearing his gravity inversion boots that he had fastened snugly to his ankles. Hanging himself upside down for five minutes he could imagine the entire 75 kilos of his body stretching his entire spine that would release the pressure his lower vertebrae were putting on all those nerve endings.

The next night he played batman again, this time hanging upside down in his bathroom's entryway for a full ten minutes. But the next day his back was hurting even more than it had before he had started his inversion treatment.

But the pain was affecting much more than just his lower back, which his gravity inversion equipment normally could correct within two days. The pain had spread to his buttocks, his thighs and down his lower leg. But only on his right side.

The MRI at Pattaya Bangkok showed that several of his vertebrae in his lower back were compressed to the point of actually touching each other. Which was nothing new because he had the same diagnosis in the U.S. fifteen years ago when he started using gravity inversion boots to stretch his vertebrae. So whenever he started feeling his lower back start to go out he found two or three days of gravity inversion to be just enough to avoid any further pain for two or three weeks.

The pain was getting to be so bad that he could hardly sleep at night and often lay in bed for hours in so much pain that he almost started to cry like a little baby. He couldn't even contemplate having any women visiting him now because he knew that having sex would be much more painful than the pleasure he could derive from it so he decided to avoid female companionship.

Until Kit messaged him one morning. "I want eat Shabushi."

Kit arrived at his condo at 6:00 p.m. on a motorbike taxi. Fast Eddy paid the driver 140 baht, and took Kit upstairs to his condo where she immediately sat on his couch and logged into her favorites on Netflix. Fast Eddy watched her face as she sat completely absorbed in picking out a television series that might interest her.

"We must go now Kit. If we don't get to Big C by 6:30, we might not be able to get a table."

He drove fast, weaving through traffic getting up to 30 miles an hour when there was no one directly in front of him. Five minutes later he was pulling into Big C's motorbike parking area. Although it was practically full, Kit immediately saw a parking spot that was open. Without saying a word she pointed at a narrow gap between two motorbikes.

They were soon walking through the shopping center, Kit walking quickly while Fast Eddy walked beside her. Once again he thought about how so many Thai women walked so slowly and lazily as if they had all the time in the world.

They were in luck. Shabushi still had several tables left. An employee of the restaurant seated them at a vacant table as Kit explained in Thai exactly what she wanted. When the attendant left, Kit went to the drink section to get him a glass of water and a glass of punch for herself.

Fast Eddy was already filling one plate with Chinese dumplings while picking out over half a dozen types of Sushi. By this time Kit had taken their drinks to their table and had joined him.

Shabushi has a track that wanders throughout all the tables in the restaurant. On this conveyor small plates of raw shrimp, eggs, pork, and vegetables are constantly moving past the restaurant's patrons. Who can cook whatever they want on a special contraption that is filled with water and heated by electricity.

An alert Thai woman is expected to put all the raw vegetables,

252

noodles and meat in the cooking implement and to remove everything as soon as it's cooked. The Thai woman then places all the cooked food into her companions bowl with a special Thai hot sauce. So other than having to go to the other end of the restaurant for more pot stickers, sushi and other small items, Fast Eddy doesn't have to do a thing. While Kit's constantly putting food on his plate and returning to the beverage section to refill their glasses.

By the time they get back to the condo, Kit is anxious to get back to Netflix. While Fast Eddy can only think about relieving the pain that is starting to flare up in his back, buttocks and groin.

"Kit. I'm giving you two-thousand baht tonight, but we are not going to have sex. I hurt too much. But I want you to help me now." Motioning to her to join him in the bedroom he strapped the gravity inversion boots around his ankles and motioned for her to follow him to the inversion bar.

"This is very dangerous. If I have an accident, maybe I die." Starting with his feet on the floor, Fast Eddy pulled his legs over the bar which takes him a few second to fasten two hooks from his gravity inversion boots around the bar while lifting his entire body weight until he is able to flip himself into an upside down position with his head only a few inches above the floor. But when one of the hooks slides out of the bar, Fast Eddy is left hanging from his right leg. Thankfully his muscular arms and strong stomach muscles enable him to force the disengaged hook around the bar. until he is able to fasten it around the bar.

"You see, Kit, I almost have big accident. If I fall on my head maybe I die. But now I'm same same bat."

Fast Eddy knew the average guy isn't in good enough shape to get up on that bar by himself. But even though he had never had a problem inverting himself, he knew that the first time could always be the last time. His stomach muscles could tighten up which could leave him hanging upside down without being able to get off the bar. He might for one reason or the other lose consciousness. Or both hooks might slip off the bar and he would wind up falling on his head. So it is good having Kit watch because if something goes wrong she could always run down to get the security guard.

"It's so good to have her here, instead of another girl, who might be too stupid to even think of going down to get the security

253

guard. Now I know why I want her and not any of these other girls."

After doing his imitation of a bat, Fast Eddy took Kit into the other room where she sat next to him watching Netflix. He had two ice packs in his freezer and took one of them out, and went back to the couch. Then he took off his shorts and jockey shorts, and put the ice pack around his balls. For the next half hour he kept shifting the ice pack around his groin as he observed Kit watching Netflix...in total amazement over how she could watch it for hours on end, and how she could quickly switch from one t.v. show to another. He had never seen a girl who could be so utterly transfixed by whatever she was watching while being so unaware of her other surroundings.

Electric Acupuncture Saves Fast Eddy's Back

"What happened to your back? It seems you are able to at least get over to a few bars now, even if you are getting around on that crutch of yours."[28]

"Good point, Wolfgang. I guess I enjoy the bars too much."

"So what are you doing about that back of yours? I see you have driven your Triumph here."

"Yep. Even though I've got a clutch and a five-speed gear box, which makes the Triumph much tougher to drive than my Yamaha Nmax, sometimes I just like to drive in style. So I sort of wedge a single crutch between the left mirror and handlebar and just manage as best as I can. I've got a back condition that's called a sciatic nerve problem. It affects only one side of a man's body. In my case my right side. And believe it or not, I've found out I have more pain in my right buttock than I have in my lower back"

"How did you find that out?"

" Bangkok Pattaya Hospital wants to operate on my back and my insurance company has told me I'm covered. But my nephew is an emergency room nurse in the U.S. He keeps telling me not to let them operate on my back, unless there is nothing else I can do and the pain becomes unbearable. I've even let the hospital inject cortisone in my back. Which is pretty extreme and can lead to some nasty side effects. It wasn't very effective though. But from past experience I've found that a good chiropractor can do wonders."

"Did you find one?"

---

[28]Due to reoccurring back injuries Fast Eddy keeps a pair of crutches in his condo

"No. I couldn't find a chiropractor anywhere close to me."

"So what did you do?"

"I learned about an Englishman who practices acupuncture and other methods of treating back injuries in South Pattaya.

"Did you find the guy?"

"Yes. I took little Miss Kit along and had her ride behind me on my motorbike. I had figured out about where the Englishman's office was . . . within a hundred meters of it. But I had trouble finding it. It was not on Pattaya Tai, and my GPS indicated it being on Pattaya Thai. But I got Kit to walk around the area with me and we found this little street that was little more than an alley. We found a run down looking place there with the Englishman's name on a sign board. I could tell that Kit wasn't very impressed, but we went in. And out pops this middle-aged guy with a bald head and a pot belly. It turns out he was the so-called chiropractor."

"What did he do?"

"He turned me over on my belly on this narrow table and manipulated my spine a little the way chiropractors do. Then he told me he was going to perform acupuncture on me. So while I lay on my side facing Kit, he pulled out this large needle that had an electrical cord attached to it. And when he stuck it in my lower back . . . wow, when that current went into my spine I knew that something big was happening. Then he told me that my spine was not my major problem. He said the nerves in my right buttock were all screwed up and that was the main problem area although the nerves still carried pain to my lower back. He then stuck that needle into my right buttock and shot a lot of electricity through it."

"How many times did you have to go back?"

"Didn't have to. Nigel charged me only one-thousand baht, and when I asked him when my next appointment was he told me I didn't have to go back because I would feel a lot better by the next morning. And Nigel was right. By the next morning I was hardly feeling any pain. But, as I would later find out, I had some problems walking. And now I'm thinking all that electricity that had obviously affected my nerves had also done something to my locomotor skills of my right leg."

Kit on Death's Door

"What do you mean by the electric current affecting the locomotor skills of your right leg, Fast Eddy?"

"Let me give you an example, Wolfgang. Big Jim and Angry Pussy were becoming very successful with the Angry Pussy bar right from the start. One of the reasons was they had a series of parties at the bar and they actually had live entertainment there. When Angry Pussy turned 39, they had a birthday party for her. I think you were even there, Wolfgang. They had a hog cooking right outside the bar and a lot of food on a long table inside. And they had a small karaoke group playing music."

"Yes, I remember that. The head singer was a fantastic looking lady boy."

"That she was. I thought she was a lady at first, and she looked great to me until finally Kit told me she was a lady boy."

"I remember your bringing Kit to that party."

"Do you remember when I fell down just outside the bar while I was shooting video of the karaoke group?"

"Yes. I remember. Were you as drunk as I was?"

"No Wolfgang. But I was trying my damnest to get the best video possible for Big Jim and Angry Pussy. But I couldn't get around very well without using a crutch. It had been only a week or two since Nigel shot that electricity through my back and buttocks and a high-powered pain killer. I felt 100 percent better after that but my legs started feeling really weird once I got that electricity jolting up my spine. Every so often when I'd start getting up from a sitting down position at a table, my right leg would suddenly start to go out on me. I even fell down a couple of times because my right leg wasn't supporting my body. I expected it to but as soon as I'd get up, it was like I didn't have a right leg at all, and I'd just topple over. And that's exactly what happened to me while I was shooting video at Angry Pussy's bar. There was a little drop off where her bar meets the street. And whereas I had been using the crutch so I could peg leg myself around while shooting video of the karaoke group, I tried getting up close to the lead singer without using the crutch. My right leg crumpled underneath me and suddenly I was sprawling down onto the concrete."

"Did Little Miss Kit enjoy the party?"

"I think so. She got drunk again, and Kit always enjoys herself once she's had a few drinks."

"Did you ever manage to start boom booming Meow again?"

"I tried to, but after she saw me bring Kit into the two Soi 33 bars, she'd hardly ever look at me again. One night right after Angry Pussy had that big party I got pretty wasted at Cocktail bar. Yah asked me to bar fine Meow, and when I informed Yah that Meow hated me, Yah told me Meow was in love with me. Before I could stop her, Yah started talking to Meow in Thai. But when I took Meow back to my condo, she just sat there on my couch like a stone. Didn't move a muscle and when I asked her if she wanted a drink, she told me, no. And when I asked her to go into the bedroom with me, she told me she didn't want to. Then she said she wanted to go back to the bar. So I drove her back to Cocktail bar. But I will say one thing good about her though. She paid me back the bar fine I had given Yah."

"Which all led up to Kit almost dying on you?"

"No leading up to it at all, Wolfgang. It all happened pretty fast. By this time Kit was coming to my condo three or four times a week. She always went back to her room before three in the morning. One morning we set up our usual time for six p.m.. But Kit started complaining about having stomach pains which she attributed to acid reflux. But Kit's tougher than nails. At six p.m. she arrived at the Bahthaus doubled up in pain. But that night Angry Pussy was having another big party. And I had promised her and Big Jim that I would be sure to come because they were expecting me to shoot a lot of pictures and video which I'd put on You Tube."

"I was hoping Kit would come around so I gave her some anti acid pills I kept in the bathroom. Terry had promised to go with me to the party, and I wasn't going to disappoint him because he hadn't been out drinking for a long time. Angry Pussy was having a birthday party for a group of guys from Finland whose friend had set the whole thing up with her. Kit's stomach was hurting her a lot by the time Terry and I had planned to go to the party, so I put her to bed and promised her I'd be home by one a.m."

"What happened then?"

"Those Finns were big drinkers and real party animals. They really hit if off with Terry. And all of us got drunker than snot together. Angry Pussy had a couple of free lancers from another bar come in to do shows, and I started to show them how to pole dance. I even got Terry up with those two free lancers[29] trying to dance. I don't know how much Terry and I drank with the Finns, but later Terry said he must have had over twenty mixed drinks. So I was completely toasted by the time I got back to my condo. I must have passed out immediately right next to Kit who was already asleep. And then at about three a.m. she woke me up."

"Is that when you took her to the hospital?"

"Yes. I must have still been drunk at three a.m. But I quickly came to my senses when Kit told me she needed to go to the hospital. I honestly didn't know where to take her. I knew that taking her to the emergency room at the Si Racha Hospital was out of the question because it would take me over half an hour to get there and I was still drunk on my ass. I had heard only bad things about the Banglamung public hospital. Because I could get her to Bangkok Pattaya Hospital in five minutes I decided to take her there thinking her condition was not all that serious.

But I could get her to Bangkok Pattaya Hospital in just five minutes."

"You should have just taken her to the nearest motorcycle taxi driver and let her fend for herself," Wolfgang replied while taking a long drag off his cigarette.

"I couldn't do that to her. And I don't even remember how she managed to get on my motorbike considering all the pain she

---

259

must have been going through. But when I got her to the emergency room, they started to work on her right away. They gave her a shot of antibiotics, and then they took her somewhere and brought her back while I sat there and waited. There was this really young guy hanging around the emergency room, who I figured to be the boyfriend of one of the nurses. The nurses had her partitioned off behind these curtains so the rest of the emergency room patients couldn't see her being undressed or anything else they were doing to her. After what seemed an eternity to me, the young guy motioned for me to go with him into the partitioned area where the nurses had Kit lying on a narrow hospital bed. Turns out that the young guy is a surgeon. He tells me right away that Kit's suffering from a burst appendix and that she will die if he doesn't operate on her right away.

"Wolgang, You can't begin to understand my dilemma so I'm going to describe my exact conversation with the doctor."

"How do you know she has a ruptured appendix?" I asked the young doctor.

"They just did a cat scan on her. Her appendix has ruptured and she's got a lot of infection inside her. We have her on an IV right now which is injecting some pretty powerful antibiotic into her. The choice is yours. I want to operate on her at eight a.m. Does she have insurance?"

"No, she doesn't."

"You will have to give the hospital cash or credit card," the doctor replied.

"I don't have that much cash so it will have to be on my credit card."

"The hospital needs 200000 baht for me to operate on her. It'll cost more than that but I will try to keep your costs as low as I can considering she doesn't have insurance."

"I didn't have to think twice about it, Wolfgang. For one thing she was the love of my life. And even if she hadn't been, if I didn't pay the money and she would end up dying because I hadn't, I would never be able to forgive myself as long as I live."

At the Bangkok Pattaya Hospital

"There was no point to my staying the rest of the night at the hospital. Kit would be unconscious anyway. And the nurses would be sedating her early in the morning to get her ready for the operation. So I drove my motorbike back to my condo where I managed to get several hours of sleep before hastening back to the hospital, Dick."

"Where was she when you got to the hospital?"

"Either still on the operating table or just starting recovery."

"And how did you spend your time while you were waiting for her to get back into her hospital room?"

"I went down to the lobby and got a large cup of Starbucks coffee and something to eat. I'm wondering if Kit's going to die from all the infection she has from a burst appendix. I've got my phone with me and I'm reading everything I can about ruptured appendixes, and how dangerous it is to have your appendix actually rupture. From what I'm reading there's a lot of toxic bacteria that builds up in the appendix when it starts getting close to rupturing. And this leads to sepsis.

"I'm no doctor, Dick. But normally when a surgeon removes an appendix, he wants to keep the hole as small as possible. So he tries to perform some kind of Microscopic surgery. I forget what they call it. This way the scar is kept as small as possible. And the recovery time from the appendectomy is considerably reduced. The problem is when the appendix actually ruptures the infection is no longer confined to the appendix. It spreads all over other vital organs. In such cases the surgeon's objective is to make a large incision so that all the pus and infection can be gotten out as soon as possible."

"So what did the surgeon do to Kit? Did he make a small or large incision?"

"I didn't know until I actually saw it and that wasn't until after one p.m. She has a 6 inch cavity in her abdomen. Which the doctor didn't sew up until five days after the operation. He just left that huge wound wide open. And the nurses put some gauze into that cavity which they would change two or three times a day. The idea was to let all the pus inside of her wound seep out as fast as possible."

"So how did it go between you and Kit while you were with her in the hospital?"

"I was with her day and night for four days in the hospital. Bangkok Pattaya Hospital has these beautiful large hospital rooms that are up to the standards of a five star hotel. Each room has a little couch that a guest can transform into a bed. There's a microwave in each room and a coffee maker. There's an ample sized closet. I made my own coffee every morning. Then I would head down to Starbucks for breakfast or lunch, or to Au Bonne Pain, which has the best club sandwiches in Pattaya. At first the nurses would make Kit eat this bland hospital food they kept bringing to her. But later on as she started getting stronger, she would go with me down to Au Bonne Pain or Starbucks in a wheel chair."

"I'll bet that was a big pain in the ass, Fast Eddy."

"No, not at all. Because Kit's not a big complainer. She's a pretty brave little girl. They had this IV stand next to her hospital bed. At first she'd be getting glucose in her veins through an IV. She had another needle in her arm which was constantly transmitting high powered antibiotics into her veins. Every time she had to go to the toilet the nurses would have to help her go to the toilet and they'd carry that IV stand in for her. But I would oftentimes take her to the toilet and guide her inside by taking her arm. She would be leaning against me as we guided the IV stand down the floor and into the toilet. I was only too happy to be doing all that for her."

"Anyone come visit her?"

"No. Not one of her so-called friends came in to see her. But Terry came to visit her, bringing with him his new Thai girlfriend, Pineapple. Terry's main problem with his old girlfriend, Mut, is she kept asking him for too much money. After buying her a house in the village he soon found out that this wasn't enough. By the time she asked him to set her up with her second bar he'd had enough and sent her packing. Finding her replacement took just one night. Which was the first night he came into the Angry Pussy Bar where he met one of Angry Pussy's bar girls, and got drunk on his ass. When Angry Pussy had to call a taxi for him, the bar girl went with him back to his condo. And they've been together ever since that night. So when Kit was in the hospital for appendicitis, Terry and Pineapple came into her hospital room to visit her. Terry had bought Kit a nice vase of flowers which he put on a table beneath the television set."

"What did you and Kit do when she finally got out of the hospital?"

"I took her straight back to my condo where she stayed with me for the next two weeks. It takes at least two or three months to recover from an operation such as hers. Unfortunately I had a huge emergency in the U.S. with our family business which I share with my sisters. There was no way I could avoid having to deal with it. But I almost did on account of Kit. I booked a flight, and then I canceled it because I knew I needed more time with her. Finally, I had to get on a plane so I asked Kit to stay in my condo until I could return from the U.S. in about eleven days. I even had a key made up for her which I left with the condo office girls. But Kit told me, "I will only stay with you if you stay here with me."

"The first day I got her back to my condo from the hospital Kit is weighing only 29.9 kilos, when she's already too skinny at her normal 35 kilos. My main goal is to get her weight up to 33 kilos, and then 35. Perhaps more, but for me, she's a one of a kind at 35 kilos. Her lower legs are pixel thin, but at 35, her thighs are very firm, tapered and on the verge of actually being muscular. Her arms are very slender but she's always had very thin arms as long as I've known her."

"But at 30 kilos, she's just 66 pounds. She's not strong enough to fend off pneumonia or other diseases that normally wouldn't be fatal but might be for her in her weakened condition. I have a scale in my master bedroom where she sleeps just outside the main bathroom, so I weigh her once or twice each day. And mark down the date, time and her weight on a sheet of paper. I'm taking her to two restaurants a day in order to get her weight back.

"When you went to the U.S. for 11 days, did Kit stay alone at your condo?"

"No. And that's why I nearly didn't go to the U.S. and canceled my original flight. With my paying Kit 20000 baht a month I figured she was a big money maker for the girls living around her who would always be trying to borrow money from her which they would never pay back. And that shitty Thai boyfriend of hers.

That cancerous little reptile. I was sure he hadn't been getting any money from Kit for a while, and now I figured he will be back as soon as she sets her little foot back in South Pattaya.

Kit has to get injections Again

"Fast Eddy, my hand hurts again. I need to go hospital."

"When?"

"Can we go Tomorrow?"

"Okay. Meet me at my condo at five a.m."

Fast Eddy knew he'd be taking her back to the hospital at Si Racha. For the rest of her life. But he hadn't been figuring that her next day of reckoning would come right on the heels of her nearly dying from a burst appendix.

This time Kit had to spend three days at the hospital where Fast Eddy visited her every day. Surprisingly, Kit's injections were limited to her left hand.

Ko Larn Island

"Has Kit moved in with you, yet?" Angry Pussy asked Fast Eddy.

"No. But she should."

"Yes. She really should," Angry Pussy replied. "She's never going to ever meet someone like you. So how's she doing?"

"She's running short of money. I haven't paid her since I went to the U.S. I was paying her when she was in the hospital and for about a week or ten days while she was staying with me. When I had to go to the United States, I wanted her to stay at my condo. She said she would but only if I was staying with her. So the morning I left for the airport I put her on a motorbike taxi to her room."

"Why weren't you paying her when you were in the U.S.?"

"Because she had decided to stay with some very bad people. I think she'd be dead if she hadn't stayed all night with me when you had that birthday party for the Finns. And there's no way I think those people living with her would have gotten her to a hospital on time. She nearly lost her left arm because no one was looking out for her when she needed those injections. If she had stayed at my condo while I was in the U.S. I would have given her money for those eleven days."

"What makes you think she didn't have money, when you came back from the U.S.?"

"Because she started asking me to help her with her room. I didn't know what she meant when she asked me that. She might have meant that she wanted to move in with me. She said she didn't like the people living with her anymore and that she wanted for me to get her another room somewhere near Pattaya Klang. But I told her I would not do it."

Fast Eddy and Angry Pussy were on their fourth beer when Kit started text messaging him. He enjoyed buying drinks for Angry Pussy. Because even though Angry Pussy was about as hard core as a Thai woman could get, she had many years of experience having to deal with Western men. Especially American men due to Dick Fitswell's being American and having been her boss for so long. And most importantly Fast Eddy appreciated the fact that

Angry Pussy had brains, which he considered to be an asset nearly all bar girls sadly don't possess.

"Is that Kit who's messaging you?" Angry Pussy asked.

"Yep. And now she's telling me she wants to move in with me."

"Do it then. Have her move in tonight."

"Damn good idea, Angry Pussy. I'm typing a message to her right now, "Come now. Stay with me."

Angry pussy watched him conversing with Kit as she sipped her glass of Singha, giving him a few minutes before inquiring, "What did she say, Fast Eddy?"

"She says she can't come tonight because she's still busy packing all her things, and she has even posted a picture of all these bags and boxes on her floor."

"Tell her to hire a real taxi. Have her get a car."

"I already did, but she keeps saying she's doesn't have everything ready yet. She's also telling me that she wants to sneak out when no one's watching."

When three days went by and Kit had still not moved in with him, Fast Eddy decided to pull out his ace of spades. Which was the uncertainty that had to be having a huge effect on Kit. "I'm going to put Little Miss Kit right over the edge," he finally decided. Then he went online and made a reservation at the Xanadu Resort on Koh Larn Island. He reserved his room for November 18 after deciding he'd stay another night or two if necessary, which he could do once he arrived on Koh Larn when he could feel out the situation.

"He started text messaging Kit at 18:00 on November 17."

"How long you stay on Koh Larn?" Kit asked as soon as he dropped the bad news on her. Which was that she could not really count on him to bend to her time table.

"I don't know?" he replied. "I stay one night. Maybe two nights or three."

There was no reply. Until 10 p.m.

"Can I come with you?" Kit finally responded.

"Sure you can. But we go early. In the morning."

"What time?"

"We leave my condo at 8:30 in the morning. We must have time to take my motorbike and park it for the night, and then we take the ferry to Koh Larn."

"Okay," she typed back to him. "I not sleep tonight so I very tired tomorrow."

Fast Eddy was very surprised when Kit drove a small motorbike to the Bahthaus with another girl following her on a second motorbike

"My motorbike," Kit replied when he asked her what she was up to. "This friend me. She drive her motorbike home. I stay with you now."

The sudden turn of events surprised him. Kit had only brought with her a small bag of clothing and other essentials. But bringing her motorbike to his condo showed him for the first time in nearly three years that she was finally doing what he had been wanting her to do—for, it seems nearly forever. Kit's motorbike was a small Honda Wave with a manual transmission. But whereas most Honda Waves have 100 cc. or 125 cc. engines the motor on Kit's motorbike seemed too small to even be a 100. Fast Eddie noticed that the small motorbike had obviously been repainted. While he also noticed that the motorbike had no license plate on it.

"Who's your friend?" Fast Eddy asked Kit.

"Her name, Knot."

"Sawadee kap, Knot. You young lady, Knot. How old are you?" he finally asked the girl.

"She only sixteen," Kit replied. She cannot work bar. But she friend me."

By this time Fast Eddy had found a parking place for Kit's motorbike, and was wheeling it between two motorcycles belonging to other residents when Danny suddenly appeared in

267

the motorbike parking area.

"Sawadhi Kap, Kit," said Danny as he eyeballed Kit's young friend. "Who is this lady with you?"

"Her name Knot," Kit replied (while pronouncing her friend's name as Nut).

"Nut very pretty lady, Kit. How old is she?"

"Nut only 16."

"Fast Eddy. Be sure to get Nut's phone number. Perhaps you and Kit, Nut and me, we can all go over to have dinner together at Surf and Turf," said Danny who was obviously intending to boom boom Nut as soon as possible.

*****

"So how did you and Kit enjoy Koh Larn?" Danny asked Fast Eddy after Kit and Fast Eddy returned to the Bahthaus.

"Let me put it this way, Danny. Kit stayed awake all of six hours once we arrived at Koh Larn. I rented a motorbike at the end of the main pier and took Kit up and down the big hill to our hotel. Where she slept from noon until six in the evening. I spent several hours swimming and walking up and down Samae Beach. Got bored, got into bed with her and crashed until dinner time. We had a great dinner at Xanadu's restaurant with a spectacular view of the beach. Eventually I fell asleep while Kit played games on her phone. And that was about it."

Kit Gets a Thai Driver's License

"Dick, there's three things I feel Kit needs. First is her health. Although she came out of the hospital weighing only 30 kilos, after several weeks she was still at 32 kilograms. I am disappointed by her lack of progress. I've been waking her up pretty early in the mornings so she would be sure to have breakfast. And paying far too much in restaurants at night. But I'm willing to pay a lot more for food than I normally would so long as she gets better. The second thing I'm hoping for is that she will view my condo more as her primary home, and eventually her only home. I think the more time she spends there and the more she gets used to the condo layout, gets better acquainted with the condo staff, and with the Seven Elevens and Family Marts nearby, the more comfortable she's going to get. And the third thing is I want to increase her self esteem. And to want her to recognize that she is much more than the average bar girl and the kind of people most bar girls hang out with."

"I disagree with you there," Dick Fitswell replied. There's the old saying that "you can take the woman out of the bar, but you can't take the bar out of the woman."

"I agree with you, Dick. But my friend, Madonna, in the U.S. was a hardened prostitute. She wasn't even a stripper dressing like a stripper or to be more precise undressing like a stripper. She made her money at the Chameleon Club where the girls never wore g strings and she wore a lot of clothes compared to the strippers at the topless clubs. She made her money by fucking guys, and if she didn't fuck a guy she didn't make any money. Not by lap dances because they didn't even do lap dances at Chameleon. And not off drinks either because Chameleon wasn't charging much for drinks the way the other clubs in the area were doing. Madonna had a heart. And later when she married Jerry, she became a great housewife who prided herself on taking good care of the house and her man."

"But she was American," Dick pointed out, "which makes all the difference in the world."

"How's that, Dick?"

"I can't speak for all Thais, but being a bar owner I sure as hell can say a lot against bar girls, their families, and the friends they keep around them. They are very poorly educated. The average bar girl has only six years of schooling behind her. Thais of the poorer classes are brain washed by the upper classes into thinking their country is the number one country in the world."

"But we know differently, don't we Dick?"

"Yes. Americans are much less well educated than they used to be. Their average IQ used to be 100. Now it's 98, whereas the IQ of the average Englishman is 100, and it's even higher for Koreans, Japanese, Chinese from Singapore and so on. But the IQ of the average Thai is only 92. And this counts the really smart Thais and the one's who have a lot of money. I've heard that the average bar girl only has an IQ of 80. Yet these girls think they are smarter than us. And most of them prefer having Thai boyfriends who are constantly trying to brainwash them into thinking they are much smarter than their customers."

"I agree about that, for the most part."

"But there's even more. Most of these bar girls come from Issan, which as you know is primarily rural. They are village girls so to speak. They are used to living in houses that are hardly more than huts with chickens crawling around underneath the floors. And when they come to places like Pattaya and Bangkok, they are already acclimated to living in pretty primitive conditions. They are comfortable sleeping four or five people in a room together, and huddling around on the floor eating together. What I'm trying to tell you is they are living like rats, and they prefer to keep living like rats. You can take them out of the bar, and have them stay with you in your nice air-conditioned condo. And most of them will because you are paying them a lot of money to stay with you. But they would much prefer living with three or four other Thais sleeping on the floor in a hot room that is cooled only by a fan."

"Like rats," Fast Eddy nearly shouted back at Dick Fitswell. "I like it. Rats."

"They are all rats," Fitswell replied while tapping his forehead for emphasis. "Or at least all of them we are likely to be meeting. And don't ever forget it. They prefer living in Rat Dom with all the other rats. Since you are not Thai and not a rat, they will always feel uncomfortable with you. While feeling at ease with all the other rats who speak the same language and have the same culture."

"I think, I hope Kit is different, though. She's not an Issan girl for one thing. She's a northern girl from Prae where the schools are better in general than they are in most other places in Thailand. And she speaks in a much softer clearer voice than most of these Issan bar girls. And I notice a lot of things that put her well ahead of the rest of the pack."

"As, for instance."

"For one thing she has a much greater attention span than most of the other girls . And she's much more alert than these other girls. For example, when I"m taking pictures of her with a professional camera she's always trying to pick it up and play with it. She's also so much quicker at coming up with new things to do such as suggesting a restaurant I've never been to before. Or going to a market I never knew existed. And she moves and thinks so much faster than most bar girls I've been around."

"So you are actually thinking that she will change and want to give up her rat like ways?"

"I am hoping she will, Dick. Which is why I've been constantly training her to wear a motorbike helmet which I can practically guarantee you most of her friends are not doing. And why I've gotten her a passport, which once again most of her friends don't have because they can never even contemplate going anywhere outside Thailand. Next thing I want to do is to help her get a Thai driving license."

"Which most of her friends don't have," Dick Fitswell replied.

"Exactly. I am hoping that with the passage of time she will see herself as three steps above most of her peers. She obeys the traffic rules which most of her peers don't. And you know what I mean. Most of these bar people routinely run red slights, don't wear helmets, and drive the wrong way against the flow of traffic. They really are a bunch of ignorant imbeciles, and hopefully I want Kit to realize down the road that she's not at all like them. So if she gets a Thai driving license she will start to think that she's superior to all these idiots she has living all around her. She already drives a motorbike very well, but when she finally learns in driving school the driving rules and what happens when you don't follow them she will hopefully start thinking less and less of herself as a bar girl."

*****

271

"Did Kit ever get her Thai motorbike driver's license, Fast Eddy?"

"Yes, we got it done, Dick. It took Khun Toe and me four days of running her back and forth to driving school, but now she's got it."

Kit Disappears Again

"Dick, everything was going great with Kit. She had brought her motorbike to my condo, then her clothes. After she started feeling better, she started cleaning. And much later, when it was too late for both of us, I found out that she had even started to organize my household. All of which goes to show that Kit had been planning on staying for the long haul. I had helped her get her passport, and her Thai drivers license, and just before she left me, I even got her a health insurance policy with Aetna."

"Now why in the hell would you do that, Fast Eddy"

"For one thing her appendix operation wound up costing me three-hundred-thousand baht which is about $9000 U.S. I had thought about getting her health insurance months before because I knew she would be coming to me for anything that required medical care. I had taken care of her injections for the tumor in her arm and hand, not once but twice. And had even gotten her tooth pulled when it went to hell on her. But I never figured on having to pay a $9000 hospital bill although I was still planning on paying for her future injections.. While I did figure on paying for even more injections for her. Which is a preexisting illness for her and would not be covered on any hospital policy I might buy. But wow, that sudden appendicitis hitting her was a real eye opener. So I took her to Aetna as soon as I could."

"And got suckered into buying her health insurance," Harry piped up suddenly as he emerged from his usual beer stupor.

"Not suckered at all. You guys just don't get it," Fast Eddy replied condescendingly."

"Oh Yeah, well just tell everyone here how Kit left you."

"There's not too much to tell you guys. The shit hit the fan while Kit's still staying with me, and she's still just 32 kilos and not recovered from her operation. I'm getting her up early in the mornings to make sure she has a good breakfast. And checking her weight every day. But she hates having to wake up. I'm like a mother checking her weight every day and making sure she gets a lot to eat. Then she gets her Thai driving license, and all of a sudden she's wanting to go out with a friend who went with us to get a driving license. She went out drinking that night with the friend who had another friend who had come down from Bangkok.

273

Kit never came home that night.

The next morning Kit was still gone. But at nine a.m. she was knocking on my door. When I asked her what happened, she said she had gotten very drunk and passed out on another Thai woman's floor. I tell her she's lying again as usual. She tells me in a little voice, "I haven't done anything wrong." Then she disappears down to Terry's condo to talk with Pineapple."

"So you locked her out of your condo, then," said Harry. Well good for you, Fast Eddy."

"Please be quiet for once, Harry. I want to hear Fast Eddy's story, not yours. Please go on, Fast Eddy. So what did Kit think about your changing the locks on her?" Dick Fitswell asked.

"I didn't think Khun Toe was working that day so I went to my favorite locksmith and got him to come to my condo and change the locks while Kit was still downstairs talking with Terry and Pineapple."

"You are not going to believe what Kit does next, Dick."

"Let's have Fast Eddy tell us in his own words, Harry."

"Alight then. I am not wanting Khun Toe to be with me while we are changing the locks. I've got the locksmith with me. I'm planning on showing Kit as soon as she comes back to my condo that she will no longer have a key to come and go as she pleases. So I'm not planning on having Toe know anything about my changing the locks. But all of a sudden Toe's at my door, and he's wondering what's going on. So I let him in my condo and we are both watching the locksmith change the lock. The locksmith finishes the job in a few minutes. After Khun Toe and the locksmith leave, Kit comes back from Terry's condo. Maybe I made a big mistake. But I showed her that I've had a new lock put on the door, and then to rub it in, I show her a picture of Toe watching the locksmith changing the lock."

"Why are you calling that a big mistake? I just don't get it," Dick Fitswell replied.

"Because Kit was by this time seeing Toe as a friend. Now I might be wrong, but as soon as she knows I got Toe involved changing the lock, she's no doubt lost a huge amount of face."

"I understand what you are saying," Dick Fitswell replied.

"Fucking whore. They are all fucking whores and they get what they deserve!" exclaimed Harry.

"Please let Fast Eddy finish his story, Harry," an annoyed Dick Fitswell replied.

"From then on, Kit's not acting her usual self," Fast Eddy continued.   She's still with me in the condo for the next few days. But sometimes I see her in bed, and she's crying. I have never seen Kit cry before. She's not crying aloud like a baby though. She's just quietly sobbing to herself in a voice I can hardly hear. But I'm starting to notice something very different about her. She does the laundry, but she doesn't hang her clothes up in her closet. Which is not like her at all. Her clothes are on the closet floor. I even tell Terry that she's planning on making a get away."

"And what did Terry make of that?"

"It doesn't matter now. I turned out to be 100 percent correct. Kit did a runner. She left practically all her clothes in my place and just disappeared.

Back at the Angry Pussy Bar

"I am really starting to like Angry Pussy, Dick. It's too bad you let her leave you to start that Naklua Bar with Big Jim."

I thought it would be the best thing for us, Fast Eddy. We need more followers. I haven't gone up to Naklua to look in on her. So can you tell me in your own words your latest thoughts about her and the new bar?"

"Angry Pussy has the knack very few bar managers have of taking an interest in her customers and telling them what they want to hear, Dick."

"Can you give me an example of how she's accomplishing that, Fast Eddy?"

"For instance, the last time I went to Angry Pussy's, Angry Pussy asked me, "You hear from Kit?""

"No. I have no idea what she's doing, I told her."

"She really needs you, Angry Pussy replied. You do everything for her. She is very lucky to have you."

"Tell her that, Angry Pussy," I remember telling her. Or something on that order."

"She will be back. It's just a matter of time," Big Jim added to offer his two cents worth as he was knocking back a few gin and tonics with Angry Pussy and me.

"She will be back, Angry Pussy replied. "I agree with Big Jim here. Because Kit knows that you can't stop helping her. Whenever she gets in a bad way, she knows you will want to get back with her. I think she put a spell on you, Fast Eddy. I never see you this way with any other lady."

"Angry Pussy was too busy keeping track of her other customers and the constant interruptions from her bar girls to even notice my sudden preoccupation with my phone. While Big Jim kept flirting with one bar girl after the other as they kept coming up to their table to keep him and Angry Pussy informed about the bar's customers."

"Hi Fast Eddy, how are you?" Kit starts messaging me.

"I am okay," I messaged Kit back.

"I so sorry for everything," Kit replied.

"Why you sorry? For what?" I ask Kit. While thinking, "Is Kit sorry she's no longer getting any more money from me, or is she truly sorry that she's no longer living with me?"

"Where are you?".

"At Angry Pussy Bar."

"Do you have lady?" she asks me.

"No have lady."

"I want come Angry Pussy Bar."

"Where are you?"

"On Soi 6."

"You work in Soi 6 bar now?"

"No. I only drink with friends. You want me?"

"I do. But I am not sure."

"Can I come?"

"Before I can reply, she is suddenly calling me on line. However, the noise in the bar does not allow me to hear a single word. But I can see her clearly enough because her call is a line video call."

"Without saying a word to anyone I rush into the toilet to listen to Kit speaking in that melodic voice of hers that I had always found so refreshingly different from the annoying voices of too many Issan girls. But even in the toilet I still can't hear her over the music and loud voices in the bar."

"I finally give up and go back to the table. Angry Pussy and Big Jim don't even seem to notice that I had been gone for a full ten minutes. But by the time I finish my beer, Kit starts video conferencing with me again."

"Want me to come?" she asks me.

"But I'm thinking she wants to bring some lesbo girlfriend of hers to Angry Pussy's so they can sponge off me. So I decide to head right down to Soi 6 and look for her."

"Did you find her?"

"No, I didn't, Dick. So I went to Sex in the City Bar where I had become friends with the manager. A guy named Kevin, who managed the Nature bar for a while. Kevin's Malaysian Chinese, and you don't know how much I dislike most Chinese. But Kevin speaks English almost as well as we do, and he's a free thinker. I figure I can have Kit meet me at Sex in the City so I start messaging her from there. But there's no reply, so I decide to have a few beers. When I get home, I discover that Kit's tried to call me three more times but for some reason I don't discover this until I get back to my condo."

"So what did you make of that, Fast Eddy?"

"I really think she was really wanting to get back together with me. But when I try to call her back at Midnight, she never calls me back."

Three friends Turn up Suddenly

"What's new in your life, Wolfgang asked Fast Eddy at the Centara Fitness Center? I haven't seen you at Big Dicks lately. Are you playing house with Little Miss Kit?

"I haven't heard from Kit for quite awhile. Haven't been to Big Dicks that much either, although I had been going to Soi 6 even more often. Like every other night. I've had two good friends suddenly turn up."

"So now you are using them as an excuse to go out even more often?"

"Yes. First, Canada John suddenly calls me that he's just ten minutes from the Bahthaus. Which is just like Canada John. He lives in China near Hong Kong now and he's doing all sorts of engineering projects for the Chinese. He makes a lot of money on his projects but he's so busy that he oftentimes won't even spend the time emailing me that he's coming back to Pattaya. So I have little or no warning at all."

"Who's your second friend?"

"That's Leon. The last time I saw Leon was about four years ago. He met me online and then he asked me to meet up with him in Pattaya. I recommended the Lek Villa Hotel and he followed my advice by booking a room there. He had a good friend who lived down the street from him. So his friend came with him. His friend's a homosexual, but I mean who cares. Mike's a great guy. So when Leon and I would have dinner together at Queen Victoria on Soi 6, Mike would often join us, then the three of us would hit a couple bars together. But Mike wouldn't stay with us for long. Like I said, he's a homosexual so he was always going to Boys Town to meet homosexual Thai men."

"Did Mike like the lady boys, Fast Eddy? Because there's loads of them on Soi 6."

"No. He didn't like lady boys at all. Anymore than he liked women."

"So you and Leon spent a lot time together on Soi 6?"

"You bet your ass we did, Dick. We hit a few go-go bars on

Walking Street. We also spent a lot of time at the bars on Drinking Street."

"So you and Leon really hit it off."

"That we did. Leon's so easy going. We might go to a Soi 6 bar and when I'd hook up with a woman I liked chances are he'd just run off and find another Soi 6 bar. Then eventually we'd wind up together later on."

"Why did Leon take four years before deciding to finally come back to Pattaya?"

"The year after Leon and I got together in Pattaya, his friend Mike came, but he came without Leon. I had dinner with Mike a couple of times and he told me Leon had gotten married to an American woman. But it so turns out Mike was only joking with me. Maybe Leon was too busy working in the U.S. or maybe he simply didn't have enough money, but whatever the reason I suddenly found out he was back in Pattaya. I came back to my condo one night and there was a note the security guard had put under my door. Leon had already checked into Lek Villa, and on this note he had put down his room number and telephone number."

Richard Pump Up

Leon was smoking a cigarette on his balcony at Lek Villa when he heard Fast Eddy knocking on his door."

"Come in, Fast Eddy. It's so good to see you again."

Although Leon was from North Dakota, he was much more like a Southern country boy than a Northerner living in the city. A big man Just over six feet, Leon was slightly overweight. Leon is the epitome of the country boy who never takes anything too seriously. Three years ago Leon had gone into a Soi 6 bar while Fast Eddy was banging one of his whores in another bar. When Fast Eddy joined Leon at the bar Leon was visiting, he found that all the bar girls were lady boys. Which didn't seem to faze Leon one bit. When Fast Eddy mentioned to Leon and the lady boy sitting with Leon that he had once had sex with a lady boy, Leon's face broke out into a huge smile.

"You never told me you had sex with a lady boy before, Fast Eddy," said Leon.

"It was purely an accident," Fast Eddy replied. The lady boy was damned good looking. And pretty smart too. But I just didn't suddenly run into this lady boy out of the blue. An American guy renting a condo near me really liked the lady boy. Back then my girlfriend was still living with me. And we kept running into Floyd at all these restaurants with his lady boy lover. And I'm telling you this lady boy was much better looking than over 90 percent of all the bar girls I had ever met. Now this lady boy was so presentable that I wouldn't have minded having her on my arm. I could have taken her everywhere especially after that time some of my friends and I were having a few with Floyd and the lady boy in his condo."

"Sounds interesting," Leon replied. "So what happened?"

"My girlfriend was with us in Floyd's condo, and so were several of my American friends. So while my girlfriend was out on Floyd's balcony with my American friends, Floyd's lady boy lover asked me to talk with her in Floyd's living room. It turns out both Floyd and his lady boy knew that I had been successful in getting my girlfriend a visa to the U.S. And now the lady boy starts asking me all kinds of questions about how she can get a visa to the United States. I'm, of course thinking the lady boy is deeply in love with Floyd. So I start giving her ideas on how she and Floyd can get her a visa to the U.S. I'm really impressed with the lady boy's intelligence and her good English skills. But of even greater interest to me is the lady boy has had an operation and had her dick removed. We talked a lot about that also."

"Did you believe the lady boy actually had her penis removed?" Leon asked.

"Yes. Absolutely. Because Floyd had also been telling me that his lady boy lover had a man-made vagina. Thing was Leon, I had never associated the lady boy with Soi 6. But I soon found Floyd hanging out at a Soi 6 bar with his Emmy. Then every so often I'd run into Emmy hanging out at that Soi 6 bar by herself. Eventually after seeing Emmy standing in front of the bar, I decided to have a drink with her figuring she'd be about the best company I'd find on Soi 6 that night."

"Oh no. I can smell this one coming," Leon replied.

"I was a little drunk, Leon. So we went into the bar together and ensconced ourselves in a booth where we started drinking tequilas. Now, as I have mentioned Emmy spoke very good English, so she was excellent company for me. So when she started to rub my dick, I started thinking, "Why not. This is probably the only chance I will have in my entire life to bang an artificial pussy."

"You didn't, did you?"

"Well yeah I did. I told Emmy not to tell Floyd. And when Emmy swore she wouldn't, I took her upstairs."

"What was it like, Fast Eddy?"

"It was good, Leon. Emmy had a great body. Better than most Thai women have and she performed great oral sex on me. But . . . and you are not going to believe this. As soon as Emmy undressed, I found out that everyone had been lying to me. Because Emmy had a dick. I was mortified at first. Even Floyd had been lying, and not only to me but to everyone. But I was too drunk to know better, so we had sex together. Which would have been okay. I mean who would have known, but the next day Floyd asked me on the telephone, "Did you have sex with Emmy?" I lied to Floyd, of course, but it all just goes to show that you can't trust any bar girl or lady boy to keep their mouths shut

282

about anything."

"What a story!" the lady boy sitting with Leon and Fast Eddy cried out. That is wonderful story. Look at me now. I not same Emmy. I have no dick. I have pussy."

In that Southern drawl of his, Leon asked the lady boy, "If you really got a pussy, show it to me."

Fast Eddy couldn't believe his eyes when the Lady boy pulled off her shorts, and sure enough, the lady boy had a vagina where her penis used to be."

Leon contemplated the lady boy's pussy for a few seconds before finally commenting, "Well, I have never fucked a lady boy's pussy before. Let's go upstairs right now."

But that was four years ago, and here was Leon again, who looked virtually the same as Fast Eddy remembered him.

"Leon, did you come alone or have you brought Mike along with you?"

"Mike's back in the U.S., but fortunately or unfortunately I brought another neighbor with me."

"What do you mean unfortunately?"

"Well, he doesn't want to do anything and he can hardly walk very far."

"I have the perfect solution for him. And that's Soi 6."

"I think taking Richard down to Soi 6 will scare him to death."

When Fast Eddy suggested to Richard that he get a motorbike taxi near Lek Villa, Richard replied, "I ain't getting on one of them small motorbikes."

"Well, it's too far for you to walk," Leon told his neighbor. Tell you what. I'll take a motorbike taxi and you get on Fast Eddy's motorbike with him. We will follow each other out to Soi 6."

"I'm not getting on any damn motorbike," Richard replied. "You have to Richard. You have no choice. Now get on that motorbike behind Fast Eddy."

At only about five foot six, Richard was just over the height of the average American woman. But as he struggled to get on Fast Eddy's motorbike, Fast Eddy felt Richard's full 175 pounds perched behind him.

"Okay, Richard. I am taking us down the back way so don't you get too scared on me when you think I'm driving too fast."

Richard started behaving just like a little old lady when Fast Eddy accelerated out of the Lek Villa parking lot. Scared shitless, he put his arms around Fast Eddy's waist and hung on for dear life. By the time they got to Soi 6, Richard was completely terrified.

"First stop's Nature Bar, Richard. That's where Leon is meeting us."

But when Leon failed to show up, Fast Eddy walked down to Slice Pizza where he found Leon already ordering two slices of pizza.

Each slice cost only 75 baht. Fast Eddy had long ago discovered that just one slice was enough to hold him over for much of the evening and that two slices were actually more than enough. So he ordered two slices, from two different styles of pizza. One was for Richard and one was for himself.

By the time they were on their third beer at the Nature Bar, Fast Eddy decided it was time to try another place...a place where he could get his two friends laid.

"Richard, since you have never been to Soi 6 before, I'm going to give you the lay of the land. Then Fast Eddy added, "Just consider me your tour guide so do exactly what I tell you to do. First off most bars on Soi 6 have short time rooms upstairs. You pay the bar a bar fine, but here on Soi 6 the bar fine is just for the cost of the room rental. The bar fine is typically 300 to 400 baht. After that it's strictly between you and the girl what you will wind up paying her for sex in the room upstairs. Now a lot of the girls might ask you for one-thousand-two-hundred or as much as one-thousand-five-hundred baht, but Richard, never pay any of these girls even one baht more than the going rate, which is one-thousand baht."

"I got a problem, Fast Eddy."

"What's that Richard?"

"I have really big problems trying to get it up."

"Do you have anything physically wrong with you?"

"No, other than my not being able to walk worth a shit. Anyway, I need to pump my penis up in order to get an erection."

"Why is that, Richard?"

"I don't know. It's just that I've got like a flat tire until I pump the tire up. Then I want to fuck the girl for a half hour to one hour. Either that or get a blow job."

"Okay. That means we are going to Smoke and Kisses. I got a very special lady friend there, who will make sure that you are well treated, Richard."

Ning was in her usual position sitting just outside Smoke and Kisses where she could get a clear view of all the men walking past her on Soi 6. When Fast Eddy brought his two friends into the bar, Ning was obviously very pleased that he had brought a couple friends into her bar.

After getting the men their beers, Ning sat in the booth next to Fast Eddy.

"What kind of lady do you want?" she asked Richard and Leon."

"Ning, Leon here knows pretty much what he wants and what he doesn't want while Richard here, has never been on Soi 6 before and this is his first trip to Thailand."

Turning to face Richard, Ning tells him, "Richard, you just tell me what lady you want and I will bring her over to you."

Sensing his new friend's shyness, Fast Eddy tells Ning Richard's predicament. "Uhh Ning, maybe Richard doesn't want me to tell you this, but I think I should. Richard has big problem getting his dick big. He uses this peter pump so we will have to find him a girl who will understand his problem and pump his penis up for him."

But none of the bar girls want anything to do with Richard. Except one who's with him for all of three minutes. While Fast Eddy comments to Leon," I wouldn't fuck her with your dogs dick."

285

"Yeah, well I don't want to fuck her now, either, Richard replies. You know what she wants? She wants one-thousand-five-hundred baht, and when I told her I wanted her to blow me for one hour, she started asking two-thousand baht."

"Hell, Richard, About every time I take Ning upstairs, we are up there for an hour or more. Sometimes just talking but she takes her sweet time with the sex part also. I wouldn't give that bitch you were talking to 500 baht,

"Well, I'm not you, Fast Eddy. I gotta have somebody tonight."

"I think we need to go to Angry Pussy bar, Richard."

Leon and Richard's Addiction to Angry Pussy's

"Who are your two friends? Angry Pussy asked Fast Eddy when he arrived with Leon and Richard in tow.

"The Big guy here is Leon. We are good friends from several years ago, Angry Pussy. So Leon has a pretty good idea of what he's doing here in Pattaya. But the little guy, this is Richard. Richard lives on the same street as Leon in America. But Richard doesn't know anything about Thailand."

Trying to size up her two new customers, Angry Pussy turned to Richard and asked: "Have you ever been to Thailand before, Richard?"

"No. Although Leon tells me a lot about Thailand."

"Do you want a lady for company, Richard?" Angry Pussy asked while directing Fast Eddy and his two friends to an unoccupied table.

"Sure I do, Angry Pussy. Do you have someone you can recommend?"

"Just pick out any lady here who's not sitting with a customer, and I will have her come over to get you a drink."

" The one in blue over by the bar will do," replied Richard.

"How about you, Leon? Anyone here that you want to take care of you?"

"Don't worry about me, Angry Pussy. Just make sure someone gets me a gin and tonic," Leon replied.

"Da Da. Come here," Angry Pussy shouted at the woman in blue.

"I sit with Fast Eddy here. But do not worry. Da Da get all of us drinks. And Fast Eddy, I want to buy you a beer for bringing your friends here."

"Well boys, you aren't going to get this kind of service over on Soi 6 or in the Walking Street go-go's, Fast Eddy told his friends as

Da Da took their drink orders. Lesson number one about these Naklua beer bars is since Naklua is mostly residential with a lot of expats living here full time, the bars are not out to rip you off so much. They want your repeat business. I know guys who keep going back to the same beer bar every night. And Angry Pussy's bar and Cocktail bar next door are the best two beer bars in Naklua."

It took just two beers for Richard to decide that he wanted Da Da to go back to his hotel room with him. So he turned to Fast Eddy for advice.

"I want Da Da to fuck me," Richard said in a loud enough voice for the entire table to hear.

"Richard, I wouldn't use the word fuck around these women if I were you, Fast Eddy replied. Use boom boom instead."

"So what do I do, Fast Eddy? How much should I pay?"

"I don't know. That is up to you and Da Da, but I think she will be very happy with one-thousand baht."

"And the bar fine," Angry Pussy added. "Richard, you give me 400 baht and you can take Da Da out of the bar. Do you want her for all night or do you want her for short time?"

"What's the difference Angry Pussy?"

"Short time is for one or two hours, Richard. And long time is if you want Da Da to spend the whole night with you/"

"I want short time then."

Da Da nodded after exchanging a few words in Thai with Angry Pussy. Showing she agreed to the arrangement. Five minutes later Richard and Dada were leaving the bar together.

"I just hope Richard is able to find our hotel," said Leon to no one in particular. "Why Richard's just hopeless enough to not find his hotel even if it's only across the street from us."

"Da Da knows how to find Lek Villa," Angry Pussy replied.

"Well I hope he doesn't fall down or if he does that Da Da is strong enough to catch him," Leon replied while taking a long drag on his cigarette. And Angry Pussy, I think right about now I should take a lady back to the hotel with me."

"Which lady you want?"

"I want the tall lady over there," Leon replied as he pointed out a bar girl who was almost as tall as a lady boy.
With both Leon and Richard now gone, Fast Eddy was now alone with Angry Pussy, which was not a bad thing. Unlike his two friends Fast Eddy had absolutely no interest in any of the women there. Whereas in Angry Pussy he at least had someone to confide in.

"What about you and Kit?" Angry Pussy asked him.

"I still haven't heard a word from her, and I have no idea where she is."

"Why she not stay with you?"

"I don't know."

"She not going to find many customers anywhere. She is too skinny. Most men will not like her."

"I don't know about that. She is still awfully pretty, Angry Pussy."

"She not so pretty. She should stay with you, Fast Eddy. She never going to find a man same same you."

Two hours after leaving the bar with Da Da, Richard rejoined Angry Pussy and Fast Eddy. Fast Eddy expected Leon to come back to the bar, not Richard. But after bar fining the tall girl, Leon wound up paying her for long time."

"Where's Leon?" Fast Eddy asked Richard.

"He stay at hotel with his whore," Richard replied.

"Well how about you and Da Da? Where is she?"Angry Pussy asked.

"I send her home so that she can get some sleep," Richard replied.

"Good. Because now that she's not here we can talk about her,

Richard. Even if Angry Pussy is all ears now." said Fast Eddy.

"She was okay. She made me cum. And I haven't cum in over a year now."

"Why haven't you?" Angry Pussy asked.

"Because I only fuck whores back in America. And they won't blow me for more than ten minutes. So if I don't come right away, they just give up and then they tell me it's all my fault."

"How long did it take you to cum with Da Da?

"About 45 minutes. Fast Eddy, and finally when I came, she started jerking me off which made me spray my cum all over her face."

"Well done Angry Pussy. I think you have made Richard a very happy customer," said Fast Eddy.

Belle

Finding neither Ning nor the Drug Addict at Smoke and Kisses, Fast Eddy noticed a new woman he had never seen before. Who was incomparably more attractive than all the other girls in the bar. The girl was tall and slender, seeming out of place in a seedy Soi 6 bar. Every once in awhile he had met go-go girls from Walking Street down on Soi 6 but none of them stayed for long. Several times he wanted to kick himself for not taking them upstairs after finding out they were nowhere to be found. He would not make that mistake this time.

"Can I buy you a drink?" he asked the girl.

"Yes. I want Leo."

Which was a very good sign since beers were cheaper than mixed drinks. Even better, it would take a girl much longer to consume a bottle of beer than a ladies drink or shot of tequila, which were more often than not, watered down.

The girl finished her bottle of Leo after he polished off his Heineken. Telling himself that she just might be a keeper, he ordered two more beers and asked her to do a short time.

"Boom boom okay now?" he asked the new girl.

"Yes," the girl replied. "Take beer up."

Upstairs in the short time room the girl was even more than he expected. Her body was long and lean. She never balked when he went down on her. And when he finished he found that she was very tight when he penetrated her, which got him already thinking about spending more time with her in his upcoming visits to Soi 6. "She might even be the perfect fit for me. She's just about perfect."

It didn't take him long to cum, and after he did, she mounted him in the female superior position and started gyrating feverishly on his still erect penis. Until he had to get her to stop. But their beer bottles were still full which they took downstairs with them.

At eleven p.m. after they had four more beers together, she told him she had to go home at 12, which was one hour before the bar's closing time..

"Why must you leave so early?" he asked the girl.

"I live La Chabang," she replied. It very far."

Fast Eddy knew exactly where La Chabang was having passed it many times while taking Kit to the hospital in Si Racha. Since she lived over twenty miles from Soi 6, he figured the girl would take at least half an hour getting home.

"Do you have line?" he asked the girl."

"Yes. I give you," she replied.

Like many bar girls, the girl was very adept at making him her new friend on line, which was far more adept than he would ever be. Taking just a minute, the girl got the code from his phone which she scanned into her telephone

"Now, even if she never comes back to Smoke and Kisses ever again, I can always contact her directly and have her visit me at my condo," he promised himself.

Soapie Soapie Time

"Come to think of it, Fast Eddy, I think Richard and I ought to do a soapie. I haven't had one for years."

"I haven't had one in 12 years, Leon. Does Richard know what a soapie is?"

"I told him what it entails."

"I ain't getting one of those soapies. Sounds like too much trouble for what it's worth," Richard replied.

"This will be fun, Richard. I'm going to see what kind of girls you and Leon will pick out. And you will love a soapie. You pay one-thousand-five-hundred baht, maybe two-thousand or a little more and everything is included. They've got a big window like a fish bowl with these girls behind it. With the girls all wearing numbers. You watch them while having a beer, and believe me, each one of these gals is trying her damnest to get you to choose her."

"Well I don't want no fucking soapie!"

"Oh yes you do," Leon replied. I'm paying for your soapie. Now that is an offer you cannot refuse."

Fast Eddy was torn between wanting to make sure his friends were having a good time and wanting to see Belle as soon as possible. Which would be between six and seven. For one thing he wanted to have a bite to eat, and the closer to six, the better. He could get a slice of pizza or two at Slice Pizza, and take them over to Nature Bar or Smoke and Kisses. And still be able to start drinking with Belle, take her upstairs, and get drunk with her afterwards. So there was no time to waste due to Richard's lack of mobility. If it wasn't for Richard's problems with his hips, Fast Eddy knew that Leon and he could walk briskly to one of the soapies.

"We'd better leave right now because all this is going to take some time," Fast Eddy told his two friends. "And Richard, these are your choices. You can walk half a mile down Second Road to the soapies. And I know you aren't going to want to walk half a mile. Or, you can get a motorbike taxi and meet me on Second Road right at Soi 3. Leon can show you the way if you guys get two motorbike taxis."

"Well I ain't getting on no damn motorbike taxi. Those drivers are crazy."

"Richard, most of them really aren't that bad. And most drive a lot saner than I do. If you can ride with me, you can ride with anybody."

Fast Eddy wasn't quite sure the soapie massage places were right on Soi 3 at Second Road, but he was sure they were close enough. But he chose Soi 3 because he had a favorite massage girl who had recently started working on Soi 3. Unfortunately she wasn't there and the girls told him they didn't think she was working there anymore. By this time, Richard and Leon had arrived on Second Road at the Soi 3 intersection.

"How did the motorbike taxi work out for you, Richard?" Fast Eddy asked as he approached Second Road.

"Not too bad. You are right, Fast Eddy. The driver wasn't half as crazy as you are."

"We are in luck. I can see Sabai Land from here. It's only fifty feet from us," Fast Eddy replied.

A Thai man wearing a suit greeted them at the door and led them to a seating area in front of a long glass window where the soapie girls sat. Where each girl was watching and hoping that one of Sabai Land's customers would choose her. Much more than a waiter, the Thai man was the principal person in charge who could also serve as the bouncer if need be. The customers seating area was composed of roughly thirty chairs three rows deep. In the back two rows Fast Eddy saw small groups of Asian men in the shadows, who were likely to be Chinese, Japanese or Korean men.

"Let's take our seats in the front row," Fast Eddy announced to his two friends. "That way the girls can get a good look at us handsome men."

The Maitre d took a seat to Fast Eddy's right while Richard and Leon sat to Fast Eddy's left. Fast Eddy counted close to sixty girls sitting behind the glass window although a small group of girls sat way off to their left outside the glass partition. Fast Eddy noticed that the girls sitting behind the glass window were separated into two groups.

"Why are the girls separated into three groups? Richard asked Fast Eddy.

"Hell if I know. I haven't been to Sabai Land for over 12 years, Richard. Why don't you ask the Maitre D?"

"Will you ask him for me, Fast Eddy?"

Which made sense seeing that Fast Eddy was sitting over three feet from the maitre d. Nevertheless, Fast Eddy was planning on having nothing to do with any of the girls even if Richard and Leon would soon be taking two girls upstairs.

 Fast Eddy motioned to the maitre d and asked, Pu Ying som. Tinai. Som som," which was perfectly shitty Thai which Fast Eddy thought the Maitre di would have no clue about what he was asking. But which roughly meant, "Ladies three over there."

"Ladies. Three kinds the Maitre d replied. "Ladies there, the maitre d said while pointing at the group of girls sitting directly in front of Richard and Leon. They cost two-thousand-six-hundred baht. But ladies over there," the Maitre d added while pointing at the group of women sitting to their far right, "they older ladies. They cost two-thousand baht. Ladies tinon, they cost two-thousand-eight-hundred baht. They more beautiful than other ladies," the maitre d explained while pointing at the smaller group of girls to the far left.

Which Fast Eddy explained to Richard and Leon.

"What do I do now?" Richard asked Fast Eddy.

"Choose a girl and tell the Maitre d which girl you want."

"I would like the girl wearing that Harley Davidson t shirt," Leon replied. "That is if Richard here will finally make up his mind."

"I kind of like the girl sitting right in front of me. The one in orange," said Richard. But only if Leon takes a lady also."

Five minutes later, Fast Eddy watched Leon and Richard being escorted by the maitre d off to the left of the large window. Which he assumed led to either a back area or upstairs where his two friends would spend the next hour and a half in soapie splendor.

He walked slowly past the small group of two-thousand-eight-hundred baht girls on his way out of the club. While remarking to himself, "So these are the best lookers at Sabai Land. And even they aren't much to write home about. Most of the girls here are way too fat for me."

It took him only a five minute walk to get to Soi 6. Belle was already there waiting for him.

Banging Ning and Belle

Fast Eddy never got to the other end of Soi 6 on his motorbike when his phone rang.

"You want see me?" Ning asked in a cheerful voice that didn't expect no for an answer.

"Yes. In fifteen minutes. But first I want to get something to eat," he replied.

Since eating was not a big thing for Fast Eddy, he had developed a routine for Soi 6. Which was to head straight to Slice Pizza for one or two big slices of pizza to go. Slice had three or four styles of Pizza in a glass display case just inside the front door. Fast Eddy ordered a single slice of Pepperoni, and waited several minutes for one of the attendants to heat it up before heading down to MK Kitty Bar after paying his bin[30].

He found Lamai standing a few feet in front of the go-go bar's front entrance.

"You come have drink with me?" Lamai asked him.

"Yes. But only one."

Lamai found a spot on the long padded bench in front of the stage already occupied by three girls. Small tables were positioned all along the padded bench where up to three people could sit at each table. The three girls immediately moved to a new table farther down the couch. Lamai immediately brought Fast Eddy an ashtray even though the club officially didn't allow smoking inside. Since they couldn't ever tell the Japanese and Korean customers to put out the cigarettes, the waitresses always kept several ashtrays handy.

---

[30]Bill

297

"Where you go?" asked Lamai.

"Smoke and Kisses. In a few minutes," Fast Eddy replied.

Fast Eddy had made it a habit to never smoke cigarettes in front of girls he was about to have sex with, unless the girl was already a smoker. And since neither Ning nor Belle smoked, he hardly ever went to Smoke and Kisses before finding another bar where he could smoke a cigarette or two with his first beer.

By the time Lamai had finished her first ladies drink, which took less than five minutes, Fast Eddy was almost done with his Heineken. So he check binned. By the time the waitress came back with his change, he was all set to make a fast getaway to Smoke and Kisses.

"You come back later?" Lamai asked him.

"Maybe. I don't know."

*****

As soon as he got back to Smoke and Kisses Ning took him over to a vacant booth, and went up to the bar, while asking him if he wanted a drink.

"A Heineken, Ning. And a drink for you also."

"Kap kun ka[31], Fast Eddy."

"I don't see Belle here."

"Maybe she come later.   She live far away."

"Why she live so far away, Ning? La Chabang must be 40 kilometers from here."

---

[31]Thank you

298

"She have boyfriend, Fast Eddy."

"Thai or falang?"

"Thai man."

"If she come tonight, I boom boom you, not her. I don't like for lady to have Thai boyfriend. Because she gives the money I give her to Thai boyfriend."

"I wouldn't care if I were you. Belle have many problems with Thai boyfriend. They argue all the time."

But before he could finish his beer, Belle finally arrived at the bar. Fast Eddy saw a tall slender girl just outside the front entrance that led to the outside portion of Smoke and Kisses, but he wasn't sure it was Belle until Ning told him she had just arrived.

"You want Belle to have drink with us?" Ning asked.

"Sure. Bring her in."

"What do you want to drink?" he asked Belle as she sat up close to him on his right while Ning sat a couple of feet away from him on the left side of the booth.

"Leo."

Which got Fast Eddy thinking. "Belle just might be a keeper. Leo's just about the cheapest beer you can buy and it's going to take her a good twenty minutes to drink just one of them. Unlike most of these other girls drinking these coca colas, ladies drinks and watered down tequilas."

But by the time she started to lightly massage his legs, he was almost sure that Ning must be teaching Belle a lot of her old tricks.

"Which one of us do you want to boom boom?" Ning asked.

"I want to boom boom you, Ning. Because you called me and I told you I would come to you in fifteen minutes. But next time Belle and you are both here, I want to boom boom Belle."

When they finally went upstairs, Fast Eddy took his clothes off and put them on the clothes stand with its tripod base that kept it

299

upright from the floor. When he got in the shower, Ning brought him a small bottle of Listerine mouthwash.

When he finished showering, he lay on his back naked on the bed while he waited for Ning to get out of the shower.

He was completely relaxed by the time she started to hover over him. Telling him to relax and to close his eyes, she started to gently run her hands across his feet, but the time Fast Eddy disobeyed her instructions and opened up his eyes. To see that she was no longer just the whore with magnificent breasts. As their eyes met, her face was beautiful, like an angel's.

He didn't start to become erect until her hands started to rub his abdomen. He was soon feeling moist lips engulfing his still too small penis. Which didn't stay small for long. Two minutes later he felt that he was about to cum in her mouth. But Ning could feel what was coming and immediately pulled her head away. And told him, "Your job now."

Which he wouldn't miss for the world. Hearing her voice telling him, "Go easy now," his lips moved gently into her. Taking his time, he felt her getting wet. And getting wetter and wetter for a full fifteen minutes until she cried out to him, "Fuck me now." as she jerked away from him..

He sensed that she was about to climax into his mouth the same way Squirt had, and wondered if she was a squirter too. But didn't want to admit it which made her always jerk away before losing control.

Had it been another girl he might not even have cum. But her eyes kept gazing directly into his as she kept smiling at him urging him to cum and to keep cumming and to never stop.

Belle was waiting for them when they got back downstairs. Alone, although there were two customers being entertained by two bar girls in one of the booths. . For the life of him, Fast Eddy couldn't understand why the two men chose the two bar girls over Belle.

Ning left early as she usually did. Leaving him in Belle's good hands.

300

Canada John and his Friends at Smoke and Kisses

It seemed like everyone was at Smoke and Kisses due to Canada John and Fast Eddy's bringing an entire entourage with them. There was Micky, an American who lived in China close to Canada John. While Canada John also brought his Chinese girlfriend who would stay with him another two weeks before going back to China without him. Fast Eddy was also able to bring Richard and Leon along. Leon coming in a songthaew, the universal converted pickup truck that provided one of the most popular means of getting from point a to point b in Pattaya.

A burly bald forty-year old, Micky was an American friend of Canada John 's who had been living in China for years. Although in appearance Micky seemed every ounce a brawler, he spoke five languages fluently, including Chinese. Which helped enable him to earn an excellent salary teaching teachers how to teach the Chinese.

With his friends all gathered around him not to mention two very attractive bar girls in Belle and Ning, Fast Eddy was not feeling one ounce sorry for Kit who he had passed once again on his way from Slice Pizza to Smoke and Kisses. And like she had so many times before, pretended not to notice him. Yet he knew that very few customers would come into her bar that night. While she might very well be going home penniless.

But after an hour had passed, all his friends decided to go to Angry Pussy's bar, where both Leon and Richard had two girls waiting for them. This time it was Belle's turn to go upstairs with Fast Eddy. And once again she did not disappoint. But when he took Belle back downstairs all his friends were gone.

He found all three of them drinking heavily at Angry Pussy Bar. Which was pretty much to be expected. But his biggest surprise of the night was Richard. Who had Angry Pussy's iPod in front of him with Da Da sitting next to him.

For the most part, the Angry Pussy Bar played its music according to the tastes of its customers. While Richard was doing a damn good job of playing DJ on Angry Pussy's I pad. Until Da Da suddenly decided to change the music.

Fast Eddy watched Dada' grab the iPod, as his eyes followed her in disbelief as she took it over to the bar.

"That fucking hillbilly dumb shit is going to play 'Da Da' music now in spite of what practically every customer in this bar wants to listen to," Fast Eddy exclaimed to Richard and everyone nearby. "

"Up to her," I guess," Richard replied.

"No, it's not, and if you don't believe me, just watch me!" Fast Eddy replied. "You are the DJ here, Richard."

Fast Eddy caught up with the misguided bar girl just as she was putting Angry Pussy's iPod on the bar.

"You can't take that iPod to the bar," an enraged Fast Eddy told the girl. "Why you take?"

"I want play music me."

"No, you aren't. You ask Angry Pussy for her iPod?"

"My cochai,"[32] the bar girl replied.

"Well understand this. Richard DJ. Not you. "Falang pay drinks

---

[32]Means I don't understand

for drinks tini[33]. You not pay. Bar girl not pay. Music for falang. Kickiet pu Ying tini. Pu Ying ti bar my me Nune thai. My me baht. Falang me nune Thai."[34]

"My cochai," the girl replied looking completely bewildered by Fast Eddy's inept attempt to explain to her in Thai that he who has the money calls the tune.

"Well get this." Fast Eddy snatched the iPod off the top of the bar and took it back to Richard who was now grinning like a possum.

"Richard DJ tini. Cochai?" Now you listen up even if you cannot understand a word I'm telling you. Bar play music for customers. Not bar girl. Up to customers. Not up to bar girl."

Angry Pussy stood close by, hearing everything. While tacitly agreeing with Fast Eddy that bar girls had no right to over rule the music the customers wanted to play. But Fast Eddy was not finished. Not quite yet.

"Richard, do not let anyone take away the iPod. Except for Angry Pussy. This girlfriend of yours is a complete moron."

"Fuck these bitches. I'm going to play whatever you want me to play, Fast Eddy, or what I decide to play. And now I'm playing a song that says it all."

---

[33]Tini means here.

[34]Lazy ladies here. Ladies at this bar don't have Thai money. Not have baht. Falang have Thai money.

A few seconds later, Richard was playing "We are the Champions" by Queen that Fast Eddy felt fit the occasion perfectly. And turned the volume up.

"Nothing like rubbing it in, Richard, to any misguided idiot bar girl who gets in our way.

I Work for the CIA Frank Told the Russian Condo Owner

Frank was becoming well acquainted with some of the Russian condo owners starting from the first day when he met Alexander who was exercising next to him at the Centara Hotel physical fitness center. At first he didn't recognize the Russian. Until he saw him wearing the same hat he had been wearing at the Bahthaus. Fast Eddy was there also, and that's when the two Americans and the Russian bonded.

Like most Americans both Fast Eddy and Frank had been brainwashed since the time they were knee high. "The Russians were robots. They were brainwashed automatons of the Communist system. They were put in laboratories, put on steroids, and had their bodies transformed into human machines that could usually outperform Americans in the Olympics."

Frank remembered back in his grade school days how all the students got their weekly copy of Current Events that was full of anti Soviet propaganda. But he certainly knew differently now. Starting at the Centara physical fitness center where he watched Russian women exercising hard for two hours practically non stop while thinking that excelling in sports wasn't a Communist thing at all. It's a Russian thing no matter who's in power, both he and Fast Eddy concluded.

A week after exercising next to Alexander, Frank ran into Alexander's neighbor in the Bahthaus motorbike parking lot. Already smoking cigarettes with Khun Gan and Khun Toe, the stocky Russian smiled broadly at Frank and said, "Alexander say you very strong man." Which was extremely hard for Andre considering he only had a vocabulary of about fifty English words. But Andre was a different kettle of worms than just about any human being Frank had ever encountered. Because as bad as his English was, his Thai was even worse. But somehow he managed to hang out in the Bahthaus parking lot smoking cigarettes with the two Bahthaus Thai employees for a half an hour or more.

So one would think that a Russian like Andre with practically no English or Thai language skills at all would feel like a fish out of water in Pattaya. And yet, Frank kept running into Andre just about everywhere. Such as on Soi 13/1, three miles from the condo when Frank was at a small unpretentious bar where he met a Pole, who behaved just fine until Andre suddenly showed up out of nowhere.

Frank had never forgotten that time Andre was eating and drinking with a group of Russians at Surf and Turf, and invited his girlfriend and him to join his wife, brother, nephew, and their wives at his table. Frank and his girlfriend had already eaten their dinner when Andre spotted him going to the restroom. Which all wound up with Frank and Jenny having a lot of wine and beer with the Russians for over an hour. But after the Russians all left and he asked the waiter for his bill, he had found out that Andre had picked up his whole tab.

So when Frank suddenly saw Andre walking up Soi 13/1, he decided he just had to buy Andre a few beers. Andre broke into a huge smile as he approached Frank and the Pole, but when Frank introduced Andre to the Pole as his Russian pal, the Pole, who obviously hated all Russians for invading Poland, went ballistic.

Besides Andre, Alexander had two other good Russian friends who owned condos at the Bahthaus. Which was young Andre and his wife who had bought a condo on the fifth floor. Frank had become friends with all three Russian men while most of the other condo owners acted as if they didn't even know the Russians existed. This all gets a little confusing because there's old Andre and there's young Andre. But all three men and their families were Siberians from the Lake Baikal area.

And as for Russians being mindless automatons who are victims of Russian propaganda, Alexander liked Putin. whereas young Andre and his wife despised Putin for being a murderous autocrat. But even though young Andre's English was not nearly as good as Alexander's, his wife's English was so good that Frank felt she could easily be mistaken for being American.

Both young Andre and Alexander had spent several evenings drinking with Frank in his condo. And on two occasions Frank had lent young Andre one of his motorcycles so that they could ride around Pattaya together while Frank showed Andre the sights.

For two weeks, Frank was laid up with pneumonia staying by his lonesome in his condo. Out of all his friends, no one came to visit him except for Alexander who had stopped by to ask Frank to have dinner with him at Surf and Turf.

Although Frank knew Alexander was still at the Bahthaus, he had seen nothing of him for over a week. Yet Frank knew Alexander had the same weakness most of the other Bahthaus residents had.   Which was women, but unlike most of the other residents, Alexander was smarter than the rest due to his having no use whatsoever for Thai bar girls who he viewed as useless as tits on a boar. Frank also knew that Alexander liked to keep his numerous affairs with Russian women discreet to keep his image up with his Russian friends.

Well it's about high time to make Alexander pay for his transgressions," Frank nearly said aloud. I'm going to bring Alexander out of his cave, and drag his latest mistress out with us.

Somehow knowing intuitively something was up, Khun Gan, the daytime security guard followed Frank all the way up to Alexander's fifth floor condo. And watched Frank pound loudly on Alexander's door. And then Khun Gan, who seemed to be always amused at the antics of the condo residents, watched Alexander open his door.

"CIA," Frank announced loudly to his Russian friend who broke out into a broad grin.

"I want to see who you have here with you, Alexander," he added as he watched Alexander's face turn beet red.

The Russian woman was not as pretty as several of Alexander's other girlfriends Fast Eddy had met, but she had a sensational body.

After inviting Frank in, Alexander became the gentlemanly host that had long ago endeared Frank to the small group of Siberian Russian Bahthaus co-owners.

"Can I bring you something to drink, Frank? Some wine, a beer, some vodka?"

Noticing that Alexander already had a bottle of vodka out, Frank replied, "No thanks Alexander. I notice you are drinking Smirnov. That's American vodka. I much prefer Russian Vodka. No seriously. Let's just set a time to meet so we can go to a restaurant together. My girlfriend is waiting on me."

"Funny thing that you said you CIA, Frank. Because years ago I applied for a job with the FSB, which replaced the KGB as the

Federal Security Service."

"Is your girlfriend ready to go out now, Alexander?"

"I think I not take her with us. So I go alone with you and your girlfriend."

"Can you meet me downstairs in fifteen minutes, Alexander?"

"Yes. We can get taxi together."

Fifteen minutes later, they all walked over to the Siam Beach Hotel where they hailed a songthaew. Alexander suggested that they go to the Hilton Hotel where he had a Russian friend meeting them.. The taxi cost 200 baht which Frank and Alexander shared.

Teaming up with the Russians at the Hilton

The Central Festival Mall is huge by any standards being an entire city block long and a long one at that. It is advertised as the largest beach front shopping center in Asia. Although a lot of Hong Kong Chinese might argue that point. Looming high over the Central Festival complex is the Hilton Hotel. Near the top of the Hilton is a restaurant Frank had gone to a few times with Danny but that was only during the daytime. Although some of his friends spoke highly of the evening buffet, Frank had never tried it.

By the time Alexander, Frank and his Thai girlfriend got to the restaurant the buffet was finished although the restaurant was still packed with customers. Frank had found the view from the restaurant to be magnificent. Unfortunately it could only be enjoyed if one had a table near the restaurant's large windows or in the outdoor seating areas that overlooked the Gulf of Thailand. But these prime vantage areas were already taken leaving the service lady no choice other than to seat them at a small table in the back of the main room.

A large man soon joined them.

"My friend Vladimer," Alexander announced to Jenny and Frank in broken English. Vladimer is business associate of mine. He's from Siberia also."

Their portions were small and quite expensive for what you get. Which didn't bother Frank in the least other than his deciding to give the place a pass the next time. But the company was excellent which was the main point.

"Frank, Vladimer already knows our main problem. I tell him everything already."

"Then he understands how you, Canada John , and your son had to pay all those bribes, Alexander?"

"Let me tell him again the main points, Frank."

"Vladimer, as you understand, I have decided to transfer title to my condominium to my son. Which should be no problem. But in

Thai law a condominium must have no more than 49% foreign ownership. Both Frank and me. We foreigners. The rest of the condo ownership has to be Thai. Which has to be at least 51%. And I already explain to you that many foreigners buy and sell their condos as Thai companies. The problem is the Bahthaus was less than 49 percent foreign ownership. But now it is 49.8 percent foreign owned. This means the Bahthaus management and owners have broken Thai law."

"I want to interrupt you, Alexander. Maybe I can make the next point a little more clear," Frank added. Vladimir, there's this Englishman whose business is buying, selling condos and renting them out. And this Englishman has lived in Pattaya for more than 30 years. He bought a condo in the Bahthaus and put it in his son's name. But his son has a Thai mother. My point is this. By Thai law the son is Thai. But what happens next is the son's papa sells the condo to an Australian who is of course a foreigner, same as me and Alexander. But the condo ends up being in foreign name. In the Australian's name. This makes our foreign-Thai ownership ratio rise from less than 49 percent to 49.8 percent."

"I start to see the problem," Vladimir replied.

"Ok. What happens is when Alexander goes to a lawyer to have his title transferred to his son, the lawyer tells him he cannot do it. Then the lawyer tells Alexander he can do it under one condition. Which is he must do a deal with the Pattaya land office. So Alexander has his lawyer do the deal. Under the table the lawyer pays someone at the land office $1000 to look the other way. The result is Alexander's son gets the condo in his own name as a foreigner. But at the same time I've got this very good friend, Canada John. And I have a very good German friend who sells his condo to Canada John . The problem is, again, the percentage of foreign to Thai ownership is 49.8 percent. So Canada John and my German friend have to pay a $1000 bribe to the land office also. In the same week Alexander and his son had to pay their $1000 bribe."

"I see. I see big problem," Vladimer replied.

"Vladimir, this means that anytime any foreigner wants to sell his condo to another foreigner he has to pay at least $1000 bribe money to the land office. So when we talk about my Russian friends, they must pay every time. Also my American friends, English, German friends. Anyone who is not Thai. And this makes me very angry."

"Does the manager know about this, Frank?"

"Of course she does, Vladimer. As chairman I even had her go to the land office to correct this problem. Which would amount to reversing the sale the Englishman made to the Australian so the Australian winds up having his foreigner's name off the condo title with a Thai company name replacing it."

"Which lowers the value of the Australian's condo," Alexander added. "Because Thai companies that are run by a foreigner are made up of two nominal Thai stockholders who have nothing to say about how the condo is run. And all these Thai companies are illegal under Thai law."

"Getting back to our Thai manager, Vladimir; she went to the land office like I asked her to do. But when she asked one of the bosses at the land office to correct that illegal sale, the man told her it was too difficult for him to correct. And that he wanted to evaluate each new foreigner to foreigner sale as a separate case."

"Which means, that the land office official wants his bribe each time a foreigner sells his condo to another foreigner," Vladimer replied.

"Exactly, Vladimir. And this whole thing makes me wonder about Tatyana's death. Tatyana was the Russian woman who was found dead in the Bahthaus swimming pool." Alexander added.

"This is our problem, Vladimir. Both Frank and I want to stop all these bribes from happening in the future. But if either Frank or I say anything about it, Frank might just wind up dead. There are too many powerful people involved here."

"I can see that Frank will have a price on his head. Maybe you also, Alexander. Frank, do you know that the price for a hit here in Pattaya is only 10000 baht? That's just $300 U.S. I cannot impress upon you how dangerous your situation is as chairman of the Bahthaus."

"You are wrong here," Frank replied with a huge smile as he winked at his girlfriend. "Jenny tells me that my life is worth only one-thousand baht here in Pattaya. I'm not worth ten-thousand baht."

"Yes. I tell Frank all the time to quit as big boss of condo. I tell him all the owners don't care about him or what he does to help them. But Frank does not understand," Jenny replied.

This is what I recommend to you, Frank. And Alexander feels the same way I do. You need to get a lawyer from Bangkok. Not Pattaya. This is because all lawyers have this, uh, as you Americans say, good old boy network. They are all in it together. So you need someone who is far away from the good old boy network. Also, Pattaya lawyers are often scared of big shot Bangkok lawyers. This is my card, Frank. If you need any help Alexander and a lot of our Russian friends will be only too happy to pay any legal fees you might have to pay a Bangkok lawyer."

By the time Frank, Alexander and Jenny were getting back to the Bahthaus, Frank was already thinking about the future and past of American Russian relationships.

"If only these imbeciles running the American government really knew what Russians are really like, our two countries would be the best of friends."

Micky

By now, Canada John had his own entourage of friends who were visiting Pattaya from China. As well as a place to house them due to his buying a second condo at the Bahthaus. But as the deal was going through, he let two of his buddies stay at his large seventh floor condo with its magnificent sea view. Since they were all living in China, and they all lived close to each other, they had a very tightly knit group. But whereas Canada John was a gifted engineer, two of his buddies were teachers, making over $5000 a month on the Chinese payroll.

You couldn't miss Micky. Big, bald, and very rugged looking, Micky could easily pass for an ex Navy Seal or member of the elite British SAS. But underneath the tough guy veneer lurked a brain that had learned five languages, including Chinese. Micky's fluency with languages had helped him obtain a position in the Chinese education system which paid him quite well for teaching teachers how to effectively teach English.

The other teacher earned nearly as much as Micky did because he was simply good at his job. But while both men liked to drink beer, Micky was an overachiever when it came to drinking more than his fair share.

Which is why he showed up at the Cocktail bar with eight Heinekens already under his belt. A small girl on the north side of 40 watched him chug a tequila with the bartender. She sized him up as an oversexed American with a huge wallet, and decided he was a far better prospect than all the fat Germans around her.

Unfortunately for Micky, the Cocktail bar would be closing in fifteen minutes. But fortunately, Fast Eddy, Angry Pussy and Richard were all drinking together next door at the Angry Pussy Bar.

"Come on and join us, said Angry Pussy. Richard is DJ again, and Fast Eddy is doing his number one job, drinking my tequila. I see you with lady next door."

"Yeah. I think she want to stay all night with me," Micky replied.

"If you want, I can ask her to come here. Have drinks with you."

"Ask her over then. The more the merrier."

"No. Only merrier for you, Micky, if your dick want company."

"Where's Leon, Richard?" asked Fast Eddy who had arrived just before Micky did.

"Oh, that lazy loafer. He was here earlier, and then he got that gal of his to come back to his hotel. He's probably sleeping with her right now."

They were soon joined by the woman from the Cocktail bar which had just closed. But as soon as she arrived, Angry Pussy asked the middle aged woman what she wanted to drink.

"Me no care. Thai whiskey good. Beer good. I want play with Micky dick."

"Yes. Play with Micky dick," Angry Pussy replied. "He have very good dick. Micky dick very beautiful and big. It same same big ice cream cone. And very sweet."

"Fast Eddy, do you think I should bar fine her?" Micky asked guiltily, knowing that everyone knew he had a wife back in China, but nevertheless asking for approval so he could later blame his friends in case his conscience should ever catch up with him.

"Yes. You must bar fine her Micky. Because you are American, same as me. And Canada John is Canadian. So if you don't bar fine her, Canada John is going to blame all of us Americans for being weak."

"What about you, Angry Pussy, should I bar fine her?"

"You need bar fine her, Micky. She need money real bad. No have customers for more than two weeks," Angry Pussy lied while remembering that the woman had been bar fined by three fat Germans in the past several days.

After waking up early the next morning, Canada John decided to check on Micky's room to find out if his friend ever made it back from the bars. He saw two lumps in the blankets, and a pair of bare feet sticking out beneath them. While remarking to himself, "I have never seen an uglier pair of women's feet in my life."

314

An Ugly American Bites the Dust

"Hey guys, any of you here besides Fast Eddy, ever try Nam's restaurant next to my condo?"

"No, Frank. Any special reason we should?" Dick Fitswell replied.

"She's got great food, and a lot of interesting shit goes down there sometimes."

"Such as?"

"A lot of Russians come in for one thing. And for me, it can get very interesting on account of those Russians."

"What's so interesting about them?" Harry asked. "There are too many of them if you ask me."

"Well let me tell you about last night. I didn't even want to have a single beer. So I walked in just to get a bite to eat. I even resolved not to allow Nam talk me into having any alcohol. Oftentimes when she doesn't have many customers, she will drink a beer or two with me. And even if she is too busy in the kitchen cooking, she will still try to convince me to have a beer, hoping that one of my friends will see me, and join me for a few. Usually I don't mind either way because her restaurant is just 30 feet from my condo. So anything I can do to help keep her open is good for her and good for the other residents of the Bahthaus. She's a superb cook, a fun person to be with, and has a personality that won't quit. Her boyfriend is Russian. Since he's taken her to Russia six or seven times, she's totally unlike most Thai women I know because Nam knows a lot more about the world outside of Thailand."

"But very few Bahthaus residents have even stepped inside her restaurant. I think it's because of the anti Russian sentiment most of the residents feel. After all, the restaurant started off being a restaurant owned by Russians who saw Russians as being the only clientele worth worrying about. Its menus were only in Russian, so even the Norwegians, Germans, Dutch and other Europeans whose primary language was not English still held it against the restaurant for its anti-English and anti European attitudes. So it didn't take long for the restaurant to fall flat on its face. But when a Ukrainian couple took over the restaurant too many potential customers still viewed it as the Russian

Restaurant that welcomed only Russians. Even though the Ukrainian couple only had three Russian dishes on the menu while putting out a great variety of Thai, Italian, and German dishes, the Russian stigma soldiered on. And continued after Nam bought the restaurant from the Ukrainians."

"So when I see the slender American Bahthaus condo renter eating a full course dinner at Nam's, I felt that Nam was finally making headway with the Bahthaus residents even though I am having some serious doubts about the American customer. The guy is very affable every time I run into him at the Bahthaus. Which is so untrue of most of the residents who are too involved in their selfish little worlds to bother about saying hello to their fellow residents. But when I saw all the boxes on the lobby floor that someone had ordered from the Decorum furniture outlet I started to form very favorable opinions of the man who ordered the furniture from Decorum."

"When I first bought my condo from Herman the German I bought my desk, a chest of drawers, a Vietnamese floor lamp, and one of my beds from Decorum. Which is owned by the French. The chest of drawers, my desk and the bed are all made out of teak. At Decorum I saw a bed that had two little end tables, but after measuring it, I discovered that the bed would not fit in a shallow alcove that would be perfect for this bed...provided it would fit. But Nicholas, the young Frenchman, who waited on me said, "No problem. Together we design a bed just like this one that will fit your requirements." I ended up helping Nicholas prepare drawings of a desk and bed that would meet my requirements perfectly. Which in the case of the two end tables attached to the teak bed amounted to shortening the width of each end table. Three months later, Decorum delivered the bed and desk. The bed with its two shortened end tables fit inside the small alcove like a glove."

"I bought the Vietnamese floor lamp a few months later for three hundred American dollars, which is way too much for a floor lamp. But the floor lamp has an exquisite style that is uniquely French. But I also bought another bed, a coffee table, and some shelves and small tables from other vendors which seemed to be a good idea at the time. But none of them lasted more than half a dozen years. So I got Nicholas to come to my condo to measure one of my walls for a custom teak bookshelf. I had to wait several months for that bookshelf but it turned out to be sensational. Which led me to buying a second desk made out of bamboo which I placed underneath my new book shelf. I have to hand it to the

French. They sure have style."

"I fucking hate the French!" Harry exclaimed in a loud voice. "Most of them refuse to speak one word of English."

"You couldn't be more wrong, Harry. Anyway, I was more than happy to find another resident doing business with Decorum which I consider the creme de la creme of all furniture outlets in Pattaya. But when I went into the condo office to ask Kamon who this new resident of exquisite tastes was, Kamon told me about the man's dark side."

"He American. I think from California, Frank. But he not good guy. He renter, not owner. And he buy furniture from Decorum for big money expecting the condo owner to pay him back. Then he take out furniture that belong to condo owner and put it outside on the balcony where it get rained on. And he only rent here for two months and not ask owner if he can do."

"When I went inside Nam's restaurant to greet the condo renter, I notice another man sitting next to the American. The guy looked around fifty. While a young man was sitting across the table from the American renter. The young man seemed to be a clean cut young man of quiet demeanor. So I figured the young man to be the fifty year old's son."

"I start off telling the American renter, "You have great tastes to be eating dinner here at Nam's.""

"Yes. I come here a lot," the American tells me. "But tonight when I first got here there were no tables left so here I am with these two Russians."

"Nothing wrong with that because I happen to like Russians."

"You like Russia?" the fifty year old asks me. "Come sit with us. We like America."

"But as soon as I take a seat between the Russian and the American renter, I can hear the Russian order three beers. Which Nam brings to our table before I realize that the three beers are for the Russian, the American renter, and me."

"Having a beer is the last thing, Dick, I wanted, but refusing a beer's even worse, which is about like slapping the Russian in the face."

"By the time I finish my beer, Canada John comes into the restaurant. But seeing that I am sitting at a full table, he takes the booth next to us and orders a Wiener schnitzel and French fries from Nam. A few minutes later, Micky arrives to take a booth where he can sit near us."

But whereas Canada John is busy, Micky's got all the time in the world. Canada John 's out of the restaurant as fast as he can finish his food and pay his bill. By this time there are full beers and empty beer bottles everywhere with the Russian paying the tab. But whereas the Russian's English is very limited, his son's English is pretty good.

"Do you go to school?" Frank asked the Russian boy.

"Yes. I am in my first year at university," the young man replied.

"How old are you now?"

"I'm seventeen."

"What do you want to be when you graduate from the university?" Frank asked.

"I want to be engineer."

"What kind of engineer?"

"I want to be mechanics engineer."

Then we start talking about Russian literature, and I'm telling the young man that I consider it to be very deep and introspective. That I had studied Russian literature in college where I had read a lot of Tolstoy and Dostoevsky. But while we are talking about Russian literature I start hearing the boy's father and Micky speaking Chinese to each other. Which hardly surprises me. Because I already know Micky lives in China where he has to speak Chinese. But what amazes me is how good the Russian's Chinese is. Anyway, this whole thing becomes a four-way conversation between Micky, the two Russians and me. The Russian papa really likes me. He's making no bones about it while he keeps apologizing about his poor English. But thanks to Micky, who tells me everything the Russian is saying, we are able to communicate effectively."

"You mention, four way conversation," Harry adds. "What about

318

the American renter?"

"He's not part of the conversation. At first he starts to babble about Putin, and how he's a real maniac. And how Russia is trying to start a war with the U.S. So if I say anything good about Putin; for example how he's unifying Russia and making Russians believe in themselves again, the renter's calling Putin the anti Christ. Which is just what my new Russian friends don't want to hear. Then he starts talking about Obama who has nothing to do with any of the conversation going on, and how he helped Obama in Chicago while he was working with the Chicago youth before becoming a state senator. Then all of a sudden he tells everyone that he personally knew Khrushchev, who as you know, was the premier of Russia when John F. Kennedy was president of the U.S."

"So how did the two Russians take all of that?" Dick Fitswell asked.

"The boy suddenly leaves after making an excuse about having to go back to his hotel. While his papa keeps looking at me, rolling his eyes. The guy can't speak English very well, but he's clearly telling me that he thinks this American's really whacked out. Then the Russian tells Micky in Chinese that his son has a heart condition, and that it started to flare up because of all the things the American renter was spouting off. Micky tells me in English that the boy was so enraged that he couldn't stay at the table any longer so he went back to their room at the Siam Beach Hotel."

By this time Micky's had enough of the American's bullshit. So he tells the guy, "You never met Khrushchev."

"The hell I didn't."

"Bullshit. Khrushchev was ousted from power in the Soviet Union around 1964 which is 56 years ago. So you must have been 10 years old when you met him."

"You don't know what you are talking about."

"And you are a goddamn liar."

"You had better watch your mouth," the American renter replied.

"You don't know who you are dealing with so shut the fuck up."

"And you certainly don't know me and what I am capable of."

"That did it for Micky. He stood up and told the renter to give him his best punch. I'm telling you guys, Micky is around 220. And he's got these huge long arms. If you remember what Sonny Liston[35] was like when he was the heavyweight world champion, you'd be getting a pretty good idea of what Micky was like that night. I don't think that renter had any idea of how big or strong looking Micky is while Micky was sitting down. But once Micky stood up, he looked massive. Needless to say that renter never stood up, and then Nam ran up to all of us, yelling at Micky and the renter to quiet down."

"So that was the end of it?" Dick Fitswell asked.

"That was about it. Actually that Russian guy was very interesting. He was showing me and Micky a few pictures of himself in uniform. He fought in Afghanistan as a captain in the Soviet Army. He was wounded when a mine went off. And if this sounds familiar, it should. Because a lot of our American soldiers got wounded or killed by mines much later on. But back then the Russians were the bad guys. While the Afghanistani were the good guys fighting for freedom from all those bad Russians. I no longer see it that way. Those Russians were fighting for their country while hoping to bring all those radical Muslims into the modern world. The Russians built roads, bridges, and schools for the Afghanistani while hoping to keep the radical Afghanistani from infiltrating parts of their country that are mostly inhabited by Muslims. Well it didn't work out well for the Russians just as it hasn't worked out for us Americans who keep thinking we can do everything better than anyone else in the world. Anyway, Micky, the Russian and I agreed to resume our drinking in my condo since Nam was closing her restaurant so the three of us went up the street to Family Mart to buy a lot of beer. Only thing is when we got to Family Mart the Russian ran into one of his pals who

---

[35] Sonny Liston was perhaps the most feared heavyweight champion boxer in the world

was staying at Siam Beach so Micky and I lost him. Which left Micky and I drinking on my balcony until after two a.m."

"That's a funny story," Dick Fitswell replied. "Imagine that, you and Micky, both of you Americans, teaming up with a pair of Russians against a common enemy, who just happens to be another American."

"No shit, Dick. And it has an even funnier grand ending. The owner of the condo had to go to the police to stop his renter from further damaging his condo. Kamon told me later on that the renter started tearing wall paper off the walls and doing all sorts of other stuff to vandalize the condo he was renting. So now the police are making this guy go to court which will decide how much money he needs to pay the condo owner back. Then, the renter winds up getting evicted from the Bahthaus."

Canada John Buys a Second Condo at the Bahthaus

When it came to getting the inside track of what's going on at the Bahthaus, Fast Eddy knew about everything Frank did, even though he was not on the committee. So when one of the co-owners wanted to sell her condo, Fast Eddy was the first to find out about it. He had helped the woman and her husband before, when she felt she was being cheated by the Englishman who was managing their condo for them. And when it turned out that she had been right due to Fast Eddy's help, he could do no wrong in either her eyes or her husband's. And although Canada John wasn't particularly interested in buying a second condo, he had told Fast Eddy that he might. Provided . . . the price was right, he would buy a second place that he could rent out at a favorable return of investment. But when the woman emailed Fast Eddy to inform him they'd sell their unit for 2.7 million baht, Fast Eddy was elated. Because he knew the deal would go through while he would be helping three friends out. Canada John , as well as Sarah and her husband. Who had been ripped off by the unscrupulous Englishman they had trusted to manage their condo.

After the deal went through John offered Fast Eddy a reward to show his appreciation for setting up the deal. Since Fast Eddy refused a finder's fee for bringing the buyer and seller together, Canada John offered him a free meal or a long time with any girl he picked. As for the free meal, Fast Eddy could pick any restaurant he wanted regardless of cost. But since Fast Eddy was not a big eater who might eventually die from overeating, he chose sex over good food.

The Drug Addict's Evil Return

With four-thousand baht in his pocket, courtesy of Canada John, Fast Eddy decided upon Bo as his first choice. Which was not as easy as it might seem because although Bo and Fast Eddy had been friends on Line, this didn't last long. Bo told him later that she had forgotten her password on her line account. So there would be no way he could set anything up with her short of coming to MK Kitty Bar and doing it personally. Which would require Bo to be working.

So he drove his motorbike to Soi 6/1 where Ning could not spot him coming to Soi 6 and parked it behind MK Kitty bar. This allowed him to stealthily use the rear entrance to the go-go where he wouldn't be spotted walking down Soi 6 by Lamai either. Who would probably be lurking just outside MK Kitty's where she would try to latch onto Fast Eddy before he could get near any other girls. Luckily, Bo was inside the go-go up on the stage.

Bo caught his eye immediately about the same time he started to order a beer from the waitress.

"And get Bo a drink also," he told the waitress, knowing only too well that once Bo sat down with him, Lamai would leave him alone. And even if she didn't he could always use the excuse that he didn't know she was working that night. But "oh well, Bo's with me now, and no offence Lamai but I'm not going to buy two ladies drinks right now."

But when Lamai saw him sitting with Bo, Fast Eddy told her he was only staying for a single beer, and that he was setting up a long time with Bo.

Bo agreed to meeting him at MK Kitty bar at 6:30 the next night while he promised her he would pay the bar fine of fifteen-hundred baht and give her a two-thousand-five-hundred baht tip for staying with him a few hours. Which was more money than he would normally pay any bar girl under any circumstances, but he made it clear to Bo that Canada John was paying the bill.

With the business finished, Fast Eddy drove his motorbike to Angry Pussy's bar where he could enjoy a few beers without being molested by any money-hungry bar girls.

The next day Lamai text messaged him that Bo could not meet

him that night for some reason or the other that no doubt amounted to the usual bar girl bullshit. Since he had already promised Leon and Richard that he would be meeting them later on at Angry Pussy's bar, this left him very little time to come up with a long time bar girl. So he decided to head straight to Smoke and Kisses where he hoped to find either Ning or Belle. Since dinner was of no importance, he went to Slice Pizza for pizza which he would eat at Smoke and Kisses.

He found Ning waiting for him. Who told him Belle was not likely to come because her motorbike had still not been fixed.

In spite of their knowing each other for five years, Ning had never come to his condo before. But this time, Fast Eddy was confident that he could get her to spend the next few hours with him although Canada John had specified that he had to get a bar girl to do a long time with him. But even though long time by definition meant the girl had to spend the whole night with him, Fast Eddy was confident that Canada John would agree to his bringing a girl to Angry Pussy's so long as he took her back to his condo for a minimum of several more hours.

"You would really like Angry Pussy's bar," Fast Eddy told Ning. "You and Angry Pussy will really hit it off. You already know Leon, Richard, Micky and Canada John . They should all be there. We can all have a good time, then you stay in my condo for two or three hours and you can go home."

"I would really like to, Ning replied. "But my boyfriend will be video messaging me from Holland. So if I'm gone from my room for four or five hours we might have some big problem."

"You can come up with an excuse, Ning. Richard and Leon are going back to the U.S. in a few days so this might be our last chance to get everyone together."

"I just cannot, Fast Eddy. And besides, I can't drink. I have stomach problems drinking alcohol. But how about the drug addict. She's just outside the bar now. She will probably want to go with you."

"Okay, Ning. I know everyone will really like you. But if you can't, you can't. So bring our drug addict friend on over."

Fast Eddy bought the drug addict a beer and another 160 baht bullshit lady's drink for Ning while the two women discussed Fast

Eddy's proposition in Thai. Twenty minutes later he had the Drug Addict behind him on his motorbike after paying his drink tab and the one-thousand baht bar fine.

He had been hoping to arrange a little party at Angry Pussy's. But by the time Fast Eddy and the Drug Addict arrived, hardly anyone was there. Angry Pussy had gone somewhere else for the evening and Canada John was nowhere to be found, so Fast Eddy figured he was off entertaining Emmy, his Chinese girlfriend. "As for Micky, he's likely to show up eventually," Fast Eddy decided. And even though Big Jim had started text messaging him, he was at Cocktail bar next door. Which left Fast Eddy alone with Richard and the Drug Addict. And as for Leon, he had already arrived at the bar, bar fined his favorite squeeze, and gone back to his hotel.

"When is everyone coming?" the drug addict asked him.

"I think in the next hour or so some of my other friends should be here," Fast Eddy replied.

"I'm getting pretty bored. I can't stay very long."

"Like hell you can't," Fast Eddy muttered under his breath. "Didn't Ning explain the arrangement to you, in Thai. I'm sure she did. You are to be on my burner for the next five hours. That's what you are getting your two-thousand baht tip for, not to mention your bar fine of another one-thousand baht. And Canada John 's got to be here for sure, just to verify that he's getting his full four-thousand baht's worth."

"Where are you Jim?" Fast Eddy text messaged his friend. "I got a problem with this gal."

"Right behind you," Big Jim messaged Fast Eddy back. "I'm just kind of joking around here with Meow."

By the time Big Jim joined them, the drug addict was already talking about having to leave.

"Suddenly she's only got one hour to be with me," Fast Eddy told Big Jim. "I'm telling you that's not what we agreed on with Ning."

"Ning just doesn't understand," the drug addict replied.

"I might as well take you to your room now. That'll give me more time here to be alone with my friends such as Big Jim here."

"Take me home then. I'm not enjoying myself."

It took Fast Eddy just five minutes to get the drug addict back to her room on Soi Poitasan. He had taken or picked her up there several times before. On the ground level of the apartment building there was a little restaurant if you could call it that. Several falang were there drinking with several hags who apparently did a half ass job of cooking Thai food for the cheap charlies who hung out in the neighborhood. There might have been a Thai guy or two. Fast Eddy couldn't be sure because part of the place was in the shadows, and he had long ago found out that his night vision wasn't all that great, especially when he already had a few beers.

As soon as he pulled up to let the drug addict out, he pulled five hundred baht out of his wallet. Although he would have given the drug addict two-thousand baht had she lived up to her part of the arrangement, he now felt he was overpaying her by even offering her five-hundred baht.

But as soon as he mentioned that he was paying her just 500 baht, the drug addict was able to snatch his motorbike key from the ignition.

"You give me two-thousand baht!" she screamed at him as she started to run to the front entrance of the apartment building."

Fast Eddy fought back the urge to jump off his motorbike and punch her to her knees, which she certainly deserved he told himself. But he had never been one to hit women and he certainly wasn't going to start now. For one thing, there were witnesses all around him. And they probably knew her already so they would certainly side against him. He fought back the urge to call her a cunt and a bitch and a dirty rotten thief out loud. Knowing that all that would accomplish would be to piss her off enough to steal his motorbike keys (or at least borrow them for the next few hours). Which would cost him too much time out of his life

For one thing, without his keys he couldn't drive his motorbike back to his condo or to Angry Pussy's. The second problem was the key to his condo was attached to the motorbike key ring so she had the key to his condo along with the key to his motorbike. Although he had a spare key to his condo hidden beneath the floorboard of his Nmax he would still have had to walk back to his condo for another motorbike key or gotten a motorbike taxi. Whichever way you would slice this would have resulted in the drug addict having a key to his condo and his motorbike.

He decided the cheapest solution was to simply cave in and pay her the two-thousand baht.

Three minutes later a completely pissed off Fast Eddy was pulling up in front of Angry Pussy's. Pulling up a chair next to Big Jim, he ordered a Thai whisky and soda and started messaging Ning online.

Ning answered immediately. When he told her how the drug addict had completely ripped him off, Ning replied. "You will see Fast Eddy. When I finish with her, she will never work at Smoke and Kisses ever again."

Fast Eddy Takes Bo to Angry Pussy's

"So what happened to the drug addict?" Danny asked Fast Eddy.

"Next night, Danny, I head straight over to Smoke and Kisses. Ning's there, and Belle's not, although she's messaging me on line. Belle is telling me that if it wasn't for me, she'd die. But since she's way over in Laem Chabang, she can't get to work. Her motorbike is still getting fixed. I know she's got this young Thai boyfriend and he's controlling her. I wind up taking Ning upstairs where we spend an hour talking and having sex. Which is terrific. I tell you, Danny, in the five years I've known Ning, not once have I failed to cum. And I don't think she has either. So by the time we've finished I'm all done in and in no mood to try to boom boom another lady."

"Since the night was still young, it being only eight p.m., I am torn between going to Angry Pussy's bar and heading down to either the Dolls go-go bar or MK Kitty bar. It's just too damn early to head to Angry Pussy's or Cocktail bar on account of the girls being so butt ugly, with the exception of Meow who's hating my guts by now. So I go in the back door into MK Kitty bar."

"Bo's there. And since I still have one-thousand baht left from the four-thousand Canada John gave me, I offer Bo a proposition. Which is my paying the one-thousand-five-hundred baht bar fine to the bar and giving her a two-thousand baht tip. I tell her right out front that I just boom boomed one of the Smoke and Kisses girls who did such a number on me, that I'm in no mood for sex. I also make it clear to Bo that Canada John is paying me what I will be paying her. So the numbers work out to one-thousand-five-hundred baht for the bar fine plus two-thousand to Bo less the one-thousand baht I still have left over from Canada John, netting me a cost of two-thousand-five-hundred baht for a great time."

In ten minutes Bo is out of the bar with me. Then, when I show her my Nmax, Bo tells me she wants to drive it. Which surprises the hell out of me, but in a good way. Bo is looking beautiful but for me beauty is not enough. Bo is taking charge and that's showing me she thinks outside the box and that she has a lot of initiative.

I cannot explain what a great time I'm having. I'm sitting behind Bo with my crotch up against her ass. Bo drives fast, enjoying my

Nmax to the utmost. She's smiling and laughing and telling me how much she loves driving my motorbike. I direct her down the back way to Angry Pussy's. The pretty slender waitress at Danny's Italian restaurant sees us driving past the restaurant. But none of my friends are at Angry Pussy's so I take Bo into the Cocktail bar. Meow's there, with that pissed off look on her face again. Bo and I sit next to each other at the bar. Meow winds up taking our drink orders, and she makes it very obvious how angry she is. After all, she's already met Bo when I took her into MK Kitties, and when Bo's looking her best, she's quite the stunner. Surprisingly Bo orders a Leo beer. Then we have another round together but by the time we finish that second round, Richard and Big Jim are both at Angry Pussy's next door.

We have several drinks at Angry Pussy's with Big Jim and Richard. Angry Pussy's not sitting with us because she's just had an argument with Big Jim about how to run the bar. But she stops by our table a few times so she can get to know Bo better. And Bo's fabulous. She's kissing me at our table, but when Angry Pussy stops by, Angry Pussy turns on all her charm. And so does Bo.

"You have beautiful lady with you, Fast Eddy. Maybe you should move her in with you. Then you can bring her to my bar every night," Angry Pussy said in a loud enough voice for the whole table to overhear.

"Thing is Angry Pussy means every word that's coming out of her mouth. I mean Bo's a real live wire and so is Angry Pussy, so it's immediately obvious that the two women have bonded with each other straight off, and this is very rare for two Thai women who have just met."

Then I ask Bo to pole dance with me. Angry Pussy's got two dancing poles on her stage so Bo takes one while I take the other. I levitate off the platform and then I try to pull myself from my pole to the one Bo's at. I go smoothly from one pole to the other. But something goes wrong and I nearly wind up falling down off Bo's pole. Bo grabs onto me before I go down. Suddenly we are hugging and kissing each other as I press my body into hers.

"After we return to Richard and Big Jim's table, Angry Pussy finally joins us but since there's no more room at our table, she puts her sweet little butt on a bar stool that is right next to Bo. It must have been the close presence of Angry Pussy that does it, but Bo starts going into great detail about how MK Kitty bar works... from the watering down of tequila to the club's insistence of keeping close track of the girls once they leave the bar with their customers."

"At eleven p.m. Bo gets a phone call. Which turns out to be another MK Kitty bar girl. Bo asks me if it's all right if the girl joins us and if I mind buying her some drinks. Well of course I don't mind. For one thing I would like as many MK Kitty girls to find out all they can about Angry Pussy and her bar. Because eventually several of the MK Kitty girls might end up working for Angry Pussy. This could be very good for me, Dick. Because the drinks are so much cheaper at Angry Pussy's place than they are in the go-go bars. And also due to both the Cocktail bar and Angry Pussy's policies of not putting too much pressure on their customers to buy their bar girls drinks. Which means I can finally find some pretty bar girls at these two Naklua bars and not have to pay so much money buying them drinks and bar fining them."

"So did Bo's friend finally show up?" asked Danny.

"She most certainly did. She looked vaguely familiar. She was pretty good looking but she was by no means a stunner like Bo. She didn't stay long though. By this time Bo is starting to complain about being too drunk. Well I've seen Kit drink a lot more than Bo did that night. But I'm thinking that Bo might have had several tequilas at MK Kitty's before I arrive after boom booming Ning. Anyway, by now it's close to midnight. So I take Bo and her friend across Naklua Road where there are usually a couple motorbike taxi drivers sitting in front of the Family Mart hoping to find customers. So I wind up paying Bo not only the two-thousand baht I had promised her but also 150 baht taxi fare for two girls. By the time both girls drive off behind the motorcycle taxi driver, I'm thinking that Angry Pussy and I will soon see at least several new girls working at Angry Pussy's who are from MK Kitty. This is because a lot of the go-go bar's girls aren't making much money and because I feel Angry Pussy made a great impression on Bo and her friend."

*****

Fast Eddy almost made it out with Big Jim the next night. But he stayed home in his condo instead as he had too much work to do helping Frank prepare for the upcoming annual Bahthaus co-owners' meeting. But he almost felt he was back on Soi 6 because of the many text messages he was getting from both Belle and Big Jim.

330

Belle kept messaging him about how bored she was at Smoke and Kisses and how few customers there were. But while she was sending him pictures of a practically empty Soi 6 Big Jim was hitting a few Soi 6 bars while texting Fast Eddy his progress.

But what really pissed Fast Eddy off was when Big Jim text messaged him, "You wouldn't believe what I have just found out about Bo."

"Where are you now?" Fast Eddy replied.

"MK Kitty's."

"What did you find out?" Fast Eddy asked while expecting the worse.

"A couple of the girls who are drinking with me right now told me Bo has a Thai boyfriend who comes to Soi 6 every night to pick her up from work. So when she went back to her bar after leaving you at Angry Pussy's she was meeting her Thai boyfriend who'd be taking her home."

"I kind of thought that Bo couldn't have gotten as drunk as she pretended to be last night," Fast Eddy replied. "I will tell you what, Jim. I am never going to buy her a drink ever again."

Belle Moves in with Fast Eddy after the Virus Hits

"So you finally followed my advice and moved Belle in with you, Fast Eddy. I told you, Belle is the girl for you," said Canada John while slurping his second Heineken down in his sixth floor condo.

"I didn't exactly follow your advice, John. It just happened. But here's how Belle winds up staying with me.

"I'm blaming this damn virus. It's killing me. Remember John, when we were all hitting those happy hours at the Elephant bar at Centara. Man, all those girls there knew my name because I was going to Centara every day to exercise, get a massage or buy a snack from the Elephant bar. And there's a lot of other ladies, standing in front of Centara's restaurants or promoting special offers for Centara. I was trying to meet women who don't work in bars because they know how to work and how to show up on time. And even if I never date a single one of them, I wanted to find out what makes them tick. But wouldn't you know it, John, when this virus hits, the first thing that's shut down is Centara and all the other hotels. Which makes it nearly impossible for me to meet any women who aren't bar girls."

"And the next thing that happens, John, is they shut down all the bars here. So there's no chance of meeting any new bar girls either. Unless I meet them on facebook or Thai Friendly or other social media. Well, I'm not about to do that. Girls can be butt ugly, but they can put on a lot of makeup, do their hair just so, or they can Photoshop their pictures with their phones. So when you meet them they don't look at all like what you thought they would look like. And not only that, I probably won't even like their personalities once I meet them in real life. So what am I going to do? I start thinking that since I've lived here so long that I might run into girls I plum forgot about or didn't pay much attention to when they were working in a bar. And now that all these gals can no longer work in a bar, I might find them walking around on the beach or Beach Road. Anyway, since I don't have anything better to do, I decide to find out, and I'm going to get some good exercise in while doing it."

"So you decide to check out all the freelancers then?" Canada John asked.

"Yes. I start out on Soi 6 having some good English food at the Queen Vic. And when I finish eating, I start walking from Queen Vic all the way down Soi 6 to Beach Road. I am also wanting to find out if many girls are still selling themselves on Soi 6 even though the bars are all closed. Some of the bars have their doors part way open. There's a few gals eating their Pok Pok[36] just outside the bars. I'm thinking I might even find Kit walking down Beach Road as a free lancer. So I walk all the way down Beach Road to Walking Street, and then I go on to the end of Walking Street but there's hardly any free lancers on Beach Road or Walking Street. I continue walking back down Walking Street, then over to Second Road so that I can walk all the way back to my motorbike on Soi 6. When I get to Royal Garden on 2nd Road my phone starts ringing."

"And it's Belle. Right?"

"Yep. And Belle is crying. And I mean she's really crying like a wounded animal. And to be quite honest, she's really turning me off. She's crying because I had given her some money that she was going to use to repair her motorbike. And now she's telling me that her Thai boyfriend took the money away from her. Beating her up too, and that's why she's crying. When I ask her if she wants to spend the night with me, she says yes, and I tell her I'll pay for her taxi. Takes her over on hour to get from Laem Chabang to my condo. Where I start making us Thai whiskeys, then we have sex together and she falls asleep in my arms. She's got her arm around me and the whole nine yards and I am finding this to be terrific. She's got a great body, and she's tall, so she has a lot of physical presence even though she's very slender."

"You've got the right one. And she's so pretty. So much prettier than Kit."

"She's pretty all right, but she's not as pretty as Kit. Not to me.

---

[36]Papaya salad which a lot of Thai women eat every day

333

Maybe for you and all the other guys, but for me, no one's as cute or as beautiful as Kit. Even if she's god awful skinny."

Fast Eddy's Diary...In the Shadow of the Virus

April 1

We are at war, except most people don't realize it yet. Trump and his minions are now telling the American public that the U.S. might face as many as 250,000 deaths. This forecast is up from 200,000 since yesterday. But I am thinking the U.S. will be lucky if only a million Am   ericans die this year. Yet I am 8000 miles away, stuck in my one-thousand-three-hundred square foot condominium I bought in Thailand 15 years ago. Which is just 200 yards away from the beach in Naklua next to Pattaya. Which is the most infamous sin city of all sin cities in the world until now.

Thanks to the virus which has transformed Pattaya into a ghost town, all the bars have been closed. Most restaurants are now vacant. My fitness center at the Centara five star hotel shut down two weeks ago, along with its beautiful spa where I get my massages. And now, alcohol sales are being allowed only in the morning and between five and six p.m.

Lucky for me and lucky for her, I have a new lady staying with me. Her name's Belle, and she's very beautiful. Belle is very tall for a Thai woman. Standing five feet seven, she's taller than 80 percent of all American women. And she weighs just 106 pounds. But tomorrow's my birthday when I turn 61 and Belle's not turning 24 until June. So she's too young for me. While culturally we are 180 degrees apart. This should not work. But we are about to go through a world war together which in many ways is likely to be worse than World War II. This is because during the War people stayed together. But now, this virus is so bad people must stay away from each other. And perhaps for over a year.

I didn't plan it this way. Belle and I are stuck together for what is likely to be the duration. The girl would have been Kit who I had known for three years, who had stayed with me for a month last November and December. Yet it's Belle who's with me now, and as for Kit, I have no idea where she's at or what she's doing.

Yesterday the U.S. reported 912 new deaths for a total of 4053. Figures that I suspect are totally under inflated. My nephew's an

335

emergency room registered nurse in Prescott, AZ, a town of just 40,000. Two nights ago he called me to tell me to self isolate. And that there are five current cases with the virus in his hospital. But his hospital's web site is reporting zero cases. "My hospital's days behind with its reporting," he tells me.

Jeremy thinks the U.S. is slow to give the actual figures so that the powers that be can keep the stock market from collapsing while keeping Americans from panicking. Which they surely would if they knew that at least a million of them will die.

I keep noticing most falang are still not wearing their masks. The Surf and Turf Restaurant is still open with a few Westerners inside not wearing their masks. I swim in the ocean at the Siam Beach Hotel which is practically closed. Inside the buoys at the beach there's only around eight people swimming. Most of the Russians are gone. I swim eight lengths which I figure is around 100 yards out to the buoys. The waves are two to 3 feet high. I'm using the sidestroke and breast stroke most of the time because I'm not using goggles. Every now and then I swallow a bit of salt water, but I would be swallowing a lot more if I did much free style swimming.

When I get back to the condo Belle's already hungry. Kamon, at the condo office, tells me she's going to the Naklua fish market. So Belle, Kamon and I drive there on two motorbikes. As I enter the parking area at the food market a young Thai guy races by me. We almost collide when he almost rear ends me.

I am already angry at all the arrogant dim witted Westerners who are not wearing face masks. Which is the majority of them. I don't know who's worse, these full of testosterone idiot young Thai men hot rodding their motorbikes. Or all these imbecilic old falang farts who just don't get it. Who don't read a decent newspaper or keep up on what's happening in the world.

Belle and I load up on a kilo of fresh shrimp, a half a kilo of crabs, and some other sea food I had never seen before while Kamon gets herself a half kilo of shrimp. Later in the evening while Belle's cooking all that sea food Kamon sends me pictures of shrimp in the frying pan from her room.

We start off on our first large bottle of Leo beer while eating the sea food. Then it's Belle in her world on her phone while I'm in mine. My old girlfriend starts messaging me on Messenger. Since then she found herself a new boyfriend, who she had just married, and now she's over three months pregnant with his child.

We're still friends. She wants to wish me a happy birthday which is tomorrow. But she also wants to alert me to what's happening with the virus. "Two people, a man and his Thai girlfriend are already in the hospital with the virus from Wongamat Beach condo. And there's many more at AD condo," she tells me.

Wongamat Beach condo is less than half a mile north of my condo balcony where Belle and I are drinking beer together. There's an 89-year old German who used to head the committee at Wongamat Beach living there with his 35-year old Thai wife. I know both of them from the Centara Fitness Center where the old German is still able to do an hour on the rowing machine. So I know my ex girlfriend's source of information is accurate no matter how much the Thai government is lying about the virus to keep its people from panicking. As for AD condo it's just half a mile up Soi 16 from me. I have a good Austrian friend who's bought five small condos there that he can rent out for 13000 baht a month.

And this is just on my street here in Naklua. I can just imagine how infested the rest of Pattaya is getting.

April 2, 2020

Finally, the news I've been waiting for comes in. The nuclear aircraft carrier Theodore Roosevelt is infected with the virus. With 93 sailors testing positive. The entire crew of over four-thousand men in danger. Big Jim traces the aircraft carrier's movements in March to operation Cobra Gold that carried out joint military exercises between U.S. forces and its Asian allies. With the U.S. 7th fleet anchored off the coast of Thailand just offshore from Pattaya."

"It is no coincidence that the Theodore Roosevelt had sailed out of the Gulf of Thailand close to Pattaya. The U.S. Navy had at first decided that the 7th fleet's sailors should not be allowed to come ashore to indulge in Pattaya's infamous red light districts. And from what I had gleaned from internet sources Cobra Gold was to end on March 8"

"But this is not what happened. Big Jim and I had been hitting a few Soi 6 bars where we found U.S. Navy sailors drinking with Soi 6 girls in some of the bars. But after an hour or two Big Jim rushed off to visit the Angry Pussy Bar on Naklua Soi 33."

"Big Jim had been hitting the Walking Street and Soi 6 bars every night. Whereas I was helping Frank out with our upcoming big annual co-owners meeting. So I wound up missing out on the fun times my friends were having on Walking Street and Soi 6 due to my having to work until nine or ten at night preparing for the upcoming meeting."

"But every night I kept getting reports from Belle and Big Jim about the latest events on Soi 6. This was before Belle had moved in with me while she was still working out of Smoke and Kisses. She kept sending me pictures of a practically deserted Soi 6. While telling me she hadn't had a single customer buy her a drink in the bar. But I got a different picture from Big Jim who kept complaining to me how Soi 6 was being overrun by the U.S. Navy."

"Both of us expected Soi 6 to be almost totally deserted once Cobra Gold completed all of its military joint exercises with their Thai counterparts. Internet reports had the Navy leaving Thailand by March 8. But Jim kept complaining about the young Navy guys overrunning the Soi 6 bars a week later."

"But all that was two weeks ago. We had heard nothing of what happened to all the U.S. sailors who had been turned loose on the Walking Street go-go bars and Soi 6's short time bars. I had been expecting the virus to crop up in one of the Navy ships. Because after the virus had infested a cruise ship, the state department had warned Americans to forgo all cruises. So why hadn't the U.S. Navy figured out that if the virus could so easily infect a cruise ship, didn't the same apply to a war ship? But oh well, I had long ago expected such gross stupidity to come out of the anals of U.S. politicians and Generals."

"Today just happens to be my birthday. But the virus has curtailed any form of normal birthday plans. Most of my friends are self isolating. Robert has been having all kinds of health issues over the past couple of years. Big John had open heart surgery and had nearly died on the operating table. While Terry had a life threatening blood clot in his leg, which put him in intensive care for three days and another five in one of Bangkok Pattaya Hospitals five star rooms. Figuring he'd be sure to die if he ever got the virus, Terry stopped having any guests in his condo and was having his Thai girlfriend disinfect the entire place daily with Clorox."

"I had been thinking about having a small drinking party in our condo pool with all of us observing a reasonable amount of social distancing. Until Big John talked me out of it when he said, "if you have more than several people down at the pool they will be sitting so far enough away from each other that people will be shouting to be heard. And that virus can travel up to 100 feet in the air in just one second."

"I couldn't quite trust letting Canada John and his small circle of friends into my condo as they still hadn't started using face masks and didn't seem to be taking the virus seriously enough."

"But Belle and I have been taking it very seriously. We wash all our food and beer that enters the condo. We do this by putting the plastic bags of food or TV dinners into the kitchen sink in either dish water detergent or bleach solution. While we wipe down the handles of the condo's doors and the kitchen counter tops."

"But what about an upcoming birthday dinner? I want to take Belle to a Japanese Restaurant that is rated number one in the Pattaya area. The restaurant is only one kilometer from my condo in Naklua. But on the phone the restaurant tells me they are now doing carry out only due to the virus. Since no alcohol is to be sold after six p.m. we get to the restaurant at five-thirty p.m. where we are seated at a table while our food is being prepared. I use the word prepared since we have ordered a lot of sushi. We also get three bottles of sake. The restaurant gives us a healthy discount now that it's carry out only so my bill's just one-thousand-eight-hundred baht which is less than sixty dollars."

"We take it all home on my motorbike. Which comes to a pretty good assortment of Japanese food including a great tasting miso soup. I invite Big Jim over after we finish eating and have polished off one and a half bottles of hot sake."

April 5, 2020

"With the published death toll for the U.S. reaching one-thousand a day, all of us are wondering what the real figures are for

Pattaya.   Certainly it has to be a lot more than the 23 reported deaths so far."

"I am on a mission to once again look for Clorox Bleach. Terry was able to find it at Villa Market, whereas I had been unsuccessful four times."

"There's very little traffic on all the roads so I'm able to get my Nmax up to 70 kph pretty often on my way to Villa Market. The driving is terrific as I have the roads practically to myself. It's almost as traffic free as most rural two lanes are in the United States. "So living in a ghost town isn't so bad after all," I keep telling myself. "I've got Belle staying with me full time, and we are drinking beer together every night. I still have great internet. Belle's not going anywhere, an dshes not inviting any of her bar girlfriends to the condo either. Because she knows only too well the dangers from not self-isolating."

"I find I love driving a motorcycle in these ghost town like conditions. Unfortunately once again I can't find any bleach at Villa Market."

"Two hours after getting back to the condo the alcohol order Big Jim and I ordered arrives. Since Big Jim and Angry Pussy had been running a bar Jim is able to get the wholesale price. When the delivery truck arrives in front of my condo, I had been figuring a case of Leo beer would be 24 bottles. But when I start to open the first case, I discover there are just 12 bottles in the box. Which means I had gotten just 60 bottles. And not the 120 bottles I had counted on. But at least they are the large Leos holding twice as much beer as the regular size bottles."

"Since my rule is to disinfect anything that comes into my condo, I put two bottles of Thai whisky in a bucket of bleach water solution. Then I put 12 bottles of Leo beer into the bucket of Bleach solution and rinse all the bottles in my kitchen sink."

"Feeling full of myself for being ahead of the game, I call Big Jim so we can congratulate each other on our great wisdom for predicting that all alcohol sales would be frozen for 24 hours before long."

"At four p.m. I do 70 laps in our condo pool, which is not enough so I head to the ocean for another 30 minutes doing two laps between the buoys which I figure are about 80 yards away from the beach. Canada John and Micky are already out in the water

340

waving at me."

"After we finish our swim, we discuss the subject of alcohol and the Thai government shutting off all alcohol sales for 24 hours. Canada John tells me if it shuts down all alcohol sales, he knows where my stash is and expects me to cut him in. But I reply, "I have warned you to stock up on alcohol so if you don't, I am not going to feel sorry for you."

"Well Fast Eddy, I know where I can always get alcohol. It's in a little mom and pop shop where the Thais buy their alcohol at any time, day or night."

"Which starts me thinking. "If the Thais can buy alcohol at any time of the night on Soi Poitasan, that means there's lots of places they can get it all over Pattaya. And since a lot of Thais have no self control, they will be drinking in groups totally oblivious of the virus and the need for self distancing. And that means there is no way that they will heed anyone's advice on how to not spread the virus. So if the government follows up on its threats to eliminate all alcohol sales if Thais don't refrain from gathering in groups, the government's plan to ban all alcohol sales is inevitable."

April 11, 2020

"Because last night I had made tacos for Belle and me, tonight I decided that we should go a few hundred yards to a Thai restaurant for carry out Thai food. The tacos tasted great and I was very happy that Belle had liked them. Because my ex Thai girlfriend had never liked Mexican food so we very seldom went to Mexican restaurants when we had the chance."

"But I wanted to get my exercise in."

"Earlier I had been having a small argument with one of my friends. When I told him that some of the Thai girls seemed to like my trim body, my friend told me, "You are one of the most egotistical guys I know.""

"Which kind of pissed me off. So I told him, "I am egotistical and I will admit it. But you are just as egotistical as I am.""

"And I meant it. I had recently taken a picture of Belle sitting down to dinner with me. The picture showed her with her cell phone. So when my friend saw the picture after I sent it to him on line, he posted back to me, "I would make it a rule that she should never be on her phone at the dinner table."

"Now I will have to admit that it's rude to absorb oneself on his phone while eating, but most Thai women do it. And Belle's English is terrible. We don't have a lot in common, and my friend would be the first to admit that most Thai women don't give a rats ass about the outside world or anything else for that matter. Except for Thailand which they feel is the greatest, most accomplished nation on earth. So I get on my phone too since there's not a lot we can talk about."

"But Belle and I spend a lot of time together. Usually she's in the living room sitting on my couch with me. Every so often, one of us will tell the other, "let's go have a cigarette together." And then we will go out to the deck and smoke our cigarettes even if we are in our separate little smart phone worlds."

"I view my friend as a control freak when it comes to Thai woman. But I am often that way myself. One has to give these girls some sense of direction. And if a man doesn't, the Thai girl will soon start to walk all over him."

"As far as being too controlling, why sure, I've been that way with Little Miss Kit. I have always insisted that she be on time, and when she isn't, I always exact a big price on her being late. I don't give her any money. And Kit until lately has learned to always be on time. However, when she's with me I pretty much let her do her own thing. Except those few weeks ago when she was deathly ill."

"I end up swimming for an hour and ten minutes in the ocean. The waves are not nearly as high as they have been. The last time I swam in the ocean it took me one hour to swim eight lengths out to the buoys. But now I manage to do an entire 10 lengths in practically the same amount of time."

"There's no one out in the water with me when I first start out, and no one's on the beach at all which is completely deserted. When I am swimming way out to the buoys there's no chance that anyone can save me if I lose the ability to swim for any reason at all. But now, if I should die, there's no one around who will even know that I have died."

"Most of the people I know here won't exercise at all. But I'm sure the women like my body a lot better than theirs. However, I have to pay a big price in blood, sweat and tears."

"Belle's gotten a cough from all the cigarettes she's been smoking whereas I have no cough at all. And I'm sure it's all that swimming that helps to clear all the smoke out of my lungs."

"Tonight she only drinks two large bottles of Leo. For me, it's wine. I've got one of those cartoons of wine in the fridge that have those little plastic spigots on them. They take up too much room in the fridge but it's so easy to just take a glass, hold it under the spigot, and pour yourself a glass.

After watching a few of my you tube bar videos with Belle , Big John messages me that starting immediately all alcohol sales are prohibited in Pattaya until April 30th. And not only that, the new law prohibits the transportation of all alcohol also. Along with any drinking in public. That means that if Big Jim wants to give me a few beers, I cannot go to his condo and take the beer back to my condo even if I want to drink it in private with Belle."

"I pat myself on the back, commenting to myself about how Big Jim and I were pretty smart to buy and stock up on all that alcohol we got because we predicted this would happen."

"But Belle's not really into my videos. As is almost always the case, she's totally into her own little phone world. I remember again what she's told me about how she rarely watches television. And that when she does, she only wants to watch Thai content on television because she wants to be entertained. So I start to think about the differences between Kit and Belle. How Kit loves watching Netflix, and even if she doesn't oftentimes really enjoy the content I'm interested in, she still finds a lot of content in English that has Thai subtitles which helps her learn English better. And then there are times I want her to watch something in particular. Usually she watches those and actually pays attention to the movies."

But I tell Belle. "We can't go to the bars anymore, but at least I can bring the bars back to us."'

"Within half an hour of my comparing Belle to Kit, Kit suddenly messages me on line. Starting out with "Hi, how are you?" And then, "Do you have lady?"

"We've got this esp thing going again. Belle and I are watching Kit in my you tube videos and I'm thinking about her in a positive way and suddenly she's trying to contact me."

"Twice, she asks me to video call her on line. I tell her, "Not now. Bad idea" (I am thinking about Belle sitting on the couch next to me). "But later," (because now Belle will go to bed long before I do).

"By the time Belle goes to bed, I have drunk a lot more wine than I should have. I settle into a chair on my balcony and call Kit. Later I look on line to see how long we have talked. And am totally amazed that we were video conferencing for an hour and fifteen minutes."

"From the looks of things Kit's living with an older woman. For a lot of our conversation Kit is picking her nose, playing with her face, and fingering one of her eyes to make it larger. I remember telling her she's the prettiest girl in Pattaya. Kit tells me she doesn't believe any of this. But I tell her I have no reason to lie."

"Inebriated as I am from the wine, Kit has me sexually aroused. Nearly all my friends think Belle is much more attractive than Kit. And perhaps she is. But Kit's face and body click all the right boxes. Perhaps Angry Pussy was right when she said that Kit had put some kind of magical spell on me."

April 13, 2020

I want to test again to see whether or not I am sterile. My ex girlfriend who stayed with me for nine years is to have a baby in August. She's got a new boyfriend who she married last week. I have never gotten anyone pregnant in my entire life.

"So yeah, I want to know. Wouldn't you?"

I feel really weird doing this. But I'd feel even weirder having to masturbate in this little plastic vial Bangkok Pattaya Hospital has given me. When I ask Belle to help me produce a specimen of my sperm for the hospital she replies. "I go shower now"

This is the third time I've tried to get a viable sperm sample. And this time we are successful.

344

I arrive at Bangkok Pattaya Hospital ten minutes later. But I have to register outside the hospital front entrance and wash my hands in an alcohol cream dispenser. Just inside the front entrance a couple of nurses make me stand so that my feet are placed over two footprint indicators on the floor so the thermal image detector can do its work.

The nurses in Urology politely greet me, check the little specimen bottle and tell me to come back in one hour to see my doctor.

When one of the nurses leads me into Doctor Jimmy's office one and a half hour later, I notice that Dr. Jimmy is not his usual cheerful friendly self. He seems tired and depressed. Handing me a printout of the sperm sample test results, Dr. Jimmy tells me in a sad voice. "Ninety-eight percent of your sperm cells are dead. So you can't produce a child."

"You told me before that a man can still produce babies when he's over 80, Dr. Jimmy. I suppose that you are telling me I'm not Charlie Chaplin."[37]

"No, you are not Charlie Chaplin," Dr. Jimmy replied sadly.

"Don't feel badly for me, Dr. Jimmy. This means I don't have to use a condom. And last week you had me tested for HIV which turned out negative. As I knew it would be. I am really happy. I don't want "wah, wah wah" in my life."

I did a lot today. I took my desktop computer to "Pattaya to U"[38]

---

[37]Was a famous silent film star who had a child at 73

way over in South Pattaya on my Triumph, went to the hospital, and finally swam 135 laps in the condo pool.

But there's no drinking tonight which makes this the 2nd alcohol free night in a row. I must spare my liver and kidneys. I give Belle one of those antihistamine pills I use and relax watching "10000 B.C." followed by one or two episodes of "Hannibal" which is a highly-rated television series on Hannibal Lecter's cannibalistic career.

April 14. 2020

An article in the New York Times reads "Congress shoves trillions at Virus with no end game in sight". I am disgusted. No. Much more than that. Practically everyone, and I don't care if it's a Republican or Democrat, should be hanged from the nearest tree. Because I really think this will all lead to hyper inflation, which I believe to be the biggest threat to the U.S. economy. This has happened elsewhere in the world. But the most infamous example was in Germany during the 1920's when Germans couldn't even buy a loaf of bread with a wheel barrow of German Marks.

I believe that all politicians need to serve with the foremost thought in their minds being that they are not going to be reelected. This means every single one of them must sacrifice himself if need be to balance the budget whether it's the U.S. government he's serving, his state, his congressional district, city. I believe that was the goal of our founding fathers. Which is that all government representatives are elected to serve only for a short period of time during which they will try their utmost to do the best job for their country.

This printing of money as the cure all for everything needs to stop, but it won't because nearly all our politicians have only one goal and that is to be reelected at any cost. Under the threat of the virus, our senators and representatives are shotgunning unimaginable sums of money in order to bail out individuals and businesses alike.

---

[38]This is a computer repair shop

346

Take the SBA... the Small Business Association for, instance. That first two trillion dollar bailout had earmarked 500 billion of it to fund the SBA to keep the smallest and most fragile businesses from going bust. Unfortunately it's already out of money and most of that money has gone to larger businesses than this type of funding was intended for. Now our gutless senators and representatives are throwing another 500 billion to rectify the mistakes they made with that first 500 billion dollar bailout.

What we have here is the classic case of the grasshopper and the ant. The grasshopper doesn't give a thought about tomorrow. While the ant works hard all his life trying to put away enough money for that rainy day he knows is going to come. Most Americans are grasshoppers. I've heard the average tax payer can survive only until his next paycheck comes in. Most Americans have accumulated so much debt that they will never be able to pay it back. While I have saved enough to hopefully last me three years of having no income at all in case the farms my sisters and I own have three very bad years in a row. But when the U.S. government prints and throws all those trillions of dollars in all those mindless directions to eradicate the disastrous economic catastrophe induced by the virus, all that money I have in the bank might become valueless due to hyperinflation. Meanwhile all the grasshoppers keep getting their fix while the ants lose everything.

As for Trump, don't even get me started. He's beyond terrible. The fact that he's bound to become known as the worse president in U.S. History doesn't get close to how god awful he is.

So how am I doing? So long as I don't dwell on all this darkness I see ahead for my country and the world, I'm doing okay. The Thai authorities are kicking people off the beach now, even if they are swimming alone. But I can swim in our condo pool. We still have two large bottles of Thai whiskey and a bottle of rum, two bottles of vodka, and a few other bottles of various poison. Not to mention 30 large bottles of Leo beer.

Hopefully we will be able to buy alcohol on May 1 even though I don't expect any bars to be open.

Belle is pretty easy to get along with. She doesn't watch televison at all. Since she's on her phone so much of the time. I don't have to put up with that infernal racket from Thai television. So it's pretty quiet around here although Belle is starting to get into the television series "Hannibal," which is excellently done and very gory.

We regularly take cigarette breaks out on the balcony, and drink Thai whiskey or Leo beer nearly every night. Getting a little background on her now. She rarely goes home to her family and hardly ever sees her daughter. Her mother works but it's tough on her now with the virus overshadowing nearly all aspects of life here. Her grandmother never liked her, she tells me. And her father is dead. In the picture Belle showed me, he was a handsome tall man.

I gather her mother worked too hard to be able to spend much time with her. While her grandmother favored her sister. She tells me she feels pretty much unloved by her family which is why she doesn't want to go home very often. She keeps telling me, "Thankfully I have you, and I can stay here." Which might mean compared to most Thai women she could very well become very loyal to me since she's not close to her family.

She's been telling me last night a lot about the go-go bars and how Korean guys are paying three-thousand baht for short times. And five-thousand baht for long time. But she tells me the Korean guys do not like her. She has hardly any breasts at all for one thing. And they don't like her hair style.

But I don't care. Big breasts never thrilled me. And she's very tall for a Thai woman yet slender. So if we are having sex I've got a real presence next to me, and it's mainly due to her height.

April 16, 2020 The Virus is Here in Naklua

I don't have too much of a hangover this morning even though Belle and I had our fair share of Thai Whiskeys and Soda. There's a lot of talk out of the Thai visa forum of Thailand starting to open up again on May 1. But I get a call from Terry who tells me the virus is all around us now, no matter what the authorities admit. Terry tells me a doctor at the Banglamung Hospital now has the virus. That's just 3 kilometers from the Bahthaus. There's also the recent situation from Foodland in Terminal 21 which is about a mile from us.

Angry Pussy had messaged me about Terminal 21. The authorities are warning everyone who was at Foodland on a certain date and time. There's also a phone number to report to should anyone be experiencing symptoms. But Terry clarifies what really happened. Apparently someone had gone upcountry after visiting Pattaya who was tested positive with the virus after infecting others. The person had visited a restaurant in Terminal 21 and a few shops and then had gone shopping for food at Foodland.

Poor Belle though. Last night she admits to me how much she misses her friends. She's a real trooper though. She knows she's stuck here on account of the virus and she feels lucky to be here. Which is a lot more than I can say for Little Miss Kit.

They are keeping people off the beach now. Last night Canada John and Paul swam laps with me in our condo pool after going down to the beach where they saw the police kicking everyone out, even swimmers. Big Jim is out walking down the beach for exercise. He's picking up a lot of trash that's littering the beach because he can't stand the sight of it. But also if the police stop him he can show he's performing a public service. Big Jim tells me that he's been watching Thai Coast guard vessels approach swimmers and ordering them on bullhorns to get out of the water.

Out of all of us, Terry is the most worried about the virus. He tells me that he sends his girlfriend, Pinapple out to get food, cigarettes, etc only about once in three days. She uses latex gloves while shopping and when she comes back to the condo she puts all the food containers in bleach. Then she takes off her clothes and showers to get any traces of the virus off of her. Finally she washes her clothes so there's no possibility of the virus on them.

May 3, 2020

Today the alcohol ban is lifted. But who knows for how long. The primary reason for disallowing the sale of alcohol was to keep the Thais from congregating together while maintaining social distancing. Especially during Songkran[39] which was to have ended

---

[39]Buddhist Thai holiday where the object is to

on April 19. But we are well past Songkran. Belle and I are on our last bottle of Thai whiskey although I have a bottle of Puerto Rican rum which amounts to the same thing. But Canada John has found a place here in Naklua where he can buy alcohol. So we can be sure that any Thai with half a brain has many mom and pop stands where he can buy alcohol. This whole alcohol ban seems so capricious that I decide to expect it to be reinstated anytime "the powers that be" decide that prohibition is a good thing.

I get up early and head straight to Best Supermarket where I buy three large bottles of Sangsom Thai whiskey which we will drink with Soda. But around five p.m. Belle and I get another four bottles at the mini Lotus just up the street.

Tonight I start playing several movies on the external hard drive. I also play several boxing matches of Muhammad Ali and Frazier, George Foreman, and Sonny Liston. Finally I settle on Clint Eastwood's "Letters from Iwo Jima," and end up watching the whole movie, most of which is in Japanese with English subtitles.

Belle's on the couch next to me although she's sitting far away. But as always she's 100 percent absorbed in her phone.

She's just finishing her period and I'm horny as hell. So I won't be able to take care of business until tomorrow. I start thinking about Kit and how having her period never stopped her. Although she wouldn't take her clothes off, she'd at least do oral which she performed exceptionally well. I suppose I should have been asking Belle to get me off period or no period but I had always figured waiting a few days wouldn't hurt me that much. And I could use her period days to ramp up my exercise routine.   I had jogged two days in a row, although the first day I walked about a third the distance between Naklua Soi 16 and Soi 6 and back. The second day I ran over 90 percent of the way in one hour, which was good for a six mile run. It was all on concrete though and my legs and feet were hurting like hell. So today I swam over a mile, which was a lot easier on my aching body than all that running on hard concrete.

Belle shows no interest about anything I put on t.v. Which is no secret because right after she had moved in she told me she never watched television. And that her phone was her number

---

get everyone soaking wet

one source for entertainment. This is both a good thing and a bad thing. The good thing is I cannot tolerate the total crap Thai women watch on television. When my ex girlfriend was living with me, I absolutely would not allow her to put her t.v. shows on the t.v. in the living room. Which confined her to the large bedroom. I hated doing that because it took away a lot of the comradery that results from two people watching the same shows together which we used to do during the first years of our relationship.

Kit's an entirely different kettle of fish. Early on she became 100 percent addicted to my internet movie and television subscriptions. Whenever she used to visit, the first thing she'd do was to sit down on the living room couch to watch my movie and television subscriptions. Later on, when she was recovering from appendicitis, she'd usually wind up in the large bedroom where she would watch them for hours on end. But at least Kit was learning a few worthwhile things. While watching such content she could at least learn a little about the rest of the world. And since the audio was in English with Thai subtitles she was learning English and getting better at it the longer she watched it.

Belle had told me before that she wanted to be entertained and the Phone was doing that and nothing more. Like most Thais most of us are likely to associate with, Belle had developed and was continuing to develop a perfect cocoon of Thai-ness that her phone was perpetuating. Whether it was her constant contact with her friends, watching Thai you tube videos, or listening to music she was taking the easy way out. By inundating herself totally in Thai- ness in a sea of total ignorance of the outside world.

Belle's English skills are atrocious. And they weren't about to get any better. And as far as the music she liked to listen to, I am appalled to say that she loves "Da Da music." I think they only play it in Thailand. The bar girls love it. It does not even qualify as music on any level since it consists of just one beat played over and over again at various tones and degrees of amplification. As in DA DA. da da. DA DA DA. This is as primitive as it gets and I can guarantee that even the young people in the U.S. never listen to it. Because I have traveled all over the U.S. several times with my ex girlfriend and not once did we ever hear it on a single American radio station.

But Belle is a very attractive woman. In spite of all the alcohol she's been drinking which has been every night for the past

351

month except for two she's got this lanky tall body and a sensuous face. I can hardly wait to have her drape that tall slender body all over me tomorrow.

As usual Belle starts drinking a lot earlier than me. By the time I am watching "Letters from Iwo Jima", Belle's completely immersed in her phone. And I don't think she's even giving the movie a passing glimpse. Never mind the fact that between 50 and 100 million people died during World War II, and that 400,000 of those dead were American and over three million Japanese. Never mind, because most Thai women are interested only in Thailand.

And all of them are the same with rare exception. That is appallingly ignorant. So when it really comes down to it, Belle and I have hardly anything in common.

Big Jim put it another way. "All of them are rats," They want to live with their fellow Thais of the same social class.

And even when it comes down to Little Miss Kit, she doesn't care if she goes to a five star hospital like Bangkok Pattaya or not. So long as she has a lot of Thais all around her. But Big Jim said it. I didn't. Because I really don't know about Little Miss Kit who is oftentimes full of surprises.

I finally want Belle to watch just two minutes of "Letters to Iwo Jima." Half rising from my spot on the couch I look and call out to her. "Belle. I want you to look at the t.v." But there's no answer because she's glued into that phone of hers. I try to get her attention a second time. Raising my voice a little I try to call her to attention by repeating her name. Once again she doesn't even look up at me. When I ask her a third time she finally looks up, and I tell her. "Look at the t.v. for just one minute." Finally she starts watching all those thousands of American Marines assaulting the beach while the American battleships fire off their 16 inch guns. Belle watches for only 10 seconds before averting her face downwards into her phone.

Finally I invite her to have a cigarette with me out on the balcony. Where we never have much to say to each other because she's constantly on her phone. Sometimes I respond in kind while other times I just sit with her watching the street below me so that I can take in anything that remotely interests me as I absorb myself in thought.

Finally Belle lets loose the bombshell. "I want to see my mother."

"When?" I ask her.

"Tomorrow."

"Why Tomorrow?" I reply.

"I not want to tell you, but today I feel not comfortable."

While I'm thinking,"Well I can certainly see why. The girl has to be completely bored here." We can't even go to any restaurants together, let alone any bars. And she's not talking to any Thais. Terry has got a girlfriend staying with him, but he won't let her out other than to bring him coffee or cigarettes but he's not about to let Pineapple socialize with Belle. On account of his fear that Belle will give her the virus."

There's nothing for her to fall back on in my condo. She's not watching televison. She's never expressed any interest in learning English because if she would, I would get her started on You Tube classes or a computer program such as the Rosetta Stone. My ex girlfriend, who stayed with me for nine years, at least gave Rosetta Stone a try, not to mention her taking a lot of English classes for over a year.

A condo owner friend of mine has a girlfriend who studies for hours upon end. She's hoping to get a law degree he tells me. The two are nearly always together eating out at restaurants until this virus hit. And when she's not studying all those law courses in the condo she's watching t.v. with him. Not Thai televison, but programs that are of mutual interest to both of them.

So Belle suddenly wants to see her mother. Today the Thai authorities are finally letting us buy alcohol. But I still can't swim in the ocean down on the beach. And a 10 p.m. curfew still is in place.

So today they have for the first time lifted all those travel restrictions that will allow Thai and falang to travel to other provinces and from this west side of Sukhumvit to the dark side. And tonight Belle should be getting over her period, so she's certainly not done anything to take care of me during the past week. Also social distancing is still being insisted upon as even yesterday I saw all those lines drawn all over the floors at the Central Festival shopping mall. But here Belle has suddenly decided she's going to go up to the village where she's going to probably be around all these Thais who are not even wearing masks.

So far she's been awfully good about staying away from people who might be giving her the virus. She's been pretty much my shadow this entire month so she already knows about the dangers from not socially distancing. But there are lots of Thais and falang around who don't give it a moment's thought.

I tell her that I don't think her running off to see her mother is a good idea. But she tells me she will be wearing a mask. So I explain wearing masks does not protect the wearer from getting the virus at all. I even tell her even if you are wearing a mask the virus can get to you through your eyes, or even your arms or legs.

But this means nothing to her. She's obviously determined to go visit her mother regardless of risk. But she asks, "I cannot come back to you?"

I reply. "No. You can't."

Seeing her mother is bad enough. I have no idea where this virus thing is headed in Thailand because the authorities are constantly lying about everything. Falang and Thai alike are accepting the contention that there's only been 13 new cases in the entire country today and no new deaths. Well, perhaps Thailand has gotten really lucky with very few real cases of the virus. I have been reading on Thai Visa that the hospitals are not overflowing with new cases and that people have not been seen dying in the streets. It is quite possible that the heat, high humidity and Thais being better at social distancing than Americans and the English. Certainly there's a lot of sunlight here and since the sun is the best supply of vitamin D that vitalizes the immune system it might well be that Thailand is practically immune to the virus. But I am not counting on it.

I am thinking that Belle might not be planning on seeing her mother at all. I keep remembering how many times Belle has been telling me how sorry she was for her Thai boyfriend, who is only 18 years old. How he has no friends, and if she only knew he was financially secure by being able to latch onto a job, she would not have to worry about him anymore.

But good God. The useless turd beat her up. And how often did

354

he take her phone away from her to read all her messages. The guy is a piece of human excrement which he proved when he messaged me: "stay away from my wife. I can take care of her myself."

But there is no doubt that this human turd is not employed anymore. He had already been pretty much fired from his job from what Belle has told me. There's no doubt in my mind that he hasn't gained employment elsewhere because there are too many Thais out of work already. So, if she felt sorry for him then, she is certainly feeling even more sorry for him now.

I've seen it too much in the U.S.. Woman beaters are usually forgiven time and time again by their victims. Which is why the American police do not want to get involved in family disputes.

And I've read so many times that Thai women we keep getting involved with prefer Thai men to Western men only because as bad as so many of them are...their being lazy SOB's and women beaters, the girls at least understand them and are comfortable with all that goes with it. While they have no real understanding of Western men.

As Big Jim puts it. Once again. "They are all rats. They are so into their Thainess and their having been brain washed that Thailand is the number one country in the universe, and the rest of us don't count for anything."

A less likely scenario is she has gotten a better offer from one of her old customers.

As I ponder this sudden change in our affairs, I decide to have one more Thai whisky and soda after Belle tells me she's going to bed. I do not sleep well. Normally I can get my mind off all those things that disturb me by getting into a book on my Kindle that takes me into an entirely different world of events. Tonight I continue to read <u>Stillness at Appomattox</u>, which is about the last year of the American Civil War. But I am still unable to sleep.

But I knew that I could not tolerate Belle's sudden decision to visit her mother, her boyfriend or whomever. The bars are closed and will be for a long time to come. With the threat of the virus forever lurking, I can't just go out and pick up someone for a short time. Hell, I can't even or shouldn't think about getting Kit to come to my condo. I liked going to Soi 6 and not knowing how each night will turn out. For one-thousand baht I can take

355

practically anyone I want upstairs for a short time and never get too involved with any of them. And all that drinking and getting to meet new people, it is all so much fun. Although I had considered Belle to be pretty much the cream of the Soi 6 crop I still remember that horrible feeling I had when Belle called me to tell me she had been beaten up. I was in no mood to move anyone in but that virus has changed everything. I saw myself as no longer being able to free lance around and being able to pick from so many girls because of all the bars closing and the threat of being infected by the virus omnipresent. The thought of a pretty girl who was much too young at 23 staying with me seemed to be the start of a new adventure. And if I did not take her up on it, would leave me bored without female companionship. It seemed like the best choice out of a lot of bad options.

This morning I made myself a pot of coffee and went out onto the balcony. I didn't have to wait long for Belle to suddenly appear, fully dressed and ready to go. "I am going now," she told me. To which I replied, "Okay, but you know you can't be coming back." Then I added, "You could have waited two weeks before going to see your mother. We could have seen how this virus is going here in Thailand and then maybe you could go."

But she would have none of that. I will never call most Thai women we are likely to meet as being reasonable. Many expats would go so far as to say they can only think in the present. While not thinking of the past, about who has been good to them, or about what kind of life they have been leading compared to what they might have had, or about the future. Even of a future that can offer the prospect of being with a good man and having a guaranteed comfortable income.

Alone at Last

"Fast Eddy. How does it feel now that you are alone?" Dick Fitswell asked, "It will probably be a very long time before the bars will reopen. And Soi 6? Chances are it will never be the same again."

"I really don't know, Dick. But when Belle was staying with me, we were both drinking far too much. I think she was doing all that drinking to forget how unhappy she was in my condo. She had no friends there and no Thais to even talk to. Whereas Kit was starting to get along pretty well with some of our staff members and getting pretty close to Terry's girlfriend, Pineapple. Now, I have only myself to take care of. I am not particular about food so for me just opening up a can of tuna fish, pork and beans or micro waving a t.v. dinner gets the job done. I have a ton of reading to catch up on. And I am really enjoying my online subscriptions. I drive my motorbikes and swim nearly every day, so I keep very busy. But Belle, she had nothing to fall back on to keep her occupied with this virus going on."

"Do you feel sorry for her?"

"In a way. Or I did while she was staying with me. She must have been very bored staying here. And her English was very rudimentary. She was like a fish out of water. But I don't miss having to constantly look out after her and being worried if she is happy or not. I sure didn't miss having to keep picking up after her though."

"You never said anything about that. We are paying these girls so they should be picking up after us, cleaning our condos for us, cooking our meals and so on."

Belle hardly did anything when it came to any work in the condo. I did most of the dishes and most of the cooking. At least she started liking Mexican food. Which I made very spicy. But every night she would leave glasses and beer bottles near the couch where she had been sitting next to me. Then there were all those bottles of Leo left on the kitchen counter top.

"Sounds like the typical lazy bar girl."

"You can bet your ass she was. She would leave the dishes unwashed in the kitchen and then she would instantly go into the living room and get on her phone."

"You have told me Kit was always glued to her phone too."

"Kit was constantly playing games on her phone. So both girls were learning absolutely nothing on their phones."

"So what are your plans now?"

"For one thing I have very few women's line accounts on my telephone so I don't have anyone really messaging me anymore. With the bars closed I can't pick up any girls in the bars or take them upstairs on Soi 6. As for the virus. Thailand looks like it's pretty virus free now although two weeks ago it didn't seem that way. And right now I'm pretty down on Thai women. They are so much into their Thainess and so hostile to any Western ideas. Most bar girls have had it too much their way for far too long so I am hoping that will change but I am not holding my breath."

"What about Kit?"

"That last chat window we were using is now closed down due to my getting a new phone. Kit had been trying to get together with me several times, but I kept having to tell her I already have a lady staying with me full time."

"I am almost about to contact her on one of the other line chat identities she was using or text messaging her on one of her phone telephone numbers."

"Why don't you then?"

"Because like Belle I am afraid that she's just another rat, as Big Jim calls all of them. She kept on going back to her South Pattaya friends when she was staying with me. And, right now I am still busy cleaning up after Belle and organizing my place. If I have Kit coming here there's going to be all kinds of complications worrying about her. Such as making sure she's eaten well, and this means eating Thai food."

"Do you plan on seeing her again?"

"Eventually. I am thinking she will eventually try to get hold of me. And certainly so by her birthday which is in the middle of July or when her arm is hurting a lot when she needs injections. But probably before all of that just to see if Mr ATM no longer has a live in girlfriend."

"Do you miss her?"

" I shouldn't. On account of her probably being insane. And many other reasons I've already talked to you about. But she has a lot of things about her that attract me very much. And right now with this virus lock down still going on, with no hotels or bars open, there's just not much opportunity for meeting other women. I could find ladies online, but I've always hated the idea of having to do that. I like meeting girls face to face so I find out right off how attractive they really are and if there is any kind of connection there. Even here in Thailand most gals are getting fat but with their smart phones these gals can make themselves look pretty much whatever they want people to think they look like."

"So what are you going to do with yourself?"

"Because of the virus my money has pretty much dried up, so I don't want to be spending a lot right now. And I want my condo to be just the way I like it with no intrusions from lazy bar girls. I will keep swimming. And watching a lot of interesting stuff on Netflix and Amazon Prime. And my condo will be my castle. As for sex, I can't even think about that right now. The virus is still pretty scary. But the most important thing of all is, I don't want to be bailing any of these worthless Thai boyfriends out right now."

"Heard from Belle?"

"Not a thing. Maybe she is with her mother. But she might have gone back to her abusive boyfriend."

"So you figure she's gone back to subjecting herself to all that abuse again?"

"I really don't know. In the U.S. I had learned that most of these abused women keep thinking that eventually the abusive male will change. If only she does things differently and better in the future. They keep splitting up with the guys, but only for a short time. Then they keep going back to them. But here in Thailand they figure this is just Thai man style. While thinking that we falang are weak. They understand the abusive Thai male. There's the common language, culture and customs. Whereas we Westerners are aliens from outer space. Because we are nice to them. They just don't begin to understand what many of us falang have going for ourselves. They don't understand English and don't want to understand it beyond the most rudimentary level . . . to enable them to get money out of us. They don't care about the world outside Thailand. So yeah...especially Belle who is too lazy to want to learn anything new about anything. She's going back to what's familiar to her."

The Virus Leaves No Options

"Fast Eddy, I have one girl coming this afternoon. And another coming to my condo tonight, but you know how it is."

"I don't know Big Jim, how is it?"

"These whores are all the same. Chances are just 50 percent that any one of them will show up. And the closer you get to the time they should show, the greater chance that they will somehow screw it up."

"I don't know what to do for women now that the bars are all closed down," Fast Eddy replied. Unlike you, I didn't get many contacts on line. In fact I removed a lot of them over the past two years. I don't want these women constantly aggravating me with all these pleas, "I need help. I can't pay my rent. Or my son needs money and I don't have any." By now I just don't' give a shit about all their Mickey Mouse problems. A lot of men are finding girls through social networking and a lot of bar girls are using it to find customers."

"I've met a few hotties online, on either Facebook or Thai Friendly and about 50 percent of them turned out okay."

"It won't work for me, Jim. I only like girls who are slender. I don't like girls with dumpy short legs, and I don't like stupid girls either. As Canada John used to tell me, "I have a lot more girls to choose from, Fast Eddy, because my selection criteria is much broader than yours. I can go with a girl who's slightly overweight but you won't even fuck a girl who's slightly overweight with your dog's dick."

"I meet a lot of girls on Beach Road who are exercising, Big Jim replied.. "But we both know they really don't want to exercise. They are only pretending to be walking or jogging for exercise. Most of them are just trying to be picked up."

"I've jogged a few times from Soi 6 down Beach Road to Walking Street and back, but I'd say 95 percent of all the girls I see are too fat and they walk so slowly. And a lot of these girls are in their twenties. Almost all of them are slugs and the few who are slim and attractive have really hard faces. I haven't seen one yet who I want to bring to my condo. My condo's too good for them."

"So what are you going to do, Fast Eddy?"

"I'm praying that the bars reopen soon. Or tourism will start up soon, even if Thailand only lets the Chinese, Koreans, and Taiwanese in. Then Centara might open soon and I will be once again meeting girls who are not bar girls. But even then, just what the hell would I do with one of those girls anyway? To be honest, Jim, I don't know what to do other than to keep watching good internet content I've subscribed to. Their programs enable me to keep my mind on other things, while I keep exercising and wait it out to see what happens."

"You could always message Belle and get her to come back and see you. You don't have to have her live with you. Just have her come once or twice a week."

"I don't know, Jim. Maybe. Maybe not. She's quite the looker and she's got some good qualities. But right now, having my freedom is enough."

Living with Kit

When Kit called me on line video, I decided to give her another try, Jim. I know you and the guys think she's way too skinny and a pain in the ass. But she at least makes me laugh. So here, once again, she's making all these faces at me on line. While Belle only sent a few messages to me mentioning she's got a birthday coming up. But you gotta hand it to Kit. She's an original. An original what, I still can't figure out. But she sure makes life interesting. So now she's living with me. I can't say for how long, but what the hell? And all things considered she's so much better than Belle, or Meow, or any of the others."

"Come on Fast Eddy. She's a rat same as all of these whores."

"It might seem that way, Jim. But I don't think either you or any of our friends have ever experienced saving a girl's arm, or her life. There is no precedent that I know of where there is this life and death connection between a young Thai woman and an old fart like us."

"So what's she like now? I mean having her live with you?"

"When I go to bed at night she's still awake watching all that great internet content I've subscribed to. So I don't have to worry about having to entertain someone all the time. All the dishes are done when I go to bed. And there's no dirty dishes in the morning either. She's willing to cook most of the time. She's quiet."

"Doesn't it worry you that she probably has a Thai boyfriend?"

"No. Not so much anymore. I'd even put better odds on her having a lesbian girlfriend, than a Thai man. I think that scar she's got now makes her less attractive to a Thai boyfriend while it undoubtably lessens her value to potential customers. So she becomes less of a meal ticket to a Thai boyfriend Pimp relationship. But for me, I don't care if she's got an ugly scar or not. Or whether she's too skinny."

"Come on Fast Eddy. She's a rat just like all the rest of them. As for your getting her insurance so that she can now go to the best hospitals, these Thais are all the same. They'd rather be surrounded by ten Thais in a single room than having a room to themselves at Bangkok Pattaya Hospital. That's what they are used to. A rat doesn't mind how it lives so long as it has enough food to eat."

"You might be right, Jim. But I'm going to be finding out soon. I used to get really pissed off at Kit because she would not spend a single night with me. I thought she had a Thai boyfriend back then. Now she's staying at my condo practically all the time. She knows where everything is. She's probably got most of her clothes at my condo. Unlike Belle, Kit knows her way around my place and she's smart enough to know and to appreciate a lot of the things she's not getting in the kingdom of rats."

"So just what is she getting from you that she's not getting in that room she's sharing with all those Thais."

"Air conditioning for one thing. Good cooking facilities for another. And Kit's a very quiet girl. I think she likes the quiet here. The fact she can sleep until four p.m. with no interruptions from anyone. The safety of my condo. She's lost at least a couple of phones because of the assholes living around her. And I bought her that Mickey Mouse watch. She now has no idea of where it is. Some of her clothes are missing. Bottom line is she keeps changing roommates but at least one of them is stealing a lot of her shit. Fact is she might be a rat but she still has no reason to trust all the other rats. Anyways, Jim, we will see. I'm not putting any pressure on her at all. I'm not telling her when to wake up. I'm not accusing her of having Thai boyfriends, or telling her that her friends are no good. I pretty much let her decide if she wants to eat out or cook inside my condo. So what's there not to like here? And now thanks to you, and to Canada John , I think she's now starting to think that my best friends really like her and that you guys aren't boring."

"Okay. So be it. But what exactly are you getting for your money out of her?"

"Jim look. I could say that any woman who can't wake up before four p.m. or even 12 is too lazy to be worth paying. I can't keep thinking this way even today. But I'm now looking at having a number of choices, nearly all of them bad. As I've said before, I don't want to go down Beach Road trying to find girls to have sex with in my condo. It's one thing to fuck this one or that one on Soi 6 but now I am actively having to seek them out and line up their meeting me or following me back to my condo. As if they are all prizes worth pursuing. But they aren't prizes worth pursuing. Most of them are dumbshit hillbilly girls with IQs averaging 75. Most are fat who can't even begin to keep up with an old man like me. As for finding them online, I'm not about to do that and for pretty much the same reasons. Now, sure, I'd like for Kit to get up in the morning. I wish she'd actually work hard at doing something worthwhile in her life like studying English. But it really doesn't matter because hardly any of these bar girls will measure up. But Kit's still a far better choice than the rest of these bar girls."

"I don't think so. To me, Kit is the rat of all rats. She doesn't treat you well even though you have saved her life and probably saved her arm."

"The nights are the worse now that this virus has closed down all the bars, Jim. So even though Kit doesn't wake up until four p.m., I have her with me during the nights when a man gets loneliest. And when it comes to sex even though she's not giving me all that I really want she still gets me off faster and better than just about anyone else. So I'm not lying around at night getting horny. I never have to clean a dish anymore and she's starting to do all the laundry. She's quiet so she's not bothering me the way most of these Thai women would with their horrific Issan accents that makes them sound like ducks. And when I want to go out at night, say to a restaurant, I feel that Kit is very presentable. She's genuinely cute. She has very good manners. She doesn't have any tattoos. And I feel really good and proud to have her with me. In a nutshell it's one helluva lot better to have her in my life than not to have her."

"Still I can't see giving a girl 15 to 20,000 baht a month who can't get her lazy ass out of bed until late afternoons."

"That can all change Jim. It might take a year or even two years for Kit to rid herself of all those young bar girl habits she's acquired. But Kit's no longer young. She's going to be 27 next month so she's going to be 30 in three years. She also is suffering from a real disability due to her not being able to use one finger and her thumb. And she's still got that scar from her appendix rupturing. There's an excellent chance that Kit's going to become much more appreciative as time goes on. An appreciation one will never get from a 23 or 24 year-old bar girl."

"And, let me continue to ramble on. There's a good chance that Kit's been abused and she's real shy because of that. But she still can overcome her having been abused. It just takes a lot of time and patience from those who are closest to her. And that would

365

be me. The thing is, I think she's worth spending all that extra time and effort having to put up with all her shit."

"You sure about that?"

"I think so. But I'm now going to find out real fast. Jim, I want to ask you about something else. Lately Kit hardly ever watches any Western movies or tv shows. She's watching all this Thai and Korean shit now. Also, do you remember that time you saw her get on her phone and you remarked that she was accessing all this Korean stuff and you commented those Koreans she was viewing were movie stars and other celebrities?"

"It doesn't mean anything, Fast Eddy. All these Thai women are into these Korean soap operas now. It's the rage here."

"To me, it does Jim. Because I've heard that Thai women prefer Chinese, Japanese and Korean men to falang. For this reason. They look very similar to Thais. Also it means most of these women are not the slightest interested in learning English other than learning just enough to weasel the maximum amount of money out of us. What a lot of this comes down to is most Thai women we come into contact with, and they are bar girls, are much more attracted to Koreans, Japanese, and Chinese than they are to us. Also, we Westerners are much more generous and logical than most Koreans, Japanese and Chinese. Taking this one step further the women we meet have no respect for our generosity, our being logical or our pragmatism."

"Good points, Fast Eddy. Also, when these girls keep watching all these Korean soap operas they think life is one big soap opera. They are already addicted to Thai soap operas and when they start watching all these Korean soap operas their little minds keep imagining their lives as one big soap opera with all this drama that's so petty, mindless, and superficial. The same thing's true with all these Thai soap operas."

"Tell you what, Jim, it's really nice having Kit around. I like her sitting on the couch next to me. She's ten times smarter than most bar girls. And when I take her out to restaurants or that bar we go to, I feel I've got the right girl with me. But dammit, she sleeps in until four p.m. She isn't doing anything to better herself. And when I see so many Thais working hard to make less money than these bar girls do, I keep thinking they don't even deserve 10000 baht a month when they can't get their lazy assess out of bed."

You are our Leader, the Russians Told Frank

No one had ever sent Frank an email like this. None of the Americans did. And certainly none of the Germans. As for the English residents at the Bahthaus, most of them were whining, bitching pain in the asses. Frank still had half a bottle of good Siberian vodka young Andre had brought back from Irkutsk. Frank went out onto his deck to read Andre's email for the second time, after pouring himself a small glass of the gifted vodka on ice. Which was the only way to savor good vodka, Frank had long ago decided.

But this vodka tasted better than any he had ever had before. And not that it was Russian. For he had oftentimes found his Russian friends drinking good American vodka, which was Smirnov, his favorite American vodka. So it wasn't just his drinking Russian vodka now that made it so good. It was the good intent of the Russian couple who had given it to him that made the difference.

And as for Smirnov, it was that single night getting his MBA, that made it his first choice of all American vodkas. His father had always told him it was best to buy cheap vodkas and whiskeys, because one couldn't tell the difference between the expensive stuff and lesser quality vodkas and whiskeys once you made a cocktail out of them.

Thirty-five Years Ago

The Heublein Liquor case Frank and his classmates studied under Professor Kugel ran over sixty pages of text, balance sheets, and profit and loss statements. Which was a typical case study that had been pioneered at the Harvard Business School which would be implemented in MBA programs throughout the U.S. The question for Frank and his classmates to ponder was a Marketing Issue over how Heublein could successfully compete with its rivals which were producing cheaper Vodka brands.

Unlike most of its competition, Smirnov vodka was employing a double charcoal purification process that would theoretically result in a smoother vodka. However, the financial statements divulged this double purification process to be much more expensive than the single stage purification process used by Smirnov's rivals.

Professor Kugel had divided his class into five teams with three or four students on each team. The students had all been expected to study the Heublein liquor case at home which meant many hours spent digesting the history of Smirnov including its later acquisition by Heublein and a lot of financial data. Each team was given enough time to deliberate on what marketing strategies Heublein should use to gain market share over its rivals. Professor Kugel then invited each team to give its appraisal to the rest of the class of what strategies Heublein should employ. But when it came time for Frank's team to respond, Frank held up his hand hoping Professor Kugel would ask him to speak for the other members of his team.

"Okay, Frank, since you had your hand up first I will now ask you to tell us what your team's answer is to what Heublein needs to do to overcome its rivals."

"First off, Professor Kugel, vodka is vodka. It has a neutral taste so it's a great mixer. Smirnov does not need to purity its vodka through a second charcoal filtration process since people cannot tell the difference between vodka that is filtered once through charcoal and vodka that goes through two stages of this purification process. I move that Heublein direct its vodka distillers to eliminate this second filtration process. Then we take all that money which is saved and put it into one helluva lot more advertising worldwide. We can perhaps double our sales while keeping our overall profit margin the same per bottle."

"Are you sure people can't taste the difference between vodkas?" Professor Kugel asked. "You are sure now, are you, Frank?" he asked a second time in an even more confident voice."

"Sure, I'm sure. Everyone knows you can't tell the difference."

"Okay. We will soon see about that."

Two days later Professor Kugel asked Frank and one other student to wait in the hallway while he prepared an exhibit in class. After a few minutes, another student joined them in the hallway.

'Here are two blindfolds for you," the student instructed Frank and his companion. "You two are to be guinea pigs for Professor Kugel's great experiment. Put them on when Professor Kugel instructs you to."

The student then escorted Frank and his companion to Professor

Kugel's desk.

"Make yourselves comfortable gentlemen. Then put on your blindfolds," Professor Kugel explained to his two guinea pigs.

After Frank and his accomplice put on their blindfolds, Professor Kugel placed two small glasses in front of them. Then addressing the third student, Professor Kugel continued, "Now I want you to give Frank and Larry the two glasses on the left, and then I want you to hand two glasses on the right to them when they are finished."

"And now, I want both of you to slowly drink the glass of vodka you have been given. Do not chug it. I want both of you to slowly savor the vodka and while you are doing it I want you to think about what it tastes like."

Fank found that the first vodka had a harsh taste to it. After tasting both vodkas, he decided that the second vodka was far smoother although it had a neutral taste.

"Okay. Which vodka tastes better?" Professor Kugel asked. "You can take off your blindfolds now. Don't tell us your choices. I want both of you to write number one or number two down on the piece of paper you both have in front of you."

"I am now reading your answers," Professor Kugel continued. "Both of you have chosen number 2, and number 2 is the Smirnov vodka. Now, are you both sure that you have chosen the Smirnov as the better vodka?"

"The Smirnov was definitely a lot better than the first vodka," Frank replied. "I hate to admit it, but I am wrong. So we had better continue using the second filtration process."

From then on, Smirnov had become Frank's go to vodka. And he rarely mixed it with orange juice or anything else. Orange juice or a similar mixer brought the calory content of a glass of vodka up from 90 to over 150 calories, and sometimes even far more.

Since moving to Thailand Frank nearly always had a full bottle of Smirnov on hand due to its offering a lot of kick for the money while being far less fattening than beer. But he would often substitute good Russian vodka while hoping that he could find some subtle taste differences between brands.

The email he was reading from Andre's wife went as follows.

Andre, Alexander and I fully support you as our chairman running this condo. You are our leader. We feel that your heart is in the right place, and that you are doing your utmost to look after the rest of us condo co-owners. When we come back from Siberia we will bring you another bottle of our vodka. Because we hope you have finished the first bottle we brought you. Good luck with your endeavors. We will see you soon.

Elena

How did Tatyana Die?

"Fast Eddy, I am not sure, but I don't think the Russians killed Tatyana."

"Why are you telling me this, Frank?"

"Because I have been brooding about it for years now. Do you remember that night you pole danced over at TJ bar, and how you became fast friends with the three Russians and how one of them gave you the shirt off his back and then he walked bare chested back to his hotel room with his wife?"

"I sure do, Frank, but what the hell does that have to do with Tatyana's death?"

"Plenty. Because in general of all nationalities here in Pattaya I like the Russians best. They are my firmest supporters of me as chairman at the Bahthaus. And when we show them we like them and are friendly toward them they reciprocate. I mean in general. They are fun loving. They read a lot more than we Americans do. In my book they are A-okay. And much easier to get along with than most Germans or Englishmen."

"That still doesn't mean that there aren't a lot of bad apple Russian mafia guys here in Pattaya."

"Very true, Fast Eddy. But I think we could just as easily blame the Germans or English, even we Americans. And aside from all that here's the clincher."

"Go on, I'm all ears."

"The other night I was swimming in our condo swimming pool. I would swim two side stroke laps, then two breast strokes, followed by two strokes free style, then three more laps doing the sidestroke and the tenth lap I'd swim the entire length of the pool underwater. The other night I did only 100 laps, but I wanted to do the full 130 laps I normally do. The underwater pool lights were not working so it started to get pretty dark. I was getting to the point of not being able to see the bottom of the pool or the side I was swimming underwater to. I'm swimming 40 feet underwater holding my breath so I am only able to concentrate on making it to the other side without coming up for air. Anyway, I'm going pretty fast and then suddenly I hit my head on the side of the pool. I didn't realize I could hit it so hard. It didn't knock me out or anything, but I started thinking right then and there that it is very possible or even likely that Tatyana might have hit her head on the side of the pool."

"Hmm. Very possible Frank."

"Even if it was during the day, she might have misjudged the edge of the pool. She might have been swimming and blinded by the sun. Like driving a car and the sun is right in your eyes. You can hardly see. In any case according to Herman the German she suffered a head injury either the day before her death or the same day she died. This would all make sense. I think if I had hit my head a little harder I could have passed out."

"Makes sense to me. But this is all pure speculation, Frank. But if she passed out, she would have sucked in a lot of water and drowned. If you remember, Khun Toe said she didn't drown.

"Tatyana's death is baffling. I just think something happened to her that's inexplicable. But here's another thing, Fast Eddy. Remember how the owner of that red Ferrari was a possible suspect? It turns out that Alexander rented that Ferrari out for a week. Just for shits and grins and for impressing his women. But Alexander never met Tatyana. And Alexander's one of the best men you could ever meet. So, we will never really know, Fast Eddy. But it sure doesn't make much sense to me to keep demonizing these Russians and accuse most of them of being mafia types. I suppose it really doesn't matter anyway. She's dead."

At the Moon Light Beach Condo Bar

There was no question that Kit was a little vampire. Once in while she might go to bed at eight p.m. and wake up at a reasonable hour. But that was when she weighed just 32 kilos while recovering from her appendix operation. When Fast Eddy was forcing her to wake up by nine a.m. to make sure she had a good breakfast. But now that Kit was tipping the scales at between 38 and 39 kilos she would stay awake until five or six a.m.

By now she had a passport that would allow her to travel with Fast Eddy. He had made sure she had a Thai motorbike license. He had even gotten her a hospital insurance policy so that she could go to Pattaya Bangkok Hospital from now on, with the exception of the tumor in her arm and hand which would be considered a preexisting illness. And unlike before, when she had never spent a single night in his condo, Kit was now staying all night each time she visited for up to six nights in a row. And each time she sat behind him on one of his motorcycles she automatically put on a helmet. So big changes were occurring in their relationship.

Fast Eddy still worried about her, however. With the shadow of the virus still hanging over Pattaya, Fast Eddy still could hardly believe that most Thais on motorcycles were wearing masks to conform with the virus containment mandates from the government. Which used the corrupt police for their front line. Driving his Triumph or Nmax, he was mortified to see seventy-five percent of all Thais not wearing their helmets. He was even more disgusted when he observed a man and two of his children on a motorcycle . . . none of them wearing helmets.

"Such people do not deserve to be parents," Fast Eddy almost shouted hoping the whole world could hear his thoughts. "They are too ignorant to be allowed to make babies. Don't these people know that Thailand has the highest road fatality rate in the world? With the majority of all road deaths attributed to motorcyclists? Which is due to these people not wearing helmets and their moronic driving habits? And as for the Thai police. What right do they have to force anyone to wear a mask, when they allow most Thais to break every traffic law in the book and be on their motorcycles not wearing helmets. Don't these people and the police know that a human head is almost as delicate as an egg shell when it hits something hard like the concrete surface of a road?"

"I don't want Kit to get hurt or die on a motorcycle because she's not wearing a helmet or riding behind one of these useless idiots. But the people she's living around are a bunch of mindless idiots. And I'm sure that when she's with them she's not wearing a helmet. More than that, while she was living with these same clueless idiots, Kit did not get the MRI that Queen Savang Vadhana Hospital had scheduled for her. I wasn't with her then, and it would have cost eight-thousand baht. Not to mention my having her get her tooth pulled at Bangkok Pattaya Hospital. Where were her friends then while her tooth was rotting out? Kit is smart, and she will get up on time when she knows she has to. But she's a creature of habit and when she's around those worthless ignorant people she's becoming just as ignorant as they are. So above all, I would like to see her develop better habits, learn more about the rest of the world and to be safe. Which is why I want her to stay with me in my condo and to regard it as her real home while finding new friends who will be much better examples for her."

Kit was sitting on the couch next to him watching Netflix when Canada John came in.

"Tonight is my drinking night. Let's all go to Moon Light Beach and have a few beers at Leo Bar? And you, little Miss Kit, you are coming with Fast Eddy and me."

"Okay," Kit replied. "We go now."

"No, you are not!" said Canada John "You can't go like that. Put some makeup on. Fast Eddy and I will just have a little chat here while we wait for you."

Kit spent just Fifteen minutes putting on her makeup. Which made a huge difference in her appearance. Then she followed Fast Eddy and Canada John to the motorbike parking lot where Fast Eddy kept his Triumph and Nmax.

"Kit, do you want to ride to Moon Light Beach on my motorcycle or shall we walk?" It's only 300 meters."

"What?"

"The bar. Where we will drink."

"I want walk. No take motorbike."

Fast Eddy was always impressed every time he walked into Moon Light Beach. Although the typical Moon Light Beach condo was just 55 square meters, they were laid out so well that many owners hardly used their air conditioners. Starting out with a large atrium surrounded by tall white Corinthian columns that had been borrowed from ancient Greece and Rome, Moon Light Beach had an unrivaled ambience that it shared only with its two sister condo buildings, Twilight Beach and Sun Light Beach. Between the columns is a large pool that is surrounded by lush tropical plants. The pool could have been a showcase pool for swimmers had it not been for the architects designing an altogether different creation. With a depth of just two feet, and the proximity of the plants, the pool provided a home for over a dozen large multi colored carp. There is no roof for this atrium which is open to the sky with the condos forming a 360-degree perimeter rising 30 floors above ground level. Immediately to the West of the building is a 65-meter swimming pool with a sensational view of the Gulf of Thailand. A stairway meanders through tall plants to the beach from the pool. The view is not limited to the pool because a splendid view of the ocean can be seen from inside the atrium while most of the condos have magnificent balconies providing spectacular sea views. But perhaps the best part of the open roof structure of the building is how it causes a funnel effect that induces the outside air to flow throughout the building and into each condo.

Although Kit had to be impressed, she hardly showed any sign of being affected by Moon Light Beach's magnificence. But Fast Eddy knew differently. Moon Light Beach is the kind of place where movies should be made... being the living carnation out of which dreams are made. His first visit to Moon Light Beach 14 years ago, had nearly intimidated him. The whole place reeked of exclusivity where only the very rich and movie stars could live. But he knew better now. Due to having learned a long time ago that the average rental was just 15000 baht[40] while many renters

---

[40]$468.75 at 32 baht to the dollar

376

remained there for years[41]. And as for movies, there was no doubt in Fast Eddy's mind that movies had been made here, because he had already seen a half a dozen Thai movies being filmed at Centara Grand Mirage and next door at the less opulent Siam Beach Hotel.

He knew few owners at Moonlight Beach although he had met a lot of long term renters who had lived in their 55 square meter[43] condos for twenty years. But he had never been successful at getting any of his friends to move into Moon Light Beach. Until Big Jim had taken his advice and rented a 26th floor unit for 15000 baht.

The first person they saw was Leo sitting at the bar. Leo had run a successful music bar in Naklua which he allowed his Thai wife to run for him. But since he had never gotten a work permit he never as much as brought a drink over to any of his customers. The Leo Blues bar had become an almost legendary Pattaya icon due to many world class musicians coming there to play their music, most of them being retired and well past their earning years. But Leo had once told him that he had to pay 60000 baht a month to three separate police entities that comprised both the Pattaya and Naklua police departments and the Immigration police. And as to the work permit requirement that the Thai government imposed on all foreigners Leo had once explained to him: "just what the hell kind of work permit am I supposed to get? A work permit so I can be a bartender, a work permit so I can manage my own place, a work permit that allows me to cook food or to even bring food to my customers? The police even took me to jail because they caught me talking to customers. But my wife had sorted that out by paying the appropriate bribe money."

There was no doubt in Fast Eddy's mind that Kit didn't really

---

[43] 594 square feet

appreciate the predicament Leo was now putting himself in. Because the second person they saw was Micky, the bartender, all six feet of him, muscular and formidable looking with his bald head and self-assured manner. Fast Eddy knew all too well that Micky didn't have a work permit. Leo's wife, Nan, could have been bartending and normally might have been except for the virus. And all the hell that would have come down of all of them, from Leo down to the customers who were drinking in his place. So much of the time Nan sat just outside the bar entrance to observe any potential troublemakers who might descend on the bar. As for potential troublemakers, they could run anywhere from an under cover Thai policeman to the kind of potential customers likely to stir almost unsurmountable problems for the bar.

Fast Eddy wasn't sure exactly what the police might do to any of them, but he was certain that there would at least be a 100000-baht fine for drinking in a public place. With potential jail time for customers and bar owner alike. Because at this time while Thailand was still being locked down not even restaurants were being allowed to serve alcohol. Besides outrageous fines the bar and everyone in it could also be taken to jail for lack of social distancing and there being too many people in the bar at the same time.

The bar had a curtain in front of it so that anyone wishing to enter the bar had to open the curtain before he could view anyone or anything inside. Fast Eddy was the first to open the curtain and come inside the bar with Canada John and Kit following closely behind him. Upon seeing Leo sitting at the corner of the bar, Fast Eddy took a bar stool next to him and motioned for Kit to take the adjoining bar stool.

Standing in front of the bar was another Thai woman whom Fast Eddy had just met. The woman had to be nearly forty. He had seen her lounging at the Bahthaus pool and figured her to be a Caucasian woman. He had watched Micky and Canada John swim their laps together while never guessing the close connection Micky had with the woman. But he soon found out the connection due to the woman's excellent English skills and outgoing personality. The woman's mother was Thai whereas her father had been German. The two had met in Bangkok and like many foreigners her German father had supported the entire family for years. Strangely enough due to the schools she had been sent to her German was nearly nonexistent whereas her English was excellent. But down deep she was still Thai so the immediate result was Kit and her taking to each other immediately. And as for the connection between the woman and Micky, she was one of Micky's favorite girlfriends even though she was likely to be even older than Micky.

At the far end of the bar, Fast Eddy noticed James Canada John 's boat designer friend from Jomtien who made a good living designing yachts for a wealthy clientele. This was the same man who had been with Canada John, Kit, Canada John 's girlfriend and a friend of Canada John 's two years ago when he had taken Kit to the Doll House. An attractive Thai woman sat next to James, the boatbuilder.

Big Jim was there also, with a worn out multi tattooed Thai woman who was just one of his many pickups from Beach Road he was having sex with. The woman's face was hard . . . Fast Eddy wouldn't fuck her with his dog's dick.

Eventually the three Thai women all seemed to be getting along well together. Canada John kept commenting on how cute the boatbuilder's girlfriend was. But when Kit told the other three Thai women that she wanted to go to a Family Mart that was just across the street from Moon Light Beach, Canada John commented how terrific it was to see the four Thai women starting to bond together.

Fast Eddy was happy for Kit also. Because he wanted her to start feeling that Naklua and his condo was her one and only permanent home. Canada John , Big Jim, and Micky were all doing a great job at making Kit feel welcome. So the icing on the cake would be her finding Thai women she could relate to.

He found Kit to be changing in many ways. At least outwardly. She had become primarily a beer drinker. And now she was no longer 32 kilos as she had been when she had been convalescing from her operation at his condo. She was now 37 kilos and sometimes even tipped his scales at 38, whereas two years ago she was just 35 kilos. A few months ago she just picked at her food, but now she was eating like a horse. Best of all, she was now staying all night with him every night she visited him while most of her clothes stayed in his condo. As for the Thai boyfriend, Fast Eddy wasn't at all certain she had a Thai boyfriend anymore. Now he was more concerned that she had Thai girlfriends for lovers.

When they finally left the Leo Bar at Moon Light Beach they had only walked a few feet down the road together when Kit suddenly jumped onto his back and started riding him as if he were a horse. But she didn't feel as light as a feather any more on account of the weight she had gained. Had she been any other woman he would have gone on for another fifty feet and then told her to get off his shoulders. But Kit wasn't just any other Thai woman. So he went on being her horse until they had gone on for another two hundred yards when they started getting close to the Bahthaus. It was only then that Kit dismounted. And most likely because she didn't want to take a chance of becoming a spectacle for the Bahthaus night time security guard.

The second time Fast Eddy took Kit to Moon Light Beach, pretty much the same gang was there. With Micky as bartender while Leo sat at his favorite corner at the bar. Big Jim was with the same woman he had taken before. Kit and Fast Eddy pulled chairs up to the table Big Jim was sitting at with his tattooed squeeze. Once again Micky was the perfect bartender, going out of his way to make sure Kit and Fast Eddy had full beers in front of them, while making Kit feel like an honored guest.

Fast Eddy found Big Jim's "girlfriend to be sullen and very tawdry looking. While Kit exchanged hardly a word with her. Kit in contrast, was vibrant, smiling often whenever Big Jim started to tease her.

"I not like my nose," Kit told Big Jim and Fast Eddy.

"I like your nose very much," Fast Eddy replied. "Don't even think about changing your nose. My ex girlfriend wanted to have plastic surgery on her nose, but I didn't pay for it. I paid for her braces because she had a mouth like a horse, but I sure as hell wouldn't pay for her nose job. She had to pay for it herself and she didn't look better at all when she got her new nose. She even looked too high so[44]. Kit, I love your nose. I love your face. Do

---

[44]High society. As opposed to low society in Thailand's cast system

not change anything because then you won't be yourself any more."

"I want silicon," Kit replied with a gleaming smile. "I want big tits," she added while pretending to lift up that area of her chest where big breasts would have been.

"Oh yeah," Big Jim told Kit with a lecherous grin. Fast Eddie here. He big farmer. He have lots and lots of money. Ask him to get you nom yai.[45] Fast Eddy have beau coup money. He very happy to get you silicon."

"Thanks Jim," Fast Eddy replied while giving his friend the finger. "And fuck you too."

"But Fast Eddy. Kit wants nom yai. You have big money. You very rich man. Give her what she wants. She deserves it."

Fast Eddy was proud of Kit because now his friends could see the other side of her. She was no longer the shy introverted girl playing games on her phone. Micky was certainly picking up on the outgoing vivacious personality lurking inside of her wanting to get out. But this time it wasn't the presence of other Thais that was doing the trick. It had to be the outgoing personalities of his friends and their showing Kit that they truly liked her.

Eventually Canada John came in. But the bar that should never have been open was closing at 11. But this time Fast Eddy had taken Kit to dinner at the Italian restaurant on Soi 33 where Kit had two glasses of wine as he drank two Heinekens. When he took her on his motorbike just past the Bahthaus front entrance, an agitated Kit spoke out, "Put motorbike inside" Meaning that once again she wanted to walk to Moon Light Beach. But he kept driving and parked his motorbike just inside the Moon Light Beach visitor parking area.

After leaving the bar, Kit called out in a girlish voice.

---

[45] Big breasts

"I drive motorbike. John, you and Fast Eddy walk."

Canada John and Fast Eddy found Kit already waiting for them just outside the Bahthaus parking area, obviously pleased with herself.

"You are right Fast Eddy. She is really something. Now I can see why you like her so much," said Canada John seeing for the first time the big difference between Kit and every other Thai woman he had ever encountered.

Dinner at Nam's

Turned out to be a huge disappointment. Big Jim came with the same heavily tattooed woman he had been planking. This time, Nam did not allow them to have alcohol. Which is understandable due to her looking at a fine of 100,000 baht if the police came. Fast Eddy figured she would have served them alcohol had it not been for Big Jim's whore, who Nam had never met before, and who had a face which was easy to dislike.

Canada John ordered one of Fast Eddy's all time favorites, salmon with fruit salsa, which was a dish worthy of the top restaurants in Bangkok. This dish was Nam at her best, which until now had been a very high standard. But this time, Nam had scrimped on the ingredients. Perhaps it was because she had only reopened several days before after having had to close her restaurant for two months because of the virus lock-down. So it was likely that she hadn't had enough time yet to build up her food inventory.

By the time everyone could leave for Leo's bar, it had already started to rain. But once again, Kit decided against taking his motorbike over to Moon Light Beach. Fast Eddy watched her starting to run. While nearly laughing out loud as she accelerated into a crazy bow-legged gait that could only be regarded as vintage Kit. Fast Eddy started to try and keep up with her, but his stomach was too full of food for him to even want to try. When he finally entered the Moon Light Beach condominium front gate there was no sign of Kit.

He found her sitting on a bar stool ordering two Heinekens, obviously quite pleased with herself. "My God, I've better stop smoking. Kit must have just run a quarter of a mile at a full gallop," Fast Eddy told himself. Then mentally, added, "she obviously now feels very comfortable with this bar and my friends who come here."

Since Big Jim and his whore were already sitting at a table, Kit and Fast Eddy soon joined them. Canada John came into the bar half an hour later due to his having to make a phone call before he could get down to the serious business of drinking.

Micky was tending bar while Leo sat at his bar stool.

Fast Eddy watched Micky pouring drinks, washing glasses, and meandering throughout the bar to wait on his customers. Which got Fast Eddy thinking, "That Micky. He ought to star in a remake of the movie, "Cocktail" starring Bryan Brown and Tom Cruise. Pondering what role Micky should play, Fast Eddy preferred casting Micky as Bryan Brown over Tom Cruise due to his being older, more experienced and far less boyish.

Before long the talk in the bar started to focus on an upcoming cruise in a small yacht that was owned by James. Leo and one of the customers sitting close to him at the bar commented on how much Thai women hated being in the sun. While Fast Eddy kept pondering that Kit would most likely sleep through the entire afternoon. Which she had already done at Koh Larn Island and with her staying up all night and waking up at 4 p.m. made it highly unlikely for her to enjoy the outing.

Fast Eddy woke up in the middle of the night to a dream. In the dream he heard Micky's loud voice telling him, "She's a goddamn lesbian for Christ's sake, Fast Eddy and it's about time you come to start realizing that!"

By 2:30 p.m., Kit was sprawled out on the big bed in the master bedroom, her body all catty wampus yet so slender and elegant. So he decided to exercise hard on the elliptical machine at Centara Grand Mirage Hotel which had just opened up its fitness center after having shut down for two months on account of the virus. By the time he got back it was 4:00. He found Kit fully dressed, with her makeup on.

"I want to go back South Pattaya," she announced..

Fast Eddy was mortified...thinking, "Just why in the hell does she want to go back there when she's had everything she could possibly want here in my condo?" But he had already decided to let her go if she wanted to go. And not to make sarcastic remarks about her wanting to go back to see her Thai boyfriend or her "real friends". He had been planning on giving her no more than 20000 baht for the month. But the way he had been working it was to give her one-thousand baht for each entire night she stayed with him.
Then again, perhaps she had a falang suddenly message her to offer her money for a short time. As to the prospect of a Thai boyfriend, that 15-centimeter scar from the appendix operation was likely to be pretty unsightly to most men. She had never had a single tattoo although she had a single piercing in her belly button of a small rabbit. For him she had the perfect stomach

384

and abdomen, flat and unblemished. He couldn't help thinking that she had probably lost confidence in the beauty of her own body.

But he would wind up saving himself several thousand baht if he kept her out of his place for a few days. Besides, she had imposed her own schedule on him. So it was now for him to call the tune for once.

Using his phone he deposited five-thousand baht into her bank account as she sat next to him on the couch. Then he took her to the motorcycle taxis stand at Family Mart where he gave her 120 baht for taxi fare.

"I will not see you for a few days, he told her. This way you can have time with your friends while I will have time with my friends. I plan on going on that boat ride on Sunday. I don't think you would like it. And we will all probably get very drunk so I will be very hung over on Monday. So let us see each other again on Tuesday."

Fast Eddy could tell by looking at Kit's face that she was very unhappy about not being able to come back to him until Tuesday, today being Thursday. Whether it was on account of just the money, she wouldn't be making or her actually enjoying being at his condo and feeling right at home there.
But when he got back inside his condo he saw that she had done the laundry and put it on the line on his small balcony. She had also left some makeup on the small end table next to his couch and the electronic cigarette inhaler on his coffee table. So it seemed to him that she had been planning on coming back in a day or two.

"But why go back to South Pattaya?" he kept asking himself. "It seems she wants to have her cake and eat it too. Which is to get all the advantages of being with me starting out with the money I'm giving her and going to nice restaurants, while being able to party all night long with her Thai friends. On the other hand, she had just mentioned to me that she was staying with this old lady (and there was plenty of evidence that she was) along with two or three other women. And that with all the jobs having been lost because of the virus her roommates couldn't get any money unless it came from her. So perhaps this whole thing is all about bailing these losers out and because she had a big heart, which is typical of most of these Thai women."

Short Time with Ning at the Bahthaus

Living in Pattaya under the shadow of the virus was an entirely new ball game. Both for Fast Eddy and the girls who provided sex for money to all the falang who could afford to pay.

But Ning was another story. In the five years he had known her, she had made him cum every time. She was that good. And she was smart despite her only having a sixth grade education. The only problem Fast Eddy had with her is that she had never ever met him outside the Smoke and Kisses Bar on Soi 6. With the reason for this being that she had an agreement with her boyfriend back in Holland that it was acceptable for her to fuck customers due to his being unable to pay her enough money to support her lifestyle. But she could not have sex with customers outside her bar. But now Fast Eddy knew that there was no way for Ning to make any money unless she met customers outside the bar due to the bars all being closed. So he messaged her and found she was willing to meet him the following day, and that the only place they could meet would be at his condo.

By the time Ning was waiting for him at the Bahthaus front entrance, Kit had already started text messaging with him. While as soon as he took her upstairs to his condo, Ning asked him.

"What about Kit?"

"I am messaging with her right now, Ning."

Typically of Ning, she told him right off, "I haven't much time. I have to meet friends soon." But he showed her around his condo before getting down to the serious business of boom booming. He showed her the closet in the large bedroom where Kit had hung all her clothes. Which got Ning off to her usual barrage of questions.

"How long she stay with you? When Kit coming back?"

"I don't know, Ning."

"And how about Belle?"

"I had to do most of the dishes. The cooking also. She drink all the time, Ning."

To which Ning replied. "Belle does ice and she does cocaine."

But later on Big Jim would be telling him, "Ning like all Thai women wants to discredit the competition. So they will make up all these stories. There is no way Belle is a drug addict. If she was, there is no way she could be staying with you for an entire month."

After Ning showered Fast Eddy found her lying naked on the queen size bed in the small bedroom.

The sex went as it always had been between them. Which was terrific. But after smoking him almost to the point of orgasm, she asked him for a massage. Lying down naked on her stomach, she had him gently massage her back as he put his groin up against her buttocks.

It won't take much for me to start penetrating her, he told himself while rubbing his appendage up and down her backside. He was close to being inside her, when she laughed and said, "You trying to fuck my ass?"

She had told him many times that many customers had fucked her ass, almost bragging about it. While Big Jim had once told him that she had actually admitted to him that she enjoyed getting fucked in the ass.

But he didn't try it. Later while thinking about it, he considered, "Well maybe next time. That is if she really wants me to."

The Final Countdown

"The final hour is here, a confident Dick Fitswell announced to his disciples. "One among you is to become my Saint Peter, to spread the good word of the perfect fit. All of you know that twice I have met God[46] who has told me to spread the good word and that I must appoint twelve apostles. We have not quite reached that goal yet but we are not that far off. We have here at this consecrated place seven of you. Wolfgang, Harry, Scott, Fast Eddy, Big Jim, Danny and Frank. Unfortunately due to this virus enveloping the entire world, Richard and Leon are stuck in the U.S.A. so it will be awhile before they can come back to perform the chores I have set out for them. This makes nine of you so far."

"I think I deserve to be Saint Peter," Harry interrupted the great mentor in a loud bombastic voice.

"That remains to be seen, Harry. You will get your turn later," Dick Fitswell said in a voice commanding respect. "So let's start with you, Frank."

"I haven't really been out there that much," said Frank. "A lot has to do with my position as chairman of the Bahthaus. I have to be pretty low key and can't afford to be seen fucking all these girls on Soi 6 by the residents at the Bahthaus. As chairman I must command respect and not show any weaknesses. When I am no longer chairman, I can become a lot more vocal in spreading the true message of Fitswell. And I can set more of an example for the rest of the world to follow."

"Well then. You can and should remain one of my disciples. Perhaps you can be like Saint Paul, who didn't do anything for Jesus or God until long after the crucifixion when Jesus appeared to him on the Road to Damascus."

---

[46]Dick Fitswell meets God in Dick Fitswell the Man in Quest of the Perfect Fit

"That suits me just fine, Dick. For now I pretty much agree with Fast Eddy. For what he stands for and his position on the true meaning of the perfect fit."

"Then you certainly cannot be the Saint Peter for this flock of mine."

"Now, Harry," Dick Fitswell told everyone as he looked at each one of his disciples, to embellish the gravity of the situation. "You are one of several who have pretty much given up on women. While you continue to assert that if a lady boy's anus is tighter than a woman's vagina, it must be the perfect fit. However, one can claim the same thing for homosexuals and I am not nor will I ever glorify homosexuality. I don't condemn it, but I won't glorify it ether. I want you to give ample reason why you should be our Saint Peter."

"First of all, fucking a lady boy is not the same as fucking a man. I have a wise old friend who asserts that when a man is having sex with a lady boy, it comes to what is in his mind while he's screwing the lady boy. When he's doing her, in the back of his mind, is he fucking a woman or a man? I see a woman's face in front of me. Certainly not a man's. I would heave my guts out at the mere thought of having sex with a man. A lot of lady boys have fake tits. They have nice asses. Not a man's ass but a woman's ass. And I sure hate having sex with a fat assed woman. So for me, the lady boy with the beautiful ass is much more woman than an overweight woman. My cock cannot begin to get hard when it's touching a woman's fat ass or bloated stomach. So to further make my point, I'm going to ask you a question, Frank."

"Go ahead," Harry.

"Frank, I know you go to that lady boy bar in Naklua. I'm not trying to put you down or anything because we know it's a very good bar and that most of the Bahthaus residents go there from time to time. So let me ask you, when you have had a few drinks, and say you are sitting at the bar facing the bartender and a lady boy comes up behind you and starts fondling your balls, do you get a hard on, or don't you?"

"Harry, there's that old saying that a stiff dick knows no conscience. I have been to that Lady boy bar many times. Most of the lady boys there are a lot better looking than practically any group of girls I've ever seen in any beer bar now days. And yes,

I've had many lady boys feeling my dick. And it gets real hard. Now, I've never ever had a lady boy give me an oil massage. But if a sexy looking lady boy starts rubbing my cock and my balls long enough I am certain that I would erupt into a happy ending."

"See my point," Harry continued. "Now what do you think, Fast Eddy?"

"I agree with Frank. I find an average looking woman to be not attractive at all, but a good-looking lady boy is very sexy. So I am going to get hard when a good-looking lady boy is feeling me up. And if I ever got an oil massage from one of them, I will surely have a happy ending. But I love women, and I really don't care that much for lady boys."

"Okay then. I think most of us can regard Frank and Fast Eddy as heterosexuals," Dick Fitswell replied. "There is a reason why lady boys are considered Thailand's third sex. They are neither fish nor fowl, and any man who has not been here long would think a gorgeous looking lady boy to be a woman. I now want Wolfgang to tell us all his thoughts and to give us all ample reason for my making him our Saint Peter."

"I agree totally with everything that's been said about lady boys," Wolfgang replied. "I happen to like both lady boys and women. And I'd say I have sex with about 50 percent lady boys and 50 percent women. I waver back and forth. Sometimes I prefer lady boys; then I get tired of them and go back to women. But at any given moment I can change my mind. So long as I have sex with someone almost every night."

"I find that commendable, Wolfgang. Your dick has no conscience at all. But I still want you to explain to us why we might consider lady boys to be women more than men. Or at least as has been pointed out, as Thailand's third sex."

"Well Dick, I just happen to know two homosexuals quite well. They live in the U.S., not here, so they come here only to visit. I can take them to the lady boy bar or to Soi 6. Where I will have a few beers with them and take them to several bars. But neither of them will have anything to do with lady boys. Both of them will always wind up down on Boys Town which caters only to men who enjoy having sex with men. So I think this will convince you that lady boys truly are a third sex. This means if it fits, it fits, so long as your sex partner is either a lady boy or a woman."

I must now ask you, Dick Fitswell added, "Do you have a live in girlfriend now?"

"No. I had a Thai lady as a girlfriend for four years. Later, when I found out how much I enjoyed having sex with lady boys, I had this gorgeous lady boy living with me for over a month."

"What happened? Why aren't you with her now?"

"She got insanely jealous all the time. And if you think a Thai girlfriend is irrational and out of control, the lady boys are much worse."

"Then what attracts you to the lady boys?"

"Dick. I can only generalize. In general the stupidest sex workers here are Thai women. They have completely no interest in any falang. They have no interest in the outside world at all. Their English skills are terrible. Except for a few. And most of them can't even dance worth a shit. Lady boys are usually much smarter than the women here. They have lots of personality. Although most of them are total showoffs. They can speak much better English than the girls, and being part man, mentally I mean, they have similar interests as ours. For example, they tend to know a lot more about motorcycles than the women. Or if you are watching a boxing match on t.v. the Thai ladies could care less, but the lady boys as a rule really get into it. When you are drinking with them, it's a lot like drinking with the guys. They are like peacocks. The female peacocks are rather greyish in color. You will hardly notice the females. But the male peacocks are beautiful birds. Their feathers are many colors. They strut around and they are quite vocal. They have the looks and they have the personality. And lastly, the lady boy tends to feel what you are feeling so they identify with you. Whereas most Thai ladies are just a bunch of cold-hearted bitches who view all foreigners with contempt."

"Very well put," Harry added. "I like the lady boys. They want to fuck me. And they really enjoy it. But all these Thai ladies. They don't want me. They only want some puny shrimp assed Thai boy who's ripping them off for their money."

"We haven't heard a word from you, Scott. Why do you like lady boys?" Dick Fitswell asked.

"Once you start doing lady boys you will never go back to ladies ever again. Lady boys give the best blow jobs. They are much more loyal. They work out a lot more than the Thai ladies. And have all you guys noticed how fat most Thai ladies have become? They are not the same as they were 15 or 20 years ago. And they are so fucking dumb that you can hardly get them off their phones."

"Scott, we have all noticed that you keep branding your lady boys with that tattoo you have invented. "Can you tell us why you find it necessary to tattoo your favorite lady boys?"

"Dick, I think I've told you all about that before. My tattoo is based on my initials which are SP. But I've turned my initials upside down and turned them backwards to read PS. While I have been using a special script that makes the PS pretty unclear. Then I add a little symbol which starts off with a picture I've taken of my penis. Which I have transformed into a Photoshop image. I pay each lady boy five-thousand baht to permanently wear my tattoo and right after I have the tattoo done I take them all back to my condo to fuck them in the ass."

"That's pretty weird shit," Dick Fitswell replied.

"No it isn't. Not when you think about it. It's all about total control. I want all my favorite lady boys to know that they have a connection to me throughout their entire lives. So no matter who they are with later on, that person will never have that same connection over them that I've had. So I will never be forgotten and that works both ways. The lady boy quite obviously, and also the person the lady boy might love later on in life. Because the lady boy's future lover will always be pissed off about that tattoo. Also, tattoos are a bit painful and when I fuck these lady boys in the ass after I have them tattooed they will suffer even more pain. And ladies and lady boys alike enjoy pain."

"Oh come on Scott. You are speaking total bullshit," Fast Eddy added.

"The hell I am. Ladies like pain. They like to feel a real man having total control over them. That's why a lot of women enjoy being beat up. You will seldom see a woman ever give up on the man who's beating on them. Instead they think they are at fault. And that if they are nicer to their woman beating boyfriend that he will finally turn around and become better. Even so the actual pain itself causes their adrenaline to flow. Which causes them to be very sexually turned on."

"I like it," Dick Fitswell added to the flow of the conversation. "One might say there's nothing more repulsive than a man who allows a woman to control him. So one might take the converse to be a given. That a man who totally controls a woman is a man who should be revered. Think about certain hostage situations. Let's assume that the hostage is a woman or a group of women. The man holding them hostage has complete power over them. Even life and death. If this situation goes on long enough, we often find that the woman or women form an emotional bond with the hostage taker. And this emotional bond also becomes a sexual bond."

"Now we come to you, Big Jim." Dick Fitswell unknown to his disciples had contrived to save the best and the worse until last. "From what I have seen of you, you can hardly go a single day without having sex with someone. But you told me a long time ago that you have never had sex with a lady boy. Can you please explain to all of us why you think you should become my Saint Peter?"

"Dick, I am totally addicted to pussy. I think about it all the time. Which is one of the reasons I go to strip clubs at least once a week when I'm in the United States."

"Yeah. I remember the last time you and I went to the Hustler Club over in East Saint Louis," Fast Eddy replied. "I told you I wasn't going to tip a single one of those strippers and that I wanted to save money that night so I could go back to Thailand in two weeks. I figured the money I'd save at Hustler would buy me two long times with Thai women who I would find to be immensely more attractive than a single one of those Hustler club strippers."

"That is my whole point, Fast Eddy. I cannot do without pussy for even a single day or at least not thinking about it."

"Yeah, well you must have dropped at least 200 hundred dollars getting all those lap dances from those strippers. And all you got was a girl sliding around on your lap for five minutes which you paid $20.00 a dance. And you were coming back to Thailand in just two weeks."

"Yeah. But when I was doing those private dances in the private room, I also got the chance to look at their pussies."

"Did the girls let you eat them?"

"Well no. At least not most of the time. But I travel in my business in the U.S. so I get to be all over the U.S. Depending on the strip club, where it's at, and the laws governing the area the club is located in, I will oftentimes get blow jobs from the dancers. Sometimes I will even get fucked, and every once in awhile I will get one of those strippers to meet me at my hotel after her shift."

"But Jim, you have to admit that the Thai women are on average much better looking than American strippers have become. Most American strippers have gotten to be very fat."

"But not all of them. Besides, even if they are a little fat, I still like looking into their pussies."

"Okay Jim. Lately here in Thailand the authorities have closed off all the bars. And almost every night you either have a Thai woman in your room already or you are walking down Beach Road looking for a new one to bring back to your condo. And I've been with you walking down Beach Road, Jim. And you were talking to at least 15 women, some you knew and some you wanted to meet. I didn't like the looks of any one of those women, and wouldn't even fuck them with your dog's dick."

"Yeah, but most nights you are sitting at home alone, Fast Eddy, so whatever I've got in my bed is ten times better than what you've got."

"Why should I even bother with them? Almost all of them are even more stupid than the average rabbit. And you know me, I only like slender women. I hate to even touch fat women or have them touch me, and they can't even make me cum. So why should I pay them one-thousand baht? For what? And why should I even let them come into my beautiful condo? They don't deserve to be there in the first place. Just what the hell can those girls do for me?"

"You can always cum in their mouths, Fast Eddy."

"Okay guys. I've gotta play referee," Dick Fitswell interjected in a loud commanding voice.

"So let me continue on with my train of thought here. Big Jim's sent me pictures of some of the girls he's banged and some of them are pretty damn good looking. So I will get back to you later, Jim. Turning to Fast Eddy, Dick Fitswell asked: "And just what the hell are you doing with Little Miss Kitty? You've been on and off with her for three years now."

"Okay Dick. She's got a little body I am absolutely in love with for one thing. And she's smart and I have no use for stupid women. I also think that regardless of what all you other guys think that she's the most beautiful woman in all Pattaya. And let me be clear about that one. Most of the really so called beautiful women in Pattaya all have the same basic facial features. Whereas Kit's face changes. Sometimes she looks like a demon. Other times a child. Still, other times she looks like a person who is very kind deep down. And yet, most of the time she's not kind. So I am constantly wondering when and if that will ever really come out of her. She also knows by now what I like. What kind of food I like, and she can even tell without my even telling her whether or not I like someone I am having to deal with or not. All it takes is a little nod from me, and she's up on her feet ready to get away from the imbecile I'm having to deal with."

"She's a rat just like the rest of them are," Big Jim replied. What it really comes down to is she doesn't really like your condo. And she doesn't care that you have saved her arm and undoubtably saved her life when she ruptured her appendix. So long as she gets money from you, she wants to have her cake and eat it too. She keeps going back to her room so she can have fun with her stupid friends. That's the way she likes it. She doesn't want to be a part of your life. They are all the same. They only love and respect Thais."

"It seems that way. But there is not a man here, or for that matter a single man I know in the Bahthaus who has saved a girl's arm, and then her life. She will have that huge scar for the rest of her life. It might mean nothing in the end. Because nearly all bar girls have no sense of fairness when it comes to how they treat any falang. But Kamon told me once that someday Kit will wake up and suddenly realize that she only has one real friend. Me. When she sees her son, she sees him when I'm in her life and helping her out financially. When I'm out of the picture she never manages to see him. I got her health insurance so in the future she can go to Bangkok Pattaya Hospital. She got a drivers license all because of me. And a passport. And you, yourself Jim, keep saying they are all rats, and that rats wind up eating each other. So Kamon would say that one day soon she will realize that she can count on just one person, even more than her mother and father."

"You are dreaming, Fast Eddy. She doesn't want to listen to you. She doesn't care what you feel or what you are doing for her. She's like all the other rats."

"I must admit that I am hoping for something a lot better. Either from her or someone new I might meet. But right now with this virus thing going on, the bars are closed. And I'm not about to try and meet some worthless fraudulent bitch on Facebook or Thai Friendly. There's just something about her that feels so right. When she's sitting on the couch next to me, or even walking down the street with me to the 7-11. Or when we shop for food together. I've been with some pretty good looking girls, such as Meow and Belle and it's just not the same. Also if you asked Angry Pussy, none of the younger girls will begin to take care of any one of us. She tells me I should look for someone 30 or older. Kit's going to be 27 next month plus she has these physical conditions, one that nearly killed her and there's still that tumor in her left arm and hand and already she can't use one of her fingers and her thumb. So, maybe she's going to get that sense of mortality soon that an older woman oftentimes gets. And she will start to think playtime is about over. And that younger women will be looking far better than her."

"But she's not the perfect fuck, is she now? And for whatever reason you allow her to control what the two of you are doing," Dick Fitswell added.

"You sound just like Ning, Dick. Ning's always telling me that Kit's trying to control me. Which is pretty despicable of me for falling for that, I must admit. But I am thinking that Kit is a very shy person down deep and that she can only overcome that shyness when she's drinking. I am even thinking she is likely to have been sexually abused as a child and that she is very likely to have multi personality syndrom or what is now often called dissociative identity disorder. This is where the victim of this mental disease switches on and off to different identities without her being aware of it. For one moment she's an intelligent rational adult and then suddenly a switch goes off in her brain. And she starts acting and thinking of herself as a little child. This would explain Kit's jumping into a grocery cart and having me wheel her around the shopping center. Or her suddenly going catatonic on me. When Kit won't speak a single word and just looks out into space."

"Why do you even put up with her then, if you think she might be psychologically disturbed?" Dick Fitswell asked.

"Maybe I'm a pervert down deep, Dick. Danny here likes really young girls. And as Harry would say if Danny can fuck a 14-year-old and get away with it he certainly would. I don't go for these younger girls. Even 24 is too young for me to have the slightest interest in. Kit is not jail bait, but she sure acts like a very young girl. I'm certainly turned on by her. I can climax in just five minutes with her. No one else has that kind of effect on me."

"Tell Dick, your theory about horses," Big Jim smirked.

"You guys will think I'm crazy. But during World War II while my Dad was stationed in England, he had this English friend who was pretty well to do. The Englishman had a horse named Venus. Now Venus was a thoroughbred, which is a horse that is bred for racing. They are the fastest horses alive and when my Dad got off her, he told me it was something he would remember for the rest of his life. Only thing about most thoroughbreds is that most of them are downright nutty. Whereas a good Morgan horse is a jack of all trades. They are easily managed and they are very intelligent. A good Morgan horse is compact and muscular. It used to be that a farmer could put a Morgan horse behind a plow and race him the next day."

"So you are comparing Kit to Venus, a thoroughbred that could give a man the ride of his life?" replied an completely incredulous Dick Fitswell.

"That's what I am saying. I used to have a 1985 BMW K100RS motorcycle. There are much faster bikes now, but never mind. The bike would get up to 100 miles an hour in just seven seconds. It was damn fast and very thrilling to ride. But after I got used to it I kept wanting to have even more power. Power is addicting. But when I started to jump out of airplanes the speed and power of different motorcycles became pretty irrelevant. Getting up to 130 miles an hour on a narrow two lane road got to be not such a big deal the more I got used to that bike. But once I started free falling from a small airplane at over 10,000 feet, the thrill that comes from speed took on an entirely new level."

"How's that Fast Eddy?" a now totally spell bound Dick Fitswell asked.

"It's so damn scary. You start out in this little cockpit in a small Cessna. And as the plane goes higher and higher it gets colder and colder in the cockpit. Then you have to get out of that small plane and walk out onto the airplane's wing without losing your balance. Because if you do and you fall off that wing you are going to be completely off balance. And go immediately into high speed somersaults. Then somehow you must regain control because if you continue to somersault in the air you will never be able to get your parachute to open properly if at all. Which means you die. Within three seconds you are doing 120 miles an hour, but you get no sense of falling anymore. That's only in the first second or two. Now you feel like you are tied onto the front of a fast-moving train speeding horizontally at over 500 miles an hour. Trust me, there's nothing like it. You got the thrill of being a bird and the threat of death plus the need for completely controlling your mind and your body. Now that's what riding a very fast thoroughbred is like or having to deal with a woman who's very much like a fast nearly out of control horse."

"Tell Dick here about plow horses," Big Jim said with a huge grin.

"Most women we meet here are like plow horses. Outwardly they might appear independently minded or exciting to go to bed with. But the truth is they are like plow horses. Their bodies are no longer at all the kind of slender bodies most Thai women used to have. They've eaten too much food at McDonalds or 7-11. They are dim witted and slow moving. A lot of them can hardly even walk. They are just a dime a dozen. Then there's someone like Kit who I swear is the fastest Thai woman on two legs. She's got the quickest reaction time. She catches on very quickly. And she's like a skittish horse. Surprise her by a sudden movement or all of a sudden come into the room and her body and mind instantly reacts. She's no plow horse, which is a horse you can count on to get the chores done. And take a look at those legs of hers. Her lower legs are nearly pixel thin. Then they move up into her thighs which are beautifully tapered and firm. Then finally there's that nice sweet bubble butt of hers, which is very slender but has just the right curves. Yes...she is a real problem child but most thoroughbreds are also."

"Wolfgang, what do you make of all this?" Dick Fitswell asked hoping to shift the focus of the overall conversation into a new dimension.

"I think Fast Eddy's got a very valid point about horses. But I have a few problems with his thinking. A man should never glorify any single woman's body, intellect or her personality. Also, Fast Eddy has paid far too much money paying for Kit's medical bills. And he has been far too kind to his past girlfriend who he was with for nine years. The fact is all these bar girls will bounce back in the long run. They aren't going to starve, and they can always go back to their family in the village. So I agree with Big Jim. They're all rats. They live in this sub culture of ignorance while thinking Thailand is the number one country in the world. They have no interest at all in how the rest of the world thinks, its history and certainly not of its geography. Let alone the past that nearly all bar girls have no sense of the past or the future. For them it's all about now. Look, I got this 11 million baht condo. Do you guys think that most of these girls will think I'm a good catch and that if they play their cards right that they might be getting my condo? No way. Or take Little Miss Kit for example. Do you think that she really appreciates all that Fast Eddy has done for her? Of saving her arm. Or perhaps even her life? No. Because that's in the past. It's all about what are you doing for me right now. Most of them cannot control their money because it's all about today and not at all about tomorrow."

"So do you think you should be our Saint Peter?" Dick Fitswell asked.

"Yes. By all means. Because I do not differentiate at all. I suppose I am bisexual. I am only interested in right now. In getting the best orgasm I can, and then dispensing with the person who's given that orgasm to me."

"How about you, Danny? You seem to be chasing down various sex partners every day. You are a dedicated man," Dick Fitswell added.

"I would be a good choice, Dick. But I don't know if I'm in the same league as Big Jim here."

"You are correct Danny. And you spend far too much time chasing down these very young girls. Very few of them are worth a damn when it comes to providing good sex. They are babes in the wood. So you cannot possibly be considered in the same league as Wolfgang and certainly not with Big Jim."

"Dick, I disagree with you, said Fast Eddy. None of these guys here should be Saint Peter. None of them are really seeking out top quality women the way you have. But I have. I am looking for the top horse. Right now it happens to be Kit, and for all the reasons I've given you. But when and if the bars ever reopen once this virus thing is settled, you can be sure that I will be looking for a girl who's equal to or better than Kit."

"You've had that same chance many times before, Dick Fitswell replied. "For instance about two years ago when you and Kit were on the outs, and you met this nice looking Soi 6 girl. If I remember, she blew you, then she lay across your chest for the next half hour French kissing you, and then she had you bang her without a condom. But you were only with her two or three times. But when Kit started messaging you again, you chose to meet up with her instead, and that was the last night that other woman was ever seen in that Soi 6 bar. And just what are you going to do the next time Kit starts to feel a lot of pain in her arm and she wants you to take her to the hospital for that next round of injections? Are you going to tell her you have another girlfriend and that you cannot help her?"

"Uh. I guess I can't Dick. I just can't let that arm of hers just fall off and allow her to suffer from non ending pain"

"See. You are just too soft on the girl, Fast Eddy."

"Yeah. Well I am not like the rest of you guys. None of you have any interest whatsoever in what makes one of these girls tick. In getting to really know them."

"Which is one of the reasons you cannot be Saint Peter, Fast Eddy. You allow yourself to care too much. And if there is one thing you must finally remember it's, when it comes to women, nice guys finish last. Because unfortunately most women are not attracted to nice men who treat them well. They like a man who has at least a strong trace of villainy in them. One reason for this is such men always keep them guessing. Whereas a nice guy is no challenge to them at all."

"Well all I got to say to that is, I doubt if any of you have ever jumped out of an airplane or ridden a fast thoroughbred horse. I've had experiences the rest of you will never have. And as for nice guys finishing last, here's one for the rest of you to remember, "it is better to have loved and lost than not to have loved at all."

"Okay then, Fast Eddy. Whether you are right or wrong I am quoted from <u>Dick Fitswell the man in search of the Perfect Fit</u> saying "I'm the real man, the man on the prowl, looking, always searching for the perfect woman, not for brains or heart, but for the perfect fit." You tell me Kit's smart and that in some way or another she might have heart? I suppose you meant by how courageous she was when she visited you when she had

400

appendicitis or possibly even had an appendix that had already ruptured. Well that doesn't matter."

"So you are disqualifying me?"

"That I am. And not only that. I don't think you can even be one of my apostles. But you should be one of my disciples undergoing reeducation. Just as a person has to become a monk apprentice before he can become a priest. I don't know if I've used the correct terminology but you get the idea. As for Richard and Leon back in America, I have big hopes for both of them, especially Richard. Who had to use a pump up to get off but who came all the way to Thailand to completely recover from that disability. Which now brings us to the main contenders."

"Which should be me," Harry replied.

"No. Certainly not you, Dick Fitswell replied. "You fuck lady boys with reckless abandon. And you certainly don't care about anything other than having the best orgasm possible. But I don't think you can possibly measure up to Big Jim here. Who has to see pussy every day. Or Scott either. Scott, you have the right idea. You are a total control freak. And your mind is completely warped. But all three of you, listen up. Including you, Wolfgang. I don't care how sexy a Lady boy is and even if she's had her dick cut off and replaced by an artificial vagina. When it really comes down to, the next morning when you wake up to that lady boy, what do you see? Well I'll tell you what you see. You see a man. She might have seemed feminine the night before. But now that her hair is messed up and the makeup worn off, you've still got a man and you feel it the next day whereas the night before you had a few drinks and the lady boy looked really fresh with her makeup on and her hair just right. And the worse is chances are she was wearing a wig and now you are waking up to a man with short hair."

"And now I am going to offer all you the one most important thing Fast Eddy has offered for all of us to ponder. For him, Kit is the essence of femininity. He loves the way she walks and talks. Now how can any of you love the way most lady boys talk with that lady boy voice of theirs. And just watch them walk swinging their hips trying to walk like ladies. They can't. Because they are not feminine. Also Fast Eddy has pointed out how vulnerable Kit is. Again, for whatever she is and what she isn't, she's totally feminine. Still, you three are all worthy of being my apostles. But Saint Peter? No way."

"Who's Saint Peter then?" asked Danny.

"Yeah, who is our Saint Peter?" Harry asked.

"Saint Peter is Big Jim. First, he's totally devoted to pussy. Second, what the girls are thinking, or what they are like is not of any importance to him at all. Pussy is his Holy Grail. That is why I was always questing for the perfect fit and never considered assholes to be a perfect fit. Big Jim has the perfect philosophy. Perhaps not in Western countries. But here, when it comes to bar girls, they are all rats who will even turn on each other and eat their bar girl friends alive. Which is why all of you should give them their just deserts. And my last point is this. Back thousands of years ago in the primordial forest when Neanderthals coexisted with the first men, women looked for protection from their men where the strongest got the most women. Back then men didn't have to be nice. It was all about putting food on the table and being able to beat the shit out of any other man who would dare touch a real man's women."

Made in the USA
Middletown, DE
05 May 2022

65300437R10239